P9-AZX-332

Amber House

AMBER

HOUSE

KELLY MOORE • TUCKER REED • LARKIN REED

Arthur A. Levine Books
AN IMPRINT OF SCHOLASTIC INC.

Library of Congress Cataloging-in-Publication Data

Moore, Kelly (Kelly Sheelagh).
Amber House / by Kelly Moore, Tucker Reed, and Larkin Reed. — 1st ed.
p. cm.
Summary: After her grandmother's death Sarah Parsons, nearly sixteen, delights in exploring her family's centuries-old Maryland estate with new friend Jackson, but soon she is having vivid visions of her ancestors, one of whom may be a threat to Sarah's autistic brother, Sam.
ISBN 978-0-545-43416-4 (hardback) — ISBN 978-0-545-43417-1 (paperback) — ISBN 978-0-545-46973-9 (e-book) [1. Psychic ability — Fiction. 2. Dwellings — Fiction. 3. Visions — Fiction. 4. Brothers and sisters — Fiction. 5. Family life — Maryland — Fiction. 6. Maryland — Fiction. 7. Mystery and detective stories.]
I. Reed, Tucker. II. Reed, Larkin. III. Title.
PZ7.M78645Amb 2012
[Fic] — dc23
2012014729

Book design by Whitney Lyle

10 9 8 7 6 5 4 3 2 1   12 13 14 15 16

Printed in the U.S.A.   23
First edition, October 2012

FOR LUNDI MOORE –

"Commander" — our father and
grandfather, who built tree houses
and fashioned a nautical bedroom
and kept up a family history
running back to Jamestown.
Who made our lives possible.
We wish you could have read our book.

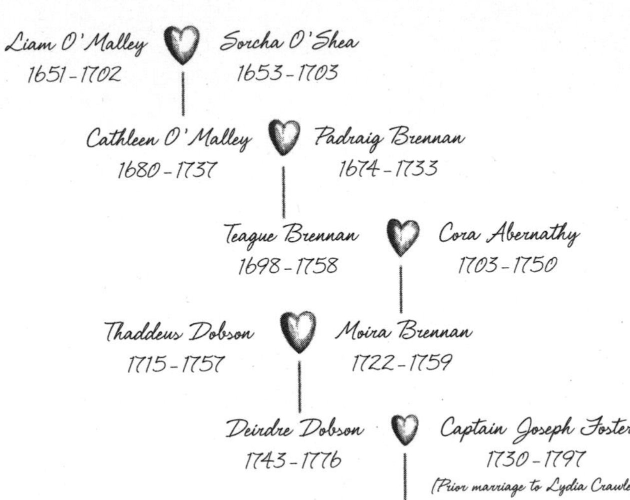
Liam O'Malley
1651-1702
Sorcha O'Shea
1653-1703
Cathleen O'Malley
1680-1737
Padraig Brennan
1674-1733
Teague Brennan
1698-1758
Cora Abernathy
1703-1750
Thaddeus Dobson
1715-1757
Moira Brennan
1722-1759
Deirdre Dobson
1743-1776
Captain Joseph Foster
1730-1797
(Prior marriage to Lydia Crawley)
Matthew Foster
1762-1775

Families of AMBER HOUSE

Compiled by Fiona Campbell Warren in 1933

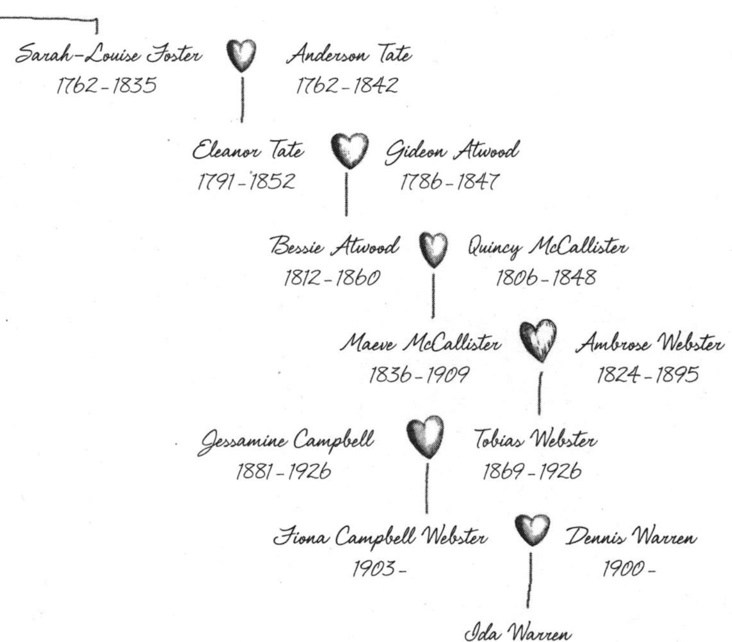

I'd been here before.

I was running down an endless hall of doors that opened into other places. I kept repeating the words I had to remember, the directions —

"If you have the chance —"

Endless doors before and behind, only I had grown too big to get through them, or too small to reach the knobs.

"— the chance to choose —"

She skipped ahead of me, glancing back with her solemn eyes, leading me on, her white dress fluttering in wind that blew all around.

"— then take the path —"

I was tired. I felt like I had grown old, running forever. It hurt. But still I had to keep going. Find the right door.

"— the path that leads —"

He was here too, someplace. Behind one of these doors, if only I could choose it. Who? I couldn't remember anymore. Only the smile. Only his wide white smile . . .

Chapter One

I was almost sixteen the first time my grandmother died.

It was mid-October. Warm still, like summer, but the trees were wearing their scarlets and golds. Back home, in Seattle, we had evergreens and faded browns. Those absurdly vivid colors along the banks of the Severn River were the first thing I fell in love with — autumn the way it was intended.

It's hard, now, to remember that first day, like looking at a photo underwater — the image shifting, in motion, never quite in focus. But there's a part of me that doesn't forget. And it's important to tap into that part, to will myself to remember. Sometimes, if I really concentrate, the memories come flooding back. All of them. Beginning to end. Then back again to the beginning. A full circle.

It started at the funeral. We were standing on the hill just west of the house, inside an iron fence filled with tombstones. Everyone in my grandmother's family had been buried in that graveyard, all the way back to the first immigrants. Gramma had picked out a plot for herself when she was still a little girl. Which gives you some idea about my grandmother's family and their morbid obsessions.

It was one of the few conversations I'd had with my grandmother that I actually remembered. I was nearly six at the time. She told me about her chosen resting place and then said, cheerfully, "One day, you'll be buried there too." I'd burst into tears.

Ten years later, I found myself clustered with a few dozen strangers on the exact spot Gramma had described to me, beneath the living half of a skeletal tree blasted by catastrophe long ago. The new slab of marble that stood in its shade, waiting to be moved into place, read simply, IDA WARREN MCGUINNESS ~ AT LONG LAST REUNITED. We stood in ranks beside the open grave like starlings on an electric wire, listening to the priest remind us there was indeed a "time for everything under the sun." One old woman dabbed at her eyes with a handkerchief, sniffing loudly. The rest of the group seemed frozen, including my mother. Dad tried to take her hand at one point, but she pretended not to see. Her eyes were focused on something in the distance.

Sammy, my five-year-old brother, was playing hide-and-seek among the headstones — humming the same six notes he always did — and I thought fleetingly of joining him. I guess that sounds like I didn't have proper respect for the dead. But I'd hardly known my grandmother — I could count the number of times she'd visited us on one hand. And we'd never been to see her here. My mother had always treated Gramma more like a distant acquaintance than a family member. So it was a little hard for me to get caught up in the proceedings.

I felt bad that I didn't feel bad.

Up the hill a bit, apart from the group, there appeared to be a father-son pair, both blond, bronzed, and sculpted, in matching black suits. I noticed a few of the other mourners covertly pointing them out to one another, and I wondered who they were.

Closer by, on the other side of the rectangular hole punched neatly in the ground, my grandmother's nurse, Rose Valois, stood with her teenaged grandson, he a full head taller than she. They were the only two dark faces in a crowd of pretty-much-uniform wrinkled, pasty white. When I glanced at them, the boy looked away, like he'd been caught staring.

My cheeks flushed. I tugged self-consciously at the suitcase-rumpled black sweater my best friend, Jecie, had lent me to wear over an old white blouse. Everything I had on was mismatched and ill fitting — humiliating enough in front of my grandmother's friends, but it sure would've been nice if my mother had warned me a couple of guys my age might be attending.

Mrs. Valois's grandson glanced back at me. His eyebrows lifted. Now I was the one who was staring.

I forced my attention elsewhere, beyond the fenced-in cemetery. To the fields baked golden. The trees lifting their heads above the bluff from their places along the banks of the river. The distant house crouched behind the thick border of gardens.

Waiting, I thought. And shivered involuntarily.

The morning air spoke to me. A breeze blew my hair into my face, whispering in my ear. The woods gossiped in hushed voices. Fallen leaves skittered across the ground like furtive animals. I heard an echo of voices, perhaps rising from some boaters on the river.

Sammy and I were the only ones who seemed to notice.

Following the service, the group massed together and headed to the house. All except the father-son pair — I saw them down on the driveway, climbing into a black SUV. I wished I'd gotten a better look at the younger one.

I slipped past the rest of the mourners, scooting out the gate and down the hill, putting some distance between me and the crowd. I wanted to be the first through the door of the family home I had heard about but never seen.

It was one of those places that actually had a name — Amber House. It'd been started in the 1600s as a stone-and-log cabin and had grown a little with every generation, almost like a living thing. Thrust out a wing of brick, heaved up a second story and a third, bellied forward with a new entry, sprouted dormers and gables and balconies. The house was mostly white clapboard trimmed in green, with lots of small-paned windows, and chimneys here and there. Which sounds messy, maybe, but wasn't. Everything came together into this beautiful whole. All of one piece.

At the entrance, I turned the brass knob, the metal flesh-warm in my hand. With a little push, the door swung smoothly open.

Shadows pooled inside, cool and deep. The air was dust-heavy and silent, empty. I saw a sweep of golden floor, thick Persian rugs, a staircase climbing and turning. Antique tables, chairs, lamps. Oil portraits hanging among folk art of all kinds. I knew without being told that generations of others had lived in this place, and had touched and used and looked upon these same things. It felt somber. Like a place where something was meant to happen. Like entering a church.

Then the crowd caught up with me, dammed into a pool on the front steps by the dumb girl rudely blocking the door, her mouth dropped into a small O.

"You're in the way, Sarah," my mother observed.

I pressed my lips together and stepped to the side.

My mother glided in — a black swan leading that flock of black-coated women. She did not look suitcase-frumpy. Even though we'd basically come straight from the airport, not a single wrinkle betrayed the sleek lines of her charcoal suit. She turned and positioned herself to greet the mourners, with maybe the smallest hint of a gracious-but-sad smile shaping her lips. Her guests shuffled past, pressing her hand, seeming a little baffled by her cold composure. They all stared around them at the house, commenting in low voices, sorting themselves into the rooms that opened off the entryway. Most went through the second door on the left, where the unmistakable clink of china and silverware announced the location of whatever food was being served.

For a moment, I regretted that I hadn't beaten the crowd to the lunch. My stomach was making those embarrassing empty noises. But I wasn't hungry enough to wait in a line with twenty white-haired ladies exuding a toxic cloud of Chanel No. 5. So when I saw Sammy scuttling past, I set off after him — my half-hearted attempt to delay the inevitable moment when he would turn up missing, and I would be sent to find him.

He must have sensed I was on his tail, because he doubled his pace. He led me into the living room and the library beyond that, and then through a door to a glassed-in gallery with two archways opening to other wings of the house, closed and unlit.

"Sam!" I hissed as unnoticeably as I could, speed walking behind him. "Sam. Wait up."

Without slowing, he veered left into the entry again. I next spotted him climbing the stairs. I followed him up, all the while trying to look at everything, trying to take in details. The eight-foot grandfather clock in the bend of the stairs, stopped at 10:37. The posts in the railing, each one different from the rest. The faces of every step, painted with a bible scene. A frame on the wall, covered in black cloth.

The stairs ended on a long landing, where a compass rose was inlaid in the varnished boards of the floor, as if a map was needed to navigate the house. I stood with my hand on the carved newel and looked in all directions. To the north was a wall of windows. South, the long railing overlooking the entry hall. To both the east and west, portals to halls that led off into gloom.

In the western wing, I glimpsed a shadow among the shadows. The back of a stray guest, just standing there, motionless. I wondered why she would be upstairs, nosing around by herself.

"Excuse me?" I called to her. "Are you looking for someone?"

Without a word, without turning, she walked away from me.

"All right, then," I said, mock cheerfully. What was I? Invisible? "Hey," I called again, "ma'am?"

She passed through a doorway out of sight.

A little offended at being ignored, I went after her. But stopped after a few steps, and stood there, wavering. Unwilling, unable, to go farther. And just completely surprised at my reluctance.

I shrugged. Shook my head. Let her snoop around. What did I care, really? After all, it wasn't my house.

I heard Sammy then, before I saw him, materializing out of the shadows in the eastern hall. He ducked through a door. Forgetting about the nosy guest, I started after him again. He'd found a boy's bedroom completely filled with nautical things — brass lamps, whaling paintings, a harpoon leaning in the corner. All of it orderly and dust free, but I could feel, when I entered, the biding stillness of the room's disuse.

Sammy was pushing himself in circles in a swivel chair before a desk. The mechanism made small, unpleasant shrieks.

Movement on the floor. "Spider," I informed him, and lifted my foot to smash it.

"Don't," he shrilled, and I hesitated just long enough for it to scurry under a slant-front desk.

"Gross," I said. "Why'd you stop me?"

"She's a good mother. She lives here," Sam said reasonably.

I sighed and shrugged. Another new nut-job notion Sam had got in his head. Whatever. "Listen," I said, trying to summon some older-sister authority, "we're not supposed to be up here, bud."

He jumped down easily enough. "Okay." I saw he was clutching some old stuffed animal.

"Put it back, Sammy."

"This is Heavy Bear. He's mine now. She don't need him anymore."

I grabbed for the bear and missed. Like a pro, Sammy twisted around me, reached the hall, and was off and running. I shot after him. "Put it back!"

"Nope!" he shouted over his shoulder, as his head disappeared down the stairs.

"Sam!" I hissed as I crested the landing — to find a sea of faces looking up at me, slightly aghast. I stopped short, flushing, and decided I was not going to make Sam my problem any longer. Holding my head as high as I could, I floated serenely down the stairs. Then I went to work, mingling. Listening.

My dad always told me that eavesdropping was a bad habit of mine. But it was really more like an instinct. Maybe it wasn't entirely ethical, but I wouldn't have learned what little I knew about the important stuff in life if I didn't eavesdrop every once in a while.

Mostly, the people around me were talking about my grandmother, which I guess is what you're supposed to do at a funeral. "Such a sensitive soul," one old woman told another. "I don't think she ever recovered from the tragedy."

I jotted that in my mental notebook — *tragedy* — and went back to listening.

Some people talked about the house, as if they had been invited to a guided tour instead of a funeral. "Oldest home in the state, you know; I'm told the antiques are all family heirlooms and priceless."

"Well, even so, Meredith wouldn't come today — says she hasn't set a foot in this house since she was twelve and saw something in the nursery —"

The last speaker spotted me listening to her and gave me a funny look. I smiled at her sweetly, and wandered on.

"I heard her liver failed, but with all poor Ida suffered, it was no wonder she drank."

Drank, I noted, and thought, *That explains a few things.*

"They say insanity runs in this family — did you see the little boy?"

I spun around at that, my hands reflexively shaping fists, but before I could open my mouth, my father put his arm over my shoulders and faced me back the other direction. "Stop eavesdropping." He leaned in to whisper to me. "Sometimes you hear things you don't want to hear."

I glanced back and had the satisfaction of seeing red stain the woman's cheeks as she watched me being pulled away. Dad gave me a tiny, tired smile and squeezed my shoulders before letting me go.

I turned my attention to the faces in the portraits of my ancestors. Mom didn't know I knew, but I'd overheard her talking on the phone, making plans to dispose of my grandmother's things through the best auction house on the East Coast. She seemed like she was in a hurry to get rid of it all and be done with Amber House. Not that I cared. Why someone would want a portrait of some long-dead stranger was beyond me.

But these faces were family. *Maybe*, I thought, *I ought to take a look.*

The newest portrait was of Gramma. I recognized her straightaway. A lovely young blonde, about twenty. It looked like she was hanging in someone else's spot, because there was a slightly larger rectangle of lighter-colored wallpaper all around the painting. I wondered who had been booted to cheaper real estate.

The oldest portraits were a time-darkened pair over the front table in the entry — a pretty good-looking man and woman, if you could get past the primitive paint job. He had dark hair and dark eyes, with an interesting scar running along his cheekbone. She was auburn haired, with a widow's peak, and eyes that seemed too big for her face. Hanging beside them, another black-draped frame, like the one on the stairs. I realized there had been a draped frame in the nautical room too. I lifted the corner of the cloth. It turned out to be a mirror. Someone must have covered all the mirrors.

"Sam?"

That voice belonged to my mom, remembering all of a sudden that she *was* a mom, and was therefore supposed to keep track of her child. If she spotted me, she'd ask me to do the track keeping. And I'd already done enough of that for the moment.

I dodged into the gallery behind the stairs. To my left was a long hall leading to closed, tall double doors. To my right, a second hall that took a bend out of sight. But instead of following my impulse to explore, I pushed through a swinging door just behind, to my left. The kitchen.

Where Mrs. Valois and her grandson turned to stare at me.

I couldn't think why I had come in here. I made my mouth work. "Oh," I said, backing out. "Sorry."

"Did you need —" Mrs. Valois started, but her grandson interrupted her.

"Would you like to sit down, Sarah?"

I stopped, startled and bemused by the invitation — in part because his voice sounded more combative than inviting. Had I done something to offend this guy? Was he trying to scare me off?

That last notion decided me. I walked to the table, pulled out a chair, and sat. I looked him in the eye and said, "You know my name?"

He held my gaze, unflinching. "Your grandmother used to talk about you."

Gramma talked about me? When we hadn't met a half-dozen times my whole life? I shook my head a little. "That's kinda hard to believe. She hardly knew me."

And instantly regretted it. I mean, what was I doing? Calling him a liar?

It didn't seem to faze him. He said, coolly, "Would you like something to drink?"

Mrs. Valois shot him a look, as if to ask why he was prolonging this uncomfortable conversation, but turned to me. "Can I get you a soda?"

He corrected her. "I bet Sarah would like one of those cherry Cokes from the stash at the back of the fridge." Then he smiled, just at the corners, and his eyebrows lifted. As if he was proving a point. As if he was daring me to contradict him.

And okay, so how *did* he know that? Had Gramma mentioned that too? How would she have known?

"Yeah," I agreed reluctantly. "A cherry Coke would be great."

Mrs. Valois went to the huge refrigerator — the only modern thing, it seemed, in the entire house. As she rummaged through its contents, I sized up this boy in front of me.

He was about my age, I guessed. This close, I could see he was scarred — it looked like he had been badly burned when he was younger. At his left shirt cuff, and up above his collar, a shiny white web of lines and patches spread across the dark brown of his skin. The scars ran up his neck and over his chin to just under his cheekbone. High cheekbones. Slightly almond-shaped green eyes. Looking into mine, watching me. I forced my attention to his hands — large and square, with long fingers. I'd always thought you could tell a lot about a person by his hands. Maybe because I admired my father's: a surgeon's hands, full of skill and intelligence. This boy's hands were like my father's.

As I stared, his right hand slipped to the cuff of his left sleeve and tugged it lower, over the scars. Mentally, I kicked myself again. I had a real talent for being thoughtless sometimes.

Mrs. Valois came back with the soda. Bottled in glass, no less. The boy took it, loosened the cap, and held it out to me.

"My favorite," I said, giving him the win. "Thanks."

"Your grandmother's favorite too," he said.

I took a few sips, wondering if a taste for sweet, syrupy soft drinks could be inherited. Nobody was talking. The boy continued to watch me, not rudely, just intently, like he was waiting for a conversation that had paused to begin again.

"I'm sorry," I offered finally, "I don't know your name."

He shook his head the slightest bit, like he couldn't believe it. *Sorry, but Gramma never talked about* you.

"I'm Jackson," he said.

"Nice to meet you." I nodded to include his grandmother. "Both."

That seemed to startle Mrs. Valois into motion. "Likewise," she said, "but I got to check on the food, clear away some dishes —"

"Oh," I said, starting to rise. "I could help you, Mrs. Valois."

"No, stay, sit," she said shortly.

Jackson nodded. "Take a break from the old birds out there —"

"Watch who you're calling old, young man." She started out the door, but turned back. "And while we're on the subject, Sarah, just call me Rose. Having someone call me 'Mrs. Valois' makes me feel every minute of my years. Anyone over the age of thirty's just a step from the grave for you kids. . . ." The door swung shut behind her.

It was evidently my turn to talk again. "Why's your grandmother doing all this work?" I asked. "I thought she was Gramma's nurse."

"Nah, not really. Gran's retired. She worked intensive care up in Baltimore for twenty years. She was just helping Ida out with the nursing thing. They were best friends most of their lives. She put this wake together out of respect."

"Oh. Well. Jeez," I said. "They must have been really good friends — did you see the spread on that dining table?"

He was amused by that. "Gran never does anything halfway. And she likes to cook."

"I hope there's some left over. Looked really good. Think I could pack some up to take back to the hotel?"

That startled him. "You aren't staying?"

"Here?" I said. "No. Not even tonight. Mom hates this place. She's selling it."

He looked down to hide it, but I saw shock on his face. And I thought, *Brilliant again, Sarah. Didn't Mom say they live on the property? She's probably selling it right out from under them.* What could I say? "I'm sorry."

He leaned back, his face composed. "I'm just — surprised. A place like this — you don't expect someone to sell it to strangers."

I shrugged a little. "I guess."

His turn to shrug. "Well, too bad you're not staying. I was hoping you and I —" He broke off, and I waited, wondering how that sentence was supposed to be completed. He looked uncomfortable.

"Hoping," he said, finally, his voice dropping, so that I had to lean in a little, "we could find the treasure."

Didn't see that one coming.

Mrs. Valois — *Rose* — came backing through the swinging door just then, her arms full of dishes. I jumped and whirled around, and my arm knocked into the Coke bottle, pushing it off the table edge. Jackson's hand caught it in midair, before it spilled more than a drop. My eyes widened. Those were *fast* reflexes.

"Getting crumbs everywhere," Rose grumbled from across the room. "Gonna have cockroaches living in the sofa." She unloaded the dishes into the sink. "None of them loved her. Why don't they all just go home?"

She pushed back out the swinging door and was gone again.

Jackson put the bottle back on the table, seeming embarrassed, not cocky like you'd expect a boy to be. But I was still focused on what he'd just said.

"Treasure," I whispered. "You're kidding, right?"

"What," he said, "you never heard about the Captain's lost diamonds? Everybody around here knows about them. I always wanted to search for them."

"So? Search. What d'you need me for?"

"Are you kidding? It's your house. I can't do it without you."

"Sounds to me like an urban legend. Sounds like it would probably be a pretty big waste of time."

"Sounds to me like a full ride at Johns Hopkins, if we find them."

"You going to Hopkins?" I was impressed.

"That's the plan, yeah. But it costs just a little more than Gran's got stuffed in her mattress. I say it's worth a look around."

I was ready to tell him no — the whole thing was ridiculous. If there was some lost stash of diamonds, why hadn't my grandmother found it? And if she hadn't, how would we? When would we even look for it? Where would we look for it?

And yet, it would suck if Mom sold the house and somebody else turned around and stumbled over a chest full of diamonds. And just imagine if the whole thing turned out to be true. Just imagine the look on my mother's face when I handed her a fistful of diamonds from this place she hated — *A gift from Gramma,* I could say. It might be worth a look around. For a couple days, anyway.

"Maybe," I said, lifting my shoulders.

He nodded, satisfied, like he'd expected me to say that. And I realized I was getting a little tired of feeling like he knew me a whole lot better than I knew him. Gramma shouldn't have talked so much about me.

"All right," I said abruptly. I stood. "I better get started looking for my brother. A place this big, I might die of old age before I run into him."

"Hide-and-seek."

"What?" I frowned a little, startled.

"Hide-and-seek? A children's game? One little kids play?"

I didn't like it. It was disturbing. Gramma couldn't have told him that Sam and I —

But then I felt stupid. It was just an idle comment. He didn't mean anything by it. He didn't know about Sammy and me. Not even my mother knew about Sammy and me.

I nodded and left without another word.

Chapter Two

It made me uncomfortable, to have a stranger seem to know so much about me. It felt unpleasantly weird. Like my life was just a story for other people to talk about.

But that thing about hide-and-seek — that was just *really* weird. The way he'd said it. Like he knew.

It was probably my only real talent, my ability to find my little brother. I wasn't beautiful and arty like my mother, or brilliant and driven like my father. As my teachers would be happy to inform anyone who would listen, I was a disorganized procrastinator with an attitude problem and (self-diagnosed) ADHD. But I had a veritable gift for finding Sammy.

I'd discovered it when I was twelve and he was nearly two. He'd just started wandering off on his own. That first time, we were in a department store in downtown Seattle. Mom looked up from the pile of silk scarves she was sorting through to find Sammy's stroller empty. She blamed me and called for him, checking all the nearby aisles. Then she started to panic. We split up, and a sales clerk summoned security, so a half-dozen middle-aged guys in uniforms were running around in circles with us. Other customers joined in, all of them calling, "Sammy," and not one of them figuring on how much the kid was enjoying himself.

But I did. I could just imagine it. I stood there, in the middle of the cosmetics department, imagining his chubby face, his wide smile, those little dimples I loved in his knuckles and knees. I could almost feel him, making himself small, giggling silently.

At first I thought I was making it up — an almost imperceptible electric vibration. But I walked toward that feeling, into it. Then it became a simple game of Hotter, Colder, like when your parents hide a present and tell you "You're getting warmer, warmer."

I found him tucked on a metal perch in the middle of a circular rack of dresses. He was delighted with himself, yelling, "Peekie, peekie!" Little twit.

My mother had no idea how I'd found him, and I never told her. I knew even then it wasn't the kind of talent she'd approve of. Mom loathed everything and anything that had to do with what she called "New Agey garbage." So I didn't think she'd want to know about my Sammy radar.

But she knew enough to always send me to find him.

"Sarah?" I jumped a little. An old lady sitting on the long sofa in the living room was beckoning to me. "Come here, dear," she said in this *I'm-really-wealthy* drawl that turned one-syllable words into two. "Sit beside me. You look the picture of Ida when she was your age."

I sat down next to her, enveloped in her lavender scent, half listening as she chattered on, first about my grandmother as a girl, and then about my "artistic" great-grandmother Fiona, who had thrown wild parties during Prohibition, and liked to dance in the moonlight, and could tell your fortune with a deck of cards. Great-gram had evidently told this woman's entire future for her when the woman was just eleven years old.

"Absolutely on the money too," she said. "Bad marriage, two daughters, typin' and typin' in a yellow house." She laughed and clapped her hands together like a child. "And I became a writah, you see? Fiona was absolutely psychic."

Sounded absolutely psychotic to me.

"You heard any stories about this house?" I asked, fishing. Okay, so I was a little interested in the lost diamonds. Maybe they were bogus, maybe they weren't, but how cool would it be to find them? Besides, I was a Tolkien fan — who wouldn't want to go looking for lost treasure?

"Stories," she said. "Oh, heavens, yes, child. It's been standin' here more than three centuries, after all."

"Like — what kind of stories?"

"Oh, you know. Murdahs. Ghosts. Secret passages. Suicides. Illegitimate children. The usual things."

"Any" — my voice dropped — "treasure?"

She laughed at me. "What? Amber House isn't treasure enough for you? Look around, child. The things just in these front rooms have got to be worth more than a million dollars. Not that your mother would dream of sellin' any of it, I'm *sure*. It's all pieces of your history."

"Yes," I agreed politely, thinking this nice old lady would likely have a stroke when she heard that was exactly what my mother had planned. "So . . . no hidden treasure?"

"*Hidden* treasure. Ah. You must mean the Captain's lost diamonds." She smiled wickedly and leaned in, as if to share some bit of juicy gossip. "Your great-great-however-many-great-granddaddy, Captain Foster, was a smugglah during the Revolution, and they say maybe dabbled in some piracy on the side. The story goes that the Captain liked to trade in his illicit wealth for diamonds. Harder to trace. Easier to carry. Unfortunately, diamonds have a way of disappearin'. They say he went mad looking for them. Who knows? Amber House holds its share of secrets. But those are in the past, aren't they, and the past doesn't give up its secrets easily."

"Sarah?"

My mother had wandered into earshot. I didn't have to be psychic to know that she was less than thrilled to catch me talking family history with the neighbors. Or to guess what her next words were going to be.

"Find Sammy, will you? Honey. Please."

I thought, as I forced myself into motion, both the *honey* and the *please* were nice touches. Added for the benefit of the guests.

I found Sammy back upstairs in the nautical room, talking to the bear.

He was sitting cross-legged on the bed, which was made like a ship's berth, all framed in wood to be its own little room, with drawers underneath and two porthole windows to the outside. Above it, a carved eagle stared from a ten-foot-wide board. A wooden mermaid leaned from a corner.

"I wonder whose room this was," I said.

"It's mine now."

"Sam," I said, shaking my head, "you know Mom doesn't want to stay here. She's booked us into a hotel."

"Nope," he insisted, "I wanna stay." He got a crafty look on his face. "Commere, Sarah."

He was up and running again, ducking past me, out the door, and down the hall. The whole *find-Sammy-and-bring-him-back* routine had been a lot easier before he'd gotten so fast.

I went into the hall. Sam was standing before another door. "Listen up, bud," I said, trying to sound stern. "We need to get back downstairs."

"Come here," he insisted.

"Fine." I took a few reluctant steps toward him. "What?"

"Look," he said, pushing open the door, holding his hands wide like a showman. "This is *your* room. I *choosed* it for you." He came and took my hand, and tugged me faster toward the door. "Look, Sarah. See?" He sounded so eager to please. "I *gived* it to you."

I looked inside.

It was a room of flowers. Not in a tacky way, like you'd see in some outdated decorating magazine. It was like the dwarfs' room in "Snow White," the way the Grimm brothers imagined it. The walls were hand painted with hollyhocks, irises, roses, lilies, and still more, maybe imaginary, blossoms in the deep, burnt shades of twilight. A canopy bed, draped in ribbon-trimmed linen, wore a quilt that was a mosaic of the same dusky colors, stitched into the image of a fruit-bearing tree. Two shelves of leather-bound books framed a dollhouse with gables and balconies and green-shuttered windows.

I realized, as I took it all in, that this room had once been my mother's. I knew it even as I doubted how my mother ever could have slept or played here, or lived here.

But I saw the way she'd propped up little things — photos, seashells — against the books on the shelves. How she'd draped a blanket over the back of a chair. These were traces of my mother that still could be found back home in Seattle, among the steel and glass and bleached wood. I stared a moment, my mouth open, wondering how she had ever gotten from here to there.

And, okay. Maybe there was treasure in the house, maybe there wasn't. But one thing was absolutely certain. There was no way I was going to turn down the chance to sleep in a room like this. At least for the few days Mom was planning on staying in Maryland.

"You got me, Sammy. This is my room."

"You're welcome," he said proudly.

"Yeah, thanks," I responded, as always, belatedly. "But listen to me. Mom's not going to let us stay here without a fight. You know that, right?"

"Right."

"So, here's the plan, Sam-my-man."

And we worked it out. People who didn't know Sammy probably would have thought I was asking too much of him. They always assumed Sammy didn't understand very well, because he was different from other kids. When he was four, they'd put a name on it — autism. Like it was a disease. But it didn't seem to me that what was different about Sam was something "wrong" that needed to be fixed.

It seemed like he had a gift for making connections in his head, and he made more of them faster than most people. Even when he was little, he had this sly sense of humor where his mind would slip sideways and he'd do something surprising and funny. And Sam was so sweet, so *not* mean. Not like other people. Not like normal people.

I thought he was the strangest, most wonderful friend I had. And I knew he was twice as smart as I was. So I could count on him to play his part. When I explained my plan to him, he smiled in appreciation. He totally got it. He was on board.

The last of the guests left about an hour after Sammy and I had finished plotting. They dribbled to the door and clutched my mother's hand, giving her a final helping of sympathy. She wasn't having any of it. She had remained cool and aloof all day. Which wasn't going to help her reputation in the neighborhood, but I guessed she didn't care very much.

Mom, Dad, Rose, Jackson, and I spent an hour clearing away, washing, sweeping, and finding room in that enormous fridge for all the leftovers until Mom finally had enough. "Let's leave the rest of this for — Rose, what is the name of the cleaning help Mother had?"

"Kate," Rose said, looking slightly offended on behalf of the forgotten woman. "Her name is Kate. She's a real nice lady."

"She's been coming twice a week?" Mom asked.

"Wednesdays and Saturdays."

"That'll work for now, I guess."

That's when my mother cleared her throat. I cringed. As charming as my mother could be, when I heard that little *ahem*, I knew Mom's capacity for tact was about to fail her once again.

"Rose, I'm sure it's no surprise to you that I intend to sell Amber House."

Rose folded her arms in disapproval. My father looked grim.

Mom swallowed and continued. "I wanted to tell you right away, to give you and your grandson adequate time to relocate —"

"No need," Rose said.

"What?" My mother's head jerked back a little in surprise.

"Jackson and I aren't moving anyplace. That cottage and land's ours."

"I'm sorry?"

"Fiona gave that land to Jackson's great-grandfather back in the twenties. We own that piece on the western line, from Nanga's cabin to the river. I got the deed."

"Oh," Mom said, a little faintly. "I never knew. Well. That's good," she added unconvincingly.

"Yes," Rose agreed. She handed a basket packed with some of the leftovers to her grandson and pushed him toward the door. "You let us know if there is anything we can do for y'all." Her short tone of voice completely undercut the genuineness of the offer, but my mother apparently didn't pay attention to that.

"I would love to have some help, Rose, going through Mother's papers and things, since you know this place better than anyone."

I don't know how my mother had the courage to utter that sentence. It was pretty easy to tell Rose didn't like her much. I guess, as Gramma's best friend, Rose might have been a little angry about the distance my mother had always kept from her. Not that I blamed Mom, necessarily. Even as a kid I could feel the presence of some old hurt or battle that stood between them like a third person, and I had never liked the sort of sweetly sarcastic way Gramma talked to my mom.

But right then I wished my mother had had the good sense to let Rose escape out the side door. An unpleasant silence welled up as Rose considered her response. I could see it just behind her lips, ready to emerge.

And that's when Sammy jumped down from his chair and took Rose by the hand. "It was so good, Rose."

"What, honey?"

"It was so good Gramma had you as a friend. Thank you."

As I stood there and wondered what had possessed Sammy to say such a thing, I could almost *see* the anger leak out of Rose. She gave Sammy an awkward little pat on the head and said, "Your gramma was a good friend to me too, child."

I noticed Jackson watching it play out with a little smile on his face.

Abruptly, Rose looked up at my mother. "I'll stop back by in the morning, make this child some breakfast. Ida always said you weren't much for cooking. Then we'll see what kind of help you need."

My mother considered being offended, but thought better of it. "Thanks," she said. "I understand we have a gardening service come by once a week, but can Jackson continue with the outside work he was doing for my mother?"

Rose shrugged. "Up to him."

Jackson nodded. "Be happy to, Mrs. Parsons. Saving for school. Thanks."

"No. Thank *you*," Mom said. "And thank you, Rose, for all the work you did for the reception. You really exceeded my expectations in every regard. The food was wonderful, and the house, the flowers, everything looked perfect." She held out a check she'd had in her pocket. "This will reimburse you for the money you spent on the groceries. Plus a little extra for all your time and effort."

Rose went back to being angry and wouldn't take the check. "You just rewrite that for the cost of the food, and I'll get it from you tomorrow. I didn't do this for pay. None of those folks stepped a foot in this house for the last twenty-five years, but I knew Ida would want a proper send-off, all the same. And she'd want Amber House looking her best."

Then she went out. And Jackson shut the door behind them.

The four of us sat down to a cold supper of leftovers around the kitchen table. Sammy was all upbeat and animated, and only I knew why — he was completely into being part of our conspiracy.

Before he left, my father made another pitch to Mom. "I wish you'd stay with me. You could have the second bedroom. There's a fold-out couch in the living room, the kids could sleep there —"

"Thanks, Tom, but I need to be close by, to get everything sorted out and disposed of. The hotel will be fine."

"Well, maybe the kids would like to spend the night. I've been out here eight months already, and they haven't once come to visit. I could show them the hospital, bring them back tomorrow evening."

"That's impossible. What would Sarah do all day with Sammy? Besides, I'm going to need her help. I want to get out of here and back home again as quickly as we can."

My father's face got tight. "Have it your way, Anne," he said. He took his jacket off the hook by the door. "You always do." He kissed Sammy on the head and stiffly patted my shoulder. I would have felt sorry for him, except I knew it was mostly his own fault. From a couple phone calls I'd "overheard," he'd gotten a little too close to Sammy's overly friendly pediatrician back in Seattle. So when he got the job offer he'd been hoping for from Johns Hopkins here in Maryland, my mother decided to let him make the move alone. She kept saying they were just separated, but I'd also overheard her talking to a lawyer. I'd thought about warning Dad, but I hadn't. Yet.

He left, and then it was just the three of us.

"Okay, guys," Mom said, "let's get these last dishes done."

Sammy cleared the table, humming his usual six notes, while I scraped, soaped, rinsed, and loaded things into the dish drainer. My grandmother had evidently had a limited appreciation for the modern conveniences. Massive refrigerator. No dishwasher.

Mom was searching through the cabinets.

"Thank God," she said, locating a stash of medical supplies in a narrow cupboard that contained mostly liquor. She pulled out a little bottle of aspirin. Then she gathered up her purse, her coat, Sammy's coat, a makeup case, the pills, and her keys. "Let's get out of here."

I gave Sammy a look, lifting my eyebrows deliberately. He gave me the smallest frown and shake of the head, disapproving of my lack of subtlety. I coughed to cover the laugh rising in my throat.

Without turning or even looking at Mom, Sammy whispered, "Nope." My brother. The *master* of subtlety.

"What?" Mom said, absolutely clueless about what was coming.

"Nope," he said, a little louder. "Nope, nope, nope, nope, *nope*!" Each time, he amped the volume, till the last one was practically rattling the windows. Then he just started to wail, wordlessly and as loud as he could.

"What is this?" my mother shouted, somewhat desperately. "What's going on?"

"I don't think he wants to go," I yelled back. Sammy continued at roughly the intensity of an ambulance siren.

Mom tried getting tough with us. "I need you two to get in that car right this instant!"

Sammy got tough back. He started to rap his knuckles against his skull and spin in circles, still screaming, with tears streaming down his cheeks. Mom stood there, speechless, hysteria bubbling behind her eyes. I held my hands out to show how helpless I was.

"Jesus, I can't take this today. I really can't. Stop it. Stop it!" She groaned. "All right!" I had expected more of a fight, but she *was* visibly exhausted. "We'll stay," she shouted.

Sammy shut off the noise like a hose, working down to a thin stream and then a couple of drips of sound. He took a deep breath and let out a long, shuddering sigh.

Freaking brilliant. I wished I could applaud.

My mother was in the cabinets again. This time she came out with a bottle of vodka and poured herself an inch over ice. I almost felt sorry for her. She'd spent all day in a place she clearly hated, being gracious to people she didn't like. And she *had* just lost her mother. Maybe it hurt and I just couldn't tell.

"Where are we going to sleep?" she snapped.

"Don't you worry about us," I said soothingly. "I'll get Sammy settled."

"Good," she said. "Good. I think I'm going to sleep in my mother's room down here. Seemed like it got pretty thoroughly cleaned. Only room in the house with a TV."

"We're going upstairs, okay?"

"Fine. Just —" She stopped to consider what she was going to say. "Don't worry about any — noises — you might hear. Old houses have a lot of creaks and groans, you know?"

"Of course, Mom. We know. Don't even think about it. We'll be fine. Can I borrow the laptop?"

"Sure. But there's no hookup, if that's what you're thinking."

No Internet? "How am I supposed to talk to Jecie?"

"There's a phone in the library."

"Yeah, sure. Never mind." Mom apparently didn't get that my friends didn't chitchat on the phone. I would have texted, but idiot that I was, I'd left my cell charger on my desk at home. "We'll be in Seattle in a couple days."

"God, I hope so," she said.

Sammy came to stand next to me. For the first time, Mom noticed Heavy Bear in his arms. A tiny furrow appeared between her brows. "Sammy, you can't have that. It's old and filthy. It will make you sick." She reached to take it. Sammy dropped open his mouth and started to wail.

"All right!" she said.

He turned it off. His lips curled up the tiniest bit.

I had created a monster.

We went out to the car to get our night bags — the rest of the luggage could wait until morning. Then Mom headed straight for Gramma's room. "Get to bed," she called back to us, and disappeared around the corner.

Sammy grinned up at me then. "You're welcome," he prompted.

"Yeah, right, thank you," I agreed. "You did good." I had to laugh, he was so pleased with himself. "Hey, champ, you got your flashlight in that bag?"

He nodded emphatically.

"You want to do a little more exploring before we hit the hay?"

He nodded emphatically.

We shut off the front hall lights, resolved to do our exploring in the dark. That way, if Mom surfaced as far as the hall, no glow would draw her out to investigate further. Plus, the overhead lighting would take the adventure out of it.

The darkness was intense, warm, velvety. The flashlight's beam stabbed through it feebly, picking out here a face staring from a portrait, there a china cat paused in a corner. As we tiptoed into the downstairs west wing, I walked just behind Sam, my hand resting on his back. I could feel his shoulder blades hunched up against the spooks just out of sight, and smiled, because I could feel mine doing the same thing.

The first room on the right side of the hall looked like an office; the one on the left was some kind of comfortable sitting room with a wall of night-blackened windows casting shards of our light back at us. A door to a bathroom on the right, and then a workroom. I saw a sewing machine with a piece of fabric still clamped in its teeth, and wondered what project had died with my grandmother. Across the hall, a wood-paneled room with one of those pool tables that have no pockets. At the hall's end, a pair of French doors that betrayed nothing of what lay beyond.

We pulled open both doors. And gasped in unison.

Before us spread a moonlit jungle of trees caught beneath a glassed-in metal web two stories high. At our left an iron stair spiraled up into the darkness, and somewhere behind the walls of greenery, a fountain splashed. We wandered stone paths that led between beds of ferns and flowers until we found the shallow pool. Its surface was a black void in the darkness, the flat pads of lilies suspended in it.

Sammy sucked in his breath, startled, then slowly raised his light. A bone white form stood facing us at the opposite end of the pool — a marble statue of a woman in a Grecian dress. We walked closer.

"She looks sad," Sammy said, staring up at the statue's downcast eyes. They were stone smooth, carved without irises. She was looking blindly into her outstretched hand, where four small red crystals sat like drops of blood on her palm. I wondered if they were loose or set into the marble. I leaned against a rock in the pool's wall and reached to touch them.

d me, Sammy switched the light off. Struggling to balance, I completely missed the statue in the sudden rkness — couldn't find her at all. Some little part of me wondered irrationally if she had moved.

"Hey," I said, turning. "Sammy? Where'd you go?"

"Sarah," I heard him whisper.

"Sam," I hissed, tracking the voice. "Come back here." I followed the sound of his steps right and right again, trailing him down the path, deep in darkness. "Sam?"

"Sarah," he said again, farther ahead.

"Sam, this is seriously *not* time for hide-and-seek." I walked faster, then started to trot, pushing through branches that reached invisibly from the dark. Left, right. I could hear him moving ahead of me. "Sam. Stop!"

"Sarah," he whispered again.

The room felt endless. I couldn't see the webbed iron walls; there were too many stars. I stopped still to listen, to catch my breath stuck like a knot in my throat. Oddly, I couldn't hear the fountain. I started backing up, trotting back the way I had come. "Sammy! You're freaking me ou —"

And I collided with him, appearing from the dark, his light suddenly gleaming.

"Sarah —" he started.

"Don't *do* that," I said, taking his hand a little too tightly.

He nodded, but said, "Do what?"

"Don't run off like that."

"I won't, Sarah. I won't run off."

The moonlight had dimmed. There were clouds where there had just been stars, and they started to empty. A few tiny splats turned into a million drops hitting the glass roof in a cacophony of sound. I felt chilled.

We crept back into the house and down the hall to the entry and fished our packs out from where we had stowed them under a bench. "No more 'sploring tonight, Sarah?"

"No, Sam. I'm done for now. Time for bed. But let's be quiet. I think Mom's still up. I hear the TV."

"Nope, Sarah. I don't hear it."

"Yeah. Just voices. Real low. So keep it down. We don't want her coming out here."

We slipped upstairs. I helped Sam find his pajamas, then headed for the bathroom with mine. I felt better in my old flannel PJs — not so chilled, wrapped in the familiar.

The light was off in my room — *my room*, I was already calling it — but a strange glow came from it. When I snuck to the door, I found Sam in there. In his Sammy way, he had found a switch on the bottom of the dollhouse and a compartment for the batteries from his flashlight. All the little lights in the dollhouse were lit. It was like something bewitched. I half expected the dolls to get up and start walking around.

"Cool, Samwise," I said. But I flicked on the room's overhead light.

Once I had Sammy settled in bed, I went back to my own room. I turned out my bedside lamp, and the darkness settled in again, complete. And the quiet was so quiet. Not like in the city, where there was always a radioactive glare and the hum of unceasing traffic coming through the window. In the silence, in the dark, my head was filled with a ringing that seemed like it should be too high-pitched to hear.

When I was younger, I'd refused to sleep without a light. It wasn't that I was scared, so much as I was too aware of what the darkness did to my perception of things, how it affected my senses.

My hearing became too keen, my sense of touch too pronounced — if I thought about it, I would suddenly itch in a thousand places and hear the thuds of my own heart thumping in my chest.

Falling asleep in that room that night was like when I was little. But it wasn't my ears or my skin that was suddenly attuned — it was some other part of me, some part that had no name. Some part that waited silently, there in the dark.

Chapter Three

I woke from a dream that floated just beyond my grasp, of voices in the dark and a statue weeping diamond tears. It was full daylight; eight o'clock in Seattle, but eleven o'clock here. Late. I threw on the jeans and shirt I had stuffed in my night bag and got moving.

Rose stood at the foot of the stairs, winding a key in the face of the grandfather clock, her left arm full of the mirrors' black drapes.

"Good morning," I greeted her. "Need some help?"

"No, child," she said. "I'm the only one who knows where these things belong." Then she added as an afterthought, "But thank you."

I was guessing that as far as Rose was concerned, I was in the same boat as my mother. Someone who hadn't done her dear departed friend justice.

I gestured at the black cloths. "What was with the drapes, Rose?"

"Just a southern superstition," she said absently as she moved the clock's hands to the right time. "To help the departed's soul cross over and not get trapped in the looking-glass world."

"The looking-glass world?" I repeated. "Like Alice?"

"*I* didn't invent the notion," Rose answered irritably. "People used to believe you could see through to the other side in a mirror. To the place where souls go after death, before they move on to their final destination. If we could see them, they thought maybe the other side can see through to us too. And maybe those souls wouldn't want to move on, but just keep hanging about being as close as they could to the ones they loved." She gave the pendulum a little push and set time into motion again. "It's just custom," she concluded. "Okay?"

I shrugged. "'S okay with me."

Mom stuck her head out of the library door. "Are you available, Rose?" Then she ducked back inside again. Rose raised her eyebrows and snorted slightly, I presumed at my mother's abruptness. But she headed through the door after her.

Sammy was sitting in the kitchen when I came in, with Heavy Bear slumped on the floor beside his chair. He was scarfing down pancakes, courtesy of Rose, I guessed. *Good thing she likes at least one member of the family.* I sat down next to him. "Any pancakes left?"

He stopped with his fork a half inch from his open mouth. "Nope." He rerouted the fork toward me. I opened my mouth and accepted his last bite of pancake. It was good — light, buttery, soaked in real maple syrup.

"Yum," I said.

"You're welcome," he said.

"Thank you," I said. "Rose is a good cook."

"Better than Mom."

"*You're* a better cook than Mom," I told him. That cracked him up. "You tell anyone about our explorations, Sam?"

"Nope."

"Good man." He nodded again.

Rose came pushing through the swinging door. She went to the cabinet beneath the sink and came up with a box of black garbage bags. "Forgot to say: There's a plate warming in the oven for you, if you want it."

"Thanks," I said, with a genuine rush of gratitude. "Sammy gave me a bite of his and it was delicious."

"Just johnnycakes. Didn't want to waste the batter. Use a pot holder and put a mat under that plate."

"I will," I promised. I decided I could live with the fact that Rose didn't like me as long as I was included in the pancakes.

I was heading for the oven, but Sammy stopped me. "Can I show you something, Sarah?"

I sighed. "What is it, Sam?"

He picked up Heavy Bear in one hand, took mine with the other, and towed me through the swinging door into the hall and on toward the living room. He stopped in front of the small side window. "Lookit."

A huge oak stood in solitary splendor on the lawn. Its branches held a tree fort, built on a couple different levels, with little wooden benches and a partial roof in one corner.

"Way cool, Sam," I said. "We'll check it out later."

"Who's that?" Sammy asked, now pointing at some bushes near the foot of the tree.

I squinted. The play of light on the moving leaves made it look almost as if someone was crouched there in the darker shadows. But the limbs of the bushes danced again in the breeze, showing it was just an illusion.

"It's no one."

"No one?" Sammy repeated.

"Right. No one's there. Can I eat now?"

I had to hunt for the pot holders I'd promised Rose I'd use. Third drawer down in the stack next to the oven, I came across a box filled with the broken remnants of some piece of china. I wondered why anyone would keep all those fragments, even though it had been a pretty little thing — lavender on the inside, blue on the outside, with three-dimensional cherry blossoms speckling the background. Looked like maybe it had been a pitcher. I picked up its handle, shaped and painted to look like a tree limb.

And I could picture it, exactly, in my mind's eye, sitting on the kitchen table. Cheerful. Full of juice. Then some young hand bumped into it, knocking it off the edge. I imagined it falling, turning as it fell. Smacking against the floor and fracturing instantly with a low chord of notes into all its many pieces. Juice spraying out around it, red, like bleeding. I could practically hear my grandmother's voice, "Oh, Anne." I could practically *see* my mother's younger face: defiant, the smallest bit satisfied.

I shook my head.

That was — strange.

I mean, I have a pretty good imagination, but all those vivid pictures in my mind — a little strange.

I set the handle carefully back in the box, but my finger brushed up against another piece. A drop of blood welled up. *Brilliant.* Finger in my mouth, I finally found the pot holders next drawer down.

Sam had followed me back to the kitchen and was sitting at the table, staring wistfully at my pancakes. Made me smile. I slathered on the butter and syrup, and paid Sammy back his bite, plus interest. He took off for the outer door, still chewing, with Heavy Bear in tow.

"Hey," I called to him. He turned back, his eyebrows lifted. *"You're welcome,"* I said, the way he always said it to me.

He grinned a pancake-filled smile.

"Stay away from the river and that tree house till I can come with you. Promise?"

"I promise, Sarah." He slipped out.

I was down to my last bite when my mother came in, carrying a near-empty coffee mug. That was her breakfast — a couple cups of coffee, black. She stared at my plate. "You didn't eat that whole stack of pancakes, did you?"

In answer, I stabbed the bite and swirled it around in the pooled syrup and melted butter, then looked her in the eye and stuck it in my mouth. My mother never called me fat, which would have been ludicrous, since I was almost too skinny. And I was used to her being abrupt and critical — I could deal. But, I thought to myself as I chewed and swallowed, deliberately and slowly, maybe being in this house was making her a little worse than usual.

She frowned and cleared her throat. "We have to go into Baltimore tomorrow. Your dad wants to show you Johns Hopkins. I expect you to get Sammy to cooperate. Okay?"

"Sure, Mom. Sammy and I both want to see it."

"Any funny noises last night?"

I shrugged with my face. "Slept like a rock."

She looked at me as if gauging my sincerity. "Well, maybe we'll just stay here another day or two. You know how I hate hotels."

Indeed I did. "Fine by me and Sam," I said. "Um, Mom?" She looked at me expectantly. I hesitated before I asked. "Did you ever break a little blue china pitcher?"

Her face shifted rapidly into an expression of anger and disgust. "She couldn't even throw away the *broken pieces*? Like every little thing in this house is a piece of a shrine? You toss them in the trash for me, honey, okay?"

"Sure," I said, lying.

"I have an enormous amount of work to do over the next couple days. Papers to go through, inventories, getting everything ready for sale. I want you to keep an eye on Sammy, make sure he doesn't get into trouble."

"Yeah. Of course."

"Where is Sammy now?"

"Just outside."

We both went to the window to check. Sammy was there, playing hide-and-seek in the bushes. It was faint, but I could hear him chattering cheerfully.

"Is he talking to himself?" My mother sounded concerned and accusatory. She was always looking for odd behaviors in Sammy, just like she was always looking for cellulite in me.

"He's only playing pretend. Talking out loud. Little kids do that."

"Yeah," she said. "So do schizophrenics."

I just had time to think to myself, *Nice*, when we heard a sharp rapping — the knocker on the front door.

"Lord," she said. "Who could that be? Do I look all right?"

"You look great, Mom." My mother never looked anything but great, her makeup flawless, her clothes crisply casual. No cellulite on that woman.

She headed to the front door. I heard her open it. "Good heavens!" she squealed, as clear as if she were in the room. "Robert, how great to see you!" she said in the same high voice.

Robert spoke in a saner tone. I couldn't hear what he said.

"What has it been?" Mom went on, full-volume soprano. "Twenty years? This must be your son. He looks just like you. I saw you two yesterday from a distance. Was sorry you couldn't stay. I'm so glad you came back, so we could actually talk. My lord, he's so tall and handsome, Robert. Can you believe we have kids this old?"

I did not catch what Robert believed. My mother kept going. "You have to meet my Sarah. She's back in the kitchen."

Oh, my God. She was bringing them back here. Me in a wrinkled T-shirt and jeans, and syrup the only thing on my face. I practically threw my pancake plate in the sink, then I bent over, pulled my uncombed hair back as tight as I could, and snapped the hair tie on my wrist around it.

"Sarah, honey —"

This strange woman who looked something like my mother walked through the door, her eyes bright, her cheeks flushed. Then I saw why. Robert, who I recognized as the father half of the black-suited pair from Gramma's funeral, followed her in. All six foot four of him, baked to a golden brown, teeth white and even. He was in his mid-forties, but even I was dazzled.

"— I want you to meet an old friend of mine, *Senator* Robert Hathaway."

He flashed me a brilliant smile. I gripped the hand he extended as strongly as I could. Didn't make a dent. "Pleased to meet you, Senator Hathaway."

"And this" — my mother gestured to someone in the rear — "is Robert's son, Richard."

Richard — the other half of the pair — stepped into frame, a smile on his face. And I thought, *Thanks, Mom. Thank you ever so much. Why don't I just shoot myself?* The father was beautiful; the son was beautiful *and* seventeen. "Hey," I said lamely.

"Hey," he returned, still smiling.

"Sarah looks so much like you, Anne." That was the senator, being gracious.

"Thank you," I said automatically, surprised to hear myself echoed in unison by my mother. She put an arm around my shoulders and added, "I'm always flattered to have someone say there's a resemblance."

Okay, I thought, *someone come fetch this pod person. I want my real mother back.*

"I've never been to Amber House before, Mrs. Parsons," Richard was saying. "I'd love to look around."

My mom and the senator looked at me expectantly. Inwardly, I sighed and wished for a breath mint. Outwardly, I smiled, hoping there wasn't any pancake stuck in my teeth. "Sure. I haven't seen much of it myself. We can explore together."

"Great," he said.

We wound our way through the library and the living room, with me making such stunning observations as, "This is the library," and, "This is the living room."

When we got to the front hall, he jumped in: "This is the entry." He laughed at me, but not in a mean way. I laughed at myself and relaxed a little.

"Sorry. Not much of a tour guide. Why'd you want to look around, anyway?" I asked.

"Are you kidding? Everyone in this part of Maryland would love a chance to wander around Amber House."

"Yeah?" I said. "Anyone under the age of thirty?"

He smiled and shrugged. "Mother was a big antiques collector. She always wanted to see the inside of this place. I guess she got me hooked."

"Was?" I asked.

"Yeah," he said, pausing. "She — passed away a few years ago."

"I'm so sorry."

"Dad and I are doing okay." He changed the subject. He gestured to the old portraits I'd noticed the day before: "These are from the seventeenth century, so they must be Sorcha and Liam O'Malley, the founders of Amber House. That clock," he said of the grandfather, as we started walking again, "is eighteenth century and looks like it has its original paint." He turned up the stairs, pointing out the bible paintings. "These are reputed to be by Edward Hicks."

I was a little flabbergasted. "Okay," I said. "You're just making all this stuff up, right?"

"Almost." He grinned. "I just used up the sum total of my antiques expertise. But it sounded impressive, didn't it?"

"Uh-huh," I said. "You should be a politician."

He laughed. "Well, it *is* the family business." We reached the compass rose landing, and he crossed to poke his head into Sammy's room. "The famous nautical room. Belonged to the Captain's son, Matthew. He died young, probably of tuberculosis."

"How do you know all this?" I said. "It's my family, and I don't know any of it."

"Fiona Warren — your mom's grandmother — wrote a book about this house. My mother had a copy."

"And you *read* it?"

He smiled again. "Not the whole thing. But it's more interesting than you might expect. She pretends to be writing a nonfiction account, but it's full of details nobody could possibly know. And sometimes she'll tell the same event twice, but have it turn out two different ways. She was a little crazy. Literally. She spent some time in an asylum."

"I come from such a colorful gene pool."

"You and me both." He headed on for the next door. My door.

"No, wait —"

He already had it open. Pajamas on the floor. Bed unmade. Suitcase open with personal items poking out. *Great.* "This, I'm guessing, is your room?"

"Yeah. Sorry about the mess. I kinda slept late. Didn't have a chance to, um, clean up yet."

He grinned. I took a moment to admire that grin. Square with just a little crooked, really wide, all teeth. It tugged his long, straight nose down a tad. No dimples — good. Strong chin — good. Startlingly blue eyes — great. He pushed back a curl that had fallen onto his forehead. Pretty nice-looking head of hair too. I realized I was staring and looked away. "That door," I said, gesturing, "is the bathroom, but I haven't opened any of these others."

"Well, I think these must lead to the Captain's rooms," he said.

I followed him into a sitting room, with a bedroom beyond. An oil painting of a ship in a storm hung over a fireplace. The walls were decorated with a collection of guns and swords that must have come from all over the world. He picked up a piece of ivory from a table and held it out to me. It was etched all over with a whaling scene. "This is scrimshaw. Sperm whale tooth usually carved by sailors. You can't even buy whale ivory like this anymore; most countries have banned the sale."

The Captain's room was littered with the stuff, on every table, the fireplace mantel, the shelves. Coupled with the weapons, all that endangered whale ivory made the room a little grim.

"I don't think I like this guy much," I said.

"He was a shipowner who smuggled guns for the Colonials during the Revolution and then got into the slave trade." He shrugged. "Or so your great-grandmother's book says."

Now I *really* wanted out of his room. "Let's go."

I left; he followed after. "Wait, we're missing one." He opened the door next to the entrance to the Captain's suite. "This was his wife's."

The room was a startling contrast to every other room in Amber House. It contained only a bed, a dresser, and a chest. The walls held a single painting of two handsome children, and a crucifix. "Wow," I said.

"Kind of a minimalist, wasn't she," he said, stepping inside. "Fiona says Deirdre Foster was sickly most of her life. The Captain kept her locked away from her children — thought she was insane."

"Another lunatic ancestor," I said from the doorway. "Lucky me."

He picked something up from the top of the dresser. "Huh. Wonder why this is here," he said, holding the thing in his hand out to me.

I started inside to take it from him, but stopped like I hit a wall. I had a strong impression of sadness filling that room. The air felt cold.

"Let's go somewhere else," I said, shaking my head. He looked quizzical, but came back out.

"Souvenir," he said. He turned my palm up and dropped the thing into it — a small green stone polished smooth, mottled with veins of peach and darker green. Odd, I thought, that something coming from that room should feel so warm.

My fingers closed around it. "Thanks." I tucked it in my pocket.

He pulled the heavy door closed. I saw then that it had an iron keyhole, set in the middle of an ornate scalloped cross pressed into the metal. I touched it, almost hearing the metallic clanks of a key turning. The thought came unbidden to mind: *They locked the madwoman in.*

Richard chose that moment to lean in and whisper ominously: "This house is haunted, you know."

I tried really hard not to flinch. "Haunted?"

"So they say. Maybe it's Deirdre."

Standing outside that desolate room, the thought of ghosts made the back of my neck crawl. But I wasn't going to let Richard see it. I shrugged. "Good," I said. "A house as old as this — there better be some ghosts."

He looked at me as if assessing, and a slow smile spread across his face. "Where next?" he asked.

I was done with these depressing rooms. "West wing," I answered. "I want to show you something."

"The conservatory?" he guessed.

Is that what it was called? "The conservatory," I agreed. He started off ahead of me, and I jokingly power walked past him. "Hey," I said. "Who's the tour guide here?"

"I thought we established that — I am," he answered, and I heard him trying to take back the lead.

I walked faster, then started to run. Instantly he was on my heels. I sprinted across the landing, shooting through the arch into the west wing. He reached for my arm; I put on a burst of speed. I wasn't going to let him catch up with me. I'd break my speed running right into the wall at the end of the hall, even, the way I used to when I was little. Laughter leaked out of me like air escaping a balloon.

Strong fingers wrapped around my arm just seconds before impact. Richard tugged me back as he slowed sharply. We collided, and I saw he was laughing as hard as I was. "Are you completely out of your mind too?" he asked.

"Not usually," I said. "But then again, don't all crazy people think they're sane?"

"I know I do," he gasped. We both stood there, breathing hard, laughing with what little air we had. And I still felt the touch of his fingers on my arm like a bracelet of heat.

Get a grip, I told myself. I yanked the curtains apart and let the sunlight fill the dark hall. "Come on," I said, opening the French doors.

We walked carefully out onto an iron-grill platform, from which the spiral staircase descended. There were birds out this morning, little bright blotches of color, singing in the branches, darting through the air. We exchanged a smile. I started down the steps, and he followed. At the bottom, I plunged down a path, trying to remember the way to the fountain.

And there she was, the statue guarding the pool. The lily blossoms open, huge and creamy. Foot-long orange-speckled fish swimming in their shade.

"Sarah?" Richard called.

"Over here," I said in a musical tone that embarrassed me.

He came through an arch of vegetation, admiration in his eyes. "Look at that," he said.

"I know. Pretty amazing, huh?"

"It should be a painting." He framed out a rectangle with his fingers. "*Girl by Fountain*."

The guy was flattering me. And I blushed. I was such a loser.

"Who built this?" I said, covering my embarrassment. "Fiona?"

"Fiona's parents, actually. Around the turn of the last century." He pointed at the statue. "Fiona asked for her specifically. Persephone. Demeter's daughter, stolen by Death to dwell in the Underworld."

And the red stones on her hand, I realized, were the pomegranate seeds that had doomed her. I saw in the daylight that the water trickling into the pool came from the statue's blind eyes, running down to fall from the tips of her lower hand, the hem of her marble gown. It was kind of awful. "She was also called Nestis," I remembered. "'Moistening mortal springs with tears.'"

"Yeah, she looks like quite a weeper," he observed with amusement. "How'd you know that?"

"My classics teacher had a poster on the wall."

"Can I show you something else pretty amazing?"

"Sure." I nodded.

"How do we get outside?"

I led him back into the west wing, down through the hall and sunroom, and out another set of French doors onto the flagstone patio. The air felt cool and clean after the trapped humidity of the conservatory. I closed my eyes and breathed in deeply.

"Sarah? You still with me?"

I opened my eyes, squinting a little in the bright light. Richard was eyeing me, a quizzical smile on his face. He gestured toward the steps with his left hand, pressed the small of my back with his right. "Race you."

Then he started double-timing it down the steps, laughing back at me. I took off after him. The flagstone steps wound down the hillside between rock retaining walls, with ferns, flowers, and vines trailing over their tops. They ended on a stone landing that opened onto —

— a dock. On the river. With a beautiful golden-orange sailboat moored there.

"Jeez," I said, in disbelief. "Is this — is this my gramma's?"

"I think she's yours now. She's called the *Liquid Amber*."

I stooped to look at her name. "The *Liquid Amber IV*." The woodwork on her was nothing short of amazing, but she had none of the shiny gadgets I was used to seeing. "She looks pretty old."

He nodded. "Everything at Amber House is, isn't it? I think your great-grandparents used to sail her, so that makes her at least a hundred."

"And she still floats?"

"Floats pretty fast, from what I've heard. Do you sail?"

"Are you kidding? I'm from Seattle. We live on the water."

"Bonus points, Parsons."

Points? I thought. *Is he keeping score?*

"We should go sailing," he said.

"I don't know if this boat's ready to take out —"

"I was inviting you to sail with *me*, on my boat. Dad and I live a half mile downriver."

"Oh." Was this guy asking me on a date? "Sure. I love sailing."

"Day after tomorrow, then?"

I wished I had my phone with me, so I could snap a picture of him to show Jecie. She'd never believe me without the photographic evidence. I nodded as coolly as I could manage. "I think I can squeeze you in."

"Great," he said easily, as if he made plans like this every day of the week. Which he probably did. "I'll pick you up here at ten thirty and we'll sail down toward the bay. Assuming you can wake up that early?"

I grinned. "It'll be tough, but I'll make the effort." He grinned back. "Don't you have school?"

"Careful scheduling. Only four days a week."

"Lucky."

"You know it," he said, still smiling widely. "We should get back."

"Oh. Right. Sure."

"After you," he said, gesturing toward the steps.

Nope. Nuh-uh. He wasn't watching my rear end climb four flights of stairs — even though I had a pretty decent rear end. "You first," I said.

Mom and the senator were sitting in the living room drinking coffee when we got back. Looking pretty cozy, I thought with disapproval.

"Dad, Sarah and I are going out on the water on Friday. You don't have plans for the *Swallow*, do you?"

"Not a one." The senator flashed the smile they probably put on all his campaign posters. "You should try to introduce Sarah to some of the other kids around here."

"Sure," Richard said.

"Oh," my mother exclaimed, struck by some thought. "I just had this *brilliant* idea. Sarah is turning sixteen in ten days. I know this is short notice, but wouldn't it be fantastic if we could get all our old friends together, Robert? Have a huge party? Richard could get the young people to come."

A party? I repeated in my head. *My birthday here? Whatever happened to leaving as quickly as possible?*

"I'm not doing anything next weekend," the senator said with enthusiasm. "We could pull it together, right, Richard?"

"If you have food, my friends will come," Richard said with that easy smile.

"We could do a masquerade," my mother improvised. "It's almost Halloween." She turned to me. "I felt kind of bad you weren't going to have a sixteenth party, honey, like I did and Gramma did and, well, all the girls of Amber House. Now you can."

All the girls of Amber House? Suddenly my mother was a traditionalist? I must have been lost in shock too long, because she prodded me again. "Is this brilliant or what, Sarah?"

They were all waiting for me to respond. I honestly didn't know what to say. If we had been in Seattle right now, I would have been hoping to see a movie with Jecie to celebrate my sixteenth. If I was really lucky, I'd get a used car for my gift. All of a sudden, I'm supposed to have a huge expensive costume party with dozens of strangers? Yet I couldn't bring myself to embarrass my mother in front of her friend, the good senator. My voice squeaked out a little queerly. "Brilliant, Mom."

The tiniest frown creased my mother's brow.

"It *is* brilliant, Annie," the senator confirmed. *Annie?* Did anyone *ever* call my mother Annie?

"But, heavens, Robert, maybe it's just impossible. I'll need a band, a caterer, a florist — Lord, a thousand things."

"It can be done," he said with assurance. "I know a young guy who's opening a restaurant in D.C. No doubt he's a little overwhelmed, but with this kind of a crowd — if he could park a van with his restaurant's name near the entrance, he'd probably pay *you* to cater it."

"If I had a caterer," my mother breathed, "everything else would be easy."

Another brilliant smile. "I'll give him a call. You'll see. This absolutely can be done." Confidence radiated off of him like solar heat. *No wonder people voted for him.* He fished out a card with the national seal and wrote on the back. "Here's my private phone number. Give me a call. Richard and I will get you names and addresses. And I can probably come up with a little more help."

"Well, I am just so excited," my mother said. "I haven't thrown a party like this in — years. Isn't this exciting, honey?"

"Exciting," I agreed, trying harder to give my voice a lift. Remembering how much Mom had wanted to leave, and wondering what *exactly* had made her change her mind. Perhaps the senator?

"I wish you could meet my son before you go, Robert. Sarah, have you seen Sammy?"

No. I hadn't seen him. I'd spent so much time being fascinated with the whiteness of Richard's smile, I'd lost all track of Sammy. And worse, now that I thought about it, I couldn't *sense* him.

Mom saw it in my face. "Find him for me, Sarah."

"Sure." *Maybe.* I went into the front hall. I took a few deep breaths, imagining Sammy, his sandy hair, his crazy smile, the twinkle in his eyes.

Nothing. Why couldn't I feel Sammy?

"Sarah?" Mom called, a little annoyed. "Wasn't he just outside?"

"Yes," I said, forcing my feet into motion.

"I'll meet him another day, Annie," Robert said. "I have to go. Do you" — he paused delicately — "need some help finding him?"

"No," Mother said. "Sarah will find him. She always does."

"That's fine," the senator said as I moved out of earshot. "Sorry to dash out like this. Richard has a tournament —"

I cut through the gallery and started running. I didn't want my mother to see me panicking, but that's where I was. Full panic mode. Why couldn't I sense him?

All I could think of was the river at the border of Amber House, running slow and cold and deep. Waiting to pull Sammy down.

Chapter Four

I burst out the sunroom's exterior doors. "Sammy!" Nothing. Calling and listening, I trotted the path that ran below the east wing and wove through the gardens on that end of the house till I reached a hedge wall. I circled back in a wide arc toward the front of the house. "Sammy!" My voice echoed back at me. I was pretty sure they could hear me in the next county over.

The senator's heavy dark sedan was just disappearing out the front gate when I reached the lawn outside the dining room. "Sammy!"

Nothing. No response.

The tree house, I thought. I raced past the front door to the oak. But the ladder stopped ten feet short of the ground. No way was he in the tree.

Mom came out the front door. "Sarah, what's the problem?"

"I don't know where he is, Mom."

"You'll find him. You always find him."

"You don't get it. I don't *know* where he is."

Maybe my mother could see the panic in my eyes. She turned back inside.

I ran around the conservatory, calling. I knew he wasn't down the stone steps that led to the river; Richard and I had just come up those. I doubled back through the west gardens and into the fields beyond. I checked the graveyard. I stood at the edge of the bluff, called down toward the river, and listened.

Still no answer. No sounds except birds. I couldn't even hear the water. The rivers back home always ran noisily over their rock beds, but the one below passed so slowly, it seemed like it was dragging against the will of gravity. I thought again of Sammy getting pulled into that slow cold current so that I couldn't feel his heat anymore.

"Sammy!" I screamed. "Answer me, Sam. Stop playing!"

He had to be somewhere else. Just had to be.

I ran on, into the woods on the west side of the property. I heard a rustling, maybe an animal, down the hill and across a little ravine. I squinted through the leaves — and caught a tiny glimpse of white.

"Sammy!" I called. "No more hide-and-seek. You come home now."

A pale sound like laughter. The rustling in the bushes started moving up the far hillside away from me, fast.

"Sammy! Stop!" I started running again, down across the hill. The little creep was running too. I could just catch flashes of white as he whipped through the brush. "Stop, Sam!"

I leapt over the creek bed at the bottom, and began running uphill. Hard work. I couldn't believe the speed that little monster was making. My legs were burning; my lungs were burning. "Sammy!"

The slope started leveling off. There was a thinning in the trees ahead, a concentration of sunlight. If Sammy knew what was good for him, he'd be sitting in that clearing when I got there.

I grabbed the stitch forming in my side and pushed on through the bushes into the open. I stopped short in front of a large, square log cabin. Smoke curled from the stone chimney despite the day's warmth. The rocking chair on the front porch was occupied by an old woman in a dark, shapeless dress. She looked at me with interest.

"Sorry," I gasped around breaths, "to intrude."

"Oh," she said, smiling, seeming oddly surprised I had chosen to speak to her. "I should've said hello straight off. It's good to see you, Sarah."

She knew my name. I figured she must be Rose's mother. She looked old enough. "I'm after my brother. See him?"

"You know me, child?" she asked, leaning forward.

"No. Sorry. No one mentioned you."

She nodded. "Guess Providence figured it was time we met." She leaned back. "Sammy ain't out here."

"Just saw him. Running through the woods. Came right past here. You must've seen him."

"Sammy ain't out here," she repeated firmly. "He's on his way home."

"How d'you know?" I asked, a little frustrated. "Who ran past?"

She smiled. "You can believe what I'm telling you, girl. Sammy's just fine. Go on home." I noticed she had the tiniest trace of something foreign in her southern accent.

"Um, okay. Thanks."

"But you come back and see me soon," she directed. "I got some things you need to hear. And you and I could help each other."

Right, I thought. "Okay," I lied and started backing away. Then I turned and ran.

"Come see old Nanga," she called after me. "Come on back again."

When I stumbled up the last rise to the house, I spotted Sammy coming out of the trees closer to the river. He was carrying Heavy Bear, walking hand in hand with Jackson. And wearing a green shirt. Not white.

"Where'd you find him?" I asked when I caught up.

"He was down by the river near our house."

"You live on the river?" Rose and Jackson didn't live with the old woman?

"Yes. He said he was playing hide-and-seek with his friend."

The kid in the white shirt. "Does some other kid live around here?"

"Not that I know of, but someone might've moved in. Always building along the river."

"I was hiding real good, Sarah," Sammy said, "and Jackson just finded me and said, 'Time to go home, Samwise.' He's a good looker too."

"Thank you," I said to Jackson.

"No problem," he said, shrugging. "Glad to help."

Mom came out then. "Sammy," she cried, a mixture of anger and relief. I could sympathize with that. Sam hesitated a second, then tucked Heavy Bear under his arm and ran up to the steps where Mom waited. She caught him up and hugged him.

"So," I said, turning back to Jackson, "seems like we're gonna stay another week or two. Think that's enough time to find the diamonds?"

The truth was, I wasn't really sold on the idea of some hoard of diamonds lost on Gramma's property for more than two hundred years. But after Richard's tour, I had a newfound interest in my family's history. I wanted a chance to poke into all the corners and cupboards of this place, and see what was there before it was gone. *Without* calling my mother's attention to the fact, because I had a feeling she wouldn't like it much.

Which meant I had to do it mostly at night. And for that, I wanted Jackson's help. I freely admitted to myself that I was too much of a chicken to wander through more of Amber House in the dark without someone over the age of five to keep me company. If Jackson wanted to search for the diamonds, then I was willing to go with him for that company. And if we stumbled across the treasure in the process, so much the better.

He was looking hopeful. It made me smile. "Maybe," he said. "When do we start?"

I shrugged. "Tonight if you want. If you can stay up. It's three hours earlier here — I can't sleep. Want to meet me in the kitchen around eleven thirty? Everyone else will be in bed."

"Sure. I'll be there."

"By the way," I said, "who's the old woman in the cabin back there?"

An unreadable play of emotions showed in Jackson's eyes. He said carefully, "The old woman?"

"Nanga. She told me to go home, that Sammy was found. Did you call her or something?"

"Not me."

I gave a small laugh, a little confused again. "Well, I hope I wasn't trespassing or anything."

"What did she say?"

"She told me to come back and talk to her."

"Really?"

"Yeah, really. I think she wanted some help with something."

"Sarah, I —" He looked like he had something else to say.

"What?"

He shook his head, changing his mind, and started back the way he had come. He said out loud, without turning his head, "Not many people get to talk to Nanga. If you can, you should."

Okay, I thought. *Whatever.*

When I got inside, I was surprised to find Rose hustling Sammy off to a bath — I guessed it was the nurse in her taking charge. He was going meekly. Not his usual behavior. He seemed to like Rose, and she seemed to like him.

She saw me come in. "You need to wash up too, young lady," she directed in a no-nonsense, do-what-the-doctor-orders voice. "Those woods are full of poison ivy and poison sumac, and I bet you don't know what either one looks like. Use plenty of soap to cut the oil. And check yourself for ticks all over. Ticks like hidden places."

Nothing like a nice walk in the woods, I thought, but I was due for a soak anyway.

First I raided Gramma's vanity for some bath salts, a robe, and a couple of heavy towels. Then I headed up to the west wing, second floor, far away from everyone else, to see if I could find a spot for a long, hot, first-class bath.

An arch just beyond the stairs led to the hall I'd sprinted down the day before. Six doors opened off of it, three on each side.

Three rooms in, I found what I was looking for: a bathroom, tiled in delicate shades of pink across the floor and up the walls, with an enormous claw-footed bathtub beneath a stained-glass window.

Perfect.

I spread one towel over the floor and looped the second over an amusing sculpted hand fixed to the wall beside the tub. I plugged the drain, dumped in half a bottle of foaming bath salts, and made the bath water as close to boiling as I could stand. Once in the tub, I stretched out my legs, leaning back against the sloped end with a sigh as the heat turned my muscles to butter. I scrubbed with plenty of soap "to cut the oil." Then I slipped down under the surface. Rising bubbles emitted glooping pops; the groans of the plumbing turned into whale calls. Up for a breath of air, then back down into the depths. I could hear my mother talking far away, the sound carried through the pipes. I could hear my brother humming in his high, sweet voice.

The sound got louder, then louder still.

Is he in the bathroom? I wondered, outraged. *He's in the bathroom!*

I surfaced in a rush of water. "Sammy, what *the heck* do you think you're —"

No one was there.

The humming seemed to echo in the hollow space of the tiled room. Sam was close. And my bath had grown cold. I wrapped myself up and poked my head out into the hall. "Sam?"

Shivering into my terry-cloth robe and leaving a trail of damp footprints on the carpet, I followed after those six piping notes. And ended up outside a closed bedroom door.

The humming stopped. My heart was thudding. I made myself open the door to Deirdre Foster's bedroom.

"Sam, you in there?"

The room was dark. Empty. The mirror on the far wall reflected my silhouette back at me. With someone right behind.

I whirled, my heart in my throat.

Sammy stood looking up at me, his blond head still wet from his bath, cocked to one side in confusion. "Did you call me, Sarah?"

"Yes," I said, and shivered.

"It's cold here, Sarah," Sammy said. "Let's go to another place."

He took my hand and led me to my room.

Dad showed up while I was braiding my damp hair. Mom didn't seem pleased to see him.

"Look, since you couldn't let the kids come visit me today, I thought I'd visit them. I want to spend time with them before you fly back across the continent." He held out a large brown bag oozing tasty odors. "I brought Chinese," he said temptingly. "If you want me to go —"

"No, of course not," she said. "Stay."

She was something less than gracious. I wondered what had happened to the effervescent woman from this afternoon.

"Come see my room, Daddy," Sammy said, taking his hand and leading him up the stairs.

"Let me guess, squirt. Are you in the nautical room?"

How'd he know that? I wondered, following them up. Then I remembered. My father had gone to medical school in Maryland. He and Mom had met and fallen in love in Baltimore. He'd probably been down here to visit a few times — maybe even a lot. Sammy and I were the only ones who had never known Amber House.

Sammy was giving him the tour. "This is my bed," he said, patting it.

"I like it, Sammy. Did you know it's a real ship's bed from a real ship?"

"Uh-huh. And this is my bell." Sammy gave it an enthusiastic ring.

"Whoa, squirt." Dad put on his best Mr. Darling voice from *Peter Pan*. "'A little less noise there, a little less noise.'"

Sammy laughed. He climbed up on the bed and patted the wide carving that hung over the top of it. "And see my eagle?" he said.

"That's a stern board, Sam. From the rear of a ship."

"Uh-huh." He leapt down and ran to the opposite corner. "And this is my mermaid."

"She's a beauty too, Sam. She's a figurehead, from the front end of a ship." Dad sat on the bed and picked up Sam's bear. "Who's this?"

"He's mine. He's Heavy Bear."

Dad looked startled. "Did your mom call him that?"

Sam took the bear. "That's his name. Heavy Bear." He turned to run out of the room. "Come on. Come see Sarah's room. I gived it to her."

Dad and I followed him out. Sammy stood in the doorway of my room, waiting for us. "Look," he said proudly.

"Oh, Sam, you found this room for Sarah? It's be-a-u-tiful," Dad said.

"Uh-huh. And see this dollhouse?" He patted its shake roof. "All the lights really light up when it has batteries. Maybe little people live in there."

"What a wonderful dollhouse. What a wonderful room. This is the room Sarah always should have had, don't you think, squirt?"

"Uh-huh."

"What I can't figure out, guys, is why your mother decided to stay here."

"I did it," Sam said proudly, spilling the beans. "Sarah told me and I did it, but you can't tell, 'cause it's a secret."

Mom called up the stairs: "Can we eat?"

"Come on," Sammy said, running out the door.

My dad gave me the look. I squirmed. "What did he *do*, exactly?"

"Just — screamed a little."

"Sarah. Come on. You know you can't encourage autistic behaviors."

"I do know, Dad. And I'm sorry. But it was so important to us. And you should have seen him. I couldn't believe the job he did. It was frightening, he was so realistic. The kid should be in movies."

"Your mother must have been hysterical." He laughed, then he mussed the hair on the top of my head. "You don't play fair, Sarah. Lord help anyone who gets between you and what you want. That's a good thing and a bad thing. Like all superpowers, it must be used wisely."

"I think you've got me mixed up with my mother."

"You know whose room this is, don't you?"

"It's hers."

"She tell you?"

"No. I just figured it out."

"You figure out a lot of things, kiddo. You always have been perceptive. Another superpower." He smiled.

I had to blink back sudden tears, surprised at how much I had missed him.

He looked uncomfortable. "Let's get down there before your mom tries to reheat the food."

"Not much danger of that," I said. "I don't think she knows how to turn on the oven."

We sat down to a dinner of sweet-and-sour pork, moo shu, Szechuan beef, and fortune cookies.

"Jackson finded me today, Daddy. I was hiding and Jackson finded me."

"Yeah?" Dad said.

"Uh-huh. He is more gooder at hide-and-seek than Sarah, even."

"Better," my mother corrected.

"He is more *better*," Sammy said.

"Not *more*, just *better*. He is better."

"That's right," Sam said, delighted. "He is!"

Dad laughed. Mom didn't. "He must be a pretty good seeker, Sam, if he's *better* than Sarah," Dad said.

Sam nodded. "Better."

Silence settled over the table. I didn't like it. "Did you hear about my party, Dad?"

Evidently not, since his face was all surprise. "You're having a party? Here?"

My mother was instantly defensive — I guess she was a little sensitive about how *insane* it was to be doing this. "She's turning sixteen. That's an important birthday. And I had a coming-out when I turned sixteen. Lord, wouldn't it be *nice* if we celebrated?"

Dad turned to me. "What does Sarah think?"

"Sarah thinks," I said deliberately, "that spending an evening with a hundred strangers is her idea of hell."

"A *hundred*?" my father repeated.

"You have no idea what you're even saying," Mom snapped at me. "In the first place, they won't all be strangers. Richard is going to be there, and you'll probably know some of his friends by then —"

"Richard?" Dad asked.

"The senator's son," I answered.

"The senator —" Lights went on in my father's eyes. "Would this be Senator Robert Hathaway?"

"Robert dropped by today to express his condolences," Mom said impatiently. "He said he would help me round up guests."

"How is Robert?" my father asked, exaggerated interest in his voice.

"He's fine. He said to say hello."

"Nice of him to remember me. Did you tell him how I was? How *we* were?"

"Of course not. I just told him you were working up at Johns Hopkins again."

"And how is *Mrs.* Hathaway?"

"I didn't ask."

"She's dead," I said. "A few years ago."

I shouldn't have said it. I should have bit my tongue and kept it in my mouth.

"The bereaved widower, huh?" my father said. "How cozy for you."

My mother's eyes narrowed. "How *dare* you criticize me? How dare you insinuate *I've* done anything wrong? Don't put this on me."

He didn't have any response to that. Without looking my way, he grated out between clenched teeth, "You don't have to have this party if you don't want to, Sarah."

Mom didn't flinch. "You're wrong about that, Tom. Sarah doesn't have any vote in the matter at all. Some of the wealthiest people on this side of the country will come to her party, and since I am selling this house and everything in it, I am *thrilled* for them to see Amber House all lit up and glowing. You can't *pay* for that kind of advertising. So we are having this party, and Sarah will be there with a smile on her face. You are certainly welcome to come if you want."

Then she dropped her napkin onto her plate and walked out. I stared at my food, completely miserable.

"Come on, Sarah, squirt," Dad said. "We don't want to waste this feast. Let's eat."

"Nope," Sammy said. He started to rap his fist against his head.

"Hey, enough of that." My dad caught Sammy's fist in his hand. "How 'bout some ice cream instead?"

"Nope! Nope, nope, nope!" Sammy shouted. He wrenched his hand free, jumped down from his chair, and ran out of the room. I could hear his feet on the stairs.

"This is my fault," I said. "I shouldn't have brought up the party."

"No, don't you do that to yourself. *None* of it is your fault." Dad sighed. "She doesn't want me around. Maybe I should stop intruding."

"But you'll come to the party, right?"

"If you want me there, I will." He stood. Awkwardly, he bent and kissed the top of my head. "I need to check on Sammy, okay?"

"Yeah. Better go."

Dad rubbed the back of his hand across his eyes. I pretended I didn't notice. "I'll be right back," he said. "To help with the dishes."

Nobody had opened their fortune cookies. Sighing, I cracked mine: "The mirror's reflection should show someone you wish to see."

I rolled my eyes. I always got the crappy fortunes.

I had most of the food put away by the time Dad came back down. "He's asleep," he said. "Just fell on the bed with his arm around his bear and went out. He'll be okay."

"Yeah, he will," I told him. "He's really a pretty upbeat kid."

"You know where he got that name for his bear?"

"Heavy Bear? No. Why?"

"Your grandmother gave me a tour once. *She* called that thing Heavy Bear. I think that's pretty odd. Don't you?"

"Maybe she told Sammy about him on one of her visits."

"Maybe." Dad picked up the scrub pad and started in on a plate. I stopped him.

"Don't worry about that. It's getting late; you need your sleep. Get going. I don't want to be the cause of a malpractice lawsuit."

"You sure you got this?"

I shrugged. "It's practically all done already."

He gave me a hug before he left. *A product of separation*, I thought. He never used to give me hugs back home in Seattle. I finished up. I wished, as I went from room to room, hitting the lights, that I had a TV. But the only set was in Gramma's room, with my mom.

Nine o'clock. Two and a half hours to go. If I'd had Jackson's phone number, I would have called and cancelled.

I went upstairs and fished my cell out of my luggage, thinking I would call Jecie, but it was dead. And, of course, I'd forgotten my charger.

I snuck into Sam's room and took his flashlight out of his backpack, then went back down to the library. I thought I remembered seeing a phone in that room.

It was there, on the table between two chairs. It had a dial, like one of those things from a Bogart movie. It took me a second to figure out how to make it work.

"Jecie. It's Sarah. Remember me?" I cringed. I always sounded stupid on the phone.

We talked for a little bit. She told me she'd gotten a tattoo — Hebrew letters from the Talmud: "If I'm not for myself, then who will be for me? But if I'm only for myself, then what am I?"

"Way to rep the Hebrew people," I told her. "I'm pretty sure tats aren't kosher. Does the rabbi know? Never mind that, does your mom know?"

She just laughed. I told her about the party, but she couldn't come. Even if she could have afforded the plane ticket, she had dress rehearsals for *The Secret Garden*. I told her about the senator's delicious son.

"Model status?" she asked.

"Model status," I confirmed. I promised I would e-mail some photos as soon as I could get to a place with Internet. I missed my computer.

Still an hour and a half to go. I explored the library. It was enormous — floor-to-ceiling shelves built around the doors and windows on all four walls. As far as I could see, the books were all hardbound, most of them leather covered. Small brass plates identified different subject matters. There was a section of French authors and a section of German. A heavy Oxford unabridged dictionary lay open on a stand near an ancient globe.

I sat in one of the tufted leather chairs and examined the stack of books my grandmother had left on the table, unshelved. Conan Doyle and Christie, Lovecraft and Poe. Her taste, evidently, had run to the macabre. On the far side of the table, a large book lay open to a picture of a house on a bluff glimpsed between the trees. I stood and examined it right-side up — it was Amber House. I checked the cover. *A Place in Time* by Fiona Campbell Warren.

This was the book Richard had told me about. Of course my grandmother had a copy. I closed it and tucked it under my arm. Maybe it would help me kill some time.

I sat at the kitchen table. The window in the outside door stared at me like a great black eye. I thought about switching chairs so I didn't have to see it, but I didn't quite want it at my back either. I opened the heavy book flat on the table.

The page after the title was filled with a photo of the author, my great-grandmother. She was pretty striking. Finely carved features, great figure, and a mass of thick hair piled on top of her head. She looked a little like my mother. The next page was the editor's explanatory preface:

> *Fiona Campbell Warren is an extraordinary woman with an extraordinary vision. In the pages that follow, she has woven together historical fact, family lore, and fictional re-creation so skillfully, you will believe she traveled the places, lived the times, and met the people she describes. Then, as if thinking better of her own invention, she will start with the same facts and characters, and alter them slightly, taking you to another place, another outcome — in Fiona's own words, an "otherwhen."*

He went on in a scholarly vein, but not with me. I flipped past. After the preface came a poem, entitled "Otherwhen." I wasn't much for poetry, but I was curious. I read it:

> *We chase the turnings of a maze confused,*
> *Drawn on by hope, pursued by history.*

By fortune we are soothed, by sorrows bruised,
We stumble on, purblind, toward mystery.
Yet Time hies round thee, hushed, on unshod feet,
Lest hearing, thou should wake to Her, and rise
To seek the point where past and future meet.
Though choice seems chance, though happenstance belies
Intent, learn thou that fate is in thy hands.
Discern the joint that shatters Time, that bends
Her flow, her heedless whim, to thy commands.
Thus heal the wound; thus make all good amends.
Hast thou a chance to choose it all again,
Then take the path that leads to otherwhen.

So, what was that even supposed to mean? Did she actually, *literally* think time could be changed, or was I just missing the metaphor? "Otherwhen," huh. Somehow, I wasn't surprised that the woman had spent some time in an asylum.

She'd laid out sort of a family tree — "Families of Amber House," in which she listed all my ancestors who had actually owned the property, starting with the pair Richard had mentioned, Liam and Sorcha O'Malley. I found Deirdre Foster in the mid-seventeen hundreds, four generations later, and her husband, Captain Foster of the whale ivory and weapon obsessions, who had evidently been married to someone else before the unfortunate Deirdre. My eye ran past a roll call of solid American names: Tate and Webster, Gideon and Quincy, with a Maeve McCallister for some more Irish leavening. Maeve proved to be Fiona's grandmother. The tree ended with Fiona's daughter — my grandmother — Ida Warren. I guessed she was the last to be born before the book was published, and as Fiona's only child, the one who had been destined to be the next owner of Amber House. My mother would be the last. I would never belong to that group.

My eyelids were sagging. It wasn't even eight o'clock back home. I closed the book and leaned forward, intending to rest my head on my arm for just a minute.

And I dreamed.

The priest stood over Gramma's grave, reminding us there was indeed "a time for everywhen under the sun." Gramma stood beside him, watching me, a little smile on her face.

The black-coated women were gone, but other women were there, dressed strangely, standing before different headstones all over the graveyard. Each of them was watching me. Gramma said, "One day you'll be here too."

I tried to say, "Never," but the word wouldn't come from my mouth.

I seemed to hear an echo of voices, rising, "Sarah, Sarah —"

Chapter Five

"Sarah."

I jerked upright, the sound of many voices still in my ears. It took me a second to understand I was sitting in my gramma's kitchen.

Jackson poked his head in the door. "Sorry." He smiled. "Couldn't stay awake? I thought you said it was only eight thirty your time."

I cursed myself for being a lightweight. "Must have been all that exercise I got this afternoon, running through your tick-infested woods."

"Oh, yeah," he said. "You're sitting smack in the middle of the tick capital of the nation, if not the world." He closed the door behind him. "The trick to avoiding them," he said, flipping up the hood on the sweatshirt he was wearing to demonstrate, "is body armor." He grinned, pushed the hood back down, and unzipped his jacket. "Where are we going to start?"

"Why don't we go up the main stairs to the third floor? I haven't been up there yet. Have you?"

"No. Let's go."

We crept quietly out of the kitchen and up the stairs. After we passed the second-floor landing, the staircase turned once and became instantly utilitarian. The narrow steps ended on the third floor in a short hall with three closed doors. I opened the first one on the right.

Light from a moon one-third full illumined the room, which held just four things: a small table, a chair before it, a standing brass lamp, and a small glass-fronted bookcase filled with identical slim leather-bound volumes. *Something to come back to*, I thought.

The door to the left opened on an old and dusty scene of chaos: a broken easel knocked on its side, still clamping a torn canvas that was once a pretty landscape, and a case full of paint tubes spilled on the floor, their guts stomped out.

On the other side of the third door, our stabbing lights revealed a long, narrow garret room, with a slanted ceiling and a single window at the far end. Midway down the attic, an ancient lightbulb hung from a pipe, a string dangling below it. Jackson went over, tugged the string, and, miraculously, the bulb glowed. Its feeble light revealed a graveyard of forgotten objects shoved toward the shadows at the sides of the room, mostly filling the V at the base of the slanting ceiling.

I ran my fingers over the handle of a worn-out wicker baby carriage and thought of the infants who had ridden in it, all kin to me, all dead and buried. A headless dress dummy boasted the painfully carved waist of a corseted era. A bald china doll sat in a wooden high chair with a busted seat, her empty eyes staring out over the memory of a nursery.

I opened a trunk. The tulle veil of a yellowed wedding gown disintegrated into dust at my touch. Beneath it, the groom's tuxedo lay above the frills of old-styled baby clothes, a child's sailor suit, a layer of high-topped leather shoes. A silverfish slithered away from my searching hands.

"Yuck," I commented involuntarily. I dropped the clothes back into place and returned them to darkness.

Jackson snorted. "I never thought of you as squeamish."

Thought of me? I shrugged and said, "Silverfish. Gross."

"Okay," he said, "I'll give you that one. They *are* gross." And he flashed me a big smile, wide and relaxed. He seemed — *happy*. I realized he always seemed a little tight to me, like he was under some kind of strain. But for once, he just seemed easy.

"It's our warm, wet weather — we got a million bugs. Some you don't see anywhere else: a beetle that only lives in the cliffs on the Chesapeake, and a spider that's only been found along the banks of this river."

I shivered. "I hate spiders. I have this theory that they all come from some alien thing that fell to Earth on a meteor a billion years ago."

He chuckled. "A little bit arachnophobic?"

"Nah," I said. "I'm just scared of spiders."

He started to explain to me the meaning of "arachnophobia," but then realized I was making a little joke. "Ah. Humor," he said, smiling. "Difficult concept."

He kept up the small talk as we worked, cracking jokes, peppering me with questions: "What's the most amazing thing you've ever seen?" Me, the northern lights; him, a hurricane coming in across the Chesapeake. "If you could travel anywhere in the world, where would you go?" Me, Paris; him, New York — "That's where my parents met." "Which are better, cats or dogs?" Both of us — "Dogs." I didn't mention that cats reminded me too much of my mother. I found myself telling him about Jecie, and the time she'd led a cow up an exterior staircase at our school, and how they'd had to get a crane to lift the cow back to the ground because cows couldn't walk down stairs. He put his head back and laughed at that one. "Jecie's pretty cool," he said, like he knew her from that one story. We talked for the better part of an hour as we pulled one box after another into the light of the single bulb to poke through their contents.

I could tell fairly quickly that it wasn't likely that anything up there was going to get us closer to the Captain's fabled diamonds. Most of it was interesting to me — like that little box at the bottom of one of your mother's drawers that contains three baby teeth and a curl of soft fine hair — comforting, connected, and kind of disgusting all at the same time. The boxes held documents, old clothes, broken treasures, once-loved toys — things not even the inhabitants of Amber House had deemed worth saving from the slow moldering of time. Each box wheezed out a gasp of dust and decay that settled on my skin and wafted into my lungs. After a while, it began to get to me. It seemed proof, silent and inescapable, that all the pieces of my life would one day come to this — this soft, sad, gray disintegration.

"I can't take much more of this," I said, struggling with the sense of suffocation. "Is there a lot left?"

Just like that, the easy-going companionability I'd been feeling from Jackson disappeared. The relaxed lines in his face retreated behind that smooth, bland look he wore so often. "Nope," he answered. "I looked over everything from here to the window. Old china and linens and papers and junk."

"I want to get out of here, then. I just have a couple more boxes. I wish we'd brought some tape." I pointed to a small collection of cartons I'd set to one side. "I'd like to seal these back up, keep the mice and moths out of them."

"I could run down and get a roll from the kitchen drawer," he said.

And leave me up here alone? I thought unhappily. But I said, "Yeah, that would be great. Thanks."

"No problem." He left through the open door.

I pulled the last couple boxes into the light. Twice, as I worked, I craned my head around and looked over my shoulder, some part of me compelled to check the room behind me. I wondered what was taking Jackson so long to return. Even if he took the stairs slowly, he should have been back.

When I finished the final box, I didn't want to wait anymore. I'd come back and tape everything up another time.

I spotted Jackson's sweatshirt slung over the back of a broken chair and tucked it under my arm to free up my hands for a box of photos I wanted to take with me. I realized, belatedly, that I would have to turn the overhead light out before I left. It made me feel a little sick — the thought of being swallowed by the attic's shadows. With one last glance around to reassure myself, I switched my flashlight on and tugged the light's string to shut it off.

Wedging the flashlight under my elbow with the sweatshirt, I bent to pick up the box. As I stood back up, fully burdened, the flashlight slipped loose, deflected off my leg on the way down, and thunked to the floor. I froze there in disbelief, helpless, with my hands full, and watched it roll away from me as if in slow motion. It came to a stop deep under the slanted roof, its glow trapped by the dusty mounds to either side of it.

With the darkness crowding me, I set the box down and bent low, then got on my hands and knees. Wishing fervently that Jackson had not gone, feeling keenly the place between my shoulders, naked and exposed, I reached in and under the angled ceiling. My fingers brushed a pile of something cold and metallic that made me flinch away.

And the light snuffed out.

Blackness wrapped around me like floodwaters. I felt like I was drowning, like the air had departed with the light. I backed up and stood, seeking blindly for the hanging bulb's string, my arms up, my hands searching. I kicked something, staggered, paused.

Silence rang in my ears, almost a buzz, a hum, a sigh. A rapid pulse of air. Which resolved into panting.

Huh-eh-huh-eh-huh-eh-huh-eh-huh-eh-huh-eh-huh.

The sound came from in front of me, from the farthest corner of the attic.

My blood all turned to water that rained down inside me, freezing cold. I was pinned on the sound of that breath, immobilized. All of my senses riveted.

I could see a little now — the charcoal piles of relics in the shadows, a slanting column of thin moonlight coming through the room's only window. I squinted to penetrate the darkness beyond it. Maybe I saw a pale shape. Maybe it was crouching there, just beyond the reach of the light. Maybe it was looking at me.

The panting stopped. The silence rose, agonizing. I strained to listen; I strained to see. I waited for the sound of movement from the attic's end.

And heard steps behind me, on the stairs.

Jackson.

Wild with relief, I turned. But could see, could sense, that the attic door was closed. *Jackson left it open; I know Jackson left it open.* I could sense, could feel, that whoever had climbed the stairs was now standing just beyond that closed door. Standing; not moving; not speaking. Not helping.

Behind me, the sound of chain sliding over wood.

I felt so cold, so squeezed, I could hardly draw in breath. A tear oozed like blood from the corner of my eye.

I made myself turn. I made myself look.

A woman stood in the shaft of moonlight. She was all darkness to me, backlit by the window. I could see thick curls of black hair, the curves of muscled arms, a shapeless drape of translucent gown. All motionless. She might have been carved of stone. A spider ran down a lock of her hair, and air escaped me in the smallest gasp. I wanted to shove my fist in my mouth to stop the scream rising in my throat.

She spoke. The voice was rough, ragged, hissing, soft.

"Are you listening? Can you hear me?"

Yes, I thought. *Yes, yes, yes, I can hear you. Yes.*

"You know I cannot be trapped here. You know I can leave this place any time I wish. You know you cannot stop me."

Richard said the house was haunted. Richard said they kept Deirdre locked away. Dead, demented Deirdre. Oh God, oh God, oh God.

Her head tilted sideways. The voice rose almost to a scream. "You think you are safe? You think I can't hurt you? I can. I can get you. I can find you in your dreams."

I heard, behind the echo of that scream, a small one-note moan coming from my throat.

"Do not sleep," she crooned as if to a baby. "No, no. Do not ever sleep. Because I live there now."

And then she started to move, started to come for me. A rush of chains, a flutter of cloth. And the shriek I had kept locked in, behind my teeth, finally escaped.

"Sarah?" Jackson yelled from the stairs. "Sarah? What is it? What happened?"

I whirled and ran for the door. Saw Jackson's flashlight reach up from below. Saw too late that the door was not closed — was still open. I smacked into its edge. Flashes of color starred my vision. I sagged.

Jackson caught me. He sank down to the floor, letting me lean against him, curled into his arm, resting against his chest. I felt a massive ache in my forehead. I ran a shaking hand over it. A huge bump was already forming.

"She was right behind me," I whispered.

"There's nobody here, Sarah."

"Turn on the light. *Turn on the light!*" I was screeching, and I didn't want to be, but I couldn't help it.

He stood, found the string. The light returned. I tried to stand, but collapsed, white spots blotting my vision. Jackson caught me again.

"Rest a minute," he said. "Tell me what you saw."

I looked around to make sure that she was gone. "You'll think I'm crazy," I said.

"Tell me."

"It was a ghost," I said into my lap.

"No . . ." He struggled with his words. "It wasn't . . . You didn't see . . . a ghost," he said.

"You don't know. I saw her. I saw her!" My voice was getting loud again.

"Shh," he said, trying to calm me. "It wasn't a ghost. It's . . ." He was shaking his head, almost as if he didn't want to say the words that were coming from his mouth. "It's . . . the house. It's Amber House."

I stared at him, the pain in my head suddenly unbearable. "What are you talking about? There was a woman. I saw her. She tried to hurt me."

"No," he said. "No. Ida saw things too. She called them echoes. When she touched certain things, little bits of the past came to life for her. She said they were the house's memory."

"Echoes? The house's memory?" *What? Besides* — "Why didn't you tell me? If you knew about it? Why didn't you warn me?"

He looked down, shrugging slightly. "I wasn't sure you'd see them. Didn't know for sure that they were real, 'cause Ida was a little —"

Crazy? I silently finished for him as he went on.

"And then you said Nanga wanted to talk to you. And I thought" — he made another little shrugging motion — "it was between you and Nanga." He paused. "Ida said they can't hurt you. It's just the past. Like little windows on the past. And you can see into them. It's a special gift that only some of the women in your family have."

The crazy ones, I thought. I wiped my face with my hand. I realized I was rocking slightly, like I sometimes do when I'm upset. I made myself stop. "They can't hurt me?"

"No. That's what Ida said."

"And Nanga knows something about this?"

"If anyone does, she does."

"Who is Nanga?"

"She's . . . a relative of mine. I think she could help. Ida always said that Nanga wants to help, that she has some kind of plan."

I looked back into the attic's depths. "If she wasn't talking to me, then who was she talking to? Who was behind the door?"

"I don't know."

I stood up shakily, Jackson helping.

"Are you all right?" he asked.

"I don't know," I echoed.

He found my flashlight, still glowing, and handed it to me. "It went out," I told him, plaintively, like a little child.

"No," he said, "it probably was just dark in the vision. You were in the past, in the darkness of the past. The light never actually went out."

She was trapped in the dark, I thought. I remembered, then, when Sammy's flashlight turned off in the conservatory our first night here. *Had I slipped into an echo without even knowing? How had I gotten out again?*

"Can you make it down the stairs?" he asked. I nodded.

He tucked my box under one arm and turned out the light. I followed him closely to the landing on the second floor. He gestured with the box. "Where do you want this?"

I went into my room and turned on the small bedside light. I pointed to the bed. "Can you shove it under there?"

It disappeared behind the bed ruffle. He headed out, but turned back at the door. He started to speak, stopped, then started again. "If you tell your mother about this, she'll leave. You'll never come back."

"Maybe I want to go."

"Maybe you don't," he said. His eyes were pleading. And I thought, *How can the diamonds be so important to him?*

"I don't know," I repeated.

"Please do one thing for me," he said, "before you decide."

"What?"

"Talk to Nanga. Go back to her cabin, if you can, and talk to her. Please." He turned and left.

If I can? I thought, as his footsteps faded away.

I noticed, then, the TV set murmuring downstairs. I hoped Mom hadn't heard us stumbling around. Maybe she'd drifted off with the set on.

I brushed my teeth and got into bed. Thinking about nothing. Remembering Deirdre's words. "Don't sleep," she'd said. I wished not to. I lay there, silent and frozen, listening to the voices rising in the dark.

"Sarah."

I woke out of the fragments of a dream I wished I could have back. I tried to nudge together the pieces — a woman's smiling face, a sense of peace, of coming home — but they were spreading like smoke.

The moonlight filtering through the lace curtains at the window cast strange patterns on my bed. It felt like I had only just closed my eyes, but the clock on the table showed that several hours had passed.

The air in my room felt cold.

"Sarah?"

I knew the voice. It was Sammy. He was in my room. But though I told myself I was crazy, I was afraid to answer him.

"Sarah?" the voice came again, flat and unnatural. "Where's my box?"

I snaked out one arm to the lamp beside the bed. *How do I turn it on?* I thought a little frantically. My fingers found the knob. I twisted. Light bloomed.

Sammy was standing there. His eyes were open. But he wasn't awake. Walking in his sleep. He'd done it before, lots of times, ever since he was about three. "Sam?" I said, and got out of bed.

"Where's my box, Sarah?"

I took his arm. He let me lead him without any resistance, placidly, easily. In the old days, Dad had taken care of this part. Now I guess it was my job. I guided him to his bed, sat him down, and lifted his legs onto the mattress. I pressed his shoulders down until his head fell against the pillow.

"Where's my box?"

"Shh, shh," I said, pulling the covers over him, tucking them up under his chin. "We'll find it in the morning, bud. Go back to sleep."

His eyes closed. His sweet lips fell open. He snored lightly. I surrendered to an irresistible impulse to kiss his forehead.

I went back to bed.

Chapter Six

When I opened my eyes the next morning, I gingerly and reluctantly began to examine the freakish thing that had happened to me the night before. What had it been? A hallucination? A ghost? Thinking back on it, it didn't really seem like she'd been talking to me. It was more like a piece of film being shown over again. Déjà vu two hundred years later. Life on endless replay.

I wondered if she could feel it happening.

When I sat up, my skull began to throb in time with my heartbeat. I touched my forehead carefully and found a lump the size of half an egg. Brilliant. What was I going to tell my mother? Especially with that fun-filled day of Baltimore errands ahead of us. Not to mention the thrill of meeting all my dad's coworkers. What was I going to tell any of them?

I found a bottle of foundation and dabbed that on, gently, then combed some hair down and across my forehead. I checked the effect in the mirror.

Yeah, I looked horrible.

I was eating a bowl of cereal in the kitchen when Mom came in. "Sarah, I'm expecting you to ride herd on Sa —"

She interrupted herself, disbelief in her eyes. "Oh my *God*, what the *hell* did you do to your face?"

"Tripped over my suitcase in the dark and fell into the bedpost," I offered, wondering if it would float.

She sighed and shook her head. “See, Sarah? There’s a reason why civilized people try to keep their rooms neat.”

Terrific. With that explanation, I got to be a klutz *and* a slob. I’d have to think of something better to tell the rest of the world.

Sam came in then, and his eyes widened a little when he saw me, but he didn’t say a word. He just stopped in front of me and reached up to put his two little hands on my cheeks. He pulled my face toward him, then he planted the softest, gentlest kiss on my lump. “Owie, Sarah.”

Who wouldn’t love a kid like that?

Mom saw Sammy had Heavy Bear in tow and was going to say something about it, but I shook my head no. My newfound authority. She pursed her lips a little, but decided to let Sam and me have our way. “Just get in the car,” she said.

I was stuck with shotgun, since Sam had to sit in the back, but I turned toward the window and visibly spaced out. I didn’t want to make small talk with Mom — I wanted to think. I knew if I was going to say something about what I’d seen, I should do it now, before Mom started spending money on my birthday bash. But I also knew if I said anything, I would never set foot in Amber House again. And I wasn’t sure I wanted that. I wasn’t sure at all.

This thing that I could do in Amber House was — unbelievable. Maybe a little scary. But Jackson said they couldn’t hurt me; they were only echoes. And they were *my* echoes — people who had contributed bits and pieces to the puzzle of me. I had to admit — I was interested. We’d be gone in two weeks anyway.

Maybe I would stay and see what happened.

We reached Baltimore in less than an hour. Mom navigated the streets with all the confidence of a former resident. She had gone to school here — the all-girls College of Notre Dame. She’d met Dad at a mixer, a dance to which the young and eligible from other nearby schools were invited. Dad was from Connecticut, going to school at Johns Hopkins; he came to the mixer with a cousin who was a midshipman in the Naval Academy at Annapolis. The rest, as they say, was history.

I had assumed we'd be heading straight to the hospital, but Mom had other entertaining destinations in mind. Our first stop was McCauley's, "the oldest stationers in Baltimore," Mom told us. The place was dark and full of every imaginable paper product. We went to a counter in the rear of the store where an old guy looked up from his work.

My mother's face split into a beaming smile. "Mr. Perkins. You're still here." I was always amazed how musical her voice became when she was being charming.

"Is that Miss — McGuinness?"

"Oh, my Lord. You got it! What a memory you have."

"A man doesn't forget a beautiful girl like you."

"At my age, that kind of flattery keeps one going." She touched the back of his hand. She was *flirting* with the old guy. Ugh.

"What is it we can help you with today?"

"Well, I'm hoping you *can* help, because I'm nearly frantic," my mother began. She poured out her story for him: how we were called away suddenly from Seattle by her mother's death, how she had given up the idea of giving me a proper coming-out party, but now "Senator Hathaway" had promised to help her throw one here, which was "an incredible piece of luck," but it was all very "rush, rush," next weekend, could he possibly do anything?

"Hmmm," Mr. Perkins said speculatively. "What exactly are we talking about?"

"A card, heavy stock, with R.S.V.P. enclosure. It would be *per*fect if it could be midnight blue with gold script. Embossed. Say, two hundred fifty?"

Two hundred fifty? I repeated in my head.

"You have the text?"

Mom offered him a page from the leather notebook in her hand.

"Very nice," he commented. He pursed his lips and mulled it over. My mother waited breathlessly. "Okay," he said. "For you and the senator."

"Oh, good heavens, thank you! What's your soonest?"

Mr. Perkins made a call to the warehouse. "We have the stock you need — darkest indigo. With a little shifting around, I could have them for you this evening." He shrugged apologetically with his face. "For a significant premium."

"Of course," my mother gushed. "You're a miracle worker, Mr. Perkins."

Mom clenched her fist in a little victory gesture as we walked out, but I felt sick. That number just kept ping-ponging around in my head. Two hundred and fifty invited guests to Miss Sarah Parsons's sweet sixteenth. What in God's name had she gotten me involved in?

Our next stop also wasn't the hospital. We drove to the pricey commercial district below Mt. Vernon Square, where Mom pulled up to the valet parking for a narrow brick building that turned out to be a woman's boutique. Sammy started humming.

"Mom," I said, "I don't think Sam can take another errand. Can't you just drop us at the hospital?"

She swung her long legs out of the driver's seat, handed her keys to the valet, and came around to Sammy's door. She crouched down in front of him. "Last stop, honey, and then we'll go get you a malted at this fabulous deli I know. Can you hang in there?"

He stopped humming. "Can Heavy Bear have one too?"

I could see her start to say no. I could see that she *wanted* to say no, but she sucked it up. "Sure, honey, he can have one too, but you have to promise me that you and Heavy Bear won't misbehave in this nice store. Can you promise?"

"Uh-huh," he said.

Good luck with that, I thought.

Inside the store, we headed for a room set off by a short flight of stairs and two huge stone urns filled with expensive flowers. The dress centered in the view was a bridal gown.

This wasn't looking good.

An attractive woman, impeccably dressed, came up to us at once. "My name is Marie," she murmured to my mother. "May I help, madame?"

"I need two gowns, full length, one for each of us. Something a little conservative for me, I think, but not too conservative. And something really extravagant for my daughter. It's her sixteenth birthday party."

"Of course, madame." She guided us to some leather-covered couches, flanked by glass tables bearing tall vases of lilies. "May I get you something? Champagne? Hot cocoa for the young man?"

"Champagne sounds wonderful. Sam? Hot cocoa?"

He nodded. "Two. One for Heavy Bear."

Mom shared an exasperated smile with Marie, then bent down to speak seriously to Sam. "Sweetie, I think you and Heavy Bear can share a cocoa —"

"TWO!" he shouted.

My mother flushed, but Marie interjected smoothly, "Of course we will get Heavy Bear his own cocoa."

Marie's assistant hurried off to fetch the refreshments, while Marie started filling a rolling rack with dresses. I watched them with mounting anxiety, cringing at the idea of trying on all these gowns. But the rack disappeared into a back room, and, moments later, the first dress came back out snugly fitted on one of the salesgirls, who apparently were hired as much for their modeling skills as for their abilities with a cash register. Valued customers were not to be put to the trouble of actually trying on dresses. Particularly when said dresses showed so much better on the models.

So I sat there, sharing Heavy Bear's cocoa, watching Sam crayon in blank spaces in a coloring book that Marie's assistant had magically produced for him, while my mother quietly shook her head at gown after gown after gown. About eight dresses in, I showed some fleeting interest in a sleek black number, at which my mother merely frowned. Marie seemed to realize then that my input wasn't particularly needed or wanted and directed all her attentions toward Mom.

About fifteen dresses in, a rose-pink thing with a lace bodice got my mother's "maybe." *For her*, I thought, scowling, *I hope.* Otherwise, the dresses swam by in an uninterrupted stream, the same two models alternating in an endless variety of colors and styles. Marie was looking more than a little frustrated when a dark green dress appeared, a classical Grecian cut worked in a silk organdy that both clung and billowed softly with every step the model took. My mother's face lit up.

Marie leapt on that as her cue: "I thought this would be very becoming on *you*, madame, with your figure."

Evidently Mom thought so too. One down. But the rack was emptied and there was nothing for me. *Yet*, I thought grimly.

"I am sorry we were not able to find something for the young lady," Marie apologized.

"I'm just stuck on the idea of putting her in autumn gold," my mother said. "It would set off her skin, make her shine. But I really liked that cream gown with the embroidered tiers. Did you like that one? Honey?"

Oh. Speaking to me. Someone wanted my input now? Um. Did I *remember* that one? "Yes, absolutely. It was great," I lied. If we weren't doing something like that black sheath I'd liked, I just didn't care.

"When is the dress needed?" Marie asked, reinvigorated by the prospect of another commission. "If madame would like, I could check with the designer. Perhaps she could render it for you in gold."

"That would be perfect."

Marie made the call. They took my measurements. The dress would be ready a week from Friday in Arlington. It was up to my mother to arrange for delivery.

I had no idea how much money my mother had just spent, but it had to have been a lot to put such a big smile on Marie's face.

We stopped at the delicatessen next, in a less ritzy neighborhood of Baltimore. Sam got his promised chocolate malt and his standard turkey and lettuce on white. Then we finally headed for Dad's hospital.

Dad met us at Johns Hopkins's old main entrance. He exclaimed, "Golly, honey, what happened to you?" as he bent down and shined into my eyes one of those little flashlight dealies doctors always carry. I guessed I passed the test, because he moved right on to the next featured event: a V.I.P. tour. This involved climbing all the stairs in the hospital's old rotunda right past the several RESTRICTED AREA signs, up into the cupola at the very top.

I counted steps as Dad started in telling us all about the hospital's founder, *Mr.* Johns Hopkins. The Hopkins family were Quakers who freed all their slaves sixty years before the rest of the country did, forcing Hopkins to drop out of school and work the fields in their place.

At about one hundred steps into our climb, Sammy and I were hearing all about how Hopkins went on to make a fortune in business, but he also had a piece of bad luck: "He fell in love with his first cousin, Elizabeth," Dad informed us.

Not smart, I thought to myself, still counting — *137, 138. You don't want to fall in love with your cousins.*

Neither one of this tragic pair ever got married, Dad continued, which left Hopkins with a ton of money and no one to leave it to. So he came up with this genius idea of starting a hospital wedded to a medical school. *169, 170.* I was breathless, with the start of a stitch in my side.

"That union of school and hospital," my father informed us, wheezing quite a bit himself by that point, "sparked a scholarly pursuit of medicine that produced some of the greatest medical discoveries of the twentieth century."

We all concentrated on climbing as we spiraled up around the inside of the cupola, ducked through a trapdoor to another platform, and hit a last sixty-six steps that were so narrow you had to turn your feet sideways to fit on them. One more trapdoor — *231, 232* — and suddenly, all of Baltimore was below us. My legs felt like lead, but the view was worth the climb. I took some pictures to send to Jecie.

And Dad finally caught his breath. "Just think," he said, "if Hopkins had been able to finish school, or if he'd married his cousin, or if he'd fallen in love with somebody else, he probably wouldn't have founded this hospital and university. And then the thousands of people treated in the hospital, and the millions of people who have benefited from Hopkins research, maybe would have died. All of history is like that — built on an infinite number of almost random events that come together to push things this way or that. If one little thing was changed, well . . ." Dad shrugged.

I finished the sentence in my head. *The whole world might be too.*

We had dinner with Dad and then hooked back up with Mom. The drive home was quiet. Sammy dozed. Mom focused on the road and her thoughts. I could tell she was feeling satisfied with the progress she had made pulling together whatever huge public display she was planning. She'd picked up both her dress and the invitations, and they were safely stowed in the back of the car.

When we got home, the house was dark, except for the exterior light. Sammy and I stumbled inside while Mom emptied her hands so she could turn off the front light and turn on the hall light.

"Sarah," Sam whispered to me. I bent down to hear. He raised his finger, pointing. "Why's she in the mirror?"

"What?" I turned to look. The lights blazed.

And I didn't see anything in the mirror — no reflected portrait, no pattern in the glass, no face at all. I turned back to Sammy. "What do you mean?"

But Sammy had already moved on.

Mom carried her invitations to the office on the lower floor of the west wing and settled in for what I assumed was some party planning, so I took the opportunity to poke around the east wing. "Come with me, Sam," I said. I wasn't up for solitary explorations yet.

Gramma's room was on the right, toward the river. It was a large room with its own private bath and this cool octagonal nook in one corner. The bedding, a little sofa, and two chairs were all done in a modern floral chintz, and most of the rest of the furniture was of recent vintage, which surprised me. Maybe Gramma just didn't want to be surrounded by the past in the room where she slept.

The only exception to all the twentieth-century coziness was an antique cradle in the corner. I wondered if Gramma could touch that cradle and still see her baby sleeping in it.

Across from Gramma's room was the Chinoise Room, which was filled with all kinds of things from the Far East: vases and boxes and artwork, and an elaborate dresser trimmed in brass. I shut the door without going in — looked like a bunch of stuff that Sammy could easily break.

The final room in the wing occupied its entire end, from the riverside to the front. It was mostly empty, with a rich, patterned parquet floor — I guessed it was a ballroom. At one end, there was a little fenced-in area that I assumed kept the musicians safe from the whirling dancers. The far wall was all French doors that led to a brick porch and stairs beyond.

The empty echoiness of the room got me to wondering if I could *make* myself see something from the past — if I could summon it up at will. While Sammy spun in tight circles in the center with the evident purpose of making himself dizzy, I went over to touch the gate to the musicians' area. I gripped the wood until it was pressing a pattern in my flesh, bent my head and concentrated, and heard, saw —

Not a thing. I finally let go, feeling a little ridiculous. *How do psychics do it?* I wondered. It was not much of a gift if I couldn't even control when it happened. If it ever happened again.

I shrugged and twirled back across the floor toward Sam in a remembered step from second-grade ballet, imagining the music of a waltz. I hit the light switch and reached for the door handle —

And a golden glow blazed behind me. Real music replaced my imagined notes, together with the sounds of feet sliding across the floor, of dozens of people talking. I turned around to see a dance, a ball in full progress, with women in hooped dresses all doing the exact same steps opposite a line of men in tailed jackets. *An echo*, I thought, surprised and pleased. *I found one.*

My eyes were drawn to a pretty girl in palest pink with ivory skin and hair almost black. She looked — familiar. *A relative?* She might have been one of my distant grandmothers. *This isn't so bad*, I thought, *isn't so frightening*. It was, in fact, something like magic, like being *in* a movie, and I stood, caught by it, enchanted, until I heard my little brother's voice.

"Wake up, Sarah. I want to go."

Then the vision of pastel dancers disappeared like a TV set shutting off, and the room returned to darkness. I felt a little disappointed; I wanted it back. Which made me smile at myself. When the echoes didn't involve a crazy woman screaming at you in a pitch-black attic, they were pretty okay. Interesting.

"Fine, Sam, let's go."

As I followed my little brother down the hall, I was humming a snatch of music that I had never heard before, music that had not been played inside those walls for centuries.

Chapter Seven

The girl in the mirror had a pleasant face surrounded by ringlets of darkest brown. She — I — caught up a stray lock with a hairpin and nodded at my reflection, satisfied. I exited my room and knocked on the next door down the hall. "Are you in there?"

"Sarah-Louise! Come in."

The boy sat at a table spread with tools and pieces of wood. He brushed glue on a dovetailed edge that he fitted to the exactly obverse dovetails of another piece. His face was pale and hollowed. My brother. Matty.

"Dearest," I said. "You should not be working."

"I am all done with the hard work, Sarah," he said. "Now I have only the pegging and gluing to finish."

"Do it tomorrow, or next week, when you are feeling stronger."

He smiled and shook his head. "You and I must not pretend with each other. We must always be truthful."

Tears welled up in my eyes. I wiped them angrily. "Forgive me."

"Sit. Help me. I want to finish this thing. I want people to see it a hundred years from now and say, 'What a clever young man he must have been.' You shall have it and you shall keep your most valued treasures in it and always think of me."

"Yes," I said with tight huskiness, as I — she — sat down to help her brother.

He smiled and touched her hand. "Sarah."

❧

"Sarah."

I could hear Sammy's voice from a faraway place, but I did not want to answer him. It was safe here in the boy's room, and there were cold shadows all around, at the edges of my vision. I did not want to leave.

"Sarah. Wake up, Sarah."

Sammy was patting my hand with his small, pudgy one. I sat up into the morning's cheerful light with my dream still caught in my head. I thought I knew those faces. Had seen them in one of the paintings on the walls.

Such an odd dream. So sad. So real. *Have I been hearing echoes in my sleep?* I wondered. *But then why did I seem to be* in *the echo, instead of just watching it?*

Who in the world would know the answer to that? I put the question aside; I had no time to think about it at the moment. I had a big day ahead. Sailing with Richard, the senator's son.

"What are you up to, Samwise?" I asked.

"Up *for*, Sarah. I am up *for* breakfast. Come with me." He tugged at my hand.

"Okay," I said, smiling.

It was French toast that morning, fried a golden brown. Another irresistible offering from Rose, who was still helping Mom, and still taking nutritional mercy on Sammy and, as a seeming afterthought, me.

When we were through with the toast, I parked Sammy in front of a cartoon on the TV in Gramma's room and took a shower in the bathroom near the kitchen, which was a *lot* warmer and cozier than the tiled bath upstairs. As I headed to my mother's room to borrow her hair dryer, I detoured to answer a knock at the front door. I opened it to a middle-aged woman who, thankfully, didn't look like she was going to care too much about my towel head.

"Can I help you?" I asked.

"I'm the calligrapher," she said, a bit impatiently.

"Um, what?"

"I'm the calligrapher." She looked at a slip of paper in her hand. "Anne Parsons hired me? To do the invitations?" I must still have looked confused, because she added, "I handwrite addresses."

"Oh, God, really?" I said, letting her in. I guessed that must have seemed a bit rude, because she frowned at me. But honestly, there were people who did that for a living?

I showed her to the office and rushed back to Gramma's bathroom — my hair was drying into a wavy mess. Thirty minutes later, it was blown, straightened, and sporting a slight curl on the ends. I'd done my best with the lump-concealment routine, and then I'd managed a quickie manicure. A spritz with floral-citrus Sunrise, a little eyeliner and lip gloss, and I thought was looking pretty good. For me. With a black-and-blue contusion. Sigh.

I'd decided on a white tank layered under a wide-striped blue and white shirt, with my favorite jacket, a couple of bracelets, and a beaded necklace. I looked in the mirror. Okay, skip the necklace. Didn't want him thinking I was trying too hard.

Except — it just didn't seem right. The jacket was a little too baggy. Plus, it bunched oddly if I didn't tug it down all the time. Which I'd probably forget to do.

God. Back up the stairs to my suitcase. What about long sleeves? Too stuffy. Capris? Maybe if my legs were tan. I clenched my teeth against mounting panic.

After ten minutes of manic changing, I headed into the kitchen in the outfit I started with — *sans* earrings and bracelets, plus necklace.

Rose gave me the once-over. "Got yourself all ready for your date?"

"What? No." I could feel myself flush. "It's not a date, Rose, we're just going sailing."

"Mm-hm." She handed me a plastic-wrapped package. "I made you some brownies to take along. Can't go empty-handed — that's low-class."

Ouch. I hadn't even thought about bringing anything. "Wow, Rose, that's incredibly thoughtful of you. Thank you."

"You keep an eye on that boy. I hope he's better behaved than his father was at his age."

"Don't worry about me. I'm not a little kid."

"No indeed." She snorted. "You're almost sixteen. Need some aspirin? That still hurt?"

"What? Oh." The bump. The concealment thing was evidently not doing its job. "I know where the bottle is, Rose, thanks." She turned to go. "Um," I stopped her, "is Jackson around?"

"He's working in the garden. Behind the east wing."

"Thanks," I said, and ducked out into the gallery and through the French doors. I came out on a stone path that led to the left, branched right along a hedge wall, and became a set of steps between formal flower beds. I spotted Jackson bent over one of these, trowel in hand. Despite the warmth of the day, he was wearing a long-sleeve shirt to work in. When he saw me, he sat back on the low wall of the bed.

"Planting," I said, "or digging up?"

"Planting," he answered, pointing to a pile of bulbs. "Ida asked me to put these in about a month ago. And I thought I'd just do that last thing for her. Fall is the best time to put in narcissus." He added for the botanically impaired — me, "Daffodils."

"Ah."

He changed the subject. "You look very nice." And I thought to myself how formally polite that sounded. I wondered what had happened to the guy who'd been chatting with me so casually in the attic, but maybe, given the way the night had ended —

"Thanks," I said. "I'm going sailing."

"With Richard Hathaway."

He knows? How? Like it's any of his business. I swallowed my annoyance, saying, "I'm just glad to have a chance to get out on the water. I love to sail."

"You can take the *Liquid Amber* anytime. I got her all ready for you."

"For me?" I repeated, a little stupidly. *Right, genius. That was* you *plural, as in* your family. *New subject.* "That was nice of you. Do you sail?"

"Ida used to let me take the *Amber* out. She said a boat that didn't sail regularly lost her wings. The *Amber* is old, but I bet she's faster than Richard Hathaway's boat."

He waited. I scrambled to find words. "Look," I said, "about that echo thing —"

"Yes?"

"Maybe I'm okay with it. For now. I mean, it's still pretty creepy, but I'm willing to keep looking, if you want."

He did that thing again, where you could see a whole series of thoughts or feelings flickering in his eyes while the rest of his face stayed perfectly impassive. I wondered what was going on in there; I wondered what he was hiding so carefully.

"Tonight?" he said.

"Yeah. Same time, same place?"

"Sure."

As long as I had him cornered, I decided I'd ask all my pending questions. "How come you called my brother Samwise the other day?"

"Just a little nickname. Seemed to settle him."

"That's what I call him."

"Really?" He shrugged. "I guess that's why he responded to it."

"You like Tolkien?" I asked. Which of course was where I'd gotten the nickname, from my favorite hobbit — Samwise Gamgee.

"Not so much," he said with a tight smile. "I have a friend who loves The Lord of the Rings. I read it because of her."

He must really *like her*, I thought, *to wade through twelve hundred pages of a fantasy he didn't enjoy.* "It's one of my favorites too."

He nodded. Silence settled over us, and I realized he was watching me again, like he was assessing me. "Well," I said shortly, "gotta go."

He responded with a bland look. "Have a good time. Don't let Hathaway kill you."

"I'll try," I said faintly, and turned on my heel. I headed back to the kitchen to collect Rose's package of brownies, then went to the office in the west wing to tell my mother I was leaving.

Mom was hard at work beside the calligrapher, stuffing envelopes and crossing names off a list the senator had sent over.

"I'll see you later," I said.

She looked up. Her face softened into a smile of approval. My ensemble had passed the test. "Have fun."

I resented the relief I thought I read in my mother's face. I mean, I knew she thought I should have had a boyfriend long before, or at least been "dating," whatever that meant anymore. Not that she'd said anything. *Directly.* Just made those little side comments that kind of drive you crazy, like "Oh, *Jecie's* going to prom?" She was probably *thrilled* I was finally doing *some*thing with *some*one. *Whatever*, I thought.

"Thanks," I said. And headed out the sunroom doors.

Richard was waiting when I got to the bottom of the stone stairs. The *Swallow* was larger than the *Amber*, and much newer. A beauty.

"Nice boat," I said, admiring.

"Nice necklace," he said, doing the same. "What happened?"

Confused, I felt for my beads.

"No," he laughed. "I meant to your *head*."

Oh, right. Wonderful. "Yeah, see, I had this really *big* idea last night . . ."

"Ah-ha-ha," he said in mock hilarity, smiling.

Silence settled — it was evidently still my turn. Slightly panicky, I held out the brownies and blurted, "Provisions. In case we get marooned." And instantly regretted it. It wasn't funny, it wasn't even cute, it was just —

"Great," Richard said, smiling. He took the heavy bag from me and hefted it speculatively, as if it weighed a ton. "Bring any for yourself, Parsons?"

Now see? That was cute.

I gave him a grin, took the hand he offered, and climbed aboard. He put the brownies on top of a bulging picnic basket, jumped to the dock, cast off the line, and heaved the hull forward. As it slid away from the dock, he skillfully leapt back aboard. "You're at the tiller, okay?"

"Fine by me," I said. He did the sweaty stuff and I got to navigate.

My dad had started me sailing when I was just a kid. The waters in the Puget Sound were rough and cold, so it was important to learn some skills *fast*. I used to crew for Dad. Lately, Sammy crewed for me. Begin young like that, and it gets in your blood.

The current carried us to mid-channel, where the breeze filled the sail. It was all magic from there.

Sailing is a dance between the boat and the wind. You have to keep the sail set to trap the wind as you tack your way in the general direction you want to go. If you can get a full sail with the breeze at your back and your bow pointed toward your destination, then you're "running before the wind." Which is more or less like flying.

Moving down the Severn, the wind wasn't at our back; it was blowing in a northerly direction off the Chesapeake. So the game was me steering and Richard adjusting the sheets to snag what little wind we could. We'd build up speed tacking northeasterly, then swing about to the southeast using our momentum and the flow of the river.

I say river, because that's what the maps called it, but the Severn from Amber House east was more an estuary of the bay. The Chesapeake spread fat fingers of water up the beds of every stream that fed it, so the water was fresh, but the current was buried and sluggish. It was hard work fighting our way downwind.

Since I was at the helm, I had some time to watch the scenery: some modest homes, but mostly a series of huge houses sitting above velvet lawns. Docks sprouted before a lot of them. About halfway down to the bay, the river belled out around an island. The channel widened and turned north there. We picked up speed as we rounded the bend. The houses along the south bank grew closer together until they congealed into the city of Annapolis. A harbor filled with ships and boats of all sizes spread out before a campus of pale gray granite buildings — the United States Naval Academy. Tacking south into the mouth of a smaller river, I saw the colonial heart of the town, all charming, steep-roofed buildings shouldering side by side. Then we came about northeast, heading away from shore.

The bay opened wide before us, the waters pushed into small, choppy waves by the wind. A huge steel ship cut through the deepest channel, heading north, slowing in its approach to the harbor in Baltimore.

Richard smiled at me, mischief in his eyes, and called for me to tack. I eased the rudder over. The sail billowed as the *Swallow* lumbered northwest into full flight.

We skimmed the waves, just barely rocking. My hair flapped wildly around me, collecting moisture from the air. I was laughing and didn't remember having started. We came even with the steel giant, and I waved at the seamen at the rails, who were watching our run. We passed them, still flying.

When we got ahead a little, Richard called for another tack.

He wanted us to cut in front of the tanker. A maneuver that was not only illegal, but just short of insane. I opened my mouth to scream, "Don't do it," but Richard had already blown the sheets, letting our sails luff wildly, skewing our path to port. If I hesitated, I might slow our flight — fatally. So, I pushed the tiller with all my strength, turning the *Swallow* across the wind. Instantly, we started to lose speed. The ship at our backs plowed on indifferently, still distant, but looking more and more like a skyscraper bearing down on us.

"Keep turning her," Richard yelled. He trimmed the jib to port to catch a little more wind.

This is not good, I thought. We had passed the halfway point, but now the tanker's bow wake was pushing us sideways as we crept toward clearing its path. I couldn't see anyone at the rails anymore. The steel sides just rose up and up into the sky itself. The ship sounded its horn, and the blare smacked me like something physical.

But then the *Swallow* started to cruise along the ship's spreading wake like a surfer down a wave. We were clear and stealing speed from the huge amount of water the tanker displaced.

Richard was roaring with laughter. *"Yeee-haw,"* he yelled, then, "Amidships," as he hauled the mainsail in the last few inches, trimming the sheets flat. "Keep her heading southeast till we clear the stern, then bring her about."

When the ship passed, we were a good ways east, well clear of the propeller wash. I turned her ninety degrees once more, back toward the mouth of the Severn. Richard let the sail swing starboard, where it again filled with wind. We ran along at a good clip past the marsh tip on the south side of the river mouth. As we neared Annapolis again, both the *Swallow* and my heart finally slowed.

We tacked back upriver as far as the island. When we got close, Richard furled the sails and dropped anchor. He was still grinning widely and wickedly. "How'd you like the ride?" he asked.

"Some ride," I said, managing a smile. "Adrenaline junkie."

He laughed, enjoying himself. Then he dove into the picnic basket. "Ham or tuna?"

I wondered if I still had an appetite in me. "Ham," I said. I unwrapped the sandwich and found I did. Apparently something about fear left me absolutely famished. We worked through two sandwiches each, a slab of pie, and a brownie, all washed down with Coke.

"You sail like a guy and eat like a guy," Richard observed. "More points, Parsons."

He was still keeping score. And, I realized, I wanted to do well.

The trip back to Amber House was more leisurely. Richard set the sail and took the tiller, so I could sit back and relax. And sneak peeks at the pilot. He did more of his tour-guide shtick, telling me how the Catholic settlers brought over from Europe by Lord Baltimore displaced the Piscataway tribe from the territory on both sides of the Severn. "They were related to

Pocahontas's tribe, but they were a separate people. A smallpox epidemic got most of them."

He pointed to a large, rectangular brick mansion that he and the senator called home. It was not as old as Amber House, he said, "but then, nothing else around here is."

As the channel narrowed, its sides rose. The trees climbing the bluffs to either side added to the late afternoon shadows as we approached Amber House. Richard skillfully slowed the boat as we entered the estuary, coming about just in time to run parallel to the dock. He tied the *Swallow* up. All very neatly done.

He held out his hand. I took it and jumped down beside him, failing to land with his same catlike grace, but coming close. I was looking for more points. He grinned, as if he could read my mind.

"A group of us are having a party tomorrow night," he said. "Wanna join us?"

"Wanna join us" was not a date, I noted unhappily. An invitation, but not another date. "Sure," I said. "How do I get there?"

"I'll pick you up. It's on the south side of the river, near Herald Island. I'm going right past your house. If you give me your number, I can text you."

"Yeah, can't. Sorry. Forgot my charger at home."

He laughed. "Okay. Then how 'bout we say . . . nine o'clock?"

"Sounds great. Thanks." Rose's words about low-class people rang in my ears. "Can I bring something, you think?"

He nodded soberly. "You are not stepping foot in my car unless you've got another big bag of brownies on you."

Chapter Eight

When I got back, Sammy was sitting in the kitchen, sucking on a frozen juice bar, his mouth the color of smashed strawberries.

"What you been up to, squirt?"

"Been playing hide-and-seek."

"Oh, yeah? Who with?"

"No one."

I smiled tolerantly. "Kind of hard to play hide-and-seek with no one, isn't it?"

"Nope. I just gotta be the finder. But I'm a good finder. Like you, Sarah."

"Where did you get the juice bar?"

"Rose made 'em for me. You can have one, if you want."

I fished one out of the freezer and thawed it from its plastic mold under running water in the sink. I took a lick. "Yum."

"You're welcome," Sammy said.

I sighed. "Yeah. Thanks."

"I know something you don't know. But you gotta say please."

I nodded. "Please, Sam. *Please* tell me what you know."

He smiled a strawberry smile. "Daddy's coming."

"For dinner?"

"For a sleepover."

"You're kidding. He's staying till tomorrow?"

"Till tomorrow after tomorrow. Mommy said he could."

Wow, I thought. And then, *No*. With Dad in the house, it'd make my planned nocturnal investigations that much harder to pull off. *Perhaps I ought to bag it*, I thought. *Perhaps I should call Jackson.*

"He knows already."

"What? Who?"

But Sam had already disappeared through the door.

I spotted Rose on her way out.

"Richard Hathaway invited me to join his friends for a party tomorrow night and said I should bring some more brownies. I was hoping you'd give me the recipe."

She looked at me skeptically, but turned and fished a little card out of a cookbook on a shelf. She handed it to me. "It's your gramma's recipe. You know how to do this?"

"Sure. I can follow directions. What could be so hard?" I started to look it over.

"I'll be gone Sunday and Monday, so —"

"Um, Rose?" I noticed my rudeness. "Sorry to interrupt."

"What?"

"Where can I find the double boiler thingy?"

"It's in this cupboard." She turned and fished out a pair of stacking pots. I stared at them. "You put the water in the bottom one," she said suspiciously.

"Right," I said. *Maybe Gramma had a box of brownie mix around here somewhere.*

"I expect you're gonna need some help making these." Clearly she recognized I had inherited my mother's cooking skills.

"I can figure it out."

"I don't want you burning the pots or setting the house on fire. You be in here at ten o'clock tomorrow morning, we'll give you some help."

"Thanks, Rose. Sorry to be such a bother."

"No bother to me," she said, snatching the card back to return it to the cookbook. "You just promise you'll make sure Sam gets a decent breakfast while I'm gone."

"I promise," I said. "Where're you going?"

"Down to Alexandria to visit my mama."

"Your mama?" I repeated, confused. "But I thought Nanga was your mother —"

She rolled her eyes a little. "Nanga? My mother's name is Sylvia."

Mom walked through the door then. "Sarah," she said, "can you make the bed in the Chinese room for your father? The linen cupboard is next to Gramma's room."

"Sure, Mom," I said.

Dad came, lugging more carry-out — Italian, this time. We four sat down to a reasonably cheerful meal together. It might have helped that I didn't mention Richard or the party once. Not that I had much of a chance to. Mom launched into this long, boring story about one of her client's paintings. Only, Dad didn't seem to find it boring. He kept prompting her with questions and chuckling in the right places. My mother laughed and gestured with her hands, elaborating, looking more beautiful and graceful than usual. She seemed young. Not hard. Vulnerable. It made me realize, a little bit, what my parents must have been like back in the beginning, when they were still in love.

After dinner, Mom headed off to her TV, but not before she asked me how my sailing date went. I told her "fine" in the most noncommittal voice I had. She frowned a little bit, itching to ask more, but knowing better than to do it. I got a perverse pleasure out of that.

I asked if I could go with Richard to the party the next evening.

"Yes, of course," she said, and added in that unthinking way of hers, "The senator wanted you to meet some of the local kids. That's probably why Richard invited you."

And just like that, I realized that Richard probably wasn't interested in me at all, that he was just doing his old man a favor by taking me around. It hurt. "Thanks," I mumbled.

I was sitting there wishing violently that my mother would enroll in an introductory course on tact, when she looked at me oddly and asked, "Did you say something?"

"I said, 'Thanks.'"

"After that."

"No."

I hadn't, had I? I hadn't cursed her out loud? I looked at Dad to check, but he was busy with Sammy.

"Okay," Mom said. "Good night, then."

Dad and Sammy and I talked for a while, just about nothing stuff. Dad asked me what I thought of the senator's son, and I shrugged. He seemed comforted by that. He asked Sam if he'd met anybody, and Sammy said, "No one." Short and sweet and summed it up — classic Sammy talk. Dad and I laughed.

Then Dad announced he was "turning into a pumpkin." I told him I could put Sam to bed, so he headed off to his room. Sam, Heavy Bear, and I went upstairs.

It was nearly ten, and I was anxious for Sam to get to sleep before Jackson arrived for our explorations. I was also hoping for a few minutes to call Jecie. I wanted some sympathy from her for my latest Richard Hathaway disappointment.

Sam, unfortunately, was not anxious to cooperate. "Did you see, Sarah?" He was standing in front of the dollhouse on the shelves in my room.

"Yeah, bud, you showed me — it lights up."

"No, Sarah." He undid the clasp in the front of the house and opened it. The front half of the house split in two and swung to either side, forming a U of displayed rooms. "Lookit," he said. "It's Amber House."

It was. Once you started looking for it, it was obvious. The desk in the front hall, the trestle table, the main stair, the nautical bedroom — all the way the house had been before they'd added the two wings and a few miscellaneous architectural details. It even had tiny oil portraits hanging on the walls. Were these people obsessed with their house, or what?

Every room was a perfect replica of the rooms as they had looked back — I guessed — when the dollhouse was made, probably in the 1700s. Which meant it had no bathrooms and there was a pump in the kitchen sink. No updating at all, except for the tiny glass bulbs in every chandelier and lamp.

Even the Amber House family was there — four-inch-tall china dolls of a black-haired mama and three children dressed in satin, plus an African-American doll in plain linen clothes. I was fascinated. I wandered the rooms — opened cupboards, took books from the shelves in the library, set the table with quarter-sized rose-painted plates. It was amazing.

"Lookit, Sarah." Sam was pointing at the fireplace in the living room. I bent down to see what he saw.

A pair of tiny boots were dangling from the chimney. I grabbed one and pulled, and a daddy doll dressed in a military uniform tumbled out. "Huh," I said.

Sammy looked at him solemnly. "Maybe you should put him back, Sarah."

"I have a better idea," I said, gathering up the doll family. "It's time to sleep. Let's put them to bed." Swiftly, I tucked them into what I assumed were their places: the boy in the nautical room, the two girls in a white bedroom on the southwest corner, the mommy in Deirdre's room, and the man in the sword-strewn suite. "And now for you too. Off to bed. I'm tired."

"You don't seem tired to me."

"Well, I am," I snapped. "You've got to go to bed."

My desperation must have been apparent, because Sam sized me up as someone ready to sweeten the deal. "Read me a story," he demanded.

I may have been an easy target for some arm-twisting, but I wasn't stupid — I had been down this road with him before. "I will read you a story, *if*" — I ticked off the conditions on my fingers — "you brush your teeth, get a drink of water, put on your pajamas, *and* get under the covers," I told him.

"Okay," he agreed a little too quickly. I had missed something important.

"*And*," I added, "if you promise to stay in bed till morning."

His face fell — that was the loophole he had been counting on.

"Okay," he agreed, more reluctantly. I thought I was safe.

He got ready for bed while I went to his backpack for a book of fairy tales we were reading. On the floor next to it, I saw a heavy frame, its face to the wall. I thought it must be a portrait, because Sammy didn't like pictures "watching him" and was always turning them around in any room he stayed in alone. I tipped it to see, but it turned out to be a mirror.

When he came back from the bathroom, I asked him, "Sam, how did this get here?"

"I did it."

"You shouldn't be taking things off the wall, bud. Why'd you take this down?"

"Don't want no one watching me."

"You don't want *any*one watching you," I corrected.

Sam gave me a questioning look, a mix of confusion and impatience. "No one's in the mirror," he said.

I picked up the mirror, turned it around. "That's right. No one's there." Sam didn't look satisfied. I was getting a little exasperated. "Want me to put it back where it was?"

He nodded again, and I leaned it back facing the wall.

Sam climbed into his berth, and I squeezed in beside him, so he could see the pictures and follow along as I read. Through the portholes to our little room-in-a-room, I saw clouds drifting over the half-full moon outside. Drops of rain started to spatter the glass.

I read Sam a tale about someone named Jack, and it struck me as I read that they are all Jack — the guys who are simple and despised by their smarter brothers, but who always figure out how to follow the princess into her enchanted realm and bring her and all her sisters back. Then Jack marries the princess and gets half the kingdom and everyone lives happily ever after.

Sammy, nearly out by the time I finished, murmured to me, "Jack finded her. Like you find me, Sarah. You're my Jack."

I smiled. "You mean I'm not the beautiful princess in our story?" But he was already asleep.

It was almost eleven by the time I was all done with Sam. I went to fish the flashlight from his pack but came up empty, and then remembered I had left the thing in the kitchen the last time I had borrowed it. I sighed, gritted my teeth, and crept into the hall.

It was pitch-black. I felt along the wall toward the stairs. The tall, wide, empty space tugged at me, almost a vacuum. I reached out and grabbed the railing to steady myself.

The soles of my sneakers squeaked slightly and the sound bounced back on me. I felt small and clumsy, worried that the noise would wake up — whatever should stay sleeping. I stole down the steps and sped lightly down the hall, trying to make no sound, trying not even to breathe, trying to outrace the feeling there was someone at my back, someone I was running from.

In the kitchen, I snapped on the little light above the stove. And the world righted itself. I smiled at my overactive imagination and sat down to wait, watching the clock above the door.

At eleven thirty exactly, Jackson's face showed in the kitchen window. He came through the door soaking wet. Water was running down his jaw and dripping to his chest. "Didn't know when it would start raining. Sorry," he said, gesturing to the growing puddles on the floor.

"You came over to help me — I'm the one who's sorry. Any towels in here?"

He started toward the cupboards.

"Don't move," I ordered. "I'll get them. Let's keep the flood in one spot."

"Bottom drawer." He pointed. "Dish towels."

I shook out two and handed them to him. He started drying his hair.

"Let me have your coat."

"That's all right, I can take care of this."

"Just give it to me." He shrugged out of it, and I hung it from a peg, tossing another couple of towels under it to catch the drips.

We switched to paper towels to wipe down his shoes. While he sat and did that job, I mopped up the floor with a few more.

"Not too good at predicting the future, are you?"

He started. "Why do you say that?"

"Where's your umbrella?"

"Oh." He managed a half grin. "Guess I'll never be a weather forecaster. Where are we heading tonight?"

It didn't look like I was going to get a second helping of the easygoing guy who'd shown up the other night. This evening's Jackson was back to being withdrawn and a little on the uncomfortable side. Maybe he was feeling guilty for not having done more to warn me about the echoes. And maybe he should have. Although, to be fair, what could he possibly have said that I would've believed?

"I want to go back up to the third floor," I said. "I want to look at the books in that glassed-in shelf."

"The third floor? You sure?"

"I'm not going in the big room. And you're not gonna leave me by myself. Right?"

"Right."

"So we're good," I said, shrugging. "Let's go."

There was no electric light in the little room with the shelves — the lamp on the worktable used oil. Jackson picked it up. "It sounds like it's still got something sloshing around in there. Shall we see if it lights?"

While I pointed his flashlight, he removed the globe and glass chimney and touched a lighter to the exposed wick. It caught with a steady golden flame. It didn't smell like kerosene. I had some vague idea that lamps in the nineteenth-century used actual whale oil and wondered if we were burning the last drops of Moby-Dick.

Jackson put the chimney and shade back over the flame, and set the lamp on the table. It gave off a warm pool of light that didn't reach much beyond the work area. It made me feel like I had stepped into the past. It was a feeling I was beginning to get used to.

I sat on the floor in front of the opened cabinet, so Jackson settled on the chair. The "books" the shelves contained proved not to be books at all, but rather, a large set of leather-clad journals. Inside, page after page was filled with dated entries, all in the same elegant handwriting.

"Looks like they're all diaries," Jackson said.

The one I had in my hand had numbers stamped into the cover: *1850–60*. I pulled another one from the shelves. It said, *1900–10*. Another said, *1770–80*.

"Two hundred and fifty years of diaries? By one person?" I said. "Know what I think these are? I think they're my great-grandmother Fiona's notes. For her book on Amber House. She must have written it here, at this table." I ran my hand over its surface, imagining her sitting here, day after day, month after month, filling all these volumes with her careful writing. It was hard to reconcile her with the party girl that old lady at the funeral had described to me.

"I want to flip through a few," I said. "Maybe they'll have some clues about the diamonds." I pulled some more from the shelves at random and made a stack. "Okay," I said. "I guess we should get out of here."

I stood and started for the door, but he caught my elbow. "Hold up a sec." He walked over to the rear interior corner of the room. "There's a handle here." His fingers found and traced the outlines of a door, worked into the paneling. "What do you say? Shall we open it?"

I felt like telling him no. I was a little leery about the things that lurked behind the closed doors on the third floor of Amber House. But I told him, "Go for it."

The door opened onto a single large space that must have topped the entire west wing of the house. The wall between the main part of the house and this attic still showed the clapboard siding of the old house — they had not bothered to dress it up in this utilitarian storeroom.

Jackson carried Fiona's oil lamp into the attic, and I scuttled after the light.

Dormer windows poked out in the slanting, bare wood ceiling, and the brickwork of three chimneys showed on the two ends of the room. The open space between was spotted with mounded islands of boxes.

"Still game?" he asked me.

"You think we're gonna find the Captain's diamonds in one of these?"

"No," he said. "But maybe some other treasure. Aren't you curious what's in them?"

I shook my head no, but added, reluctantly, "Okay, I'm curious."

Jackson dusted off an old chair with a sagging seat, set Fiona's lamp on a water-damaged table, asked me to sit, and started putting boxes in front of me for my inspection.

Most of the boxes were filled with papers — financial records of one kind or another. One held moth-eaten linens. Another few had Christmas decorations. There was a chest of miscellaneous hardware. A long pack of wallpaper remnants. Two trunks of baby clothes that seemed like they came from the sixties — clothes my mother must have worn. A box of baby toys from the same era.

I couldn't resist. I had to try to *see*. I lifted out a child's brightly painted circus set, opened it, and began to take out its jointed animals and clowns.

Like a switch had been thrown, the light brightened around the smiling lion I was holding. The sound of voices grew sharper until I could distinguish words. Then I saw an auburn-haired toddler with my mother's eyes putting the lion in its barred wagon.

My grandmother — young, with close-cropped hair — knelt beside her. "That's right, Magpie," she was saying, "the lion goes in the cage." The little girl mimicked a lion, and Ida roared back. They laughed together.

And I thought: *Once upon a time, forgotten now by everyone, my grandmother had been happy.*

I dropped the circus piece back in the box. The light bled to darkness. All felt normal again. I traded the box of toys for another carton Jackson had brought.

A box of empty pickling jars. Boxes of dishes. A stereopticon packed with rows of double-sided pictures. A case of canned food from the 1940s.

Jackson set a trunk in front of me. It was filled with canvases, standing on end. I drew one out. Globs of paint resolved into the riches of a wisteria vine heavy with flowers, trailing over the porch posts outside Amber House's kitchen door. I held it up to the glow of the lightbulb to look for the signature.

"Huh," I said.

"What?"

"The artist. Annie McGuinness."

"Isn't that —"

"My mother," I finished for him, nodding.

"Wow," he said. "That's pretty good."

I pulled out another. The daubs captured the face of a pretty, auburn-haired girl, smiling slightly, forever. She looked like Mom, but with the soft curves of a child's face. I checked the signature. Annie McGuinness.

I flipped through the other canvases: a sailboat on the Chesapeake, racing ahead of a storm; sunlight breaking over spring-green fields around a tiny Amber House; another self-portrait of my young mother sitting on a bench surrounded by leaves; one of a toddler in a Victorian dress, clutching Heavy Bear. All filled with light. All reflecting the eye of someone cheerfully captivated by the things she saw. I checked the signature on each. They were *all* Annie McGuinness.

I had never had any idea my mother could paint. I felt betrayed, somehow — like she'd hidden herself away with these paintings decades ago. Left me with a replacement, a changeling, who only looked like the person who once had been Annie McGuinness.

As I put the canvases back, I spotted a sketchbook tucked sideways in the end of the trunk, small and easy to hide. It was my chance to look back into the mind of my mother before she'd stiffened into the person she'd become. I pulled it out, then made myself shut the trunk's lid.

I looked up to see Jackson watching me. His face was gentle, but I didn't want his pity. It wasn't a big deal. I set my teeth and shrugged. "Anything else?"

He shrugged a little too, his face shifting to that smooth, neutral look he used so often. He pushed forward two identical file boxes. "These are the last."

I slit the tape on the first. It was full of family photos. The newest were of me as a baby. They went back from there, through the decades past my grandmother's childhood in a pale wool coat and black button-up shoes, to a soldier from the Great War and a family in a horse-drawn carriage.

"I want to get these out of here," I told Jackson. "I want to 'find' them someplace else, so I can look through them without having to explain them to my mother."

"Can you carry one box down the stairs?"

I tried lifting one. "I think so."

"I've got the other," he said, tucking it beneath his left arm, taking up the lamp with the right. We ducked through the door.

I balanced my box on my lifted leg, and then I sealed that part of my family's past back in its resting place.

We shoved the boxes under a bed in the west wing, then Jackson left through the conservatory. Sammy's light was on when I headed for my room. I stuck my head in and found him whispering to his bear. He looked up at my entrance, blinking a little.

"Sam. What are doing? You're supposed to be asleep."

"Okay, Sarah. I will go back to sleep."

"What woke you up? A bad dream?"

He lay down, and I went in and pulled the covers up over him. He said, "You want to hear my song, Sarah? It's about a spider."

I sat next to him and leaned to hear it. I was guessing "Itsy-Bitsy." "Go," I said.

He smiled and pulled his hands out from under the covers. He began in a chanting, spooky voice: "Beware the good mother, you'd better beware!" He shaped his fingers into claws: "She lurks in the attic and under the stair." He walked fingers up one of my arms, in time with his lyrics: "So if you go a-creeping, you gotta take care." He was milking it, going for maximum sinister: "'Cause she'll BITE anybody" — and I jumped as his fingers leapt to my neck to deliver a bite — "who enters her lair." He dissolved into giggles. "I got you, Sarah."

"Yes, you did," I said, and I gave him a few finger spider bites of my own on his ticklish spots. Then, "Shh, shh," I scolded him, and smiled. *God bless him.* No matter what kind of garbage I had to take from the rest of the world, I always had Sammy.

"G'night, Sarah," he said, smiling in return.

I reached for the light. "G'night, Sam-my-man."

Chapter Nine

"I hate to be leaving you here, Cait. God bless you and keep you. Good-bye."

In a small, dark room nearly filled by two cots, I — she — was hugging a girl of about sixteen. The girl was wearing a nightgown, and she was weeping. I was in a long skirt and cloak. I could see my breath on the air.

I kissed her cheek, slung my bag over my shoulder, and turned into the hall. A fat, red-faced man stepped out of another door.

"Stay until I can get another bond girl to take your place. I'll pay you good wages."

"My term was up at midnight. I'll not stay another minute under this roof."

"I won't let you go." He reached out a thick hand to touch my breast. I knocked it away and struck him with my open palm.

His red face turned scarlet, but still I could see the white-red print of my slap upon it. He raised his arm to strike back. It was caught midswing by a tall young man who had come up behind him. The young man slammed a fist into the other's gut, doubling him over. Then he brought his fist up hard, and I heard the wet crunch of splintering bone. With blood spurting from his nose, the fat man fell backward like a chopped tree and lay still. I picked my way around the body and threw myself upon the young man, kissing him fiercely.

Then we left that place.

We were on a sailboat, standing side by side in the prow. I saw a river mouth beside a reed marsh. I pointed. "There."

The riverbanks narrowed and rose. "No other folks up here," he said.

"The pox took a lot of the Indians, but still a fair number about. You should stay closer in." As he angled the craft in to shore, a rain began, a soft drizzle turning to harder drops.

"Let's wait a bit, Sorcha, for the storm to lessen," my young man said.

But I could not wait.

I hurried up through the woods slicked with rain. Wet earth gripped my feet and small branches slashed at my legs and arms. Vines tried to trip me. I stumbled and fell, but didn't stop. I pushed up the rest of the way on all fours, fighting the mud that tried to spill me back and down.

The trees thinned. I used a sapling to pull myself up to my feet. I walked out into the meadow on the bluff's crown, in which stood a single tall tree.

Above me the clouds leapt with light, then cracked open — a bolt arcing down to the lifted branches of the solitary tree. The boom smacked into me, stopping my ears with ringing; my skin crawled with the nearness of the discharge. Half the tree split away and fell, smoldering.

I saw something tumble from the heart of the tree. Liam had caught up with me and took my arm to stop me. But I shook him off and walked forward surely. I knelt down at the foot of the stricken tree and it was there in the grass — a clear, burnt-yellow drop with something in the center of it, some dark flaw at its core.

I lifted it high. "Let it never be forgotten."

I closed my fist around the stone.

I woke, and lay in bed remembering my dream. Knowing that it had been something more than a dream. That maybe it had been Sorcha and Liam, the way they really were. My great-great-I-didn't-know-how-many-times-great grandparents.

The thoughts my dream provoked left me brooding and moody, but fortunately, nobody was in the kitchen when I went down. As I stood spooning up the last few bites of Cheerios I'd fixed for myself, Mom made the mistake of calling for me instead of just sneaking quietly into the room. I assumed she was intent on advancing some party-related agenda, and I was not interested.

I dumped my bowl in the sink and ducked through the door to the outside. I sprinted down the path and around the corner of the house, hoping she hadn't spotted me through the window. If I could hide until ten o'clock, then Rose would be there to help me with the brownies, and I could completely evade whatever it was my mother wanted from me.

The hedge wall stretched to my right; a dozen yards down, an archway cut through it. Seemed like a good place to stay out of sight. I ran inside. It opened into a long, green corridor floored in grass and flagstones.

At its end stood a little girl, maybe six or seven, with a halo of dark hair, in a gauzy white dress.

And I thought: *She's beautiful.*

She looked my way, turned, and skipped left behind the hedge.

Without stopping to consider, without even wondering who she was or where she came from, I ran after her.

At the corridor's end, the passage continued both left and right. I cut left and ran to a corner that bent left again. I realized then I was in a hedge maze.

Halfway down the next corridor, two passages crossed, and looking right, I saw a flash of white. "Hey! Wait!" I sprinted faster and hit another choice of turns. A left took me to a dead end.

I'd lost her. I felt an indefinable pang.

I walked back, turning right at the first branching. Seeing three dead ends in all directions. And realizing I'd lost myself as well. I was certain I'd needed to make a right and then a left. I figured I must have missed a turn. I tried going back, went left and left again, and found myself in another dead end.

It occurred to me then that I might end up being late for my brownie-baking session with Rose. Maybe very late.

I decided I'd better be a little more methodical. I started pocketing any rocks I saw to mark the turnings I took. The maze wasn't endless. Eventually, I had to find the way out.

Ten minutes later, another dead end lay ahead, so I started to backtrack, following my stone warnings to avoid any previously explored corridors and thinking how very clever I had been. At the next choice of turns, one opening was already marked. I was veering away from it when the rock caught my eye. It was the mottled green pebble Richard had found in Deirdre's room. I'd left it in the pocket of the jeans I had on. Impulsively, I stooped to pick it up again — an ordinary stone could mark that corridor. Then I went around the next corner and discovered, sitting on a bench, someone I was completely surprised to see. She started, looked toward me squinting, and a smile spread across her face.

"Sarah, girl, here you are."

"Nanga! Thank God I ran into you," I said, meaning every word.

She laughed. "You a little lost, are you?"

I laughed too. "*Entirely* lost."

The hedge behind her was shorter than elsewhere, revealing the drop to the river below. I'd worked my way to the far side of the maze without even knowing it.

"Don't worry, you're only a few turnings from where you started. I'll tell you the way."

She named the turns. I repeated it back to her and then repeated it again.

"Thanks for the help," I said. "I was getting a little nervous. It's a big maze. I saw a little girl in here — will she be all right?"

"Don't you worry about her. She knows the way in and the way out."

"So she lives around here or something?"

"Yes, indeed. She's my little friend. She comes to visit sometimes to make my heart lighter."

I found it strange that Nanga was wandering around the grounds of Amber House. Unless that's what she was used to doing, when Gramma was alive.

As if she were reading my thoughts, she said, "Ida never minded when I dropped by. I hope you don't mind either." She smiled. "Sit a minute. Please."

The old woman didn't seem as . . . discomfiting . . . as she had the first time I met her. Maybe because she had just finished saving my butt. She seemed, oddly, younger up close.

"What's that in your hand?" she asked as I took a seat. I glanced down, surprised to find I was still holding the green pebble. She looked as if she wanted to reach out and touch it. "Why, that's —" She stopped. "That's verdite. It's a kind of stone that can only be found in Africa, near where my people come from. Hold on to it. For luck."

I tucked it back in my pocket. "Jackson said I should go back and talk to you. What did you want? Before."

"Before? In your room?"

"No. What? No. Outside your house."

"I promised you a chat."

The way she said it, it sounded almost like a question. "Yeah. You said there were some things you needed to tell me —"

"Sammy all right?"

"Sammy's fine," I said, wondering why she would even ask.

"You know," she said, "I been around here such a long time, I know just about all of Amber House's secrets." She nodded at me, like she was cuing me to speak.

"Um." I didn't really feel confessional, but she continued to watch me in that encouraging way. "So, you know about the — *gift?*" I was embarrassed saying the word aloud.

She nodded again. And I experienced a kind of relief. Someone besides Jackson was telling me this was real. It wasn't all just in my head. "What is it?" I asked her. "What happens?"

"Well, your grandma used to call 'em echoes, but that's not quite right. You know how you can make physical marks on a thing, like a scratch or a chip? I think maybe our thoughts and feelings can make other kinds of marks on the things we touched and used and loved. Or hated. And the women in this family — the ones with the gift — can see those marks, especially when they're in tune with 'em. That make any sense to you?"

"I guess. Kind of. So, they aren't ghosts?"

She shook her head. "There are no ghosts in Amber House."

No ghosts, I repeated to myself, and felt a little better. "What do you mean . . . 'in tune with them'?"

"Like calls to like. Need pulls an answer."

"You mean my thoughts can set off a vision?"

"More like your feelings. Or troubles. Or worries. Sometimes, I almost think the house is trying to help."

I digested that. "Can you see them?"

"No, child. I can't see the past."

"Where does it come from? This gift."

"A long way back. Fiona said the grandmother who first come here had it. She could find lost things and knew about people just by touching their belongings. Had to leave her home 'cause they thought she had the evil eye. Sold herself into bondage to pay for her passage."

"Sorcha," I said.

"You've seen her," Nanga said. "Then maybe you know there was something about this place that drew her. Something that fed her gift. It may be this was always a place of power. Or it may be the power come here just because so many powerful women been drawn here, like the cause and effect of it, the then and the now of it, don't really matter."

"Why is it only women?" I asked.

"Don't know. Women are a lot different from men. They listen different. They're like spiders, always spinning connections between themselves and others, always tending the web."

I nodded, even though I didn't really understand. And didn't like being compared to a spider.

"You ever need help, Sarah, you can trust Jackson. He's a good boy and he will do his best by you." She cocked her head a little, regarding me. "You know you're related to him? Cousins way back in the family tree."

"Really?" That was a disturbing piece of information. On so many levels. Richard had said the Captain was involved in shipping slaves, but I hadn't ever specifically connected slave-holding with my family. I don't know why. I hadn't wanted to think about it, I guess. And if Nanga was saying Jackson and I shared an ancestor, that meant one of my male ancestors had — what? I couldn't bear the thought. Had *hurt* Jackson's distant grandmother? I felt disgusting.

"I know what you're thinking, girl." Her eyes grew distant. "It was a terrible thing. An unforgivable, unforgettable thing. But a lot of fine men and women came from that evil act. And that woman got justice — justice then and justice in the end." She nodded, her eyes sharp again. "It's often seemed to me that in Amber House, time has a way of curing itself."

Evil act, I repeated mentally, shaking my head. I hoped that woman got justice. I hoped she got revenge. I guessed I would never know for certain. I needed to think about all of this more. "Okay." I stood. "I got to hurry." Rose was probably already waiting. "Thank you, again, for — everything."

She smiled and waved off my thanks with her hand.

"Good-bye," I called back, as I started walking.

Nanga lifted her voice after me. "One more thing. Almost forgot. You ever get to feeling confused in one of them echoes, a mirror'll always show you true."

I was busy repeating the turns in my head, thinking about the slave — Jackson's ancestor — hurt so cruelly by some slave-owning scumbag — *my* ancestor. Reflecting on my connection to this place and its people. So I was halfway out of the maze before I even registered that last sentence.

I found the long green corridor leading out. As I passed through the entrance, I spotted Jackson sitting on a stone wall.

"Hi," I said. "What're you doing here?"

"Sammy . . . told me he saw you go in. I wanted to make sure you'd come back out."

I nodded and laughed weakly. "Thanks. Did you know we're cousins?"

He lifted his eyebrows. "Yeah, I know. Ida told me about the woman who was my great-great-gran, about seven generations back. She sounded like an incredible woman."

"I didn't know. Gramma told me about her abolitionist great-grandmother. Somehow she never thought to tell me about our slave-owning ancestors."

"How'd the subject come up now?"

"Nanga was in there. She was the one who told me how to get out."

"Nanga?"

"Yeah. She's — nice. A little strange, but nice."

"Nanga . . . I remember Ida used to say that Nanga'd do anything for her friends, but she isn't a good person to cross. She never forgives and she never forgets."

I lifted my eyebrows. "Don't know if her memory is all that perfect — she didn't really seem to remember our first conversation. Guess that kind of thing happens when you get that old."

He nodded, amused. "She's got a few years on her."

"You know what time it is? I think I'm supposed to be in the kitchen right about now. Your grandma offered me help baking some brownies."

"I know," he said. "I'm the help."

Oh. Really? "*You're* gonna do it?"

"Well, not for nothing. We're doubling the recipe — I'm taking half home."

"You actually know what you're doing?" I must have sounded a little incredulous.

He snorted. "It's just brownies."

He knew exactly where everything was — the pans, the cocoa and nuts, the flour and sugar. He tossed me a stick of butter and told me to grease the pans.

"*Grease* them?"

Sighing, he took the butter back, cut off a small chunk, and plopped it in the pan. "Use your fingers to smear the whole inside, especially the corners, so the batter won't stick. Haven't you ever made a cake before?"

"That's why there are bakeries," I said. "Do I *have to* use my fingers?"

"Yes. You have to use your fingers. But wash 'em first," he said, rolling up his own sleeves and reaching for the soap. I tried really hard not to look at the increasingly thick scars creeping up his forearms. He caught me anyway.

He shrugged slightly. "Car accident when I was three. Burned me pretty bad all over my left side."

I didn't know what to say. I mumbled some kind of "sorry."

"I don't really remember it," he said, "except sometimes in dreams. Gran says I would have died, only I'd climbed out of my car seat. The explosion threw me clear. Got a head injury and a few broken ribs, but I survived. My parents didn't."

"Do you remember them?"

"Not the way they were."

Not the way they were?

He must have realized how strange that sounded: "I — I've heard loads of stories about them from Gran, of course, and I have pictures in my head of them, how they might have been, how *we* might have been . . ." His voice trailed off.

If things had been different, I finished in my head. I thought to myself if we ever did find the diamonds, I would make sure he got half. He had as much a right to them as I did. And he deserved better than what life had given him.

He shook it off. "We better get moving," he said. "The brownies have to cool before we can cut them."

After I did that greasing business, he showed me how to flour the pans. Then step-by-step, he took me through the recipe. A *tbsp* was a *tablespoon*; one used a *double boiler* for melting chocolate; one *did not* scoop broken eggshell from a moving mixer with one's fingers —

He grabbed my wrist as I reached for the disappearing chunk of white shell. "You looking to lose those?"

— and when one inadvertently mashed eggshell into the batter, one poured said batter down the sink and began again.

He took over at that point, efficiently re-measuring the dry ingredients, whisking butter into the melted chocolate, scraping, mixing, pouring vanilla without even measuring, mashing the nuts up with the palm of his hand. He definitely knew what he was doing.

"Too bad you want to be a doctor," I said. "You'd make a great chef."

"I'm not going to be a doctor. Going into research."

"Research," I said, surprised. "I just assumed — why would you want to bury yourself in a lab? You're such a people person. Even Sammy loves you, and he hardly ever likes anybody."

"Sammy's a great kid," he said flatly, keeping all his focus on smoothing the batter in the two pans, and then unnecessarily smoothing it again. I sensed I'd said something wrong, but I didn't know what. When Jackson looked up, though, his face was smooth. And bland. Again. He changed the subject. "Let's get these in the oven."

I started working on the mess while he prepared the frosting. When the timer dinged, he showed me how to check for doneness and declared the pans "cooked."

"Sit down," I ordered. "I'll finish the cleanup. I can do cleanup."

"If you insist," he said. He rolled down his sleeves and sat like he had when I met him — leaning back, his long legs stretched out over half the kitchen.

"How soon can we spread the frosting?"

"Give the chocolate a few more minutes to melt. It's called *ganache*, by the way. Chocolate and cream mixed together."

"Okay," I said, "now you're just showing off."

A genuine smile, warm and relaxed. Like the one in the attic. "Who, me?" he said. "Never."

I laughed, and that's when my mother walked in. Her lips

were tight; she was irritated. "Sarah, I saw you earlier, running down the path to esca —" She interrupted herself and walked closer to me, staring. "Jesus, how did you manage to get flour all over your face?"

"You looking for Sammy?" I asked hopefully.

"No. I'm looking for you. Sam went to Annapolis with your dad this morning."

"This morning?" I repeated, confused. "Didn't you say —" I turned to Jackson.

He was already heading for the door. "I'll come back and frost both pans a little later, Sarah." He slipped out.

I turned back to my mother. "Why didn't they wait for me?"

"*I* needed your help today."

"What are we doing?" I asked carefully.

"We *were* meeting with the planner, the caterer, and the cake designer. But they left thirty minutes ago."

"Sorry, Mom," I said, working hard to sound contrite instead of pleased.

"Yeah. I bet. Doesn't matter. You need to get ready to leave for Annapolis now. Change your clothes. Comb your hair. And could you throw on a little lip gloss and mascara, please? We *are* trying to make a good impression around here."

I stood there, feeling instantly inadequate, and wondering for the millionth time if Mom heard herself when she said that kind of stuff, or if it just spilled out unconsciously. She walked away, seemingly oblivious.

I mean, I got that I was a disappointment to her. I couldn't have been more — not like her. Not beautiful. Not chic. Not sharp. But, you know what? At least I *tried* to be nice.

Also not like her.

Maybe she just didn't understand that people actually did have feelings. *Not like her.*

I trudged upstairs, trying to figure out how the girl who had painted those amazing pictures in the trunk in the attic could have turned out to be my mother.

I opened the door of my bedroom and stopped. The bed was made. My clothes weren't hanging all over the chair. And something else was different —

It was the walls. They were only partially flowered.

I heard someone humming.

Part of me just wanted to turn around and get out, but I didn't. I needed to see the person hidden on the other side of the bed.

A girl with long auburn hair sat on the floor, her legs curled under her. She had a palette of paints in her left hand. With the brush in her right, she was making a hollyhock rise up the wall, sprouting leaves and blossoms as it went.

I walked around the end of the bed till I could see the girl's face.

My mother. About eleven years old.

I watched her a few moments. Busy. At ease. Occasionally humming a snatch of some familiar tune. A little bit of a mess, with paint on her hands and jeans and face. She seemed like a girl I could have been friends with. She seemed — happy.

I wished I could reach across time to speak to her. I wished somehow I could protect her from whatever it was that took that happiness from her.

I spoke without thinking: "I love you, Mom."

The girl stopped humming and cocked her head, like she was listening. She looked puzzled. Then she dabbed her brush in the paint and went back to her task.

I fled back out the door. I didn't want to know about the past. I didn't want this gift. It didn't change anything, and it only made me feel worse, somehow.

When I peeked in again, my mess was restored. And the garden was all done.

My mother's Eden. With a quilted apple tree on the bed.

I dressed hurriedly, finished my makeup, and went back downstairs. "Sorry I didn't help with the party planner," I mumbled.

My mother gave me a partial smile and a shrug. "It's not really your thing, is it? It's fine. It's pretty much all organized. It's going to be a fabulous party, if that means anything to you."

"I'm sure it will be."

When I knew what to look for, I could still see that girl from upstairs. In the eyes mostly. Her head still cocked. Still listening.

I heard myself saying it again. "I love you, Mom."

She got the strangest look on her face. Then she said, "I love you too, sweetie." Immediately she turned away, walking toward her room. "I'll be ready to go in ten minutes," she said over her shoulder, her voice a little high. "Meet you at the car?"

"Sure," I agreed.

I wanted out of the house. I went outside, rolled down the car window, and waited for her in the front seat.

In Annapolis, Mom pulled into a parking space in front of a clothing store.

Ambushed again. "Hey," I objected, "I thought we were meeting Dad and Sammy."

"I never said that. We're going to church tomorrow and you need something to wear."

"Church?" Since when was my mother religious?

"Robert invited us to join him and then head on to the club for brunch and the annual Chesapeake Clubs Regatta."

Ah. The senator. This was turning into one of those good-news-bad-news kind of things. I loved sailboat races. And Richard would probably be there. But a day with Robert at church and "the club"? My face must have betrayed my distinct lack of enthusiasm.

"Look, Sarah, it's important that we connect with as many people as possible before the party. Some of my old friends will be at church, a lot more will be at the regatta. The race is open to the five biggest yachting clubs on the Chesapeake. So we are all four going to go and smile and be friendly and have a good time. Right?"

"Sounds fabulous," I said flatly. I wondered how I was supposed to treat Richard. Didn't exactly want to be doing that flirty as-good-as-a-guy thing in front of my parents. My mother headed for the racks, while I found a chair to sit in. Halfway through an enlightening article on "Ten Spicy Ways to Do It In the Summer!" in a two-year-old issue of *Cosmo*, Mom came to find me with an armful of outfits.

Nobody to model them for me here.

She tried to talk me into something pink, but I settled on a silk sundress painted with watery red and orange poppies, belted at the waist with a thick black ribbon. Worried that it wasn't right for the season, Mom found a little cashmere sweater to cover my arms.

The store clerk offered a pair of matching ballet flats. "What did you do to your poor head?" she asked, oozing cheap sympathy.

I felt like telling her it was just a really big zit. "Got hit with a croquet mallet," I said, and smiled sweetly.

"She tripped and fell into a bedpost," my mother corrected.

The clerk tried to hide a smirk.

"Now, let's find something for the party tonight," Mom said briskly.

I'd had enough. "If I can't go in jeans, I'm not going at all."

"You don't have any idea what anyone else will be wearing, do you?" she said accusingly.

"Unless we hit a time warp when we flew in here, they better be wearing jeans. And if they aren't wearing jeans, then I'll be the only one there who isn't a total loser."

That said, I started praying they'd be wearing jeans.

Chapter Ten

The wardrobe run to Annapolis (of course) left me short on time to prepare for the party, and my makeup session (of course) ran a little long that evening — I kept trying, futilely, to smooth a paper-thin-but-fully-opaque layer of foundation on my mashed forehead. I ended up pinning my bangs down to cover my efforts.

Richard pulled up and honked right on time. I hurried out to the front hall, still tugging things into place and hoping to give myself a final once-over in the mirror by the door, but Mom was already there, touching up her lipstick.

"You and Dad going out?" I asked in surprise.

"I'm having dinner with — some old friends. I think your father prefers to keep Sammy company," she answered coolly.

"Did you even ask him?"

"Isn't your date waiting for you?"

"Not a date," I said, snagging the bag of brownies I'd left on the table there, "just a ride."

"I don't have to worry about you, right, Sarah? I know how these wealthy kids' parties can be."

"No, Mom, you don't have to worry about me. I'm still one hundred percent vice free."

"Smart girl."

I rolled my eyes. "See ya."

"Have a nice time."

You too, I thought to myself. But did not say. And did not mean.

"Sorry to keep you waiting," I offered as I climbed into Richard's little black convertible BMW.

"No problem," he said cheerfully.

We took the same route toward Annapolis as Mom and I had earlier that day, only it went by a lot faster. Richard liked to drive the same way he liked to sail. I kept a smile on my face, stuck my hands under my legs so I wouldn't white-knuckle the dash, and entrusted my life to whatever passive restraining devices the Beemer had to offer.

Richard made a sharp turn into the drive of one of those generic mansions, a kind of Tudor beam-and-plaster thing with a lot of rock facing. We decelerated past rows of other luxury vehicles wedged into the pansy beds, to a spot someone had saved us in the garage. We climbed out of the car into the vibration of the bass from the music inside the house.

I followed Richard in. The interior was all marble, cream carpeting, bleached wood, and softly stuffed leather seating. I should have been impressed, but Amber House had spoiled me. To my eyes, it just looked like a catalogue house: lots of money, no style.

Richard found the hostess, gave her a big hug, and introduced me. Turned out my jeans were not appropriate at all. Kathryn was wearing a bikini.

I smiled unhappily. "Richard didn't tell me this was a pool party."

"Dickie's such a forgetful boy," Kathryn said proprietarily. "But you can borrow one of my suits."

Gross, I thought. "Great," I said. I held out the brownies. "A contribution," I explained, wishing I had ignored my earlier impulse to bring them.

"Oh, God," she said with some excitement. "Do they have anything in them?"

"Walnuts," I said.

Richard started to laugh. Loudly. I cursed myself silently.

Kathryn stuck an elbow in Richard's ribs. She leaned forward and gave me a hug. "That's so sweet of you," she said. "I bet everyone will love them."

She led me into the kitchen, its marble counters strewn with prepackaged party foods and assorted beverages. We added the brownies to the spread.

The kitchen flowed into a den, complete with a state-of-the-art entertainment center. The soaring ceiling was open to the second story, reached by a flight of winding stairs. Kathryn started up the carpeted steps, her nearly naked bottom exactly two steps up and directly in front of my face. *No cellulite*, I noted.

"I am dying to go to your party," she said over her shoulder. "I got the invite this morning, but I heard about it Wednesday. Richard called and told me to get people to come. And of course I did. It'll be awesome."

Wednesday. That's the day he and his dad came to see us. He didn't waste any time recruiting.

"Thanks so much for your help," I offered.

"Pfffft," she said dismissively, fluttering a hand. "I saw this fantastic dress four weeks ago in Neiman's, and I asked Daddy to buy it for me, but he said he wouldn't unless I had somewhere to wear it. And now I do! I can't wait for you to see it. It's all pink, and tight, and I'm going to get wings attached at the back. What's your costume like?"

"I, um — it's gold, I think." She turned, her head cocked a little to one side, waiting for some relevant details. Unfortunately, I couldn't remember a thing about it. "It's lacy. Nice," I added.

She smiled at me like I was four years old. "I'm sure," she said, and continued up the stairs.

Kathryn's bedroom was crammed with luxury — a canopy bed draped in magenta raw silk and mounded with eccentric tapestry pillows, a flat-screen TV, a velvet love seat, a three-thousand-dollar computer, a crystal chandelier. Clothes were strewn over the bed and on the floor — expensive clothes. I found her lack of organization a positive quality.

A shelf above her desk held two dozen framed, autographed photos of Kathryn standing beside one celebrity after another. "You know all these people?"

"My dad's a music producer. He flies me out to visit him every awards season. Most of those are of me and one of his clients." She crossed the room and opened two doors, revealing a closet bigger than my bedroom back home. The bikini she pulled out and held up was more string than fabric.

"Um," I said, trying to find the right way to request the one-piece I sensed she did not own. She nodded, as if in agreement.

"Yeah, I'm thinking pink is not your color. This one?"

She held up an almost identical red bikini covered in little white hearts. It had boy shorts, however, so I lunged for it. "Cute. Thanks."

A chill breeze was blowing in off the water. Most of the guests were floating in the heated pool, but a fairly unbelievable number had gathered in the hot tub. Kathryn had to make people scoot over so we'd have room to sit.

It was uncomfortable, not to mention awkward — all of us crammed in there, with legs and arms and feet brushing up against one another. A pretty brunette to my left leaned over the top of me to talk to a guy all sharp angles and brown skin, like some Bollywood movie star, sitting on the other side of Kathryn.

"Guess what, Chad," she said, her words slurring slightly. "I licked mercury once. I broke a thermometer and this stuff came out and I licked it."

Kathryn rolled her eyes and sighed. She whispered into my ear: "That's Olivia. I'm sorry. I don't know why she's even here. I didn't invite her."

"Shove over, Kath." I craned around. Richard wedged himself in between me and Kathryn. "Did Kath introduce you yet, or what?" he said to me.

"I was just about —" Kathryn started.

Richard shushed her with a wave of his hand. "Sarah" — and he slipped his free arm around my shoulders and pulled me close as he addressed the group — "this is everybody. Everybody, this is Sarah Parsons."

"You're the chick who's throwing the party at the haunted house," Chad said.

"It's not haunted," I protested weakly, wondering what he knew, what he'd heard.

"My grandmother said she went there once when she was our age," Olivia said with lurid enthusiasm, "and just started weeping, she didn't even know why."

"They got a damn cemetery right on the property," said a kid behind me. "Even the slaves were buried in it. Some of them have got to be pissed off, right?"

"*I* heard someone was *murdered* there," Chad contributed. "Found dead in a bathtub, Stephen King style."

"My dad said all kinds of people have gone crazy in that house," the girl opposite me added, "and some retarded girl got killed on the front lawn back when he was just a kid."

I tried again: "It's not ha —"

"Oh, it's haunted, all right," Richard interrupted. "I've been there. You can feel it. But it's a *Halloween* party, right? It's *supposed* to be creepy. Right?"

"Right," I said faintly, thinking dismally that the ghosts and I might be the only ones to attend. "I hope you'll all come."

"They're coming," Richard said confidently, taking another slug from whatever it was he was drinking. "My old man called in a favor. Ataxia is playing."

"Omigod," a girl in braces squealed. "Ataxia?"

I had to stop myself from squealing also. Ataxia at *my* party? Was he *kidding*? Everyone within ten yards heard. I watched the news that the country's top-selling punk rock band was gigging at my birthday get handed on and on. It was brilliant. I suddenly felt more relaxed than I had for days. Haunted or not, maybe people would actually come to this thing. Maybe they'd even have a good time.

Olivia leaned close to me again, this time talking to my face. "Hey, didn't Richard take you sailing?" Her voice had an unhappy, accusatory tone.

"You went sailing with Dickie?" a dead ringer for Will Smith asked me, grinning. "Did he pull the ship's-wake trick on you?"

"As a matter of fact," I said, nodding.

All the guys roared with laughter. Will Clone said, "I swear Richard memorizes the shipping schedule for Baltimore Port."

"Won't need manufactured waves to beat you tomorrow, Morgan," Richard said.

"Are we talking about the regatta?" I asked.

"Richard and Chad won our class the last two years," the clone — Morgan — said. "But not this year. This time, the *Backdraft*'s gonna bring it home."

"Want to back that up with some money?" Richard taunted.

"What're we talking about, Dickie? Five hundred?"

"Chump change," he said, smiling. "Make it an even thou."

Morgan didn't look happy, but he accepted the bet.

"Can anyone compete in this thing?" I asked.

"Whoa. I think she wants in on the action." Morgan smiled condescendingly, shaking his head. "Sorry. Just club members."

"That's not what I —"

"You want to put your old girl in the regatta, Parsons?" Richard said with amusement. "I don't think they have a class for *antique scows*, but I could probably get you in our race." He shrugged with his mouth. "If you wanted in."

I hadn't actually. Wanted in. But I had a kind of knee-jerk reaction to disparaging sarcasm, maybe because I heard so much of it at home. "Sure, Hathaway," I heard myself say. "That'd be great. Sign me up."

Richard looked surprised. Kathryn laughed.

"Hundred-dollar entrance fee," Richard said. "All for charity."

"I can cover that."

"Who you gonna get to crew? Your baby brother?"

"Well, Sammy might be able to take you," I said, smiling.

Richard didn't like my teasing. "You want to make a side bet too?"

"Giving my money to charity is one thing, Hathaway; helping with the payments on your Beemer is another."

That seemed to placate him. His mouth lost its tightness and he managed a grin.

The crowd in the hot tub thinned over the next hour. Richard was off somewhere — I deliberately hadn't kept track of him. I was pretending vigorously that I was still enjoying the warm water. It was down to me, a guy propped up in the corner snoring, a pair necking across from me, and two girls who were ignoring my presence. I wondered if my dad would come get me if I snuck inside and found a phone. But I didn't even know what address to tell him.

"Sarah."

I looked up into Kathryn's face.

"You're turning into a prune. Come help me, hon."

Lord, yes, please, give me something *to do.*

So I stood and spooned frozen fruit and ice cream into a blender for Kath. She was making smoothies. In between the roaring of the blender, we talked.

"You've known Richard a long time?" I asked.

"We've been in the same schools together since we were four. He's practically a brother."

A brother. That sounded promising. "You must have known his mother."

"Oh, sure. She was always at the school parties and stuff."

"Was she nice?"

Kath choked a little on her taste test of the latest batch. "Um, sure. What do I know? I was a kid. She just seemed a little . . . loony. You know? Liable to go off? And she *hated* your mom. She was, like, *obsessed* with her."

"My mom?" How did Richard's mom know mine? Mom had moved away to college and never really gone back — had they been in high school together?

"I remember once we walked by this trophy at school with your mom's name on it, and Mrs. Hathaway started going on and on about how your mom didn't deserve it. This other time, when we drove past your house, she told us your family were all devil worshippers." She giggled. "Can you believe th —"

Her eyes widened slightly, and her voice got a little louder. "So I didn't know whether I was supposed to wear a mask or what. Are people wearing masks?"

"What?" I said, utterly confused.

I felt a hand on my shoulder. "Parsons!"

It was Richard. He grabbed a strawberry-peach smoothie, took me by the elbow, and led me away. "Yum," he said, tasting it. "You make this, Parsons?"

"Not really," I said. "I just followed orders."

"Kath can run to bossy," he said. "What d'you think of her?"

"That's not what I —" I tried again. "She seems like she's —"

"— deep as a puddle, right? Her dad's got more money than God." He stepped in front of me, snagged one of the belt loops on the boy shorts. "Wanna find someplace more private?"

I should have been expecting it; I should have been prepared. But I wasn't even sure what he was asking. What was it exactly that people were doing in the "more private" places? The truth was, I had never even been kissed. And this guy was clearly the type who was used to girls throwing themselves at him. It was hard to admit even to myself, but he scared me.

"I gotta get home," I said in a rush of words that poured from my mouth like they had lives of their own. "Gotta get up early. We're going to church with your father. Should I call home for a ride?"

He took it better than I expected. A snort, a little shake of the head to let me know what a punk kid I was. But he said he'd drive me home. "I gotta get up for church too, don't I?"

I went upstairs and changed back into my clothes, then tracked down Kathryn to say good-bye. She gave me a big hug, like we'd been best buds forever. "See you tomorrow," she said.

Right. At the race that I — like some idiot — just agreed to compete in. What in God's name is the matter with you, Parsons?

I walked with my head bent, out to where Richard was waiting in the car. But as I left, I noted with some satisfaction that every single one of my brownies had been eaten.

Richard gunned it when we hit Amber House's gravel drive. The tires spun, the rear end of the car slewed. I had a death grip on the armrest. We skidded to a halt before the front door.

"Thanks, Richard. It was great to meet all those people. Tell your dad how grateful I am for Ataxia."

"No problem, Parsons." He flashed me one of his crooked smiles.

"Well," I said, "good night." I opened the door, but he caught my arm. I didn't even have a chance to worry about my lack of experience. He just pulled me toward him and kissed me.

Soft lips. Stubble. Strawberries. The smell of cologne. The tip of his tongue just barely brushing my lips. His hand still tight around my arm. The stick shift mashing into my ribs.

Not what I had imagined, with infinite variations, for the past five years. But very interesting. I don't think my lips had ever *felt* so alive before.

He let me go and I snapped back in my seat. I had just been kissed for the first time by the boy of every girl's dreams, and I didn't know what to think about it. Did this mean I wasn't a hopeless loser? Did this mean — he *liked* me?

"Night, Parsons."

"Night, Hathaway," I said, attempting a breezy tone. It was just a tad too high-pitched. But it provoked a satisfied and crooked grin.

I got out, shut the door behind me, and made my legs start walking. I didn't look back.

Richard revved the Beemer's engine, kicking up gravel. He shot down the driveway.

And Jackson stepped out of the shadows in front of me.

"Oh, God!" I gasped, first startled, then embarrassed. "You scared me."

"Sorry."

"Um. That" — I gestured vaguely — "wasn't my idea." Why on earth was I making excuses? "It's so late. I didn't expect you to be here."

He shrugged, then nodded toward a flashlight sitting on the steps. "Thought we could poke around a little more."

I cringed inwardly. I was home late from an exhausting night of tension at a party where I hadn't known a single soul, and had been given my very first kiss by a guy who could make me stammer, and truth be told, right at that very moment, I just didn't feel like opening even one more silverfish-contaminated box.

My reluctance must have shown. Jackson's expression clouded over. "Never mind."

"I'm sorry. I'm just tired, is all. I don't think I can face bumping into any echoes tonight."

"It's all right. Some other time." He reached up to undo a strip of leather tied around his neck. He lifted it by the cord, from which hung a smooth drop of burnt yellow stone. It caught a glow from the porch light.

"I've seen a stone like that before. What is it?"

"It's amber," he said. "Ida told me once that it's supposed to have some kind of blessing on it. All I know is, when I wear it, I feel a lot more confident that things will work out the way they're supposed to." He held it out for me to take.

I took it from him. It was warm in my fingers. There was something dark in it — *jeez*. My skin crawled. The flaw in the amber was a spider, its long legs still spread in the stance it had taken when tree sap enveloped it millennia ago. Graceful and deadly. Hideous and beautiful at the same time.

"I — I think you're supposed to have it," Jackson said.

"I can't take that from you." I handed it back to him.

He took it, stepped behind me, lifted the pendant over my head and around my neck. He tied a careful knot, then pulled a stray lock of my hair free, his fingertips brushing across my skin. It made me suck in my breath.

"What's the matter?" he said.

"Just — got a chill," I said, and primly tucked my hair behind my ear.

He turned the amber so the spider crouched on my heart. "It's pretty late," he said. "Maybe we can try again another night."

"Maybe," I agreed. "I have a lot to do tomorrow. Which reminds me —"

"What?"

I took a stab. "You know the *Liquid Amber* better than anyone. How 'bout crewing for me in the regatta?"

"Down at the club?" he asked, and shook his head. "You got to be a member."

"Richard said he'd get me in." I looked him in the eye. "I want to beat him. I can't do it without you."

He raised one eyebrow. "Beating Richard Hathaway would be fun," he said. "But maybe not such a good idea."

He might have been right. But —

"If I'm gonna race," I said, shrugging, "I race to win."

He grinned at that, a wide smile, his teeth shining in the darkness. "You and me both, coz."

He stuck out his hand — large, warm, strong, sturdy — and I shook it.

Done deal.

Chapter Eleven

It had been years since I'd been inside a church. My mother liked religion about as much as she liked anything else supernatural. But she led the way up the steps the next morning.

The church was all brick and stone, with a pointed arch over the front entrance filled with stained glass. Inside, the arch's point was repeated in a thousand delicate stone ribs arrowed toward heaven. Five golden spires crowned the altar. The pews were deep, but space was limited. Just large enough to hold all the right set — the old money in this part of Maryland.

We were the obvious outsiders, and we received a good number of questioning stares as we made our way up the aisle to our seats at the front. The senator had saved us a place in the pew behind his. He was all smiles until he saw my father walk up with us, holding Sammy's hand. Even then, he kept his smile in place — it just dimmed considerably. One hundred watts down to forty.

Richard flashed me his own blindingly white grin, and I returned it, trying to hide the embarrassment that made me want to stare at the floor. I wasn't quite sure how to behave with a guy who'd kissed me the night before.

Mom and the senator both worked the crowd after mass. Richard grabbed me by the arm and introduced me to some more of my future party guests. I tried to memorize names, but I found it hard to concentrate. My mom kept squealing in the background: "Joe, it's been ages! Liza, my God, you haven't changed an iota!"

Dad and Sammy sat quietly on a bench to one side, waiting for all the hugging to end. After an eternity, we all loaded into Mom's car and followed the senator to brunch at the club.

I ate with Sam and Dad. I don't think my mother ever once sat down or took a single bite. With a champagne cocktail in one hand, she circled the room, continuing in her meet-and-greet mode. It seemed like she knew everybody south of Baltimore.

Her non-presence in our little family grouping gave me a chance to slip Dad a question I'd been dying to ask: "Gramma told me once that Mom used to paint," I lied. "Really well. Did you know that?"

"Yeah, I knew."

"Why'd she stop?"

He considered. I wasn't sure he was going to answer the question, but he did, carefully. "I think she felt it had gotten to be too big an obsession. That it controlled her, and not the other way around."

That sounded a little obsessive all by itself. "Why?"

"She was working on a canvas once when she should have been doing something else, and it —" He rethought the end of that sentence. "It had some bad consequences. So she stopped."

"What sort of —"

"That's all I'm going to say on the subject. Let's talk about something else."

Jeez. Fine. As quickly as I could after that, I excused myself and went outside.

I walked down the dock, checking out the floating real estate. Not just sweet little sloops like the *Amber* — although there were plenty of ultra-modern versions of those — but also yachts, with levels, motored or (for the sailing purists) double masted. Boats you could pop on over to Greece in.

The club had set up a small bandstand to seat the regatta's spectators. I sat and stared out toward the Chesapeake, thinking to myself that maybe it would be better if I didn't find Richard in time to sign up for the race.

In which case, I probably should have found a less conspicuous place to sit.

Richard came and sat beside me, all casual grace. "Saw you go out. Trying to ditch me, Parsons?"

"Ditch you? Wouldn't dream of it, Hathaway." I leaned back, attempting to match his casual style. He reached out to finger a lock of my hair.

Involuntarily, I made some room between us. He smiled and let the hair fall back into place.

"I owe you an apology," he said. "For last night."

"No, not at all," I said.

"Yeah, I do. Our parents are friends. I shouldn't have done that. I hope you didn't tell your mom."

"No, of course not," I said, trying to pretend it had been no big deal, but thinking how perfect it was that my mother was the one who was killing this for me. Although what "this" was, I had no idea. Just that I didn't want it dead quite yet.

He shrugged. "Thought I should apologize."

"It's okay," I said, wishing I were brave enough to add, *"I liked it."* But I wasn't anywhere close to being *that* brave.

So then he smiled, and said in a confident, teasing voice: "What do you say, Parsons?" He nodded back toward the boat club. "Shall we go sign you up, or have you chickened out and decided you'd rather just cheer me on?"

"Let's go," I said.

"You don't back down," he said, amused.

"Well," I answered, summoning up what courage I had, "I don't want to lose points."

It was an almost-under-the-radar flirt, but he caught it. He grinned, and on the walk back, he draped an arm over my shoulders. It was kind of a strange feeling. On the one hand, I felt awkward, because I didn't necessarily know Richard well enough to be wearing his arm. On the other hand, some secret part of me was absolutely loving being this guy's armrest.

I mean, it was every girl's fantasy, wasn't it? I decided to relax and enjoy it.

It took a while to find someone who could sign me up — we were passed from one person to the next. Finally, we found this old gentleman with a club insignia stitched to his jacket.

He seemed reluctant to add me to the entrants. "Well," he said, hedging, "not a member. Whose boat're you going to sail?"

"It was my grandmother's boat. The *Liquid Amber*."

"The *Amber*?" he said. "You're Mark and Ida's granddaughter?"

"Yeah."

"Well, then," he said, suddenly effusive, "of course you should race. Your great-great-grandparents helped *found* this club. You're practically an honorary member." He got out a clipboard with an entry form. "You sure you want to give me this?" he asked, taking my wad of wrinkled cash. "Smart money is on your boyfriend here," he said, clapping Richard on the back.

My boyfriend? I thought, expecting Richard to correct him. But Richard just smiled. I said, "It's for charity, right?"

"Yes, indeed. You know, she could give you a run for it, Richard." He smiled broadly. "The *Amber*'s taken home the trophy before," he told me. "It's been a few years, but I remember when your grandparents crewed her in this race a few times.

They were a good team, back then. Damn shame what happened." He shook his head. I hoped he would say more, but he'd already changed subjects. "That girl's always been a fast boat," he finished. "Made for these waters."

The old guy gave me a chart of the course and pointed out over the water to general areas where the marker buoys could be found. He shook my hand. "Best of luck to you and the *Amber*," he said.

Richard and I headed back to the dining room. "I don't know, Parsons," he said, "maybe I oughta start worrying. After all, the *Amber* won this before — what? Seventy years ago?" He laughed heartily at his own joke.

I laughed too. "Just watch your back, Hathaway, 'cause I'll be coming up behind you."

"*Oooh*," he said in mock terror.

He went back to his table and I went to join my family. Dad and Sammy were polishing off their desserts when I got there. Mom had finally parked herself next to them and was nibbling a piece of dry toast. I asked Dad for the keys to the car.

"What for?" my mother asked with some suspicion.

"I've got to change."

"Why?"

"I'm sailing in the regatta, and I'd rather not do it in a dress."

"You're *what*?" Mom blurted.

"Hey, kiddo," Dad said. "That's great."

"Did Richard ask you to crew?" Mom asked, disbelieving.

"No," I said. "I entered myself. I'm sailing the *Amber*."

"The *Amber*? This is *not* a good idea, honey —"

"It's all settled. I paid the entrance fee and everything."

My mother's mouth was tight. "I wish you'd ask me before you go off and do things like this. You could ruin everything." She crooked her finger, signaling me to lean in close. She put her mouth near my ear and whispered, "You'd better not win."

I changed into some capris and a sweater, stowed my dress back in the car, and headed down to the municipal dock. It was noon. Jackson was just tying up the *Amber*.

I pulled out the map the old guy had given me.

"Let's go out and check the course," Jackson suggested.

"Was thinking the same thing," I agreed. We put up the sails. We'd sail out far enough to spot markers, and use the practice to get into a rhythm together.

The race started in Spa Creek, just beyond the mouth to the Old Harbor. It ran northeast into Severn Bay, looped around a marker in the cove that cut into the Naval Academy's northern acres, then swung east into the Chesapeake to a second marker. From there you bore south to Howard's Point and made a careful circle around the rock island that held a lighthouse a small distance from the shore. This would be the trickiest part of the run, since the shoals, Jackson informed me, were shallow and rocky. But fortunately, by that far along in the race, the pack would be spread out, so there wouldn't be too much jockeying for position. Then the course ran back to the mouth of the Severn, around the cove marker, and southwest back to Spa Creek. The first boat to pass the Old Harbor won.

The race kicked off at three, just after the under-fourteen sailors finished up a much shorter course. There were eleven entrants in the fourteen- to eighteen-year-old class, all of us in a cluster, backed up Spa Creek. Richard's *Swallow* was in the front, as was Morgan's new sloop. Jackson and I were in the last group of two.

When Mom saw me take my place with Jackson as my crew, I could feel her displeasure, even at a distance. But Sammy jumped and cheered: "Go, Sarah! Go, Jackson!"

I found both reactions pretty gratifying.

The wind was blowing northwest, whistling through our small forest of masts, teasing the slack, luff sails, rocking the boats. Coupled with the current of the river, the wind's direction would make for a fast start, since the first leg of the race was all northeast to the marker buoy.

In every sloop, crews were ready to set sheets. The pack leaders fought not to drift across the starting line and lose place.

The starting flag dropped, the horn sounded, and Jackson smoothly pulled our main sheet into place, while I held the rudder slightly to port. The sail snapped into a perfect curve and the *Amber* strained forward. I threw my weight starboard to keep the hull even in the water and help build up speed.

As the creek mouth widened, the pack started to thin. We came about in front of our neighbor's nose and leapt forward. The *Amber* was shallow but well-balanced. Fast. Like everyone else, we chased the *Swallow*, in the lead, shadowed by the *Backdraft*.

I didn't do much more than point the nose of the boat in the general direction of the buoy that marked the first turn. Jackson worked the sails — setting, trimming, adjusting the jib — to get the greatest possible thrust from the wind.

By the time we hit the Academy's cove, half the pack was trailing. Slower boats, less capable sailors. I could see Richard still running first, with Morgan and two other boats pursuing him. They were past the first buoy, heading southeast almost directly into the wind, and I could see that Morgan's crew was having difficulty tacking — the zigzag maneuver that was required. The *Backdraft* fell to third, then to fourth, with us coming up hard.

The lead boats veered northeast close around the marsh headland, but Jackson called a course that swung us wider. More distance to travel, but it paid off. First, we milked speed from the end of the river flow, and then I felt the *Amber* catch hold of a new underwater current.

"The tide," Jackson yelled. "Turned a little while ago."

The other boats, cutting closer to land, hadn't got as much of a push from these two invisible hands. The *Amber* gained on them. We caught and passed Morgan's boat, and then the two in front of him. Suddenly, we were in second place.

We were closing on Richard as we approached the next turn. Richard shifted sails and Chad started to turn. Since Jackson had already reset our sails, I leaned on the rudder.

"No, wait!" Jackson shouted.

Confused, I tried to abort, but the *Amber* was already coming about. I hadn't seen that at the last second, Chad had straightened the *Swallow* out, so that my turn began before his. Richard grinned wide enough for me to see it across the water.

"Take a penalty, Parsons," he yelled.

I'd been suckered. According to the rules, a following boat was not allowed to start its turn around a buoy before the leading boat did. The penalty was a forced tack and jibe — two unnecessary turns that would slow us down. Jackson and I executed the clumsy maneuver and slipped to fifth.

I caught Jackson's eye and mouthed the words *I'm sorry*.

He shrugged, smiled, and shouted back, "We'll catch 'em."

With the wind blowing up the bay, the next leg southwest to the lighthouse was torture for any crew unskilled at tacking. Jackson, fortunately, was a genius with the sails. And I didn't know how, but he had it timed out perfectly for our last, long westward tack to take us directly, and at the greatest possible speed, into the turn around the lighthouse.

I was anxious to slow up. I could see the rocks shoreward; I did not want to slew too wide and end up on those jags.

"Luff sail," I shouted to Jackson, pleading with him to dump the wind from the *Amber*'s sails and slow her up. He shook his head.

"We'll make it," he shouted back. "Trust me."

I slammed the tiller far to starboard, holding my breath, silently cursing him. *If he crushes the* Amber*'s hull with this stunt* —

I watched the *Amber* swing south, then south-southwest, then more and more westerly. We struck rock — I could feel the small shudder in the hull as it scraped past some underwater obstruction. But then we were free, sails full, leaping east-northeast. We'd held an amazing amount of forward momentum around that turn. As the leaders struggled to regain speed, we pulled even with and passed all but Richard and Chad.

Their sail was full, as was ours, both of us running north-west now, before the wind. Approaching the north-shore cove, Richard pulled sail, slowing for a tight counterclockwise turn around the buoy, poised to catch me with a repeat sucker punch.

I yelled to Jackson, "Sixty degrees west."

He got it, grinned, shifted sail. We turned in front of the buoy to swing around it the opposite direction. We sailed wide of Richard and Chad, losing some ground, but saving more of our speed. And when we completed the turn, we were in close haul, forty degrees athwart the wind. Richard and Chad had come out of the turn full against the wind and needed to tack across it.

I wasn't certain, but I thought we'd pretty much pulled even.

"Eighty to port," Jackson hollered, and I pushed the tiller and leaned back as the sail swung. We cut across the blade of the wind and tacked again, swinging back west. Richard and Chad were on an opposite course, skimming east toward us.

We both turned again — they tacked west, we tacked east — separating. I could hear the crowd cheering across the water now. We were close. The boats turned again, nosing toward each other, both of us entering the mouth of Spa Creek. Richard came about so we were running side by side. The *Swallow* was in the lead, but we'd been on this tack longer, so we had more momentum. The finish line was just ahead.

We passed between the marker buoys, and I couldn't tell who had won. I looked at Jackson and he shrugged — he didn't know either.

It seemed like Richard had it. I thought for sure he had it.

Until I heard him choking out a few choice four-letter words.

Jackson was grinning pretty wide as he tied the *Amber* up, but he didn't join me for the award ceremony — "Not a member," he explained. I could understand he felt a little awkward, because that's sure the way I felt when I went up alone, mentally cursing him for a coward. Dad and Sammy cheered loudly, but Mom was nowhere to be seen.

I tracked down Dad in the crowd to tell him I was leaving.

"How are you getting home?"

"Jackson said he'd give me a ride on the *Amber*."

"Your mom's not going to be happy. First you win, then you duck out on her."

"Yeah, well, when is she ever happy?" I said, shrugging.

On my way back to Jackson and the *Amber*, I spotted Richard again. He was sitting slumped over at the end of a dock, staring out over the choppy waters of the bay. His second-place trophy lay on its back beside him. I thought about telling him it had been a hell of a race — so close I'd figured he'd won it. But I didn't. I just slipped on by. I almost wished I'd listened to my mother.

Chapter Twelve

Jackson fixed the sail to catch the northerly breeze and took the helm for our trip back up the river. Stillness fell around us like a curtain.

"You're a good sailor," Jackson told me.

"You sound surprised," I commented in mock puzzlement. "You're never surprised by any of the things I do."

"Really?"

"Yeah, come to think of it. Really. Why is that?"

I could scarcely see his face anymore, but I could hear the humor in his voice. "Why am I surprised? Or why am I not surprised?"

"Either. No. Let's start with the 'not surprised' part."

"I'm not surprised by some things, I guess, because they fit who you are. Or maybe Ida said something about it to me."

"Gramma must've spent a whole lot of time talking about me," I said. "She must've gotten pretty boring."

"You think I know you that well?"

"Seems like it sometimes."

He laughed. "Maybe you're just predictable."

"Maybe," I said, vexed but amused. "I guess I'm the one that's boring."

"Not at all," he said graciously. "Just think about poor Richard Hathaway — you surprised the hell out of him."

Back at the house, we left the *Amber* shipshape and climbed the stone stairs. Jackson said good night and was about to go, but I stopped him.

"Hey," I said, sticking out my hand, "congratulations on a great race."

He took my hand, but didn't shake — just held it in a firm, warm grip. He looked me in the eye and smiled. "A winning team."

"Yes," I said, and shook his hand once. He let me go. "Want to do some treasure hunting?" It would be maybe a couple of hours before Mom, Dad, and Sammy finished watching the club's fireworks and returned home. And I didn't want to be in the house alone.

"Sure."

We found tape, scissors, and some flashlights in the kitchen.

"Where are we going?" he asked.

"How about we go to the top of the stairs in here?"

He looked puzzled. "No stairs in the kitchen."

"The dollhouse has some, so I just thought —"

His face went from thoughtful to excited. With a sudden sureness, he went to the stretch of wall to the right of the massive fireplace. The wall held a narrow full-length closet door, next to a cupboard stacked over a set of three wide drawers where Gramma had kept things like aluminum foil and rolling pins.

Jackson opened the closet, which proved to be mostly empty except for some cleaning supplies and an ironing board. He rapped on the left wall, sounding it like a watermelon: two shallow raps and then a solid *thunk*. "It's hollow here," he said. "But how do we get to it?"

He bent his head, considering, then went to the double doors of the cupboard to the left of the closet. They concealed a stack of many small drawers, each one with a sliding hasp that held it closed. I looked in some of them — they held various pieces of silver nestled in form-fitting, fabric-lined holes. I carefully closed all the drawers, sliding the catches back into place. It seemed like the old kitchen stairs must have been removed many years before.

"See these?" Jackson said, pointing.

Just barely visible at the base of the set of locking drawers were two horizontal lines of dark metal.

"Hinges," we said at the same time.

Again Jackson bent his head in thought and again he looked up with a new purpose. He felt his way along the upper frame of the panel of drawers. On the right-hand side, a three-inch piece of wood pressed inward with a small click. At that, the top edge of the panel popped forward a fraction of an inch.

My mouth dropped open in amazement. The entire set of upper drawers was designed to fold out and down, over the front of the wide lower drawers. Now I understood why all the little silver drawers locked — so they wouldn't dump out as they were inverted.

Jackson smiled at me. Then he pulled on the handle of the uppermost drawer.

The top edge of the panel of drawers tipped out and down on mechanical arms designed to slow the drawers' descent. The hidden backside of the drawers proved to be a short set of steps that rose to more steps inside the newly revealed opening.

A secret staircase.

"Wild," Jackson commented. "I wonder if Ida knew this was here."

I shined the flashlight in the opening. The stair was dark and narrow and twisting. "Shall we try it?" I asked dubiously.

In answer, he picked up his flashlight and started climbing. I flicked off the kitchen light and followed. He stretched back a hand to help me, and I took it, seeking courage more than support. I had to duck to pass through the small opening to the stairs, and once I was inside, Jackson pushed a smooth wooden lever at one edge of the opening. It released a weight that pulled the door closed as it dropped. I backed up as the steps folded into place.

Dust was thick on the stairs, and every corner hung with webs. I tried not to think of the things that lived in the dark — centipedes and cockroaches and beetles and black widows. The stairs twisted and twisted again, a series of small triangular steps. I longed for a handhold, but couldn't have made myself reach out and touch the rail for anything in the world.

I rounded a corner and stepped wrong, losing my balance. I fell toward the wall, reaching blindly to catch myself, my hand pushing through a net of webs. I shrieked. Jackson pointed the flashlight down at me.

"Hey," he said. "Stay out of the webs."

"Gladly," I said, wiping my hand on my pants.

"No, I mean it." He spotlighted something just a few feet from me — an orange spider vibrating furiously in her web. "See her?"

"Ick," I confirmed.

"She's called a good mother. Very protective of her nest. She'll bite you if you get too close. And she's pretty poisonous. If a bite doesn't kill, it leaves a wound that never goes away. I don't think you have any on the West Coast."

"Jesus," I said, edging around it carefully. "I don't think I've ever heard of them before. Except maybe in a kind of nursery rhyme Sam told me the other day."

"I know that one."

"Wonder where he learned it?" I said, keeping my arms in and doing a thorough flashlight examination of every web I climbed past.

Jackson kept leading us higher, past a landing on the second floor. The stairs got narrower there, harder to negotiate, and the air stale. I was grateful he had gone ahead to clear a path through the accumulated webs, but I didn't like the feel of the darkness following behind me, rushing to close over the intrusion of our flashlights.

He halted abruptly. He'd reached a door of heavy planks, bound top and bottom with iron, and set with a keyhole. If it had ever been locked, it was not now. The knob turned, and Jackson pushed with his shoulder, forcing the complaining door open.

Our stabbing lights revealed a long, narrow, empty garret with a slanted ceiling and a single window at the far end. The air was chilled — I almost expected to see my breath ghosting out in front of me — and I felt reluctant to enter. Then my light found a wooden chest settled into the dark at the heart of the room.

I stopped breathing. I could actually feel the blood surging through the veins in my temples. My fingers had found Jackson's arm and were grasping it, clawlike. And I thought, *Oh, my God, this is it. We found the diamonds.*

Jackson unhooked my fingers, took my hand, and led me to the chest. Up close, we could see that it sat on an old Persian rug. And a heavy lock held it shut. And there was no visible key.

"What do you want to do?" he asked me.

"Are you kidding? Let's open it. Don't you want to?"

He didn't answer. "Keep your light on the lock." He used the butt end of his flashlight to hammer the ancient padlock repeatedly. The clanging rang brutally loud in the silent air of the attic. He paused. "I don't know if this is a good idea. Maybe someone wanted it left shut."

I couldn't believe what I was hearing. "I think the operative word in that sentence was *wanted*. Past tense. Judging by the layer of dust, no one has been up here in a long, long time. I think *we* get to decide now. Keep going!"

His face, distorted by the shadows and the unsteady lights in our hands, looked hungry. "I — I just have a bad feeling about it.

I want it opened, but you're the one who's always facing the things in the dark corners —"

"The visions can't hurt me. I'll be fine. Open it, already."

He hit the lock one more time and it busted loose. He twisted it free of the hasp. The lid rose with a metallic groan.

He stood back a little, pointing his flashlight at the chest and its contents. Evidently I was to have the privilege of searching it.

I was so excited my chest was tight. I knelt down and my hand came to rest on a little pile of beads that had been dropped long ago on the old rug. I lifted them up into the light: a silver rosary.

Time opened up. I heard, first — a woman weeping. Then she appeared in my peripheral vision, kneeling beside me — in the act of clicking a lock shut on the chest's hasp, the very same lock Jackson had just broken. I saw her yank on it to make sure it was closed.

I knew her face — she was beautiful, even with smears of dark makeup bleeding down her cheeks in the tears under her eyes. It was Fiona Warren. I'd seen her picture in her book. The fiery color of her hair surprised me — the old photo had been in the sepia tones of a century earlier. As I watched her, she started to turn her face toward me, and I had the irrational thought that I had to snuff out this vision before she *saw* me. I let the rosary spill from my fingers. She disappeared.

"You sure you want to do this?"

"What's your problem?" I asked, feeling a little irritated. This whole treasure hunt had been *his* idea. We were about to find the diamonds. Why was he hanging back now?

"Haven't you ever heard the old saying — sometimes the things that come out of a box can't be put back in?"

I shook my head a little, disbelieving. Deliberately, I turned my attention to the chest's contents. They were a jumble. The diamonds could be in anything — a bag, an envelope, the hem of a coat, even.

I saw the tops of a pair of black boots, the end of a little wooden box, the handle of a riding crop, the crumbling silk of a dress. I reached in and picked out a glint of gold — the clasp on the end of a string of coral beads, with a large piece of carved jade at their center. I held it out to him, triumphant. "Look at th —"

But the words I started to say died on my lips as full daylight filled my vision. Before me I saw a little girl with golden ringlets, in a pink satin, hoop-skirted dress and the same coral necklace. She was bent over a wooden washtub, splashing in the water.

It seemed . . . odd. It looked as if . . . there was something in the water. Something moving. I leaned to see —

Oh, God. Two little fists flailing; the dark curls on the top of a small head submerged under roiling water.

A black woman ran up, shoved the girl back, and snatched the baby from the tub, drying him gently as the infant coughed up water. "Sh-sh-shhh," she crooned. "Mama's here now, you're safe."

The little girl stood up and brushed herself off. She said to the woman, calmly, "Lay a hand on me again, girl, and I shall have you whipped." She cocked her head to one side and shrugged a little: "You can't save it, you know. The gypsy told Papa it has to die."

A violent wish that I could shove that child back into the dirt kicked me loose of the vision, which drained down to darkness. Appalled and horrified, I dropped the coral beads back in the chest. *Who was that little girl? Please, not related to me.*

Jackson was watching me. "Shall we stop?" he asked.

I felt something like nausea twisting inside me, but I wasn't ready to quit. "No," I told him. I reached back into the chest. "There's good stuff in here." I fished out a dagger, its handle made of gold set with glinting gemstones.

Candlelight settled around me, gentle and wavering. I recognized that I was in the parlor downstairs. Sarah-Louise stood, quietly weeping, above a seated black-haired woman, with a uniformed man behind them. Matthew lay on a quilt spread on the table. I had never seen a dead person before, not even my gramma, but Matthew's ashy-white pallor was unmistakable.

The man — the Captain — gave directions to someone I couldn't see: "We'll bury my son come daybreak."

The woman leapt up then to cover Matthew's body with her own. "He's not dead," she said, horror in her voice. "He's sleeping. I've seen him in my dreams. His spirit comes to me. I won't let you put him in the ground."

I knew she had to be Deirdre, the twins' mother. I'd seen her before, in the ballroom, whirling across the floor. And I realized I'd heard her before too — in the attic, shouting in the dark.

"He's dead, you lunatic," the Captain grated, taking her by the elbow and yanking her off.

She slammed back against the sideboard. Candlesticks toppled; china smashed on the floor. She caught herself there, then shot out a hand to grab something up. "No," she screamed, turning and swinging the thing in her hand down in an arc.

He saw her at the last second and parried the thing with his forearm. Then he swore, reaching for the gem-set handle suddenly protruding from his shoulder.

He pulled out a handkerchief to staunch the blood streaming from his wound, but a grim smile curled his lips. "Lock her in the nursery," he said. "I never want to see her again."

The last thing I saw was the fear on Deirdre's face. I dropped the dagger to make it all go away.

"What did you see?" Jackson asked.

I felt dizzy and shaken. So many visions so fast. And all of them so — ugly. He had been right, I conceded in my head — better not to have opened this box. I didn't want to see any more.

"Shall we pull the rest of this stuff out, see what's on the bottom?" Jackson had piled things on the floor beside him.

"We don't have to. The diamonds aren't in here. That's not what this chest is for. Please put it all back." He looked at me, confused. "Just put it back, now," I said between clenched teeth. I snatched up an armful to shove back into the open lid and instantly, a different darkness filled my sight.

"Where did you hide it?" a male voice growled. A fire somewhere behind me threw dancing light and shadows across a bare dirt drive in front of the oak on Amber House's lawn. A man in breeches and rolled-up shirtsleeves paced in the dirt, rhythmically striking his boot with the riding crop he gripped. His face was dripping sweat, and fury boiled just beneath its composed surface. It was the Captain again, maybe a decade younger than at his son's funeral. He stopped in front of a black woman, stripped naked to the waist, bound by her wrists to a low branch of the tree. "Where's the child, you damned witch?"

She did not answer. The crop whistled as it arced down to land on her bare back, where red and bleeding welts crisscrossed the white stripes of old scars on both sides of her spine. Dark drops sprayed from the blow, and I could see that the crop's leather was stained wet brown.

I would have thought the woman was dead — blood soaked the ground beneath her, and she was hanging limply from the ropes tied to her wrists. But each fall of the crop pulled a low mewling from her. Her groans mingled with sobs from a black-haired woman sprawled in the dirt — Deirdre, her face bruised, with blood seeping from a fresh split on her cheekbone. Beyond her, almost hidden in the shadows, the little girl with blond curls watched impassively.

I let the crop fall from my grasp and sank to the floor, back into the cold darkness of the attic. I knew now why all these things had been locked away. Perhaps they simply should have been burned, but the past was hallowed in this place. In Amber House, even the ugliest memories were not destroyed.

"Put it all back," I said again, and Jackson did as I asked without another question. He shut the chest and put the loop of the broken lock back through the hasp. Then he helped me to my feet. I felt old. I wished I had not seen.

I leaned on the arm he offered me, feeling the hard ridges of the scars beneath his sleeve. I wanted out of here; I did not ever want to come back.

Near the door, I noticed a large framed canvas tucked into the eave. I stopped. "Would you turn that around for me?"

He lifted it out. It was a portrait that had been slashed from corner to corner. Gingerly, I pushed the pieces back into place. A man stood before a velvet drape, his blue jacket splendid with gold buttons, a hat tucked under his arm. He had deep-set eyes over a long, slightly curving nose and a full, smiling mouth. I thought to myself, crazily, the words from the fairy tale: *What big teeth you have.*

He was the Captain. The man I had just seen beating a woman nearly to death.

I jerked my hand back from the pieces. It occurred to me, then, that if I could measure this painting, I would find that its frame fit the pale spot in the entry hall exactly.

"Who is it?" Jackson asked.

"I think, coz," I said, "that's our great-great-whatever-grandfather."

And I asked that he return him to his dark niche.

I followed Jackson closely to the landing on the second floor, where he stopped to shine the flashlight around the edges of a section of bare wood wall. With sureness, he reached up and pushed a small, hidden catch. The wall sprang in a crack with a metallic groan, and Jackson inserted his fingers and pulled it all to one side. He'd found a hidden opening just across from the door to the nautical room. We spilled out, dropping down a few feet to the hall rug.

I looked back at the hole. A three-foot piece of wall — from the waist-high molding to the crown molding — now hung behind the neighboring wall. Jackson tugged the end of the sliding wall. It glided back into place with a quiet *snick* and the opening disappeared.

"How did you know?" I said.

"How did I know what?"

"How did you know how to open that?"

He shrugged. "It — just seemed logical." He changed the subject. "Do you want me to keep you company until your family comes back?"

I shook my head. "Thanks. But I think I'd better take a shower, wash off some of the dust."

He nodded, touched my face briefly. "You want to tell me what you saw?"

I nodded back, but said, "Just not tonight."

"Okay." He turned and headed for the west wing. I guessed he was going to slip out through the conservatory again.

I shut myself in the bathroom near my room and turned on all the lights. The girl in the mirror looked a mess. Tears had made tracks through the dust on my face. I hadn't even realized I'd been weeping.

I felt a little better after a steaming-hot shower. I put on my PJs and headed back to my room carrying my filthy clothes. I was going to have to find a way to wash them myself — they were a mess, and there was a hole in one of the shirtsleeves from a splinter of wood that had gotten stuck in the rolled-up cuff. I picked it out and wondered what I should do with it, wondered what it had broken off of.

"Sarah."

Had Sammy come home while I was in the shower?

"Sarah."

I headed toward Sammy's bedroom. I felt like I was moving against a current, walking into air that rejected my presence. It was the same kind of feeling I'd had, come to think of it, a bunch of times, starting with that night in the conservatory.

I made myself open the door. The pale boy whom I'd just seen lying dead looked up from where he sat at the table.

"It's all done," he said. "See?"

A girl — Sarah-Louise — stepped forward from where I stood in the doorway and stopped behind him, her hands upon his shoulders. I could see he had gotten weaker. His skin clung to him tightly and seemed almost translucent. I wished I could tell them, warn them, death was almost there. But they knew. They didn't need my warning.

Sarah-Louise smiled down at Matthew's box. It was finished, polished.

"It is beautiful, dearest. How did you do this work?" she asked, running her fingers over the intricate pattern of inlaid hardwoods. She flipped open the top, and inside it was lined in velvet like a jewelry box, a mirror in the lid.

"This is the best part," he said. "You push it here —" He slid one end of the box a quarter of an inch to the side. "Then you push this whole piece —" The back face moved one quarter inch into the void left by the first panel. "Then you can slide this one, and this one." The bottom edge of the front came out entirely. "And see? — A hidden drawer. You can keep something in there and nobody will ever know."

"You're so clever, Matty."

The other Sarah hugged her brother. Hugged him tight.

I tucked the piece of hardwood in my hands on the molding above my head, where it would be safe. Then I backed out of the room and closed the door.

Downstairs, the front door slammed. “Sarah!” Sammy’s voice this time, definitely. “Sarah! Look what I winned!”

I went on down. Sammy shouted his news, punctuating it with little jumps. “We played bingo, Sarah, and I got the bingo! I winned knives!” He held up a box of wood-handled steak knives.

Just what every five-year-old needs, I thought, smiling a little.

Mom placed a steadying hand on Sam’s shoulder. “Go up and get ready for bed, sweetie.” I turned to go with him. “Not you, Sarah.” She cleared her throat. *Bad news.* “What exactly was the point of that performance today?”

“No point, Mom. I was racing.”

“But what were you *thinking*? Did you stop, even for a second, to think of what you had to lose?”

“So what if I beat Richard Hathaway?”

“Gee, I don’t know, Sarah. Let’s just think about that for a moment. Here you have a nice, good-looking boy who is taking you around, obviously making an effort to show you a good time. And you respond how? By going out of your way to humiliate him in front of all his friends? Is this why you’ve never had any boyfriends? Because you don’t have the faintest idea of how to treat them?”

I knew I was talking back more than I should, that I should have just let Mom vent so we could get to the end of it, but I couldn’t stop myself. I was too exhausted, too drained, to hold it in. "I didn't realize you were keeping a scorecard for my love life, Mom." My smile was brittle.

"Not keeping score, honey. Just keeping track."

"I'm not going to pretend to be incompetent just to make some boy feel good."

"Richard aside, you're not paying attention to what's important here. I am trying to assure my children's future by maximizing the sale of the assets that have been left to me. You sabotaged those efforts by offending Richard's father. You remember him — the senator?"

"I was just sailing, Mom." The words came out of my mouth like bullets.

She paused, regarding me for a moment, puzzled. Perhaps she saw my weariness. She finished her point, but her tone was mild. "You were hardly 'just sailing' and you know it. You were *competing*. That particular inclination of yours doesn't kick in anywhere near often enough — in school, for example. But when it does, God help everyone in your path." She sighed and shrugged. As if to say, spilt milk. "Good race."

"Thanks," I mumbled. "Sorry."

"The trick in life, honey, is to think more and apologize less. I'm going to need your help again tomorrow morning. A writer from *Southern Home* cornered me today. She knows about Amber House, and she thought your party might make a good article for the magazine. She wants to come over to take some preliminary photos so she can pitch the idea to her editor."

"That's great, Mom." Me in a ball gown at a coming-out party, captured for posterity and displayed in every magazine rack in the south. I wasn't sure the money was worth it.

"It *is* great," Mom said. "You'll help me, won't you?"

I swallowed my sigh. "Absolutely."

"I'll see you in the morning, then." She turned toward her

bedroom, but stopped, turned back. "You feeling all right, honey? You have some pretty dark shadows under your eyes."

"Oh, yeah, I'm okay. I just — want to go home, you know? I miss being home."

"Me too," she said. "But, it's nice, I think, for you to have had this chance to get to know Amber House."

As I turned back up the stairs, her words kept echoing in my head: *get to know Amber House.* It seemed that even in my mother's mind, Amber House was more like a person than a thing.

Chapter Thirteen

I kept my promise to Rose the next morning — I found and scrambled a few eggs for Sammy and me. Put enough ketchup on them, they were almost edible. Sam didn't complain.

"Sarah, how can you tell if it's a dream?" He shoveled a bite into his mouth, as he pushed the little bits scattered on his plate into a pile with his fingers.

"How can I tell *what* is a dream, Sam?"

"You know" — the pile of little bits got pushed up onto his fork — "the stories that happen. *All* the stuff. How can you tell?"

"Well, like, give me an example, bud."

"Well, for 'xample, I met this pretty lady who gave me a great toy." He stuffed in the bite. Some of the little bits made it, some did not. "But now I can't find the toy anywhere."

"*Where* did you meet her?"

"In a dark room with no walls."

"Oh," I said, "then I'm pretty sure that one was a dream, Sam. Did you wake up after it?"

"Maybe I did," he said dubiously. "I can't remember."

"See, Sam, that waking up thing is a pretty big clue. You gotta look for that part —"

A knock at the front door ended our philosophic musings. When I went to answer it, it turned out to be a florist delivering two large buckets of assorted flowers. The idea being, I supposed, to make the *Southern Home* writer think we had five hundred dollars worth of flowers around the house every day of the week.

Mom put me at the kitchen table with a pair of clippers and a dozen vases.. My pronounced droop made her shake her head. "You've got to adjust to Maryland time, Sarah, and get some more sleep. You look like hell." Ordinarily, I would have taken offense at the remark, but since I *felt* like hell, I thought it only fair.

She plunged on. "I need two big ones about this tall" — she held her hand up over a vase — "for the dining room and the living room. Start with the branches to give yourself a framework. Then" — she gestured to the smaller vases — "just assorted sizes for elsewhere. Give me one that's all roses. Put a different mix in each of the little ones."

She grabbed a couple of dust rags and a bottle of liquid wax, and I realized I had the better of the two jobs. So when she asked me dubiously, "You got it?" I said, "Yeah," making myself sound certain.

"Sam?" she said. "You come help me dust."

"All riiight," he said excitedly. I smiled. I was never sure if his odd enthusiasms were just little-kidness or the autism. Not that it mattered. I liked them.

I'd hoped my assigned work would keep my mind occupied and off more unpleasant subjects, but it proved to be the perfect task for mental wandering. And all my wanderings took me back to a woman lashed to a tree and a baby being drowned in a bucket. Both acts committed by psychopaths in my family tree. It was kind of a hideous contrast to the cheerful faces of the asters, Peruvian lilies, amaryllis, and echinacea — each package had a little sticker to inform the ignorant. Which would be me.

I finished one. Not bad. Pretty good, in fact. I polished off the other one to the same effect. *All right*, I told myself wearily. *Way to go.*

My mother came through the swinging door just then, glanced at the arrangements, and deftly shifted a few stems.

Instantly, the vases had a beauty that had not been there before. Long varied with short in an artful, careless rhythm.

That was Mom. Better than perfect.

She took up one large vase and headed toward the dining room. “Good job,” she said briskly. “Keep going.”

Sometimes it sucked to be me.

I slogged my way through a half-dozen more vases (long and short, balance the colors), when someone else came to the door. “I’ll get it,” I called, putting down the clippers.

Mom and I reached the door at the same time. It was a FedEx guy with a special package all for me from my school back home. One week’s worth of assignments.

“You’d better get started on that,” Mom said.

Did I mention that sometimes it sucked to be me?

I opened the envelope in my room, since I figured it would be infinitely easier to ignore if nobody else took an inventory of the contents. I dumped the two-inch stack of paper on my dresser and skimmed off the top half inch. Five work sheets with explanatory pages for geometry. I took two. Instructions from my history teacher for an essay “summarizing the causes of WWI.” Not today. A packet of ten work sheets for *Français. Merci*, Madame Anderson, *reine* of busywork. I set her whole packet on top of my two geometry sheets — my immediate to-do pile. I stuffed everything else back in the envelope. I’d worry about the rest later.

With the groan of the condemned, I found a pencil and started pushing it. Two hours later, I felt I had been sufficiently virtuous and put the remaining French work sheets aside. *Une autre fois* — another time. But at least, all the while I’d been working, I had not once revisited in my mind the agonies of the beaten slave woman.

I wished I knew who she was. I thought I might find some clue in Fiona’s journals. Since the man was the Captain, the whipping had occurred in the late 1700s. I pulled out the four volumes I'd stuck under my bed and opened up the earliest volume. I ran my fingers over the tracings of script etched into the heavy paper. Some part of me heard the sound of a pen scratching, but I forced that thought aside. I only wanted to read about the past, not visit it.

Leafing through the first few pages, I saw that the entries were not in order. The dates jumped from month to month, year to year. All of them, however, fell within the decade written on the cover, 1770–80. I picked an entry at random and read.

> *July 26, 1775. The twins had a birthday. Sarah-Louise got the dollhouse made to resemble Amber House. Camilla was there. She called it a "baby toy." Sarah-Louise did not seem to heed it.*

Camilla? Who was that? I wondered briefly what color her hair was.

> *Then the Captain had Joseph pick up Matthew and carry him all the way to the dock. Matthew's gift was a yawl, single masted and sleek, the first to be named the* Liquid Amber.
>
> *Matthew wanted to climb in and take her out that moment; the Captain said Matthew must get a little stronger first. But sailing would do him good and "toughen him up."*
>
> *I know already that Matthew never sailed his boat.*

Matthew and Sarah. My friends. Not merely brother and sister, but twins. I grieved for them a moment — for their loss, their separation — as if they were people I knew and not strangers long buried.

The journal entries made obvious what I had not understood before, and what Fiona's editor had never known. None of my great-grandmother's history was fiction. She had witnessed all the events in visions like mine. Which she'd recorded in these journals.

I flipped to another page:

> *January, 1778? I saw again Persephone, as I call her. I still have no idea who she is or where she is from. I wish I could help her — I cannot say with great particularity why I have such a strong sense that she needs help, but for the persistent sadness I see in her. And the fact she wanders the evil years of the Captain's machinations.*
>
> *Sometimes I have the oddest feeling she knows someone is watching.*

Persephone? A child lost in the underworld? What sense did that make? Did this mean that Fiona could see someone *else* who was caught up in the same echo? Was that even *possible*? How would she know that? I thought to myself that I could wander a long time through Fiona's disordered journals and never find the answer. But it explained her insistence on the statue guarding her pool. I wondered why Fiona couldn't help this Persephone. And whether anybody else could.

Maybe the reason Fiona had spent time in a mental institution was because of the visions. I knew, from Gramma, that Fiona's mother had been from the Deep South. Not part of the Amber House legacy. Maybe Fiona's parents didn't know about the gift. Maybe when Fiona had started seeing dead people, her parents figured she was — what was the term Mom had used? Schizophrenic.

I shuddered. I remembered reading about the things they did to people in asylums in the first half of the 1900s — electroshock treatments, lobotomies. What would they have done to Fiona to make her thoughts "more normal"? For that matter, what would my mother do to me if she ever found out about the things I was seeing?

I took my great-grandmother's book from the drawer and leafed through the beginning. I couldn't find any reference to the slave woman, but about a third of the way in I found miniature portraits of Sarah and Matthew. The caption below the pictures identified the twins and reported that Matthew had died shortly after this likeness was made. Lower on the page, another picture showed Matthew's headstone in the family cemetery, right beside that of his mother, who had died after him. Her inscription read, DEIRDRE DOBSON FOSTER, BELOVED MOTHER. 1743 TO 1776. SHE SLIPPED DREAMING TO THE FURTHER SHORE.

I checked the brief index included at the back. The entry for "slavery" took me to pages about the woman identified in Fiona's family tree as her grandmother, Maeve McCallister, who'd evidently been an abolitionist active in the Underground Railroad — the woman Gramma told me about. It was clear by the number of pages Fiona had dedicated to her that she'd been proud of this member of her family. I was proud of her too — at least one member of the family had tried to atone for the sins of our forefathers.

I picked the book up to move it to the bed, and loose papers fell from the back. They were written in a hand that wasn't Fiona's. The top sheet was dated June 20, 1969. That meant they must have been written by my grandmother.

The doctors cannot tell when or even if she will come out of it. She looks like the princess in the fairy tale, sleeping on and on, like she will wake at a touch. How can I help her? Mark tells me I should be patient and put my faith in the doctors. But I think there is something more I should be doing.

I stared at the note in my hand and felt a familiar sense of outrage. Another shocker from my mother's past. Mom must have gotten sick. Really sick. And she had never mentioned it.

It was beginning to seem like my mother had never told me anything about her childhood. Like she'd kept it all hidden. I wondered what had made her sick, what had happened after. I started to look through the pages for answers, but my mom yelled up the stairs.

"Sarah? Phone."

I put the loose papers back in the book and the book back in my drawer. Then I went down to the phone in the front hall.

"So, Parsons, you ran a pretty decent race."

I was impressed. I never thought I'd hear from Richard again, let alone get a pat on the back. "Just got lucky," I said.

"B.S. They obviously know how to train you up there in the Arctic Circle."

I chuckled. "Seattle's not quite arctic, but you don't want to fall off the boat. Water can be pretty cold. I would know."

He laughed. "Come to school with me tomorrow. Hang out with us."

Wow. Let's see. No work, don't have to pay attention, not going to be called on when I don't know the answer, just try to look good standing next to the best-looking boy I'd ever seen outside of a magazine? *And* escape this house *and* my mother? "Sure," I said.

"I'll pick you up at eight forty-five."

"Cool. See you."

"Later, Parsons."

Mom had come at the beginning of the call to loiter unobtrusively. She was eyeing me now like she wanted to grill me. I just smiled. And said absolutely nothing.

"The photographer is here and needs my help," she finally

said. "I didn't have a chance to fix your brother some lunch. Make him something?"

I shrugged. I hadn't had lunch either.

Sammy was sitting at the table when I got to the kitchen. "Me and Heavy Bear are hungry, Sarah. We want grilled cheese sammiches."

"Looks like P. B. and J., bud. What kind of jam?"

"Nope. Not peanut butter. Grilled cheese."

"And grape jam it is." I pulled the jam from the fridge and went looking for the peanut butter that had to be somewhere. "Want some banana slices in that?"

"*Nope.* We want grilled cheese. We *hate* peanut butter."

Okay. Sounds like I was being mean. But I knew the rules of this game. A kid with Sammy's mental wiring will get it in his head that he wants to eat something, and nothing else in the world will do. And, you know, he's little, and he's weird, and you want to be nice and make life easier. But my dad told me a long time ago that I wasn't doing Sammy any favors by letting him win — he had to learn to see the world differently, to accept other people had needs too. So I had to be more stubborn than Sammy, and, turns out, I was fine with that. In fact, I kind of had a natural aptitude for that. Especially when I didn't feel like cooking.

"Listen up, squirt. First, I know for a fact you don't hate peanut butter. You eat it all the time. Second, I am *not* cooking grilled cheese. I am *not* washing a pan. If I'm making the lunch, you can have peanut butter or you can have cereal. Now, what'll it be?"

"Peanut butter," he said with resignation.

I fixed two sandwiches, one for each of us. We were down to crusts when Jackson came to the back door. He stuck his head in, smiling. "I gotta get something for Gran for dinner. She'll be home this afternoon. Sam? You wanna come?"

"Me *and* Sarah," he said, taking my hand as if he did not mean to let it go.

"Okay," Jackson said in a measured voice. "If Sarah wants to come."

A trip to the grocery store? I shrugged mentally. *Sure.* "Um, if we're heading into town, I should change my clothes." The jeans were okay, but the oversized tee I'd stolen from Dad — not really fit for public.

"What you're wearing is perfect. Just get some tennis shoes. We gotta get moving."

"Fine," I said. "Just don't ask me to get out of the car."

"Come on, Sam," Jackson said. "But — maybe Heavy Bear better stay home. Okay?"

"Okay, Jackson," Sammy responded cheerfully. I was surprised by his easy agreement. Evidently my little brother had some hero worship going.

We slipped on some tennis shoes and went out the swinging door. Instead of turning toward the front of the house, though, Jackson headed for the rear.

"Hey," I said, trotting after him. "Aren't we driving?"

He shook his head. "I don't drive."

"Where we going?"

"To get dinner." He grinned.

We followed him down the stone stairs. Tied up at the dock was an ancient flat-bottomed rowboat, with peeling paint and an inch of water in the bottom. A pile of line and equipment lay in front of the middle bench, and a rectangle of rusty wire hung off the stern. The boat looked like it would start shipping water as soon as we climbed in.

"You going to drown us, Jackson?" I said.

"Just get in," he said, smiling. "She'll float."

Sammy jumped in to claim the forward bench. I waded through the water and sat aft. Jackson took the center bench, facing me. He grabbed the oars, braced his feet on the ribs, and started to row.

He clearly knew what he was doing. The boat went exactly where he wanted it to with no overshooting. The muscles in his arms and shoulders bunched and lengthened as he leaned back into his strokes. In short order we were speeding along.

I was right about the boat leaking, however. After five minutes, we were up to two inches of water around our feet. I must have looked a little worried. Without stopping, Jackson nodded cheerfully at a coffee can and told me, "You're on bailing duty."

I took the assignment very seriously. Every dozen yards or so, I poured some of the Severn back into its bed. I think it entertained him.

"You going to tell us where we're going now?" I asked.

"Crabbing. We're catching dinner."

"Crabbing!" Sammy squealed, as if this were the absolute pinnacle of adventure. "What's that?"

"You'll see," Jackson promised. "We're almost there."

We slowed up in a little cove in the river, where the trees dropped long shadows over the water. He pulled in the oars and lowered the cement anchor over the side.

"This is my spot," he said. "We're going to do this the old-fashioned way, with a line and a dip net." He took out his tackle and showed us. "Here's our lines — two apiece. We tie bait on 'em and drop them over, and wait for a crab to latch on. When you feel a crab feeding, you pull it up, and someone gets under the line with the dip net before the crab drops off. Then you use the tongs to move the crab from the net to the wire creel hanging off the stern. You got it?"

I was dubious, but Sammy nodded vigorously.

"Here's the bait," Jackson said, opening a bag. The contents' stench hit me in a wave.

"Oh, my God, what is that?" I said.

"Chicken necks. The more it stinks, the more we'll catch."

"I am *not* touching that," I said.

"I'll do it," he laughed. In gentlemanly fashion, he tied chicken necks to two lines. "Drop them over," he said, while he baited the others. "Keep a good hold."

When he had all six lines baited, he fished a bar of soap out from under the bench and scrubbed the rancid chicken off his hands. He tossed his own line overboard, and then we waited.

"What are we waiting for?" Sammy asked.

"You got to whisper, Sam. Don't want to scare off the crabs."

"What are we waiting for?" he hissed, barely less audible.

"You want to pay attention to any little tugs on your line. If you feel that, it means a crab has come to eat."

"I FEEL THAT! I FEEL THAT!" Sammy informed us.

Jackson laughed. *"Whisper, buddy. Whisper."*

"I feel that!" Sammy whispered.

"Okay," Jackson whispered back, grinning. "You wanna pull in your line real slow, see if the crab comes with you. Don't jerk it, or the crab will let go."

Sam reeled in his line, millimeter by millimeter, a crafty look on his face.

"He still on there?" Jackson asked.

"Yesss," Sammy whispered.

"Okay. Sarah," he said.

I was supposed to get involved? I stood reluctantly.

"Take the dip net," Jackson said. "Watch over the side to see when the crab comes near the surface. When you can get under him with the net, scoop him up."

I crept to Sammy's side and peered through the water intently. For a *long* time. "Pull a little faster, Sam," I said.

"Noooope," he whispered. Sammy the crabbing expert.

The chicken neck at last came into view, a greedy crab busy ripping chunks from it. I thought to myself, as I eased the net into the water, that crabs are like overgrown spiders that you can't squish or drown. The ugly thing was just beginning to look around and get suspicious when I scooped underneath it and got it trapped. I hoisted it up out of the water and held it dripping over the deck.

"I DID IT, I DID IT!" Sammy shouted loud enough for all the rest of the crabs to hear.

Jackson took the net from me. "If you could get the tongs, Sarah —"

"He's my crab," Sammy objected. "I want to do the tongs."

"Okay, Sam," Jackson agreed. "You can do the tongs."

I handed them to Sammy quite willingly.

"So we're going to grab this guy with the tongs, right, Sam? And put him in the wire creel. If you could pull in the creel, Sarah." I turned to get it. "No, Sam, wait for Sarah to bring the creel. No, wait, buddy!"

I turned around with the wire rectangle. Sammy hadn't waited. He was coming aft with the crab gripped in the tongs. I just had time to think, *This isn't good*, when Sammy's foot caught in one of the boat's ribs, and he pitched forward. He caught himself before he fell, but the crab went airborne. It landed square on my chest and snagged into my long hair with a claw and two or three of those spider legs.

"OH, MY GOD!" I said, reasonably calmly, I thought, given the circumstances. "OH, MY GOD!" I repeated for emphasis, and instinctively leaned forward, swinging the crab away from my body.

Jackson was trying to help me. I know this because he staggered toward me over the seat. His problem was, he was laughing so hard, he almost fell overboard. "Stop moving," he wheezed between gut-wrenching spasms of laughter. "S-stop moving."

I heard a high pitched noise that sounded something like *"Eeeeeeeeeeeee,"* and realized that it was me, squealing like a little girl.

"Stop," Jackson gasped. "Stop swinging your ha-*ha-ha-ha-ha*."

I forced myself to stand still. Jackson's hand shot in and caught the crab's free claw. He pulled it away from my face and, mercifully, the thing released me. Jackson opened the creel at my feet and popped the crab inside.

"Whoo-hoo-hoo-hoo," he said, winding down, sitting weakly on his bench, wiping tears from his eyes.

"You catched it, Sarah," Sam said with genuine admiration, and he jumped a little in the air, pumping his fist. "All *riiight*!"

So, then, I started to laugh. And Jackson started in again. And Sammy joined us. And after a little while, we moved to another fishing spot, where we hadn't scared all the crabs.

When we got back to the dock at home, Jackson told us he'd deal with the crabs — that it might be better for me not to risk another close encounter. Which sounded good to me. Sam and I skipped off the boat with nothing to carry and nothing to do. We climbed up the steps, singing a little crabbing song Sammy had just invented. The tune was the same six-note one Sam always hummed. I had to fake the words, but Sam was a very forgiving singing partner.

We burst through the kitchen door into the shadows of an unlit room. The woman who lifted her head to face me was my grandmother, the way she'd been forty years before. She had a glass with golden liquor in it. Her shoulders were rounded and hunched. Her face was bleak.

"Where have you been?"

I was confused for a moment. Why was this vision talking to me? Then Ida's face became my mother's, equally cold. "Where have you been?" she repeated.

"Jeez, I'm sorry," I said. "We thought we were going on a quick errand with Jackson, but then it turned into this crabbing expedition —"

"Why are you spending so much time with that boy?"

Sammy slipped out the door to the rear hall. I wished I could go with him.

"Jackson's a really nice guy, Mom, and really great with Sammy —"

"Why? You never stop to ponder that question, Sarah. What's in it for the other guy? What does he want from you?"

"I didn't think it was that big of a d —"

"You didn't think at all. That's your problem. You just don't think. What do you suppose Jackson is thinking? Haven't you noticed how he looks at you? Is it *fair* for you to be encouraging him?"

Encouraging him? Oh, God, she thought he had a crush on me. *Did* he have a crush on me?

"Look!" I blurted. "There is *nothing* going on between me and Jackson. Richard is coming by tomorrow morning and we're going to spend the day together at his school. Okay? Everything is fine. Everybody's using everyone else for their own nefarious purposes, exactly the way they're supposed to, all right, Mom? Jackson is just a friend. God! He's not even that — we're leaving in ten days. He's just someone to kill time with, okay?"

I heard the smallest noise. I turned and saw the exterior door was barely ajar. I opened it. The pot of crabs had been left on the step. Jackson was nowhere to be seen.

Chapter Fourteen

When I turned back into the kitchen, I saw my grandmother again. She was bleary-eyed and unsteady on her feet. The drink in her hand sloshed as she waved her arm, gesturing. "It's *your* fault," she shouted. "*You* did this. I told you and told you that you had to be more careful. None of this would have happened if you hadn't been so *stupid* and *cold* and *careless*."

The auburn-haired girl she was shouting at sat stone-still in her chair, staring at the table. She was my mother, younger than I, and tears rolled silently down her cheeks.

I slammed out the back door, wrenching myself loose from that vision. Gramma had been right. Everything came apart because of my mother. Because she didn't care how she hurt people.

I had been stupid. I had let my fear of her make me say stupid things. I didn't know if there was any way to unsay them. But I was going to try. "Jackson," I called. I walked around to the stone stairs. "Jackson?"

There was no answer.

I started walking on the path that ran west along the bluff. I wasn't sure where I was going, and the sky was darkening. But Rose's house had to be somewhere up ahead.

I would find him and apologize. Tell him I didn't mean it — that I was just trying to get Mom off my back. That we *were* friends. We *were* — what? I definitely didn't want to lead him on, if he *did* like me. But he knew I was kind of seeing Richard.

I walked past the graveyard, with its single plot of bare earth covering the grandmother I had hardly known. She'd been closer to Jackson than she had to me. He had been fond of her. And she had told him about her family, about us. So maybe Ida's family felt like part of his family. Maybe that's what I sensed when he talked to me like we had known each other forever. And why Mom thought he paid too much attention to me.

I entered the woods at the end of the field. The darkness gathering in the air huddled more thickly under the trees. The ground rose to my right, but the path continued mostly on a level. Trees and bushes walled me in on both sides, blackness on dark gray.

Where was their house? It was getting hard to see my way. I kept veering off into branches, and stumbled each time the path descended unexpectedly. I thought about turning back, but figured I must be close now, closer to Rose's than to the house. I could ask them to loan me a light for the walk back.

I heard something up ahead. The sound of someone running. Hard, fast.

"Jackson?" I called, and walked a little quicker. "Jackson? Ca —"

I had wandered too far left, into the bushes, and my foot found a place where the trail wasn't — where the bluff dropped off toward the river below. I teetered there, grabbing at the air, trying to find some purchase with my sliding left foot. Dislodged stones bounced down the slope, hitting dirt and wood and rock and water. Small branches bent and slid through my fingers, shedding leaves in my hands. I realized with sickening clarity that I was going over, and down.

Then a hand caught my arm.

I was pulled back onto someone's chest, and an arm went around me and steadied me. I grabbed hold compulsively, vertigo still rushing in my head.

"You okay?" Jackson asked. He was gasping for breath; his heart pounded beneath my cheek. I felt absurdly like bursting into tears.

"I almost fell."

"You're all right now," he said into my hair. "You're okay." He sounded shaken.

"You caught me. How'd you do that? How'd you know?" I was babbling. I needed to breathe more slowly. But how had he done that? How had he been there, just in time, just in the right place?

"I heard you crashing along. The trail gets really close to the edge right here. I was worried."

So he'd come running up the trail and got here at just the right moment. He'd caught me at just the right moment. That was so — Jackson. Always catching things.

I must have spoken aloud, because he said, "What?"

"You're always catching things," I repeated stupidly.

He started to laugh. Really hard. He had to back off and bend over and lean against his own knees. "Oh, jeez," he gasped, catching his breath, "you don't even know. Maybe if *you'd* stop dropping things."

He chuckled again. And I knew I was forgiven for the ugly things I had shouted in the kitchen.

"I'm sorry," I said anyway. "I didn't mean what I said to my mother. She makes me crazy sometimes. You and I *are* friends."

"No," he said solemnly, "we're more than friends."

"What?"

He smiled. "We're related, remember?"

"That's right." I returned his smile. "We're cousins."

"I'll walk you back," he said. He took my hand and guided me along the path. I let myself enjoy the feel of his hand, a solid thing, a safe thing after my near fall. It was not quite full dark when we emerged from the woods. "Think you can get there from here without breaking your neck, coz?"

"No promises," I said, "but I'll try."

"Yeah, you try," he said, smiling. "We going treasure hunting tonight?"

"Tomorrow," I said. "I think I'm going to need to lie down."

"Make sure you eat some of those crabs first." His voice came back to me from the darkness under the trees. "Good night, Sarah."

My father had come to dinner again. "Sammy called. Said he'd caught some crabs for me to cook," Dad explained.

Way to go, Sammy. I'd been a little worried about the cooking part, which, fortunately, Dad had already mostly taken care of. I was not fond of the cooking part of crabs.

Inside twenty minutes, the four of us sat down and began the serious work of extracting meat. Mom cracked the shell for Sam, but he did his own picking. He and I both had been eating crab from the time we started chewing.

Afterward Dad tucked Sam into bed while I got started cleaning up. Mom went into the dining room to work on party stuff she had spread all over the table.

Dad was going to come back and help me, but he only got as far as the dining room. His muffled voice filtered through to me.

"I don't know why you had to use Sarah as an excuse to throw this party, Anne."

I couldn't hear the words of my mother's response, but her tone was curt and defensive. I turned off the water and went to stand closer to the dining-room door.

"You are going to make a hell of a lot of money off of this place one way or the other," Dad went on. "You didn't have to embarrass your daughter for a few thousand more."

"How about several hundred thousand? Or a couple million, when you add in the auction. But let's not even plug money into the equation, Tom. Maybe I just think it'll be important to Sarah, someday, to look back on this party in her family's house. How come it *never* occurs to you that I might be thinking of someone besides myself?"

"Maybe because that's how I experienced our life together."

"Oh, great," my mom came back at him. "Let's just open up all the old wounds, shall we? Rehash it all. Because *I'm* not the one who betrayed our marriage."

I had heard enough of this argument. I went out the door to the rear hallway.

A man I didn't recognize came through the arch from the east wing. My grandmother followed after him, her face twisted in anger. "If you leave, don't come back here," she snarled. "Don't call or write or ever come back here again."

The man kept walking through the farther arch to the front hall. "I'll tell the girl you died," Ida yelled after him. "I don't ever want to see your face —" She disappeared through the archway behind him, and her voice turned off like a light.

I ran the same route after them. I had to get to the stairs before my parents' argument broke up, before my father made his escape through the front hall. I didn't want them to know there had been a witness. Somehow it was worse if there had been a witness.

I shut the door to my room and piled some clothes behind it. That would stop the light and make it harder to open the door from the outside.

But I wanted company. I wanted to be with someone who'd gone through some of the same things I was going through. I wanted the feeling of not being alone.

I got out the box of journals and photos hidden under the bed. I took up Fiona's handwritten record:

> *Late Spring, 1750? I followed Grandmother through the tunnel to Heart House. But when I reached the door, I accidentally brushed it and saw further back. A little girl in a pale dress stood in the center of the room. She was grieving for the little house. She watched slaves lay the last of the bricks that sealed the windows and shut out the light. She said to her companion, a teenaged negro woman, "Heart House will be so lonely. Who will come to see the grandparents after Papa has buried it?"*
>
> *And the older girl closed her eyes and concentrated. "They will find their way, Miss Deirdre. All the ones to come."*
>
> *I came back to myself in the inky night of the tunnel, now beamed, buried, and hung with the roots of the hedges. I thought about the ones to come whom I would never know. About the girl, and whether she would be able to do what I could not — save Persephone.*

Persephone again. This lost girl. I wondered if anyone had ever come along to save her. Who knew? Who in fact knew if she ever even existed? After all, Fiona had spent time in an asylum. I went back to her entry, which was not quite finished:

> *Then I lit the lantern I had taken with me and went back up through the trapdoor into the heart of the maze.*

A trapdoor in the middle of the maze? Oh, my God.

I hugged the book to me, genuinely excited. A tunnel. And an entire buried house. And maybe — the Captain's lost diamonds? The thrill of the treasure hunt snagged me again. I couldn't wait to tell Jackson.

Perhaps there was more.

I looked at the next entry, but it was dated 1761, years later. With no sequence to the journal's contents, there was no way to find a continuation of the story, if there even was one.

> *May, 1761. Edward has been after me again and leaving me flushed, as he will, so I suppose that is what brought this vision on. I started into the library and saw the young Captain leading Deirdre in, smiling as he backed her up behind the open door. Her face looked so eager, so tender, waiting to be kissed. But I could not get the notion from my mind, as he leaned in, his fingers on the amber hanging just below her collarbone — I thought of that line in the fairy tale:* What big teeth you have.

I shuddered involuntarily. The same words. She'd thought of the exact same words. Could you inherit a way of thinking — no, a *thought* — from your crazy great-grandmother?

I hunted for the amber around my neck. It seemed improbable that it was the same as the one Deirdre had worn. And yet, why not? This was Amber House, after all, where the past was never really over and done with.

I hid the journals back in their spot. I unblocked the door and peeked out. The house was dark. Dad must have left and Mom must have gone to bed. I closed the door and shut the darkness out again. And went to sleep with the light on.

Chapter Fifteen

Rose was back in the kitchen the next morning, kindly fixing breakfast for Sammy again.

"Morning," she greeted me. She seemed irritated. Maybe even more than usual.

"Morning, Rose. How was your trip to Alexandria?"

"Fine, thank you. Heard you and Jackson had some excitement while I was gone."

"Huh? Oh, yeah. We won the regatta. It was great. Jackson tell you about it?"

"No. He didn't breathe a word. But then he might've figured I wouldn't approve."

I was confused. Why wouldn't she approve?

"Jackson never said anything to you?" Rose said. "About his problem? 'Cause he probably should have."

I stared at her steadily, unwilling to ask her "What?" Not certain I wanted to hear the answer.

She sighed. "It's his business. I don't like to interfere. But you've been spending so much time together, you probably should know: He's epileptic. Ever since the accident. He has spells where he just blacks out. He has to avoid stressful activities that demand uninterrupted concentration. Lots of things he can't do, or won't do."

Like driving, I thought to myself. *And sailing. Or so Rose thought, anyway. And maybe that whole thing about going into research instead of becoming a doctor?*

Rose went on. "No need to tell him I said anything."

"Sure, Rose."

"Just thought you maybe should know."

Maybe I should. But I wished I didn't.

After breakfast, I had a limited amount of time left to get ready before Richard skidded up the drive, so I focused on the tasks at hand. First a call to Jackson to tell him about the tunnel thing and set up a time and place to meet that night — at the entrance to the maze. I was disappointed to have to leave a message, but it was the best I could do. I left it short and cryptic, to save some of the pleasure of showing him in person.

Then on to the ever-agonizing problem of what to wear. Richard's school did the whole uniform thing. With that as a guideline, I tried to find something to wear that was unobjectionable, but, you know, still hot. I paired a white button-up blouse with a pleated plaid miniskirt that was similar to the skirts we wore at my prep school back home — give or take a few inches. Except, I skipped the schoolgirl kneesocks in favor of a pair of caramel-hued riding boots I found on the floor of my mother's closet.

I hoped I hadn't gone overboard with the boots. But I saw Richard give me an appreciative once-over when he pulled up, and allowed myself a feeling of satisfaction.

During the drive, he explained to me that Saint Ignatius Academy was something of a big deal as a boarding school; while it was open as a day school to smart local teens whose parents could pay the huge tuition bill, it also housed the children of political leaders, celebrities, and various security-conscious billionaires. He'd had to pull strings to get them to let me on campus — if anybody asked, I was sitting in on classes because I was interested in attending. With Richard at the wheel, we made it there in less than twenty minutes, turning beneath an enormous stone arch that supported two iron gates. A guard waved Richard in.

The school was stunning — Gothic-style stone buildings smothered in ivy, housing all the modern luxuries and surrounded by groomed lawns running down to the Potomac River. Richard led me along a brick path to the main entrance. "We have to sign you in up front first."

The blue-haired lady in the main office was polite, if a tad officious. I signed a register and got a pin-on name tag identifying me as a visitor. When she turned the register back and saw my name, she said, "Oh." Then, "You're the young lady from Amber House, aren't you?"

"Yes," I said, surprised.

"That's one of the most beautiful homes in Maryland," she said. "I told Ida once that she should have opened it for tours."

"You knew my grandmother?"

"Oh, yes," she said. "We were friends, once upon a time, when your mother was a girl. We both rode competitively. Of course, I wasn't anywhere near as good at it as your gramma."

I was finding it kind of hard to picture either one of them ever actually getting on a horse. Richard took that moment to grab my arm and tug me toward the door.

"Thank you," I said over my shoulder, and, "Nice meeting you," before Richard pulled the door shut.

"You make me late to class with any more of your ten-minute Amber House chats," he said, "I'm gonna have to dock you points, Parsons."

"*My* —?" I sputtered. I was speechless. So I punched him in the arm. He pretended to be in pain.

A bell rang overhead. The first-period classes emptied into the halls. I saw puzzled look after puzzled look, eyes falling to my boots and moving up from there.

Richard put his hand at the small of my back and directed me around a turn in the corridor into a classroom. A wall of windows edged in stained glass dropped rainbow-hued light onto the desks and floor. Richard sat down at an empty desk halfway toward the back of the room and patted the one to his left. As I took my seat, three girls sat down in the desks behind us and commenced to whisper.

"Isn't that —"

"I like her boots."

"That's that girl."

Richard looked at me sideways, giving me a conspicuous smile.

"The one who beat him in the race."

He turned away, then, but not before I caught the sigh and roll of his eyes. And I was sorry, a little bit, that I'd made things harder for him.

"I bet he let her win."

"That's what I heard."

Huh. Or not.

I didn't really get much of a chance to listen to the lecture. I was too busy passing notes with Richard. His handwriting was largely illegible, but what I could make out was so wickedly funny, I kept having to choke down my laughter.

The teacher stopped us on the way out the door. I figured we were going to be reamed for being too rowdy.

"You're Miss Parsons from Amber House, aren't you?" Mr. Donaldson said.

"Yes."

"I read your great-grandmother's book about the house. I am fascinated by its history and the role your family played in the formation of the political face of North America."

"Oh?" I said. I had no idea what he was talking about.

"Richard tells us you might end up enrolling at Saint Ignatius. We look forward to having you as a student."

I thanked him as Richard tugged my arm again to pull me out the door.

"God, has *everybody* heard of Amber House?" I asked.

"Don't you know it's a big deal in Maryland? It's the reason everyone's coming to your party."

"I thought it was because of Ataxia."

"Yeah, well, that helps."

After history came lunch. A little early for me. I wasn't hungry just yet. Which was a good thing because, as the students mass-migrated in what I assumed was the direction of the dining hall, Richard grabbed my hand and tugged me into an empty stairwell. Was he going to try to kiss me again, I wondered hopefully.

"Sarah!"

Kathryn lunged down from the bend in the stairs above us. She wrapped her arms around me and gave me a big hug, all flowery perfume. "I didn't get a chance to congratulate you on the race the other day!"

"Where's Chad?" Richard asked, brushing past that subject.

"Meeting us there."

We slipped along a gap between the side of the building and the privet hedge in front of it, then dashed down some steps to a lower walkway, cutting across a lawn through some more bushes. By this time I was guessing some rule breaking was in the immediate plans. We got to the side entrance of a large building with a vaulted roof, where Kathryn knocked on the door. It was promptly opened by Chad, who smiled at me and nodded. "Nice win, Parsons."

"Thanks."

The gust of air blowing out through the cracked door smelled distinctly of chlorine; we had arrived at Ignatius's indoor Olympic-sized pool. The others dumped packs at the foot of one of the bleachers and sat down on the cushiony flooring — nothing so mundane as concrete around this swimming pool.

Chad had a sack with lunch essentials: sodas and candy bars. After a few minutes' worth of conversation about people I didn't know doing things I hadn't been around to see, he started stripping off his clothes. With each item of clothing removed, I scooched a few inches backward, until I was up against the tiled wall. None of them seemed to notice.

Chad stopped undressing when he got down to his boxers. He took a running jump and cannonballed into the pool. Kathryn — now in nothing but a matching bra and panty set — followed. Richard strolled over to the deep end and executed a perfect, streamlined dive.

Richard and Chad mostly horsed around in the deep water, but Kathryn parked herself nearby and talked up to me. After a while, she realized this was inefficient. She emerged and sprawled out on the rubberized flooring like a swimsuit model.

"I noticed at the party that you don't drink," she said. "And you don't do semi-skinny-dipping. What *do* you do?"

"Not much, I guess."

She snorted. "Except make an ass out of Richard in front of all his friends. I wish I could sail. I'd have done that a long time ago." She propped herself up on one arm and smoothed her wet hair back with her free hand. "I like your boots."

"Thanks."

"It's for the best," she went on. "He was getting *so* cocky. It was about time someone took him down a peg."

"Oh, well —"

"I mean, except for the fact that it was kind of like the *Swallow*'s last race. So that sucks."

"What do you mean?"

She lowered her voice. "His dad said he was going to sell it."

"Sell the boat?"

"I bet he won't, though," Kathryn said. "That would be way harsh."

"Why would he do that?"

"He won't," she said definitively. "But Richard was freaked, of course. I need a towel," she announced. She got up, and snatched her clothes from their place on the floor. "Come on."

I followed her into the locker rooms, to what I assumed was her locker, since she knew the combination. She pulled out a large fluffy towel and buffed herself dry. Which led me to wonder why she hadn't just gotten her suit to swim in, instead of the polka-dotted bra and panties.

"I can't wait for your party. It's all my mom's been talking about. I've never been to a haunted house before. Have you seen any ghosts?"

I puzzled over how to respond to that. I settled on, "Not yet."

"You should try some, like, voodoo or something. I've got a Ouija board. I could come over sometime and we could hold a séance."

A séance at Amber House. It was bad enough knowing as much as I did about my ancestors; I was absolutely certain I didn't want them talking to me. "Sounds awesome," I said.

"I know!" She'd ruffled through the contents of the locker and found a hairbrush. She slipped a hair tie from around her wrist and proceeded to braid her hair. "My mom was telling me about your great-grandmother. She said she was absolutely wild. Like, had twenty lovers and boozed it up all the time and did magic. Probably sacrificed chickens —"

"Sounds like your mom knows more about it than I do," I said. "Almost everyone does. The other day, Richard was quoting from this book about the house that his mom gave him before she died."

"What?" She tilted her head to one side, in just the same way as she'd done at the pool party. Her compulsory expression of confusion.

"My great-grandmother — the crazy one, actually — wrote a book —"

"No. You said 'before she died'? Where'd you get that idea?" She was giving me this funny look. Like I was stupid or something. "Claire Hathaway isn't dead. She left. Like, four years ago. *Everybody* knows that."

"Left?" *Why would he lie about that?*

"Yes. And it was a big deal for Richard, 'cause she was the one with the money. I mean, Richard's dad got the house, but Claire had piles and piles of money."

I must have looked shocked, because Kathryn put her hand to her mouth and kind of giggled. No wonder his father was thinking of selling the *Swallow.* No wonder he was so hot after my mom. If she sold Amber House, she'd have piles and piles of money too.

A bell went off.

"Oh, yikes, we gotta get going. Class starts in ten."

The guys had toweled dry too. All evidently had access to lockers. And, presumably, suits.

We snuck out the same door we snuck in. The art building was at the top of the campus. It was a hike. At one point, Richard held out his hand for mine, but I pretended to be involved with something on my sleeve. I didn't like that he'd lied to me about his mother. It made me wonder what else he hadn't been entirely truthful about.

The art teacher, Mr. Schrieber, was another Amber House *connoisseur*, unfortunately. After Richard introduced me, Schrieber launched into a mini one-on-one lecture on all the famous American portraitists, "spanning three hundred years of painting," hanging on the walls of Amber House. And this was not to mention what he called "the Hicks Biblicals" on the risers of the main stairs.

"My great-aunt Gwendolyn spent the night at Amber House once." He said this with such cheerful enthusiasm, I waited for some nice story to follow.

"Really?" I encouraged him.

"A long time ago, when she was a little girl. She used to tell us that night she had the most horrific nightmares she'd ever had in her life."

"Oh," I said, faltering.

"In fact, they were the inspiration for the Schreiber family boogeyman," he ran on, still happily enthusiastic. "If we were bad, Aunt Gwen would tell us, 'You'd better watch out, or she's gonna get you' " — his voice dropped to a spooky whisper — " 'The Mother Who Comes in Your Sleep.' " He laughed with glee. "Aunt Gwen was such a crazy, mean old bat."

Yes, I thought. *Nice story.*

I guess Richard noticed my chilled attitude toward him. After we buckled up in his car for the ride home, he sighed, leaned back, and said, "Okay, Parsons, what'd I do?"

I know I must have turned red. I didn't have any idea how to answer. I mean, it wasn't like he owed me the truth or something. But it just blurted out of me: "Kathryn said your mom isn't dead."

He didn't say a word. I saw the muscles in his jaw bunch, and then he turned the ignition and popped the clutch in reverse. We spun out of there kicking up gravel.

I was scared and unhappy that I had just totally blown it. I mean, I had basically called him a liar. I guessed we were kind of done, right? But he had lied to me.

Then he downshifted and screeched to a halt on the shoulder of the road. He talked facing forward, to the steering wheel, without looking at me. "I'm sorry. I don't know why I lied to you like that — it was stupid, okay? It's just —" He stopped, as if the words were bitter in his mouth. "I just didn't want to have to say it out loud, you know? That she up and left us. Left me. Like there was something wrong with me, you know? Or something wrong with her." He put his elbows on the steering wheel and pressed his palms into his eyes.

I felt terrible. I reached up and pulled his hand away from his face, then turned it over and laced my fingers through his. He tightened his hold, squeezing my hand. "I'm sorry, Parsons."

I squeezed back. "No worries, Hathaway. I'm sorry I said anything."

He leaned over, put his finger under my chin. He hesitated a moment, then gave me the softest kiss. I liked it. I liked it a lot.

Then he popped the car back in gear and drove us to Amber House, which meant he sped like a madman, passed six cars, and nearly spun out in the gravel of the entrance. Even so, I felt surprisingly relaxed, like a bunch of muscles I had been holding tense had all let go at once. Then I realized — I had just enjoyed a day of utter normalcy, no echoes allowed.

Richard was speaking to me. "Hm?" I asked.

"I said, how 'bout we go riding tomorrow after school?" he repeated.

"Riding? Riding what?" I asked.

He laughed. "Horses, you dope. What do you think?"

"You've got horses?" I asked.

"Yeah," he said. "And so do you. Jeez, Parsons, don't you ever go exploring? Somebody should have given you a map and a tour of your own house."

"Well, you're doing a pretty good job of that, Hathaway, even if it is taking you forever to finish."

"Yeah, well, I need excuses to keep coming over." He grinned fetchingly.

"You don't need any excuses," I said, grinning back. "You've got an open invitation. You're welcome anytime."

I was waiting, hoping, for another kiss, and he must have known it, because he smiled before he reached across me to open my door. "Your mom's waiting on the front porch," he said.

"Oh," I said, turning pink. "Right."

As I shifted to get out, he snagged my little finger with his little finger, like a little secret embrace. "I'll see you tomorrow, Parsons," he promised. And I smiled.

Chapter Sixteen

Mom opened the door for me. "How'd it go?"

I found I was really not interested in analyzing the day for my mother. I just wanted to slip away to my room and analyze it for myself.

"It went fine," I said. "A lot of kids said they were coming to the party. I think it's mostly because of Richard."

She must have heard something in the way I said his name — some tone that betrayed me.

"Don't start liking him too much," she said.

I think my mouth fell open. That was just perfect, wasn't it? First she was riding my case because I chased the lovely Richard off by winning the regatta with Jackson. Now she was warning me not to get too close? "I thought you wanted me to like him."

"No. I wanted *him* to like *you*. I want him at that party. I want him to bring all his friends."

I was absolutely incredulous. "That just sounds so . . . so . . . manipulative. Don't get me wrong — I'm not a big fan of the senator's, but — jeez, Mom, I didn't think you were just *pretending* to like him."

"I'm not pretending. I do like him. Of course I like him. What's not to like?"

"No." I shook my head. Was she playing word games with me? "I mean *like him* like him."

She looked at me in genuine disbelief. "Oh, God, no. I've known Robert Hathaway since he was fourteen. I know exactly what kind of man he is. Even when I was younger than you, I was never dumb enough to *like* Robert."

"So, you don't like him. You just *want* something from him."

"You know what? I don't like your tone." She came and stood in front of me, her hands on her hips. "I know you're still a child, but it's time you realize how things work in the real world: You think I'm some kind of conniving bitch because I want to use the senator's connections? I got news for you, honey: The only reason the senator is letting me use his connections is because *he* wants something from *me*."

I just stood there, shaking my head. I mean, I was relieved I didn't have to worry about my mother and her imminent piles of money, but I was still appalled. Mom was using the senator, using his son, *and* using me. And she wasn't bothered by it. At all.

"I don't know what he wants yet," she went on. "Could be something as simple as a campaign contribution and a chance to mingle with his wealthy constituents at no cost to himself. Or he could be looking for a — companion."

Okay, yuck.

"Or maybe he's more ambitious. He's single, I'm newly wealthy, and he doesn't seem to like it much when your father is around." She rolled her eyes the tiniest bit. "But here's something else for you to think about, Sarah, and I'm not telling you this to be cruel. Do you think the senator didn't say the exact same thing to Richard that I've said to you? 'Be nice. Don't mess up this deal for me.'"

Her tone was light, but brittle and unrelenting.

"I mean," she kept going, "you are a lovely girl. You don't believe that half as much as you should. Any boy would be lucky to spend time with you. But do you really think that this boy swallowed his pride and invited you to his school because he all of a sudden finds every other girl he knows inadequate?"

Maybe she wasn't trying to be cruel. But in that moment I just wanted to reach out and claw her. I turned and left the room without another word.

As I marched up the stairs to the second floor, I thought about all the things Richard and I had done — the tour of the house, racing down the hall, sailing on the bay, sharing sandwiches and brownies. Kissing. His confession in the car. All of it — just playacting? Just being "nice" to help his dad make some kind of score?

It was disgusting. It was awful.

And was that what I had been doing? Being "nice" because Mom told me to?

It wasn't. I knew it wasn't. I wasn't just being nice. Richard was perfect. Richard was amazing. What girl wouldn't want to be nice to him?

And he wasn't like that, like what my mom said. He was funny and charming. And real. He wouldn't just pretend to like me. Would he?

I felt sick in the pit of my stomach, like I wanted to throw up but never would. I went into the flowered room, closed the curtains, shut off the lights, and curled up under the covers.

Sammy woke me. The room was dark, but I knew it wasn't late yet. The clock confirmed it was only just dinnertime.

I had dreamed. I remembered just a snatch. Looking in a mirror and not seeing my face. A voice — maybe Nanga's — saying, "No one's in the mirror."

Sammy's pleading chased the fragments from my brain. "Don't you want anything to eat, Sarah? We ordered pizza."

He sounded so wistful, so bereft, I almost got up and went with him.

Almost. But not with my mom down there.

"I'm not that hungry tonight. Listen, buddy, will you do me a favor?"

"Uh-huh."

"You have to keep a secret."

"I can keep a secret. I'm a good secret keeper."

"I know you are, Sam. You're an excellent secret keeper. That's why I'm asking you."

"Tell me, Sarah."

"I'm going exploring with Jackson tonight. I think I know where there's a secret passage. And if we find it, I promise we'll take you through it. But Mom can't know I'm going. Right?"

"Right."

"So I want you to tell her I have a bad headache and I went to bed already. Then watch TV with her and sleep downstairs in Gramma's big bed. Okay? We got a deal?"

He nodded with big eyes. "We got a deal."

I quietly got ready for the night's adventure: hooded jacket, gloves, boots — everything I could think of to make myself spider-proof. I figured if I tucked my sleeves into the gloves, my pants into the boots, and my hair into the hoodie zipped up to my chin, the only spider-accessible skin I'd have left was my face. And I'd just have to watch out for my face.

The best thing about a house with multiple staircases is it makes it hard for your parents to keep track of you. Ten minutes before I was supposed to meet Jackson, I headed for the conservatory. Down the stairs, out the back, a quiet trip across the stone paths. Once I got past the windows to the rear gallery, I turned on Sam's flashlight. I veered right toward the entrance to the maze.

Jackson was already there, waiting for me. "I'm glad you got my message," I said. "Thanks for coming."

He regarded me with some amusement. "Nice outfit."

I realized, a little belatedly, I must look like a crazy person. "I have this thing about spiders," I explained. "Especially poisonous spiders."

"Well, I think you got it covered," he said, smiling. "Just watch out for your face."

Yeah, check.

I saw he'd brought a tool kit, a crowbar, a shovel, a broom, and a bigger flashlight than Sam's. He was like a damn Boy Scout, I thought, always prepared. Life never seemed to take him by surprise. But maybe that's the way you had to be when you'd been through the kind of things he'd been through.

I wondered if knowing about his condition had changed the way I thought about him. Or treated him. I hoped not. That would suck — to have people always dealing with you like you were made of glass.

"What?" he said.

"Huh?" I said.

"You're staring at me like — I don't know what."

"Sorry," I said. "Thought I — forgot something."

"A beekeeper's mask, maybe? Let's go."

He traded me flashlights and put Sam's in the kit. He gathered up his stuff.

"I can carry something," I said.

"Just carry the light."

I was a little doubtful about finding the path to the center, but I shouldn't have been. Jackson knew the way.

"There's a rhythm — right, skip, right, left, skip, left, right, skip. Then left, skip, left, right, skip, right, and left."

It sounded easy, in theory, but in practice — in the twists of the maze, in the rise and fall of the sloping ground — it was hard to keep track of where you were in the pattern. I kept wanting to turn right when I should have been going left, and sometimes I continued straight past a turn I hadn't spotted. Jackson corrected me verbally, calling me back, turning me around, but after the fifth misstep, he sighed.

"You keep doing this and *I'm* going to forget where we are in the turns. Carry this, okay?" he asked, handing me the broom. He put the crowbar and tool box in one hand and with the other took my flashlight-wielding arm above the elbow to guide me.

I was uncomfortably aware of those fingers on my arm. I held it a little away from my body, so the back of his hand would not brush my side. But he still touched my ribs whenever he guided me to the left. I wondered if he noticed.

I lost all sense of direction as we followed the twists of the maze. We'd started off west, then gone south and east, maybe, before making the last couple of turns. From there, a straight path led to the heart of the maze.

I sucked in my breath.

A little octagonal gazebo stood in the center, gleaming in the light from a three-quarter moon. It was shaped in marble and wrought iron, ringed all around with two stone steps. A delicate stairway climbed up the outer sides to the metal roof, which was girded in railing. The gnarled trunks of old wisteria vines leaned in at four of the vertices, spreading fall-naked branches along the ironwork arches. *In the spring*, I thought, *it must be glorious.*

I mounted the stairs circling up to the roof. Jackson climbed behind me. We stood at the rail, staring. The maze spread out around us and Amber House loomed above, a dark mass against the purple-black sky.

"In May and June," Jackson said, "the hedges bloom with tiny white flowers and the wisteria makes a lavender curtain all around the gazebo. Daffodils poke up between the roots. The whole place hums with bees. And there are a million butterflies."

"It would be a perfect place for a wedding."

Jackson smiled crookedly and nodded in agreement, amused, I thought, to hear me make such a girly observation. Like I was one of those twits who are always tearing pictures out of bridal magazines. "I predict," he said, with his hand to his temple and his voice oracular, "*you* will be married here someday."

I chuckled, relieved he had made a joke of it. "The odds are long against it, Nostradamus."

"Fortunately for you," he said, "I'm not a betting man."

Still a little embarrassed, I looked away again, across the moonlit view. Fresh anger at my mother bubbled up in me. How could she sell this? How could she take it away from Sammy and me? We had a right to be here. I felt — connected — to this place.

I looked up and imagined the generations of my ancestors standing in the windows, looking back at me. If my mother had her way, I would be the last one to remember them. The last one to hear the echoes of their voices.

I felt it like a loss already suffered. But what could I do about it? There wasn't a single thing I could say to change my mother's mind. If she had any idea about my connection to Amber House, it would only make her want to get out even faster. I remembered the hyperexaggerated distaste in her voice when she'd pronounced the word *schizophrenic*. An inherited disease.

I shook that thought off me like a bug.

"Let's look for the tunnel entrance," I said, a little harshly.

"After you," Jackson answered, apparently not offended by my abruptness.

We went down and I put my attention into the task at hand. I walked all around the outer edge of the gazebo, poking at the ground with the crowbar to see if the earth hid a trapdoor or a closed-over entrance. But it all seemed solidly packed dirt. Jackson watched me patiently.

"You gonna help?" I asked, a little indignant.

"Why don't we check inside the gazebo?"

It was a simple open-sided room with a couple pieces of garden furniture and a floor made of large squares of black and white marble. Nothing hidden, all open to view. Jackson bent low and shone his flashlight over every inch of the harlequin tiles. He crouched and said, "You see this?"

"What?" I bent down beside him, trying to spot what he was talking about.

"The grout between the squares here. It's not quite the same color as everywhere else."

He pulled a Swiss Army knife from his pocket and swiveled out a blade. He poked the cement between the marble tiles. It gave away under the blade like chalk.

"This is it," he said, excited.

He got the crowbar. Carefully, he inserted it into the crumbling grout under the edge of the tile. He wedged in a little wooden block for a fulcrum, then pushed the bar back and down, levering up the marble. Sand and chunks of the soft grout sifted down. "Can you hold this?" he asked, indicating the lever. "So I can get a grip on it?"

I took his place. He came around in front of the tile, lifted it out, and set it aside carefully.

We turned the beam of light on the void in the floor. It was filled with rough wood boards. Jackson smiled up at me. "I think if we pull out the other three tiles, we'll have ourselves a trapdoor."

I felt another genuine treasure hunter's thrill. *A secret door. A place other people don't know about. That nobody has entered for decades — maybe not since Fiona did.* Whether or not the diamonds were hidden down there, how cool was it to be able to explore a place like this, full of forgotten secrets? How many people would ever have the chance to do something like this?

When we'd levered up the three remaining tiles, we'd uncovered the iron hardware of a door. Jackson took a can of oil from his kit and wetted the hinges liberally.

"How'd you know to bring that?" I asked.

He shrugged with his mouth. "You said 'trapdoor.' Stands to reason there might be some rusty hinges."

He braced himself with his legs to either side of the door and started pulling on the ring handle, straining so hard that the muscles in his arms and back bulged. Sodden notes of movement sounded all around the edges; the hinges grated. Jackson pulled harder. With a final rasping *pop*, the front edge lifted above the marble tile around it.

Jackson backed up, lifting the door higher. The hinges screeched but gave. The door creaked fully open. An invisible cloud of dank, stale air rose out of the black hole below.

"Okay, I don't want to sound lame, but —" The opening spread at our feet like a pool of ink. I pointed the flashlight down and in. The beam seemed feeble, as if the darkness was pressing against it. I saw the heavy wooden steps of a ladder, what looked like a stone floor. "Yeah. I don't think I can go down there."

Jackson shook his head and grinned at me. "What? You going to let me have all the fun?"

To be honest, I definitely thought he could make this exploratory run all by himself.

"Give me the broom, will you," he said, "and shoot me some light. Please."

He swiped the broom all around the opening, swept off the upper steps on the ladder, and gave the ladder a couple of whacks for good measure, I presumed to chase off any remaining bugs. Then he started down, giving each step an experimental stomp first to make sure it would hold him.

As he descended into the pit with the light, it grew dark in the gazebo. I got out Sammy's little flashlight.

"What do you see?" I called down to him. "What's down there?"

"I think you're going to have to come down and see for yourself."

"You're kidding, right? Tell me what you see."

"Well, for one thing, no webs. I think we're pretty safe on the spider front."

"Really? I can trust you?"

"Yes, you can trust me. No spiders. Really." He made a great show of sweeping down the rest of the ladder. "Okay? Now come on. There's nothing down here that can hurt you."

I sat and swung my feet around to get on the ladder. Maybe I could do this.

Maybe not.

"Come on. Don't be a wimp," he said in a pleasantly taunting voice. "My opinion of you is slipping, coz."

"Oh, well, I can't let that happen," I answered in exaggerated dismay. I took a deep breath and started down.

The walls of the passage were made of mortared stone, the floor of rough granite. It ran off in two directions into a darkness that continued beyond the reach of my flashlight. Water seeped from the sides and ran in a thin stream down the middle.

It gave me the creeps. "Where do the passages go?" I asked.

"I dunno," Jackson said. "That one" — he pointed to my left, in the same direction the water was running — "could go all the way down to the river. The Captain was supposed to be a smuggler. This would be great for that. They built the stone tunnel on the hardrock of the bluff, then filled around it with dirt. Planted the maze on top to hide it. It's a fairly elaborate setup."

I took off my glove, let my mind drift, and touched the ladder. Immediately, I saw people climbing down it, dressed in ragged clothes, their frightened dark-skinned faces looking for hope from the man who stood close by me, holding a lantern.

"Well, I think someone else besides just the Captain knew about it, because this trapdoor was used by runaway slaves. At least once, anyway. Which makes sense. Fiona wrote about her grandmother — my great-great-great-grandmother, I guess. Said she was an abolitionist and used Amber House as a stop on the Underground Railroad. Fiona was pretty proud of her. I think her name was Maeve."

"Yes," he said. "Ida told me about her. Oddly enough, I had a great-great-great-grandfather who helped runaways too. They caught him and killed him."

Even in this, life hadn't been fair to Jackson and his family. Maeve had died of old age, at Amber House. I didn't want to think about how Jackson's great-great-great-grandfather must have died. It struck me that if we ever did find the stupid diamonds, Jackson didn't just deserve to have "a share." After what my ancestors did, he and his family deserved to have them all.

I knelt and touched the stone floor beyond the ladder, seeing men in sailors' garb hauling crates down the long passage. "It looks like you're right about the tunnel being used for smuggling at one point."

He looked at me with interest. "You pulling up another vision?"

"Yeah."

"What's it like?" he pressed.

I thought about how to answer that. "It's not always the same. Sometimes it's like I'm standing in the middle of the past, but I'm invisible to everyone around me. Sometimes, I just get a blurry image, or it's like I'm imagining it. A couple of times I've dreamed I was someone from the past, while I was sleeping. And sometimes I only hear voices."

"Yes," he said, nodding.

I pointed my little flashlight beam up the tunnel leading away from the river and presumably toward the house. "So, no spiders?"

"No," he said, "no spiders." He ushered me past him. "Just keep an eye on your footing, because the rock's a little uneven."

I took his advice and trained my light on the ground, but kept flashing it ahead as well. I wasn't going to walk face-first into a web. Or let anything else surprise me from the shadows. I started to point my flashlight at the ceiling, but he stopped me. "Don't look up."

"What?" I said, suddenly panicky, certain there were spiders everywhere above me.

He caught my hand. "Don't look up," he said again.

I yanked my hand back, gave him my sternest look, and said, "I need to see what's up there."

"Okay," he said, smiling, "but don't forget I warned you."

I pointed my light at the ceiling and peered into the gloom among the roots. There weren't any spiders; he hadn't lied. But the black tar of the ceiling was spotted all over with white blotches. I squinted, trying to see —

"Oh my god!" I shrieked and dropped the flashlight. "Ohmygod, ohmygod." The ceiling was covered — *covered* — with two-inch-long albino crickets. Hundreds of them. Thousands of them.

"Ohmygod," I repeated for emphasis.

Jackson unsuccessfully hid his smile, took my arm, snagged my fallen flashlight, and started me forward again. "They're cave crickets," he explained. "Completely harmless. Stop screaming and they won't fall off the ceiling."

"Ohmygod," I whispered, "ohmygod."

"We're almost there," he said. A wooden door showed in the darkness just ahead.

I reached out and took the latch in my hand.

Sudden daylight filled my vision, and Sorcha was there, the woman in my dream of Amber House. She was looking back at me — no, beyond me — at Liam.

"It's beautiful, my love, everything my heart has ever wanted."

I closed my eyes, pushed open the door of the buried house, and went in.

The room beyond was heavy with dust. The gray coating clearly had not been disturbed for years, perhaps since the beginning of the last century. The little house had been waiting in darkness and silence since then.

I grabbed the large flashlight from Jackson's hand and directed it up at the ceiling. No crickets. Not a one.

With the smaller flashlight, Jackson found an old lamp hanging beside the door. He gently shook it. Its contents sloshed. "Wonder if it will light." Setting the lamp on the floor, he lifted off the glass chimney. "Stand back a little," he warned. He pulled a pack of matches from his pocket, struck one, and held it to the wick. It smoked greasily, then caught. He rubbed the glass chimney against his pant leg before he fitted it back over the flame. When he set the lamp in the dust on the table, the contents of the room came into soft focus.

The table the lamp sat on was simple planks on a square base, with three mismatched chairs around it. Beside them, a massive fireplace, well blackened. In the corner, a rope-strung bed frame rotted with age. At its foot, a simple dresser with its back against the wall and a mirror over it.

On either side of the entrance, I saw the windows that Liam had carefully built into the stone walls more than three hundred years before, now blind with bricks holding out packed earth. On the wall opposite the fireplace, there was a built-in cupboard with thick moldings and a hand-painted design. Beside it, a second door, waiting to be opened.

I gestured at it. "Would you?" I asked.

Jackson lifted the lever handle and tugged. The door creaked open on rusted hinges. I brought the lamp over to reveal what lay beyond.

It was a small space, only slightly bigger than a closet. A child's bed, collapsed in on itself, filled the end of the room. Under another bricked window to my left sat a wooden trunk and a primitive rocking horse, its body a cut log, its legs and neck thick branches. The straggling wisps of real horsehair still hung as mane and tail.

I realized I was afraid to touch that horse, afraid to see the generations of long-dead children who had ridden it in imaginary pastures. I backed away and out of the room.

"Will you search for the diamonds?" I asked Jackson. I noticed I was talking in hardly more than a whisper. It felt . . . unseemly . . . to speak out loud in a place where silence had ruled so long. I thought this must have been the way archaeologists felt when they finally opened an ancient tomb. The world of noise did not come there anymore.

He nodded and got started in the main room, opening drawers and cupboards. It felt like a violation. I didn't want to watch.

Some little flicker of movement caught my eye — it must have been Jackson's passing reflection in the mirror. I went over to the mirror. It was a sweet little thing with a hand-painted flowered border. I wiped the worst of the dust from the glass face with my gloved fingers. The black-specked silvering of the mirror was revealed. I sucked in my breath and made myself look.

Face after face surfaced in the glass and sank away, replaced by others. I waited and watched, and the multitude of reflections drifted back, allowing one image to swim forward: Sorcha's face. Her hands were covering her eyes as Liam guided her by her shoulders to stand directly in front of the mirror. She lifted away her hands and her face lit with delight — the glass, perhaps, was a surprise gift.

Another face swam forward, a little Sorcha-like face, all pert prettiness, frowning as she pulled a comb through her hair.

Another face, a handsome black woman — the woman who'd saved the baby. She was wiping the glass, but paused, seeming to stare for a moment right into my eyes. Another face, familiar to me — a white woman, wan and dreamy, touching the glass and looking beyond it. Then many faces, all dark skinned, this one calm, this one fearful, this one wiping tears away, this one looking in the glass with wonder, as if he had never seen his face reflected back to him before.

Then my mother's young face appeared, her features sad and urgent, her mouth shaping words I could not hear. Why was my mother's face in this mirror? I wondered. Had she been here? Had she also found Heart House?

"Sarah?" Jackson said my name, and the image disappeared. "Something you might want to see."

He had a picture in his hands, an old framed photograph the size of a postcard, of a woman and child from the Civil War era. The little girl was looking back, past her mother's shoulder. She had a mass of curls escaping the ribbon tied around her head, the curls of a Renaissance angel.

"You know who this is?" he asked a little oddly, drawing my attention back to the woman.

"Not really," I told him. "Maybe Maeve — the grandmother who used this place to hide runaways."

"And who's that?" he asked, pointing to the corner.

I looked. There did seem to be a third person there, back under the tree. I rubbed, working the glass clear. The figure was indistinct, blurry — another "ghost" caught in the long exposure times of early photography. He — no, *she* — seemed strangely dressed, maybe even wearing pants. I could not see, could not make out her features —

"I think I know who it is," Jackson offered quietly.

"Who?"

"I think it's you. Isn't that your shirt?"

No. I shook my head in utter denial. It could *not* be me. My skin crawled. I looked again.

I had a shirt like that, a baseball tee, and the figure looked like she was wearing jeans. *Jeans!* It might have been me. Maybe. But how? And when? I had never been back to that time that I remembered. And was the little girl in the picture *looking* at me?

It was the creepiest feeling, seeing that ghostly image in the old tintype, as if part of me had lived and died a long time ago.

I stuffed the picture in my jacket's pocket.

"How do you think —" he started.

"It's not me," I said flatly, closing the subject. "Let's get out of here."

He looked as if he wanted to say more, but thought better of it. Without thinking, I reached down and grabbed some of the things he'd taken out to set them back in the trunk they'd come from.

It was a mistake. Almost instantly I was carried to another place and time.

I saw the doll first — the doll now dangling from my hand — held tightly in little arms. It was held by a sweet-faced child, about six years old, her soft curls falling in masses around her face. *Like a Renaissance angel*, I thought numbly. She was the girl in the photo Jackson had just shown me. She was dressed all in snowy cotton and her feet were bare. She turned away from me and ran down the tunnel. The doll fell from her hand onto the earth as it fell from my hand onto the floor.

I had seen this child from the past before. I had seen her at the entrance to the maze.

She was the little girl in white.

Chapter Seventeen

Who — *what* — was this girl? When I'd seen her in the maze, she'd seemed to interact with me, see me, respond to me. Not like she was locked in the past. Not like the woman in the attic. So what did that make her?

Nanga had insisted that there were no ghosts at Amber House — that I didn't have to be afraid. But what if she was wrong? What if she was just absolutely *wrong*? Maybe Nanga didn't know all of the house's secrets. Or what if she was lying?

And if there were ghosts in Amber House, was I safe? Was Sammy safe? *Maybe*, I thought, *we* should *get away from this place.*

I didn't know what to think. I just wanted out of that blind, silent, buried house.

Jackson must have sensed that I did not want to talk. He put the rest of the things in the trunk, closed all the doors and drawers and cupboards, and blew out the lantern. Then we left Heart House, all without speaking. He shut the trapdoor and set the tiles back in place. The opening was still marked by the missing grout around those four squares, but Jackson said he would find something to refill the cracks. Somehow it still seemed important to keep it a secret.

We said good-bye at the maze entrance.

The house was dark when I slipped in through the sunroom doors and up the front hall stairs. Sammy and Mom were asleep. I was exhausted. I was learning in this place that adrenaline crashes left me nearly catatonic. Thinking all this through would have to wait till the morning.

A new day's sunlight steaming benignly through my window calmed the prior night's fears somewhat. I thought about how I'd felt when I'd seen the girl in white — I hadn't had any sense of danger. My every instinct had been to meet her, to speak to her face-to-face.

As I brushed my teeth, I remembered something I'd seen written in Gramma's pages. I went back to my room and took them out of the back of Fiona's history.

I scanned the notes, looking for the entry. I found it near the bottom of the stack. The writing was smudged and partly illegible.

> *I see — girl everywhere. She is dressed — a ——tgown, and her dark hair hangs loose around her — I look and look, thinking if I could only meet her — I could lead her out of the —e. Sometimes, I think I even see her in the —r.*
>
> *Where are you? When are you?*

When are you, I repeated in my head. Only at Amber House would such a question be asked. Was this entry about my little girl in white? Had Gramma searched for her too? Was this Fiona's Persephone?

"Sarah!"

That was Mom. I tucked the book back in the drawer and went down.

My mother was moving briskly, as usual, some task at hand. "I'm packing up Gramma's clothes and medical equipment. I'd like to get them to the Salvation Army drop tomorrow so they'll be gone before the party."

No doubt she wanted help, but I wasn't feeling particularly supportive. She might not have even noticed the ugly things she'd said the day before, but I hadn't forgotten. I just stared at her.

Mom faked a smile. "Thanks for leaping right in and volunteering, but fortunately, I can handle the job myself. What I'd like for you to do is keep an eye on Sam for me. Keep him out of trouble. Okay?"

"Sure," I said.

"Great," she said. "Feed him something, then go outside for a change."

Yes. Outside. Sunshine. Fresh air.

I found Sam in the kitchen, ready for his lunch, my breakfast. Feeling generous, I went all out — I cut up banana in our bowls of toasted oats.

As we slogged through our cereal, I told Sam about my great idea. "I didn't know this till yesterday, bud, but we have horses."

"Horses? I *love* horses. Are they live ones?"

"Yes." I laughed. "Live ones."

"Um, Sarah, are horses scary?"

"No, they're not scary. But they're pretty big."

"Yes, very big. Horses are very big. But not scary."

"No," I agreed, "not scary. But you have to be careful because they are so big. So you have to listen to me and do what I tell you to do, okay, Sam?"

"Yes," he said. He jumped from his chair. "Let's go!"

"Finish your cereal first."

He shoveled several large spoonfuls into his mouth. Milk dribbled down his chin. He held out his bowl. "Fimmished," he said around a mouthful of soggy oats.

I nodded tolerantly. "Chew." I scooped up a couple more bites as he sat back down and ground his mouth's contents to a pulp. He swallowed hugely, several times, then opened his mouth for me to inspect. "Good enough, Samwise."

He jumped up again, looking at me expectantly.

I cleared the bowls to the sink. “Let’s grab some carrots for the horses,” I said.

“Carrots?” he said. “I *love* carrots.”

“So do horses, bud.”

According to a map in Fiona’s book, Amber House’s stables and barn were on the northeast side of the property, which might explain why I had never noticed them. If Gramma had indeed once been a world-class rider, she must have thrown out all her ribbons and trophies, because I’d never seen even one of them. But she’d kept the horses. Mom said she wouldn’t be without them.

Sam and I had to hike back through a cover of trees to find the tidy stone-and-board stables, white painted and wood shingled. I unlatched the outer door and swung it wide.

A woman walked in before me, down the wide interior hall. She wore a perfect riding outfit: black boots, jodhpurs, white blouse and black vest, a riding crop in her hand. Her red hair swung in a ponytail. It was Fiona. Who had evidently taught her little girl — my grandmother — how to ride.

I heard a man’s voice. “Let’s skip the ride and find some other way to amuse ourselves, shall we?” The man caught Fiona by the arm and swung her around. She brought the crop down smartly against his thigh. He released her. “Ow,” he said, rubbing the spot.

“Behave yourself, Edward, or I shall do it again.” She smiled archly and disappeared into a stall with the man at her heels.

Gone. *Thank God.*

“Gimme the carrots,” Sam shouted. “I see a horse.” He tugged at the bag in my hand.

A large roan had stuck its head out of its stall. Sam worked a carrot free of the plastic and started for the horse. I snagged him by the collar and pulled him back.

"Hey!" he protested.

"What did I say to you back in the kitchen?"

"Finish your cereal?" he offered.

"I said horses are big, and you had to do what I said."

"That's right," he said.

"So, listen to me. Horses have great big teeth. You have to be careful when you feed them carrots or you could lose a finger."

"Lose a finger? Where?"

"The horse could bite it off."

"Horses eat people?" Sam was incredulous. "I don't like horses, Sarah. I don't."

"No, bud, they don't eat your finger on purpose. But they might do it by accident if you don't hold your fingers flat."

Sam dropped his carrot and put his hands very flat on the front of his pants.

"No, Sam, I mean when you feed them carrots." He didn't move. "Look, Sammy," I said, picking his carrot up off the ground, "I'll show you. Come over here —"

"Nuh-uh."

"Sam, I promise you it'll be all right." I moved him by his shoulders, positioning him closer to the roan but well out of reach. He still had his hands pressed on his pants. I snapped off a piece of carrot and put it on the palm of my hand. "See how I'm holding my hand flat while I give the carrot to the horse?"

"No, no, Sarah!" Sam's eyes were tragic.

I held my hand out to the roan, who leaned down and gently felt for and grabbed the carrot chunk with her velvet lips. Then I showed Sam my hand, all five fingers intact. "You see?" I said. "You get it?"

"I get it."

"You want to try it?"

"Nope."

"You sure?" I asked. I broke off another chunk of carrot and held it out to the roan, who grabbed it up with lips covered in orange-colored slobber. I pulled back a hand smeared with carrot saliva. "Ew."

"I'm sure, Sarah."

Sam and I settled on dropping one carrot into the feed bin in every occupied stall — five in all. The stalls were well mucked out, with fresh straw spread in each, and hay in the bins. I wondered who did all the work, until the door on the far end of the stables opened, and Jackson walked in.

"Jackson!" Sammy shouted.

I said, "Hey," smiling, but wondering, not for the first time, why he didn't seem at all surprised to see us. It gave me an unpleasant feeling of being watched, of being studied. Was there something else he wanted from me? Something besides the diamonds he didn't seem to be looking for all that hard?

"Not in school?" I said.

"Early release." He walked to the roan, who pushed her head against him. He scratched her along the chin line.

"Why did my grandmother keep these? They must have cost a lot of money. She didn't still ride, did she?"

"No," he said. "I never saw Ida ride. But she spent a lot of time with them. And she taught me to ride. I think —"

He'd stopped, as if words had failed him. "What?" I prodded.

"She was sad, you know? The sadness of having no one left to be connected to, of being — unmoored. Everyone is gone. And there's silence where there should be voices." I thought of Jackson's parents. He went on. "I think these horses were a kind of a last living link to that lost connection, to the people she'd loved." He shrugged the smallest bit and seemed a little embarrassed. "I don't know if I said it right. Does that make any sense?"

"Sure," I said. "Sure. Everyone needs someone to be connected to, or you drift. That's why I ended up glad Sam decided to drop into our lives." I reached out and pulled my little brother into a quick hug.

Jackson regarded me. "You're connected," he said, "to more people than you realize." He shifted his attention. "Sam, I got something to show you. Come on."

Sam didn't need any further invitation. He walked carefully down the middle of the aisle, his hands still tight on his pant legs. Jackson lifted his eyebrows. It made me laugh. "Long story," I said.

Sam and I followed him to the barn beyond the stables. Straw bales formed geometric hills in the half loft, and an old tractor took up most of the space below. The shafts of light that poked through holes in the board siding sparkled with rising dust motes turned to gold. Jackson was crouched down beside a watering trough. "Come look." Sam and I peered in. The trough was lined with hay, and, nestled on top of it, a calico cat curled around four tiny kittens.

"Ohhhhh," Sam said. "I *love* kittens."

We stayed awhile. Sam named each kitten and learned from Jackson how to make them chase a twitching straw. Jackson sat there easy, his legs stretched out before him, patient with Sam's enjoyment. And I told myself, I had to be crazy to think this guy was trying to get something from us underhandedly. It just wasn't possible. How could anybody be more open and honest than Jackson?

On the way back to the house, I spotted a lump on the grass under the oak with the tree fort in it. "You go in, bud," I told Sammy. "I'll be there in a minute."

The lump was Heavy Bear, still damp from spending a night out on the lawn. "What are you doing out here?" I asked him.

I checked out the foreshortened ladder again, trying to estimate how many rungs would have to be added to get up to where the old rungs still hung on the tree. I was craning my head up, looking at the fort, leaning against the tree, when I heard voices.

"Did you bring everything? Give me the bag."

"*Me* the bag, Annie."

"No. I'm bigger. I'll carry it."

An eleven-year-old version of my mother walked around the tree, which now showed a complete ladder. She was followed by another girl who looked like a smaller twin. Same eyes, same mouth, same hair.

"You go first, Maggie," my young mother directed, and the littler girl started up the tree.

I yanked my hand off the bark. The two girls disappeared.

Maggie, I thought, outraged. *Magpie*.

My mother had — a younger sister. Someone I had never even been told about.

I felt like I had just lost part of my solidity. I didn't know who my mother was. Not at all.

And what had happened to my aunt? Why hadn't anyone ever mentioned her name? Was there something wrong with her, something bad? Was there some kind of family feud? Why pretend like she'd never existed?

Why were there so many secrets in this place?

Chapter Eighteen

I marched toward the house, fully intending to have it out with Mom right then, fully intending to get some answers. But I met her coming out the door, car keys in her hand.

"Where are you going?" I blurted. "I need to talk to you."

"Well, you can't right now," she said. "I've got appointments, errands to run. I'm already late. I'm taking Sammy with me. Sam?" she called back into the entry. "Sam!" Sammy trotted into view. "Hurry now. We'll get some ice cream. How does that sound?" She nudged Sam before her out the door and down the front steps as she groomed hay from his hair. "What on earth have you guys been doing?"

"Hey!" Sam said to me as he went past, reaching. "You found Heavy Bear." I handed it off. That reminded me of the treehouse, and Maggie, and I opened my mouth to stop my mother, to make her give me some answers — but how would I explain what I learned?

They drove away, leaving me with the same questions I'd started with.

I wasn't in the same lighthearted mood I'd been in earlier, but it wasn't enough to make me call Richard and cancel our riding date. I went inside to get ready.

My riding outfit wasn't going to be quite as snappy as my great-grandmother Fiona's. No jodhpurs, no vest, and no little black riding crop. But I did have the brown riding boots, and I liked the ponytail idea. By the time I got my hair slicked into a high-placed rubber band, I was looking pretty good. Not Fiona gorgeous, but cute enough.

Richard rode down the driveway right on time. He looked professional in worn brown boots over khaki pants, and a white shirt with cuffs rolled to his elbows. I admired how it set off his tan. His horse was a dappled gray, massive. When I came out, he freed one foot from the stirrup and held an arm down. "Get up behind me," he said. "No sense walking." I took his arm and lifted my toe to the stirrup. He hoisted me up easily.

The slope of the saddle pushed me tight against him. He wrapped the arm I had given him around his waist and nudged the horse into a lope. I could feel the muscles of his legs all along the inside of my thighs. I felt embarrassed. Among other things.

I was glad it was a short ride to the stables.

Richard sized up the horses for me since I was completely horse ignorant; he said the bay had the most spirit and the roan seemed the gentlest.

"I'm about as good a rider as I am a tour guide," I told him.

He laughed and said, "Ride the roan." He saddled her and held her steady as I swung myself heavily into the saddle. "I'm always surprised by the things that come out of your mouth," he told me.

"Yeah?" I wasn't sure that was a good thing.

"Yeah. You don't shovel a lot of B.S., you know?"

"I find I'm not really smart enough to shovel a lot of B.S."

He laughed again. "I don't think it has anything to do with how smart you are, Parsons."

We rode to the eastern border of the property, following a shaded, soft-earth riding trail. At the fence, he pulled up alongside me and leaned over, putting his arm around me to point, so I could follow his sight line. What I saw was nicely sculpted arm muscles under golden skin dusted lightly with freckles, like a brown speckled egg.

"There's my house," he said.

I readjusted my focus. The hills sloped down across the neighboring property — another McMansion — to the wooded estate beyond, with its house above the river. Mostly I saw roof and chimneys above a thick guard of trees. But I could just make out brick walls, white-shuttered windows, some heavy columns. The front of the house I had seen from the river.

"It's a beauty," I said.

"Yeah, it's one of the old ones, even though it's only been in my family about twenty years. Mother picked the property. She wanted to get as close to Amber House as possible. I think she thought there was something magical about the dirt around here." His voice seemed to grow the slightest bit tight when he said all this, but maybe I was just imagining it.

"Why was she so interested in the place?"

"I don't know. I got the sense she thought she should have been living there." He shrugged.

"Kathryn said she didn't like my mother much," I said. "Although, believe me, I can understand why *any*one might have a problem liking my mother." I thought again of Maggie.

"Yeah, sorry, she didn't like your mom." He was remembering. "You know who else she didn't like? That guy who lives on the edge of the estate. The dude you raced with."

"Jackson?"

"Yep. For what it's worth, and mind you, this is coming from my lunatic mother, but she told me once — how'd she put it? Something like, he was dangerous, or — there was something wrong with him, he shouldn't be here."

"Jackson? Dangerous?" I shook my head. I couldn't see it.

"He seems a little dangerous to me, Parsons," he said, smiling. "Hanging around you all the time. Should I be jealous?"

Jealous? I liked the sound of that. But I was a little stumped how to answer. So I just gave him my best Fiona-brilliant smile, kicked my heel into the roan's side, and leapt away. He nudged his horse to a canter and followed after.

We crisscrossed the eastern half of the property for about an hour. When my feet finally touched soil again, my legs felt oddly disjointed — full of pins and needles, and not under my control. I started to collapse, but Richard managed to get beneath me and catch me around the waist.

"Whoa, Parsons, you look like you've been hitting the sauce." He pulled me upright. I grabbed hold of my horse's saddle. The prickly feeling grew more intense, then began to subside.

"You going to be able to walk home, or do I have to carry you?"

Me, cradled in those sculpted arms, my fingers twined around his neck, looking up into his baby blues. "Tempting offer," I said, "but I think I got it."

He laughed out loud. If he was only pretending to like me, he was doing a pretty good job of it. It made me mad my mother wouldn't just let me take him for what he seemed.

He unsaddled the roan, brushed out her saddle marks with a metal comb, and put her back in her stall. He led his horse forward. "Shall we ride back to the house?" he asked.

I hoped I wasn't blushing, but it felt like I was. "Not getting me back on a horse again today, Hathaway."

So he led his gelding on the walk back. "What time should I pick you up Friday?" he asked when we reached the front drive.

"Pick me up?"

"Didn't your mom mention? They want you in Arlington for a final fitting on your dress. My dad volunteered my taxi services."

"Oh, God, I'm sorry —"

"Wouldn't do it if I didn't want to. It'll be fun."

"Yeah? Ever been to a dress fitting before?"

"I am a man of vast experience, but no dress fittings, no."

"Me either, but it doesn't sound as fun as, you know, a trip to the dentist."

"We'll find some trouble to get into, I promise."

Trouble, I repeated in my head, kind of liking the sound of it.

My mother was turning in off the main road. Richard glanced her way, reached up and tucked a stray hair behind my ear. He grinned. "Any time you feel like riding double again, Parsons, give me a call."

This time I knew I turned pink — my cheeks were burning. As he mounted his horse, he said, "Nine thirty on Friday, okay?"

Oh, right, I remembered, *Richard, genius of class scheduling, has Fridays off.* I smiled, nodded. "Okay," I said. Then he set off at a trot, posting elegantly. He even remembered to wave to my mother as she drove past.

Practically perfect, I thought, shaking my head. *I could get used to that.*

Mom, in her perverse bipolar way, asked if I'd had a good time and seemed pleased when I nodded noncommittally. *Don't like him, don't trust him, but enjoy yourself, honey.*

She and Sam had brought home Mexican food, or what passed for it in this part of Maryland. It was just barely edible. All during the meal, I mentally tried out ways of asking Mom about Maggie, but I suspected she'd demand source material — "Where did you hear that name?" — and then what would I say? I would have kind of liked throwing in her face everything I had learned about her past, but I wasn't ready to leave Amber House just yet. I kept it inside.

Mom went back to her party plans and Sam went to the TV. I put leftovers in the fridge and got myself a bowl of ice cream. A big bowl. With hot fudge sauce. And whipped cream. And one of those disgusting red cherries that I used to eat ten or twelve of, plain, out of the jar.

Jackson tapped on the glass in the back door.

I held up a finger — "one minute" — got out a second bowl, scooped half of my as-yet pristine sundae into it (including the cherry), and stabbed a spoon into the mess. I went to the door and handed Jackson the larger half. "You just saved me," I said.

He shoved a big spoonful into his mouth and said around the melting ice cream, "Anytime."

We sat on the stone step and worked on the sundaes.

"You ever hear anything about Maggie?" I asked as casually as I could.

He swallowed a mouthful before he answered. "Nope," he said. "Should I? Who is she?"

I couldn't bring myself to say it: *The aunt my grandmother and mother never told me about.* Maybe there was a good reason she was a family secret. Maybe something shameful. I shrugged. "Just a name I saw in Fiona's notes."

"Don't know her." He scooped his last spoonful from the bowl.

I bet myself that Rose knew about Maggie.

Jackson took my bowl, stood, and put both bowls just inside the door. Then he reached down to give me a hand up. "Walk with me for a minute."

"Sure." We ducked through the kitchen and out the back. He turned onto the stone path toward the conservatory.

"I wanted to ask you earlier, but I couldn't with Sam there — are you all right? 'Cause you seemed a little shook up last night."

I mulled over how to answer that, what to say, what not to say. I finally gave up and just spilled my guts. Like I always did. "I've seen a little girl running around here," I explained, "who seems to see me. Last night, I realized she's the same girl as in the picture you showed me. Not the blur in the background — the one being held by the woman, who I'm guessing must be Maeve."

"So you think you're seeing a child from the 1860s. And you think she sees you?" He chewed on that thought. "How could that be?"

"Well, I think she's a ghost. And she's haunting me. I just don't know why."

"You don't sound frightened."

"I guess I'm not. Yet."

He looked as if he was going to say something, then changed his mind. "Will you make me a promise?"

"What?"

"Promise you'll tell me if anything gets frightening. Seems like you're going through this all by yourself, and you've got to have somebody you can talk to."

He was right. I did need someone to share my experiences with, someone I could trust. But thanks to my mom, there wasn't anyone who quite fit the bill.

"I promise," I lied. Then, "Thanks."

He smiled. "No problem."

"There's something else you could help me with, if you wanted to. I want to get up in that old tree house in the oak out front, but the ladder is missing its first ten feet of rungs. Can we rig something up? It'll have to be sometime when my mom is out, but she's got a lot of errands, getting ready for the party."

"We'll make it happen."

"I've got to find some time to take Sammy down into the secret tunnel too. I promised him last night, in exchange for him covering for me."

Amusement filled his eyes. "You going to face those crickets all by yourself?"

"Well, unless you wanted to come with us?" I said hopefully.

He nodded. "More than anything."

I smiled. "Liar."

"Not me," he said. "I may keep a few secrets, but I always tell the truth. Can you stick your head into the conservatory? I have something I was supposed to give you."

He opened the glass-and-iron door. I stepped inside and he followed. "Ida wanted you to have this. She wanted you to know she thought about you even when you weren't around." He reached behind a couple of potted ferns on the nearest shelf.

He pulled out a fantastic silver and gold mask. Small, edged around with gold feathers tipped in gold dust. It was attached to a handle, but looked like it could be detached and tied on as well.

"It's perfect with my dress for the party," I said. "I wonder how she knew."

"I never wonder how any of the women of Amber House know the things they know. You just do."

I smiled. He had just made me a member of a long, exclusive, and completely nutty sisterhood. A woman of Amber House.

"See you tomorrow," he said, and departed.

I headed up the conservatory staircase to the second floor — easier to avoid my mother by that route. My legs complained every step of the way. I was going to be stiff in the morning.

At a mirror in the hall, I stopped to see how the mask looked on.

And heard a snatch of laughter. I sucked up my nerve and opened the closest door.

A woman in a gauzy dress, wearing my mask, stood facing the fireplace, holding a champagne flute. She drained her glass, then held it out for a refill. A man scooped up a bottle from a bucket on a stand and poured.

He set the empty bottle on the mantel, slid in behind her, and untied the mask, letting it fall to the floor. Then he started kissing the back of her neck. She turned to face him — it was Fiona. He took her hands and maneuvered her around, easing her down onto the small sofa. I could see his face now, smiling that same square smile that I'd seen on the senator, and on Richard.

Fiona leaned back against the arm of the sofa, and the man bent over her to resume kissing her neck. Her head tipped back. She looked toward the door. Toward me.

"I know you're there," she whispered.

The air left me. I felt impaled. A moth on a pin.

"You're watching, aren't you?" she said.

"What, honey?" the man said, not stopping, slipping the shoulder of Fiona's dress down to reveal bare skin.

"It's all right," she said to the door — to *me*. "Sometimes I watch too."

I gasped. And backed up. And slammed the door shut.

Could she see me? Was she just talking to me?

What was going on here? I'd been able to cope with the whole echo thing — just barely. But if the past wasn't going to *stay* in the past . . . First the little girl, now this lunatic woman *talking to me.*

I forced my feet to move, down the hall, down toward my room. Only, I acknowledged to myself, it wasn't my room. It would never be *my* room. It belonged to the others. All those others. There was no safe place in Amber House.

My face — my head — was hot. I was ashamed and embarrassed, by someone who had been dead for decades. Who was that man who looked so much like Richard? Was that why I had watched? To see what it would be like to let Richard kiss me like that?

And for the first time it occurred to me — would someone be watching me someday, here in Amber House? Would someone see me mooning over Richard? See me arguing with my mother? See me licking the traces of whipped cream off my pie plate?

Maybe that's why Mom wanted to sell the house. Maybe she knew all about the echoes. Maybe she didn't want to be one. Maybe I didn't either.

I switched the light on, took out the old tintype Jackson had found in Heart House, and looked at it again. I pulled out Fiona's book and flipped to the late 1800s. I found the two clear figures, in an almost identical photo, identified as Maeve Webster and her adopted daughter, Amber. The text said Amber had died when she was seven. My sweet-faced ghost.

I touched the blurry figure in the tintype. Perhaps that *was* me in the photo. I hadn't ever experienced an echo of Amber and her mother, but perhaps sometime in my future, I would find a way back to that past, and the camera would capture me then — my spirit caught on film, the way they say ghosts sometimes are, the light-sensitive chemicals reacting to the spirit's energy. And if a camera from the past could sense the presence of my energy, perhaps a person — like Fiona — could sense it too.

I didn't understand the way it worked. When I saw an echo, was the past here with me? Or was some part of me in the past? Or both? Or neither?

The nun who taught my First Holy Communion class used to tell us that God existed outside of time, that time was just our way of perceiving things. That if you could see the way God sees, you would know that everything existed all at once. There was no past or future.

I turned out the light and dressed for bed in the dark. I felt safer in the darkness. Invisible. I fell asleep still thinking about people watching me, thinking that the eyes in Amber House were kind of like the eyes of God, knowing every failing.

Except God could forgive.

Chapter Nineteen

I sat in the center of the web, spinning my hair into silk, attaching my thoughts to each thread and casting them out from me, bait to catch hungry crabs. A thousand tiny spiders attended me, drifting their filaments over me, a blanket of soft, warm snow, weaving me a silken dress. I looked in the mirror. My face was the face of the child in white. And I thought, I always get the creepy fortunes.

Then the spiders made me a veil of white, thicker and thicker, so that I could forget my face. So that I could stay forever.

I woke up making that groaning noise you make when you're trying to scream in a dream. My hand was reaching for my blinded eyes. I opened them to daylight. *Thank God.* I shuddered, my body rejecting the feel of all those spider feet.

I'd never had dreams like that before, not till we'd come to Amber House. It seemed like I couldn't escape the voices, the eyes of this place, even in my sleep.

I took my clothes and went into the bathroom to change. Because I'd never had a vision in the bathroom. I was hoping it was, like, against the house's rules.

I went downstairs, moving like an old woman with arthritis, courtesy of my horse encounter the day before. I hobbled into the kitchen for some breakfast and some aspirin.

Sammy was at the table, munching a strip of bacon. Rose was watching him eat. "Like a couple of fried eggs?" she asked me.

"Just gonna have some melon," I said, "but thank you."

"Your mama went into town to get party supplies," Rose said, standing. "You two stay out of trouble while she's gone."

"Yes, ma'am," I said. "Um, Rose?"

She turned back, halfway through the door to the dining room. I looked at that no-nonsense face and could hardly pull together a coherent thought. I finally stammered: "Did you know Maggie?"

She cocked her head, as if she could sense the confusion behind that question. "Yes, child, of course I knew Maggie."

"Well" — I plunged on, knowing that this was probably not something my mother would approve or appreciate, but determined to get the information — "what happened to her? Where is she?"

The look on Rose's face was impossible to describe — a kind of outrage mingled with disbelief, overlaid with a surprising compassion. She walked up, took my hand, and leaned in to tell me, "She's dead, honey. Your mama never told you about her?"

I shook my head.

She nodded appraisingly. "Well, maybe you ought to ask her directly. Don't you think?"

I didn't think so, didn't think so at all, but I nodded. Rose gave my hand a little pat and turned back for the door. "Have a good day," I said lamely.

She smiled — *An actual smile!* I thought — and left. I was still sitting there, contemplating the aunt I could never know, when Jackson poked his head in through the rear door from the gallery. "She gone?"

"I think so. Aren't *you* supposed to be in school?"

"I was called to a higher duty." He stepped in and pulled an umbrella from behind his back. "Cricket protection."

I laughed. "Why didn't I think of that?"

"That's what you got me for," he said, smiling.

"You have breakfast yet?" I asked. "You want something to eat?"

He held his hands up in a *what-can-I-say?* gesture. "I'm a growing boy." He helped himself to an enormous bowl of cereal and started shoveling it in.

I considered the two topics weighing on me. I still wasn't ready to tell him about Maggie. But that thing with Fiona —

"Did Gramma ever say anything to you about people in the echoes being able to see or talk to her?"

"Nope," he said. His chewing stopped. He studied me. "Did something happen?"

I realized he was going to want to know all the particulars. What *exactly* did Fiona say? What *exactly* was Fiona doing? How could I explain to him why I had been standing there, watching? Maybe if I cleaned it up a little —

I wasn't that good a liar. "Nothing happened."

I could see him choose not to push the point. He scooped up the dishes and carried them to the sink. "How about it, Sammy? Time to get moving? Want to see the secret passage?"

"Uh-huh." Sam nodded emphatically.

I got my boots from beside the back door and put on my zippered hoodie. Jackson laughed. "Looking good."

"Shut up," I told him, smiling.

Jackson started into the maze ahead of us, but I stopped him. "Let me see if I can do it," I said.

I found it easier to manage in the daylight, when I didn't have to worry about tripping over roots or missing a turn. *Right, skip, right*, I counted, *left, skip, left. Right, skip.*

"This is great," Sammy said, trotting along beside me.

"You ain't seen nothing yet, bud," I promised him.

We got to the gazebo, and Sam went straight for the stairs. His eyes grew wide as he gazed out over the maze. "I love this, Sarah."

Then Sam and I hunted for the loose tiles. Jackson had hidden them almost perfectly with a filler of white sand. "Look," Sam exclaimed, "I found it, Sarah." His voice dropped to a reverent hush. "The secret door."

Jackson lifted the tiles out and opened the trapdoor. Sam breathed in the gust of air from below. Jackson held out a flashlight. "You want to go first, Sam?"

"Yep," he answered. He took the light, swung his little legs into the hole, and went down without a second thought. Jackson followed. I pulled my zipper tighter, grabbed the umbrella, and made myself join them.

Sam was already trotting after his flashlight beam down the passage, as if he knew the way. Jackson and I hurried to keep up. "A hidden house," he said, as he opened the door and went in. "A whole hidden house." He turned to me and said in a whisper, "No one has been here."

"Not for a long time, bud."

He ran everywhere, opening everything. He pushed back the lid of the trunk in the smaller room. "Oh, look," he said, lifting out a carved-wood toy. "The tiger — but he got old and lost his stripes." He even shined his little flashlight up the fireplace. "I can see stars, Sarah."

Jackson smiled at me. Sam's enthusiasms were infectious.

"Why did they bury this good little house?" he asked finally.

"To hide it from other people," I said, "so they could use it for secret things."

"Oh," he said, nodding, "secret things."

I was glad to leave, glad to step out into the sunlight once more. I didn't ever want to go back to Heart House again. There was no treasure there. Nothing but the past.

Jackson closed the trap and replaced the tiles. "We better get moving on that tree-house ladder, if you want to be done before your mom gets back."

"Me first," Sam cried and took off running into the maze.

"Wait, Sam! You might get lost," I said. But he didn't even hesitate. He made every turn perfectly as I jogged to keep up with him. The little bugger was smart. Smarter than me.

Jackson had stashed some supplies inside the conservatory door: his toolbox, a handsaw, and a stack of two-by-four pieces. We loaded up and headed around to the oak tree in front.

The two guys set to work. For the bottom three rungs of the ladder, Jackson set the nails and let Sam pound them in. "Swing your whole forearm, buddy. That's the way."

Jackson tacked up the next five rungs and had to climb the new steps to fill in the last four feet of missing ladder. Then he climbed back down. "You want to go up first, Sarah?" I nodded. "Make sure you test the old rungs to see if they're still sturdy, before you put your full weight on them." I started up. "You next, Sam. I'll follow you, okay?"

"Okay."

Halfway up the tree, I saw the girls again. My preadolescent mother, and her younger sister, Maggie.

"You okay, Mag?" my mom called down to the little girl climbing just ahead of me.

"I'm okay."

My mother gave her sister a hand up over the edge into the tree house. I climbed up after them. It was a simple structure, not much more than a floor on two levels, a partial roof, and a rail. Not something I would want Sammy to come to by himself.

My aunt took a backpack off and dumped it on the floorboards. Heavy Bear tumbled out.

"Let's go through the rules again, Mag," Mom said. "This is our secret spot."

"Our *secret* spot."

"We only come up here when we're together."

"Only come up together."

"No telling Mommy or Daddy about what we hide up here, ever."

"No telling."

My mother made an X across her chest; Maggie did the same. Mom finished, "Cross our hearts, hope to die."

"Hope to die," Maggie said.

Mom turned to get something from the backpack on the floor behind her. It was the wooden box Matthew Foster had made a century and a half before.

She set it carefully between her sister and herself. "Did you put it in there, Mag? Like the Old One said?"

"I put it in, Annie. Like she said."

My young mother pulled a butter knife out of a metal bucket of junk tucked under a bench. She stuck the blade under a short board and pried it up. Maggie wrapped Matthew's box in a cloth and Mom set it down in the hole under the board. They fitted the board back in place again. "Say it with me," Mom directed.

"Sister Tree, Sister Tree," the two girls recited, holding hands, "keep our secrets safe."

"This is our secret, now," my mother told her little sister. "Nobody must know."

"Nobody must know," Maggie repeated.

"Will you ever tell Mommy or Daddy?"

Maggie shook her head. "Nope," she said, hugging Heavy Bear to her chest.

And that's when I knew. Why she'd sounded so familiar to me. Why she'd been speaking in echoes the whole time.

I snapped out of it, my arms waving wildly, looking for something to hold on to against a sudden wave of vertigo. Jackson caught my hand. He and Sam had both slipped up onto the platform quietly, without breaking me loose from my vision.

"What did you see?"

"My mother and —" I still could hardly say it. I shook my head. "Her sister," I said.

Jackson looked confused. "You have an aunt?"

"Yeah. Evidently no one under the age of forty is supposed to know a thing about her. She's dead now."

"You didn't know about her before? Why didn't they tell you?"

"I have no idea," I said bitterly. "I think maybe because — she was like Sam."

"Like me," Sammy said, nodding happily.

"Only more so," I said.

"How do you know?" Jackson asked.

"She talked by repeating the things my mom said. It's called echolalia. Sammy used to do it."

"Is that why they never told you about her?" Jackson said, disbelieving.

"I don't know. Back then, people used to put kids like that in institu —" I looked at Sam and stopped myself. "I wish I knew what happened to her." I looked at the floorboards. "Do you have your Swiss Army knife?"

"Yeah." He got it out of his pocket and handed it to me.

"Move closer to Jackson, Sam," I said. I folded a little screwdriver out of the knife handle and pried up the short board at the center of the tree-house floor. But there was nothing in the hole.

Far off, I heard the sound of tires hitting gravel. I peered through the leaves to the property's entrance. My mother was home.

"We've got to get down," I said. "Right now!"

Jackson scooted to the ladder. "I'll go first, Sam. Then you come after me as fast as you can." He waited until Sammy got his feet square on the ladder before starting down. Their heads disappeared below the edge of the tree house.

I put the board back in place and shoved Jackson's knife in my pocket. Then I swung my legs over the edge and hurried after them.

Below me, Jackson lifted Sam from the ladder and they crouch-ran into the bushes by the house. Ten feet from the ground, I stepped into that sense of resisting space.

"Maggie," my eleven or twelve-year-old mother shouted as she climbed up past me. "Maggie, you promised you wouldn't come up here without me. I told you we would come together just as soon as I was done painting."

The sweet simple voice. "Not done painting, Annie."

I watched her reach the top. "Maggie, stop! Give me Heavy Bear so I can take your hand. You hear me? Don't move, Mag. Stop! STOP!"

A scream descended on me. And something fell past. Something white and fluttering and fast.

A car door slammed. I felt myself drifting backward, losing balance, and grabbed wildly. I caught a rung of the ladder and hugged it close, pressing myself into the tree bark, quieting a sob in my throat.

"Mommy," Sammy cried as he ran out of the path near the conservatory. "You're home!" He grabbed her by the hand and tugged her toward the door, away from the tree.

"Whoa, whoa, Sam," my mother said. "Let me get my packages. You can help, okay?"

"Okay," he said.

"Where's your sister?"

"Playing hide-and-seek. She hasn't finded me yet."

"Going to be pretty hard for her to find you if you go inside. You think you should go look for her?"

"Nah," he said dismissively. "Sarah always finds me."

They went inside. I scurried down the last ten feet. Jackson took my arm to steady me as I hit dirt. He led me toward the conservatory. "You all right?"

"Yeah."

"I was afraid you were going to fall. What'd you see?"

"My aunt — Maggie. She —" I could hardly get the word out. My stomach clenched around it. Tears started in my eyes. "She fell."

He looked stunned. "Off the ladder?"

I shook my head. "Off the tree house. I — I think she died."

"Oh, God," he said.

Another wave of dizziness hit me. Only this one was coming up from my guts. My stomach knotted again. "I think I'm going to be s —"

I turned toward the bushes. Jackson caught back my hair. I threw up my breakfast.

"Here," Jackson said. He held out a clean white handkerchief.

I hung my head and waved off his offer. "I can't take that."

"I brought it for you."

I took the cloth from him and wiped my mouth. "Thanks," I said, embarrassed. "You must think I'm such a freak."

"No," he said. "No. Sarah," he crouched down a little to catch my eye, "there's something I should have told you a long time ago —"

"Sarah?" My mother had come to find me. She stood there staring, like she had caught us in the middle of something.

"Mom," I said, lightening my voice. "Jackson was just helping me hunt for Sammy."

"Really," she said.

"Yeah. Have you seen him?"

"He's inside. Maybe that's where you should be too. And maybe Jackson should be in school?"

That was my cue to leave. I turned back toward Jackson. "Thanks for your help," I said.

"Any time."

I was going to slink away, but my mother's next words stopped me.

"Jackson," my mother said crisply, "after you've explained to Rose why you're not in school, perhaps you could give me a hand. I have someone coming in about twenty minutes to collect the horses."

I whirled around. "The horses? But — Sammy didn't even get a chance to ride one."

I could feel Jackson's eyes on me, I could feel his concern, but he knew he was no part of this discussion. "I'll be at the stables in twenty minutes, Mrs. Parsons." And he set off for home.

My mother looked at me levelly. "There are horses in Seattle. Sammy can ride one there, if he's so keen on it. I have to get these loose ends tied up."

"Loose ends." Nice euphemism for three hundred fifty years of family history. I don't know what possessed me, but I couldn't let it go.

"You know what, Mom? You have never even asked Sammy or me if we thought it was a good idea to sell this place. And maybe *we* think it should be kept in the family."

"You have no idea what you're saying. It's just an old house full of old stuff. You have no connection to it. You've never even been here before."

“We’re here now. And Sammy and I really like this place. We don’t want it sold to strangers who don’t belong here.”

“Sarah, *you and Sammy* don’t belong here. *I* don’t belong here. We have a life three thousand miles from here. You want us to give all that up?” She stopped me before I could respond. “Even if you had some romantic notion that we could make the move, I could never afford it. The property taxes alone would eat me alive. We’d have to cut this place up and sell it a piece at a time, until there was hardly anything left. Is that what you want?”

“Dad could help —”

“Your father’s got nothing to do with this,” she interrupted me angrily.

“We could afford it if you weren’t spending so much on this ridiculous party,” I shouted.

“The only way I can *afford* the party is by selling the house,” she shot back. “This isn’t open for discussion. Maybe if you were a grown woman with your own income, we could think about keeping the house. Maybe in the best of all possible worlds, we could have done something else. But I’ve got to solve the problem of Amber House today, at this particular juncture in time, and this is the best solution I can come up with. Are we done with this topic now?” she ended in a brittle voice. “You have anything else you want to contribute?”

And I couldn’t think of a thing to say. It looked like Jackson was out of time to find the diamonds; I was out of time to have enough money to save the house. As I turned and walked up the front steps, I thought how ironic it was that in the end, time hadn’t been on Amber House’s side.

Chapter Twenty

My mother seemed in the mood to ask questions and give orders, so I snuck off upstairs before she could do either. I detoured to the bathroom to brush my teeth, then wet a washcloth, went into my room, and lay down on the bed with the cloth over my eyes.

I had just seen someone die. I thanked God I hadn't heard Maggie's body hit the ground. I didn't think I could bear that.

And I'd thrown up in front of Jackson. He'd held my hair and been very nice about it, but I couldn't bear that either. I wasn't quite sure why it mattered so much, but I didn't want Jackson seeing me like that. I pushed the thought off to a corner of my brain and Maggie returned to the front. And the more I thought about her, the more things seemed to make sense, to piece together.

Gramma must have blamed my mother for Maggie's death. Mom had been the older child, and Maggie had been like Sammy, only more so. And maybe they weren't even supposed to go up into that tree house. Of course Gramma had blamed my mother. Only, how could my grandmother have been so cruel? If my mother felt about Maggie the way I felt about Sammy, she would have blamed herself, without anybody's help.

That must have been when my grandmother had started drinking. Must have been. And my mother — that must have been when she'd given up. Stopped painting. Stopped feeling. And maybe started hating Amber House.

That little girl Gramma had written about in her letter at the back of Fiona's book, the one she had been looking for in Amber House's memories — it had to have been Maggie. What would that be like — to be trapped in a place where the child you lost still lived in echoes from the past? Waiting and looking and longing for something that wasn't even a ghost? Just some kind of *recording* of what once was and would never be again. And my mom got to blame herself for *all* of it.

It was horrifying.

Maggie's death had cut them all open, made them bleed, left them scarred. And we were still paying for it all these years later. Me and Sammy. And Dad. And Mom. It wasn't her fault. She hadn't deserved what Gramma had done to her.

For the first time in my life, I felt compassion for my mother.

The sick feeling ebbed away slowly; I thought some fresh air might help.

I went downstairs and slipped out the front door. Through the trees off to the east, I saw the outlines of a truck and large trailer. The guy must have come for the horses. I decided to go watch "my" horses get loaded up.

When I got there, Jackson was leading the feisty bay. He had wrapped a towel over her eyes and was talking softly in her ear. The metal ramp made her shy a little, but Jackson stroked her nose and settled her. She let him lead her up into the trailer. He spotted me and nodded, but continued taking care of business.

It occurred to me then that this might be very painful for him. I had thrown a little hissy fit because Mom was selling animals I thought Sam and I had a right to keep, but Jackson had known these animals for years. He probably loved the horses.

Why hadn't Mom thought to ask him if he'd like to keep at least one?

He led the roan out next, and she walked docilely, nudging her head into his shoulder for a scratch. Jackson was her friend.

I couldn't watch any more. I went back to the house.

My mother came out just as I got there. A new truck had arrived, with GARDEN LIGHTS on the side. Two men in overalls got out to talk to her. Mom had a diagram in her hand of the garden layout. The three of them huddled over the diagram for a few minutes, then the men returned to their truck, hauling extension cords out of the back. And lights. Lots and *lots* of lights.

Mom turned to go in.

"Wait," I said, walking up to her. I realized, as I struggled for the right words to say, that even though I understood my mother a little better, that didn't change her. She was still abrupt and harsh and hard. "About the horses —"

"Look, Sarah, I'm sorry you're upset about the horses, but surely you realize we have to get rid of them."

"Jackson's been taking care of those horses for a long time, Mom. Did you think to ask if he wanted to keep one?"

"You know, those animals are pretty valuable. They come from good stock and are quality brood mares. But leaving the issue of money aside, the answer to your question is yes, I did think to ask. I asked Rose. She thanked me, but she said they didn't have any place to put it and couldn't afford to keep one even if they did. Okay?"

"Oh," I said.

She exhaled a little, like she was calming herself. "Look. I know you don't believe it, but I *do* try. I care about Rose and Jackson. They watched over your grandmother for many years, and it wasn't easy. She wasn't an easy woman."

"I know, Mom."

"I realize you and Sammy may feel differently about this place than I do. I know you might want to keep some things. You should pick stuff out. We can pack it, store it for you till you get older. You should have some things."

Some things, I thought. Pieces of my history that would have no life left in them once they were removed from this place. All the treasures of Amber House would soon be gone, auctioned off. Cut off from what gave them a voice. My throat tightened and I could feel tears behind my eyes, but all I said was, "That would be good, Mom."

She started away, then turned back. She cleared her throat. "There's something else you should know, something I should tell you." She lifted her hands and gripped her temples, covering her eyes for a moment. Then she looked at me levelly. "I sold the boat."

It took me a second to process that. "What? You sold the *Amber*?"

"Yes."

I felt like I had lost a friend. "I wanted her. How could you do that without asking me? Without even telling me?"

"I had a chance to sell it for a good price to someone who saw you win the regatta. We couldn't keep the damn boat. What would we do with it? Sail it all the way to Seattle? Do you know how much it costs to haul something like that across country?"

I didn't know how, but it just kept getting worse. It was like watching a train wreck in slow motion — one collision after another, with no way to make it stop. She shouldn't have gone behind my back. She should have had the decency to tell me up front. Words came growling out of me without my even thinking: "Every time I start to think of you as a human being, you turn around and prove me wrong."

"How dare you speak to me like th —"

"I hate you," I told her. "I'll never forgive you."

I ran away blindly, but found myself turning the corner to the back of the house, to the stone stairs that ran to the river. I went down them two at a time. *If I could find the diamonds*, I thought wildly, *I could make this all better.* Then we'd have plenty of money. I would buy the *Amber* back. I could take her out now, hide her somewhere, maybe at Richard's dock. He'd help me. He'd find me someplace to hide her —

But she was already gone. The dock was empty.

"NO!"

Then I began to sob. It wasn't just for the *Amber*. It was for all of it. I didn't know if I loved Amber House or hated it. But my mother was wrong. It wasn't enough that Sammy and I should be able to keep "some stuff," some little pieces here and there. We should have been able to keep *all* of it. Even though we hadn't grown up here, lived here, it was part of who we were. And we were part of it. It would *die* when we left.

I stood on the empty dock and cried for all of us.

"Sarah."

It was Jackson.

I stumbled toward him and he opened his arms and let me rest there, against his chest. I could feel the scars beneath his shirt, stretching over the frame of muscles, and it made me cry even harder. Life sucked, you know? He'd been scarred for life, his parents killed, when he was too young even to remember. And what about Maggie, who'd backed herself into a foolish accident that never should have happened? And what about Gramma, and my mom and dad, and Sammy? What about me?

I wept until Jackson's shirtfront was wet, and he just stood steady, his arms wrapped around me, his cheek on my hair. "It'll be all right," he told me.

I quieted finally, and he fished another clean handkerchief from his pocket. He lifted my chin and blotted my tears, then handed it to me.

"I can't keep taking these from you," I said.

He shrugged with his mouth. "Brought it for you. Blow your nose."

I did what I was told. I felt a little better. "She sold the *Amber*."

"I know. I'm sorry."

"I'm sorry about the horses."

"They'll be fine," he said. He pulled a brass cleat from his pocket. "Took it off the *Amber* before they came for her. Thought you might like to keep a piece."

I took it in my hand and heard the sound of wind and waves. "Thank you."

"You okay?"

"I don't want to leave here."

"Never can tell how things will turn out."

I smiled sadly. "I'm pretty certain."

"Didn't know you could predict the future." He smiled back.

I started to answer him, but he laid a finger across my lips, hushing me. He touched the corner of my eye — catching a last teardrop — then trailed his fingertips down my cheek. I saw such longing in his face, I was struck silent all over. His hand slid behind my neck, his other hand along the line of my jaw.

He stepped in close to me, almost touching, so that I could sense the warmth of him from my toes to my chin. His thumb ran across my lips, feeling them as if they were the softest, sweetest thing.

I started to tremble somewhere deep inside, beneath my heart. I didn't understand.

He bent his head down, parted my lips with his thumb, brought his mouth close to mine. I closed my eyes. I could feel his breath on my skin, cool and warm. His nose touched mine, and he inhaled deeply, breathing me in.

Everything in me rose, a current lifting toward that breath. I waited.

But he stepped back, releasing me, his hands dropping to his sides.

"I have to tell you something," he said thickly, looking away.

"Tell me."

"I'm afraid to. I'm afraid to tell you."

"Tell me," I said again.

"I —" He looked pained. But he had to go on. "I have a gift too, Sarah. Like yours."

"Like mine?"

"Sometimes, I can see things. Things that haven't happened yet."

A month before, I would have said, *Yeah, sure,* but now, it clicked. *Of course.* "That's why you're always catching stuff."

He smiled faintly. "Yeah."

"But that's so much cooler than seeing the past," I said, confused. Why was this a bad thing? "How much can you see?"

"Mostly just flashes of little things, like the soda getting knocked over —"

"— or someone about to fall off a cliff," I said. "Not such a little thing."

"No." He paused, looking for words. "Sometimes, I can see way down the line, months, even years in advance. The big visions. But all of them are about just one person. Over and over. Ever since I first came here."

He looked me in the eyes, searching. What could he possibly have to say that was so hard?

His jaw clenched. He made it work. "They're all about you. I knew you were coming. I knew what you looked like, how you'd be, before I ever met you."

I remembered him staring at me at the funeral.

"I knew you liked sailing and cherry Coke and The Lord of the Rings."

And you read it, I thought. *The whole thing. Even though you didn't like the books. That's a little — intense.* And as soon as I thought this, I stepped back the smallest bit.

He saw it. He looked lost. Part of me wanted to take his hand, but more of me was listening to this alarm going off in my head. I didn't move.

His mouth tightened, but he went on.

"That isn't even all of it. This is what you have to know. This is what I should have told you a long time ago."

I waited.

"There is no treasure at Amber House."

It took me a second to even process the words. "You lied?"

"It wasn't totally a lie," he said. "There *is* something here that's more important to me than anything in the world. And I — needed you. To stay. For me to find it."

"For you to find *what*?"

The question had come out of my mouth sharply, surprising me. I'd sounded just exactly like my mother. And her voice went on, yammering in my head: *It's time for you to grow up, Sarah. Everyone wants something. Everyone's using everyone else.*

Even Jackson, I thought bitterly. And wanted, absurdly, to start crying again.

He could see it. "I know this sounds bad, but I wasn't just using you, Sarah. It's so hard to explain —"

"I'm still listening." The words were little ice chips.

"When I first came here, when I was about four or five, I had a — seizure. That's what they called it, anyway. But it wasn't really a seizure. It was like the world squeezed down into darkness and I went through this tiny hole and came out in a different place. A place where I was a grown-up, and a doctor — a surgeon. And I wasn't scarred. Because there'd never been an accident. My parents were alive."

He paused. He shook his head a little. "Can you even begin to imagine? I'd grown up with them. I had them. They loved me. I wasn't alone. And I wasn't — damaged. Everything was possible."

Nothing about it was possible, I thought grimly.

"It happened maybe a few dozen times over the years. You have to understand," he said pleadingly, "I could feel that it wasn't just a hallucination or a dream. It was real. I knew that somehow things were *supposed* to have turned out *differently*."

Okay. "What's any of this got to do with me?"

"In that place I saw over and over again, that other future where I was a surgeon, I — we —" He sighed, looked down, then looked me directly in the eyes. "You and I were married."

Another puzzle ratcheted into place. Jackson behaved so oddly around me because — he *loved her*. This other Sarah he saw. I felt this nasty pressure inside my chest. He lied to me to get me to stay so he and I could *what*? Get *married* one day? It was just so crazy. *He* — was crazy.

"You know none of this is possible, right?" I said carefully.

"I don't know. Sometimes it feels like it's this world that's the wrong one, the impossible one."

"I'm sorry, Jackson," I said as gently as I could. "I don't think I can help you. I wish I could, but — I gotta go."

I turned and fled up the stairs. He didn't try to stop me. And he didn't follow.

I felt sick that I had bought into his whole hidden treasure story. That I had been encouraging his — fantasies. His obsession. He wanted me to — what? Make his parents magically back alive again? By marrying him? Because of things he saw when his brain spazzed out electrically?

That went a little bit beyond seeing dead people. Just a tad.

And, of course, there were no diamonds. They were just about as real as the idea of bringing people back from the dead. I wasn't going to be able to save Amber House after all. I laughed at myself. I was going to give him half — the Captain was as much his ancestor as mine. I'd wanted to *help* Jackson. But there was no helping him. I felt completely overloaded. Like I couldn't bear another single thing.

I wished I had never come to Amber House. I wished I didn't know about my aunt and my mom. About Jackson. About any of it. I wished I could pull it all out of my brain. Let the past stay buried.

I reached the top of the stone steps and went straight inside. I climbed the stairs to the flowered room. I pulled out the journals and photos and pages under my bed, and I dumped them all in the trash. I pulled the amber from around my neck and tossed it in on top.

I was done. I just wanted to go back to Seattle.

I kept to myself the rest of the evening. Didn't talk to anyone except Sammy. Didn't let the house talk to me.

Friday I'd be gone with Richard to Arlington; Saturday was the party. Then we would leave. I could make it through two days. It would be hard to say good-bye to Richard, but — come Sunday, I was going home. Nothing could stop me. I was through with this place.

Chapter Twenty-One

That prickly feeling between your shoulder blades — like you're being watched? I had that all Friday morning. I wanted out of Amber House.

The trip to the dressmaker's would take at least two to three hours, and the longer the better, as far as I was concerned. I had no idea why Richard wanted to go through the ordeal, but I was grateful to be escaping. And not just because of the constant sense of eyes upon me. My mother had flipped into all-out party mode, with workers in every part of the house and grounds, which was unbearable. Plus, there was that hypervigilant compulsion to avoid Jackson at all costs.

I waited just inside the front door by the window for the familiar sound of Richard's Beemer, but heard a different motor powering down the driveway. A car pulled up in front of the house right on time — a *stretch limousine*. A black-jacketed driver, inscrutable in mirror sunglasses, came around to open the door for me. I stumbled down the steps, and stood and stared.

Richard poked his head out the door. "Parsons, this is Tully. Tully, Parsons." The driver nodded. "You coming, or what?"

I climbed ungracefully into the cool darkness of the interior. "I thought you were driving," I said.

"Dad said we could take it. Got to do a couple things in D.C. This way we don't have to worry about parking. What, you don't like it, Parsons?"

"I'm pretty sure I like it, Hathaway."

It was my first time in a limo. Turned out, I liked it a lot. The inside was all black leather and highly lacquered wood. I opened all the compartments, sat in every seat. I paused at the well-stocked minibar. "Can we have something?" I asked.

"What exactly were you thinking of?" he said with lifted eyebrows.

"Cherry Coke?"

Richard laughed. "Oh, God, I thought — with all you have to choose from, cherry Coke?"

"You know what, Hathaway? You're right," I said, trying hard to not think of the last time I had indulged my addiction, there in the kitchen with Rose and — "Maybe it's time I got myself a different favorite drink, so I won't be so . . . predictable. How about some of this?" I pulled out a bottle of "all-natural carbonated spring water mixed with the juice of pomegranate and acai berry," whatever that was.

Richard put two glasses — crystal tumblers — on the drop-down table, plunked in ice from the leather-covered ice bucket, and filled both with the drink. He handed me one. Then he held his up, smiling. "I would never call you predictable, Parsons. Cheers."

We clanked glasses. Richard turned on the little TV, popped in a DVD, and we sat back to watch a comedy I'd missed in the theaters. Mostly, though, I watched the people in the other cars and on the streets, all turning their heads to try to see who was in the limo, behind the darkened glass.

The highway we took ran through D.C., where I looked with longing at the green sweep of the National Mall, wishing we could stop and do the tourist thing. Instead we went straight into

Arlington to the dressmaker's studio. It was in an industrial district of warehouses and factories, but the cars parked in front of Marsden Ltd. were all top-of-the-line imports.

We walked through glass doors into a room my mother would have loved. Ultra-modern furniture in simple, clean lines. Carpet so thick you could lose a nail in it. The whole thing done in a muted palette of peach, gold, and burgundy that warmed the indirect lighting to a suitably flattering glow.

A pleasant young man with impeccable grooming entered from the rear as soon as we walked through the door. He gave us both soft, two-handed handshakes as he introduced himself as Stephen. Then he opened a door to the interior.

Richard started through. "Nope," I said, snagging his elbow.

"What," he said in mock outrage, "I don't get a preview?"

"It's a masked party. You're not supposed to know what my dress looks like. I'm supposed to be *mysterious*."

"Oh, of course," he said, as he settled onto a couch. "You're right. You put on a mask, I'll *never* be able to guess which one is you."

Stephen ushered me to a dressing room. I gasped when I stepped through the open door. My dress hung there, glistening in the lights. I hadn't had any idea what it was going to look like — I never could recall the cream version my mother had opted for.

I should have known. The woman had vision.

Done all in a burnt gold, it had a fitted bodice of brocade in an overlapping leaf pattern that skimmed down over the hips. At the neckline and the bottom edge of the bodice, the jags of the leaves had been outlined in tiny opalescent crystals and gleaming gold. The skirt was two tiers of silky tulle layers, all of them finished with a lacy, drifting border of leaves, also detailed in gold.

"What is this?" I said, picking at the edge of a leaf. The gold flecked off on my fingers. "Is it glitter?"

"No, miss." Stephen tugged it gently from my grasp, smoothing it back in place. "It is fourteen-carat gold dust."

"You're kidding, right? Actual gold dust?"

"Approximately one-and-a-quarter ounces. Miss Marsden does not generally use 'glitter' in her designs."

"Right," I said. "And what are these little beads?"

"A mixture, miss. Seed pearls and crystals."

"Right," I said again.

"Everything you need to wear with it has been provided." He backed out the door, closing it as he went.

I opened the boxes sitting on the dressing room's table. Inside them I found a strapless bra, silky panty hose, and a pair of low-heeled satin slippers with long silk ribbons in the exact same color as the gown.

I stripped down and started layering it on. The tights from waist to thigh were woven with an elastic thread that held me firmly. No jiggle allowed. The bra was a minor miracle, providing gravity-defying lift with no straps.

I raised the dress up over my head and swam my way into it through the drifting layers of tulle. I tied the ribbon straps behind my neck in as neat a bow as I could manage.

Out in the central area of the dressing rooms, lights focused on a spot just in front of a wide U of mirrors, where Stephen was waiting for me.

He stopped me short of the mirrors, fussed all around me, untying and retying the bow, smoothing leaves, checking the fit of the waist, flouncing and smoothing the skirt. He circled me a final time, then pronounced the dress "Perfect." Gently, he guided me to the spot under the lights.

And — I could not believe that girl in the mirror was me. I looked like some kind of royalty or red-carpet movie star. The neckline showed off my shoulders and scooped daringly down to cleavage I didn't know I had in the front. My waist looked sculpted.

"Yes," I said, "it is perfect. Thank you. Please tell Miss Marsden I think she's brilliant."

"You are exactly right. If you are ready, Maryanne will pack everything up for you."

I looked once more in the mirror, for the first time actually excited by the prospect of my party. The gown was — magical.

Then I went to the dressing room to change back into myself. That's when I noticed little flecks of shine on the carpet. It looked like I would be trailing fourteen-carat fairy dust everywhere I went.

They brought everything to the waiting room, the dress packed into a very long garment bag that crinkled with the tissue paper Maryanne had layered into it to keep the tulle crisp. The rest of the things went into one pretty shopping bag. Stephen met me at the door to hand me a tiny jar.

"It's a small amount of gold dust for your shoulders, face, and hair. Give it to your makeup artist. He or she will know what to do with it."

My makeup artist? I wondered. *Are you kidding me?* "Okay," I said. "Thanks again for everything."

"You are entirely welcome, miss. Please come again."

Absolutely, I thought. I'd drop by every single time I had a ball to attend.

On the way back, we got off the freeway onto the road that circled the Mall. As we drove past the Lincoln Memorial, I pressed my face up to the window. Richard saw me and laughed.

"Tully, let us out, will you? Pick us up at the other end in about thirty minutes."

I got my chance to gawk at Lincoln's enormous stone presence, then we wandered up the north side of the reflecting pool, checking out the Vietnam Memorial, and coming to a stop at the foot of the Washington Monument. Directly south across the water, the Jefferson Memorial; due north, the White House. We continued east, between the collection of Smithsonian buildings, and on to the Capitol at the very end. It was all history on another scale than the kind that lived in Amber House.

Once inside, Richard was greeted politely by the guards at the entrance and throughout the building. He led me to his father's office, a suite of rooms filled with mahogany desks and leather chairs, brass lamps and oil paintings. He took a packet from the attractive secretary at the first desk, and then we were moving again.

When we hit the parking lot, Tully was there waiting with the door open. He drove us to a neighborhood near the Capitol buildings, all Georgian row houses in brick and stone. "One last errand," Richard promised. He had to pick up some formal wear for his dad and himself at his dad's townhouse.

It was a three-story building in greige stone with white pediments and window framing, black slate shingles, black shutters, black door. It was so exactly correct and respectable looking.

"Come in," he said as he climbed out of the limo. "It will only take a sec. Look around."

The interior of the house suited the exterior, all dark-wood floors and Persian rugs, with fancy, polished antiques. I wandered into the living room. A pair of portraits hung to either side of the fireplace — a stuffy older colonial man and his much younger wife — a beautiful woman with striking golden blonde hair.

"Those are *my* ancestors," he said, "on my mother's side. Mr. and Mrs. Gerald Fitzgerald."

"Oh." I winced. "Really? Poor Gerald."

"Yeah." He laughed. "Quite a name, huh? Come on, I'll give you the quick tour."

Formal dining room, modern kitchen, office for the senator on the ground floor; master suite, library, and guest suite on the second. Richard stopped in at his father's closet and took out a garment bag, then went to the dresser and snagged a set of gold studs that he dropped in his pocket.

"Third floor," he said.

The stairs opened into one large room that ran almost the full length of the house. One end was set up with every toy a growing boy could want: pool table, music system, huge flatscreen, weight equipment. The other end held a king-sized bed flanked by dressers, bookshelves, desk, sofa. I smiled and shook my head. "You've led a deprived existence, Hathaway."

He grinned.

I zeroed in on the silver laptop on his desk. "Oh, God," I said. "Could I send a quick e-mail? Can you believe we don't have Internet at Amber House?"

"I wouldn't believe it if you told me you did." He waved me to the chair. While he packed up his own tux, I sent an update to Jecie:

You will not believe where I am . . . in the bedroom of the Abercrombie model . . . and no, we're not doing anything except picking up some party clothes, you filthy-minded hussy. Some crazy stuff happening around here, but too long a story to tell you now. I really, really am looking forward to coming home.

Richard chose that moment to walk up behind me, so I hit SEND as fast as I could. "What's this?" I said, spotting something beside the computer. A little horse stood on a shelf, carved in miniature and wrapped in hide, its leather tackle perfect down to tiny silver stirrups and bridle.

He seemed a bit embarrassed. "My mom gave me that. It was my first old thing. That's what she called bits and pieces of the past — 'old things.'" He spun my chair around and offered me a hand up. "Let's get out of here."

He grabbed the two garment bags, and we were off again.

It was darkening when we pulled up to Amber House. The last of the day's party workers were pulling out. Richard surprised me by asking Tully to park.

"Can we talk for a minute?"

"Sure," I said.

We got out, and Tully went to the trunk to fetch the bag with my dress in it. Richard slung it over his shoulder and took my hand. He led me to the path that ran around the outside of the conservatory, giving me a chance to marvel at the genius of the outdoor lighting guys.

The plants along the path were dappled with lights. The trees that arched overhead had strands trailing up their trunks and tracing every branch, light sketching them against the darkness. Over the patios in the rear, tiny bulbs hung from invisible wires at random depths, as if bits of stars had floated down to illuminate our personal patch of night.

"Damn," Richard said. "This is going to be some party."

I just nodded my head. That was my mother. If she was going to do something, she aimed for perfection.

He gave my hand — the hand he was still holding, pleasantly, comfortably, remarkably — a little tug and pulled me on, to the door to the conservatory. We wound along the paths till we found the fountain. "Here we are," he said. "Back where we started."

He hung the garment bag on Persephone's hand and sat down on the edge of the pool, patting the stones next to him. "Park it, Parsons."

"Yes, sir," I said, all mock obedience, and sat.

"I know this is early" — he pulled something from his pocket — "but I wanted to give it to you before you got your mountain of presents tomorrow."

My attention was divided between two things: the phrase *mountain of presents* — was everyone going to bring me a birthday gift? — and the beautifully wrapped little box Richard was holding out to me.

"Jeez, Hathaway," I said, "you didn't have to give me anything. You've done so much for me already."

"Open it," he said.

I unwrapped it carefully, untying the gold satin ribbon, untaping and unfolding the heavy star-spangled dark blue paper. I lifted the lid of the little box. "Oh, my God," I said.

"The chain was my mother's," he said, sounding a little shy, "but I picked the charms out for you. I asked your mom what might be good."

I lifted the necklace from the box. The gold chain was made of alternating rectangular and circular links, sweetly old-fashioned. It threaded through a loop holding a pair of leaves, in white and yellow gold. "It's perfect," I said.

"I had it engraved on the back."

I turned the leaves over and held them up to catch the light coming through the glass from outside. *The leaves of life are falling one by one.*

"It's from this poem called the 'Rubaiyat,' by Omar Khayyam."

"It's so beautiful," I said. I put it around my neck. Richard smiled, square, with just a little crooked. He reached out and turned the golden leaf right-side up.

Then he leaned toward me, his mouth coming within inches of mine. I leaned the rest of the way. Our lips touched softly, so softly. His fingers brushed my cheek. He kissed me again, harder, more urgently, his hands holding my face, and I found myself kissing him hungrily, my fingers in his hair.

"Whoa," he said, sitting back, looking a little surprised, a little unguarded.

Did I do something wrong? Why did he stop?

"Got to go," he said, standing quickly. "Tully's waiting."

I nodded again, but I didn't stand. He lifted a lock of my hair carefully, pausing a moment. Then he gave it a little tug. "See you tomorrow, Parsons. Happy birthday."

"See you," I said, and he was out the door.

I felt raggedy, uneven. I wished he hadn't gone. I wished he'd stayed and kissed me again, kissed me longer. I touched my mouth. It almost hurt.

"Get a grip, Parsons," I told myself out loud. I thought to myself, it was too bad I liked this guy so much. It was going to be painful to let him go. And then I thought, it must have been very painful for Jackson to see how much I liked Richard. But I pushed that one away.

I gathered up the garment bag and the little Marsden tote, and started for the metal stairs under the solemn gaze of the ravished queen of the underworld.

The branches hanging into the path brushed against me. I heard distant laughter; I saw fragmented glimpses of Fiona, walking the same paths, turning back to smile suggestively at her pursuer before dancing ahead out of reach.

The trees opened up; the stair was just ahead.

My hand touched the iron railing, below another hand that belonged to my young mother. My young father caught her arm, drew her close, and bent down —

I shut my eyes and climbed higher, to the platform. And there was Gramma at the rail, looking out over the garden, with my grandfather beside her, holding her tight, nuzzling her neck. I felt dizzy and slightly feverish. I turned away.

It was like the house had been watching me kiss Richard. Like it knew how those kisses had made me feel, and had given me its own memories of those same feelings. I felt invaded, spied on. But then I thought, *That's ridiculous. It's just a house, just wood and stone.*

I concentrated on the here and now. Everything was looking a little different — ready, I thought, to be shown to the potential buyers among the party guests. Patches of moonlight illuminated the long hall of the west wing — all the doors to the rooms were open. I walked to the first door and looked in. The dustcovers had been removed. Flowers stood on a table. A wedding-ring quilt covered the bed. The arches of the canopy had been draped, ready for the public display that was at once my sixteenth birthday party and my mother's advertising coup.

I glanced in other doors as I made my way down the hall. The tiled bathroom was stocked with fat towels, and a rug warmed the floor. Fiona's bed was dressed with eyelet drapes and a comforter, and a vase of white lilies shone silvery on the table before the fireplace.

I wondered how long it had been since Amber House had last been uncovered and dressed to the nines.

And I wondered if the house liked it.

Chapter Twenty-Two

I hung the garment bag from the shelves in my room, unzipped it, and pulled the layers loose, fluffing them. A pale shower of shimmer drifted to the floor, which had been freshly vacuumed. *Oh, well*, I thought. I took off my new necklace and put it on my pillow.

My stomach was complaining. I hoped there was something left in the kitchen that I would be allowed to eat.

Rose was there when I entered, sitting at the table. Every surface in the kitchen gleamed, including the floor.

"The place sure looks nice," I said. "You coming to the party?"

She shook her head. "A real-estate open house masquerading as a costume party is not exactly my cup of tea, child. But I hope you have a wonderful birthday."

"Thanks, Rose."

"Ended up helping out a little. I'm the only one who knows where everything is." She shrugged. "Your mother couldn't even find the coverlets for the beds. And lord help me, I want Ida's house to look nice. Seems like this gonna be the old girl's swan song. A real shame your mother's selling her."

"I think so too."

"I left you a paper plate of something in the fridge. All you got to do is drop it in the trash when you're through. Don't be making any mess in here. Or anywhere else, for that matter."

"Thank you, Rose."

She took her sweater from the peg rack by the door and

looked back, her hand on the doorknob. “You ask your mother about Maggie yet?”

“I guess I’m still working up the nerve.”

“Well, you do that, child. You got a right to know what happened to your family.” Nodding, she smiled her encouragement to me and closed the door.

Rose’s words echoed in my head uncomfortably. I knew what happened to my family. Maggie’s death had ripped a hole in it, and that hole still hadn’t healed over.

I fished out the foil-wrapped paper plate she’d left me. It held four pieces of fried chicken and two small mountains of coleslaw and potato salad. I ate something less than half, rewrapped it up, and put it back in the fridge. I’d have the rest for breakfast.

Sammy and my mom were in my grandmother’s room. Sammy was on the bed, watching TV; Mom was in a chair set on top of a couple of sheets, wrapped in a coverall, having her hair highlighted. The hairdresser looked up and smiled a genuine smile as I entered.

“Good, you’re back,” Mom said. “I hope you had a nice day.”

“Yeah, it was pretty good,” I said. I still hadn’t forgiven her for selling the boat. I wasn’t about to dish up details for her benefit.

She moved on. “Angelique, this is Sarah. Sarah, Angelique. She’s going to touch up your color and give you a trim, cut off the split ends.”

“I didn’t realize I had any,” I said, a little vexed.

“Not a lot,” my mother said, oblivious as always.

“Well, thanks, Angelique. I had no idea stylists made house calls.”

“Your mom has been working so hard. I told her I didn’t mind coming out, save her some time. Besides, it gives me a chance to see the inside of this place.” She smiled and kept working.

"How's the dress?" Mom asked.

"It's good," I said. "It fit really well."

"Bring it in. Let me see it."

"You can see it tomorrow," I said, not giving an inch.

"I want to see it now." My mother gave me a look.

I shrugged. "I want to surprise you."

She stared at me a moment, like she was trying to decide whether or not to be angry or maybe push things further. Then her eyebrows lifted and her shoulders did too.

"We need to talk jewelry," she said.

The phone on the nightstand rang. It was Kathryn. "Sarah, can you talk?" she said a little breathlessly.

"It's for me," I said. "I'll take it in the library. I'm sorry, Angelique, but would you hang it up in here when I get there?"

"Sure thing, hon." She smiled.

I ran into the library, said into the receiver, "Got it," and heard the click of the other line. "Go ahead," I said into the phone, plopping down in one of the leather armchairs.

"Are you, like, a witch or what?" she asked.

I swallowed. What had she heard? What did she know? "What?" I stammered.

"What have you done to Hathaway?"

Oh. Wait. Really? "What's wrong?"

She giggled. "I've never seen him like this. I was talking to him on the phone, and he was going on and on about you. How you're so funny and you're never pretending to be somebody else. How you do so many things just like a guy. How innocent you are and how you always say whatever pops into your head."

These are good things? "Yeah," I said. "I embarrass myself a lot."

She laughed. "You *are* funny," she said, allowing me that much.

"Did he say anything else?" I tried not to sound too needy. It was tough.

"Well, he *did* ask me if I'd ever had a long-distance relationship."

Oh, my God. The phrase kept echoing. *Long-distance relationship.* Was such a thing even possible? I noticed I had fallen silent again. The little guys in my head that were in charge of speech function had to start doing a better job. "Um, Kath, the hairdresser is here and waiting to do my hair. Can we talk another time?"

"Oh, wow," she said. "A house call. I'll let you go."

"See you tomorrow, okay?"

"Everybody's gonna be there. See you, sweetie." She made two little kissing noises.

"Bye, Kath."

I hung up the phone. And smiled a little. Richard wasn't just pretending. He really did like me. That would surprise the heck out of my mother.

I told myself for the twentieth time, it was going to hurt to leave him.

Angelique was blowing out Mom's hair when I went back in. "Who was it, honey?" Mom shouted over the dryer.

"It was Kathryn. One of Richard's friends. She says everyone's going to be at the party."

"I know. I can't believe the number of people who said they were coming."

You send out two hundred fifty invites, I thought, *you can expect a pretty good crowd.*

"Get your grandmother's jewelry box off the dresser and bring it here, will you?" she said. I brought the box over and set it on the table near her. It was a little Chinese chest made of cherrywood, with jade insets. It held five drawers with silver pulls. "Open them up and let's see. You should have something for your neck and wrist."

Angelique turned off the dryer. She held up a hand mirror so my mother could see herself front and back. The cut was sleek and subtly layered, and her naturally auburnish color had been warmed slightly. Her hair looked ready for whatever upswept do she was going to put it in the next day. "That's great," she said. "If you could set up in the bath across the hall, Sarah will be right with you." Angelique gave the jewelry chest a regretful look, evidently curious about the contents, but closed up her cases and headed for the bathroom.

"Let's go through it real quick," Mom said.

"I'm good, Mom, except maybe for a pair of earrings. I already know what I'm going to wear."

"What have you got?"

"You'll have to wait and see."

She huffed a little, but let it go. I was surprised, really. Maybe my mother wouldn't be telling me exactly what to wear and what to say and what to think for the rest of my life. Maybe.

"Help *me* find something, then, and if there's anything else that catches your eye, we'll get it out, okay?"

The first drawer held rings and earrings. "Take out the ruby and the emerald rings, sweetie, and the earrings to match. I don't know if I should go with green or red gems." I also found a gold pair for me — several small strands of tight-woven gold chain hanging from a fleur-de-lis.

The next drawer held a set of diamonds, and one ornately etched gold bracelet, an inch and a half wide. The drawer below that was all silver and turquoise, and the fourth held a ruby necklace with several pendant drops, and three matching bangle-style bracelets.

An emerald necklace lay in the bottom drawer, a single large drop of green set round with pearls. It was breathtaking. "What do you think?" she asked.

"I love the emeralds," I said.

"Me too," she said. I got it out and set it on her dresser for her.

"What's in here?" The inside of the bottom drawer had two tiny tabs for lifting. Another compartment lay beneath. I pulled up the top layer.

The hidden space held a small envelope with one word written on the outside: *Annie*.

"What's that?" I asked my mother.

She looked a little queer. "I don't know."

"Is it from Gramma?"

"Not her writing." She held out her hand. I gave it to her.

She studied the cursive a minute, then drew out the envelope's contents. It was plain folded card stock. When Mom flipped it open, a newspaper clipping fell out of it onto her lap. She glanced at the clipping, then started reading the card. A look of confusion and disbelief filled her face. She looked again at the clipping, studying it. Almost to herself, she said, "Left it there so I would find it." Then she looked down and pressed her hand to her eyes. "Coward," I thought I heard her say.

When she looked up, her lips were tight.

"What is it, Mom?"

"It's nothing," she said. She put the clipping in the card, stuffed the card back in the envelope, and tossed it in the trash can full of hair. "Put the rubies back, will you?" She turned to my brother, still watching the TV. "Come on, Sam. Up to bed."

"I just want to —" he started.

"Now," my mother snarled.

Eyes wide, Sammy climbed off Gramma's bed and scooted out the door, followed by my mother.

My eyes were pretty wide too. I went to the door to make

sure they had gone up the stairs. Then I fished the note out of the hair clippings and stuffed it in my pocket. I tied up the bag lining the basket and carried it away with me to the bathroom across the hall. I'd let Mom think Angelique took out the trash.

Angelique had another chair all set up for me. I dropped the bag and took a seat.

She ran her fingers through my hair. "You have such a pretty honey tone in your hair," she gushed. "I'm guessing you've never even streaked this before?"

"Actually, no."

"Well, there's a first time for everything."

"So you *don't* like the color?" I laughed.

"One can always improve a good thing. At least, *I* can."

She worked fast and efficiently, painting in highlights, trimming my split ends with a razor. All the while, the envelope in my pocket was poking into my hip.

She blew my hair dry. It was light with movement and shine. I shook my head, enjoying it. "Brilliant," I said.

"Tell your mom you like it," she said, smiling conspiratorially. "It'll help with the tip." She started cleaning up, shaking out the sheets and bagging them. I grabbed the broom and started piling up the hair. "You don't have to do that, hon," she said.

Except I wanted that trash bag. I was going to make sure both of them went into the outside cans to cover my theft. "I don't mind. My way of saying thanks."

"What a sweetheart you are!" she exclaimed. I smiled and kept sweeping.

"Well, thanks again," I said when we were done, and headed for the kitchen, bags in hand.

"See you tomorrow."

Really? She was going to do more to me? "Okay. See you tomorrow."

With the two bags of trash safely disposed of, I had a chance, finally, to satisfy my curiosity. I ducked into a downstairs bathroom and pulled out the note.

> *December 19, 1982*
> *Dear Annie,*
> *I wanted you to know how much I miss you. I know your mom doesn't think it's the right time for us to get together, but when you and she feel the time* is *right, just know I am longing to see you. I hope you can use the enclosed to buy yourself something you really want.*
> *Merry Christmas. I love you.*
> *Daddy*

I didn't get it at first. Why had this upset my mom so much? Then I put it together. Mom had told me her dad died when she was twelve. But the card was dated 1982. And she'd been born in '68.

I looked at the clipping then. It contained a photo of a smiling, pleasant-looking man. I recognized him as the man I had seen in the downstairs hall the night my parents had been arguing. The clipping's headline read, CMDR. MARK MCGUINNESS SUCCUMBS TO CANCER. His date of death: December 21, 1989.

I put the clipping and card back in the envelope and tucked it inside the waistband of my jeans, under my shirt. I thought to myself, as I climbed the stairs to the flowered room, that it wasn't just the past that Amber House was filled with. It was broken pieces of people's lives, all still sharp on the edges. And when you brushed up against them, they cut.

Chapter Twenty-Three

I was dancing, dancing with Edward, his hands sliding over the thin silk of my dress. All around us were shadows, but we were in a pool of light. His mouth was at my ear: "Happy birthday, Fee." And I thought, confused, that it should be Richard holding me, but then I remembered this was Edward. It was my birthday. I had turned twenty-one. All grown up. Mama and Papa couldn't tell me what to do anymore.

A sharp, repetitive beeping invaded my dream. Groggy and pained, I reached for my alarm and realized slowly that the noise was coming through my half-open window. It was the sound of a truck backing up.

Before I could sort it out, the door was thrown open and Sammy hurled himself on my bed.

"Happy birthday, happy birthday, today you were borned," he sung cheerily as he danced and bounced, his little feet carefully sidestepping my legs under the covers.

"Oh, *God*, no," I moaned, my voice hoarse.

"Get up, get up. There's trucks and flowers and people in orange vests. Come on." He jumped to the floor and began to tug vigorously on my arm.

"I'm coming, I'm coming."

He bolted from the room. Sam-my-man. Always bright-eyed and bushy-tailed at the crack of dawn. I hated that about him.

I mulled the possibility of stealing a cup of coffee from my mother as I stumbled down the stairs, and had actually reached the bottom before I realized that the hall was full of men in reflective vests drinking juice and coffee from a tray on the side table.

"Morning," one said.

I froze. I was wearing sweatpants, a dirty camp T-shirt, and *no bra*. Without a word, I scurried down the hall to the cover of the kitchen. Which was filled with strangers rifling through the drawers and cupboards.

Giving up on the coffee and toast, I folded my arms across my chest and slipped back up the stairs as inconspicuously as I could. Safe back in my room, I changed into jeans, tank top, and *bra*, and wound my mess of hair into a loose braid. I threw on some eyeliner for good measure. Then I set out to find Sammy.

He was in the front field, sitting on top of a pile of gray wood posts. What was left of the pasture fence, evidently. He pointed to a yellow-orange forklift.

"Look. That truck picks up these pieces." He jumped down from his perch and proceeded to enact it for me. "The two pokers slide un'erneath and then it lifts all the pieces onto the flat truck, and the flat truck takes it to the barn, and so when the people come they can put their cars someplace."

"What a lot of work."

"It was a good old fence," he said sadly. "It's broken now."

"We can fix it," I reassured him. "What else is there to see around here?"

"This way." He grabbed my hand, tugging. "Come on."

"Not so fast, bud," I said, dragging my feet. "It's too dang hot for running." The warm weather my mother had ordered especially for my party had come with a dose of humidity that was making my light clothes stick to my body.

Sam, unrelenting, towed me to the front of the house, where three white vans were parked in the gravel drive. My nose registered the faint but growing aroma of cooking meat.

"All the food's in those trucks, Sarah," he said.

"Three of them?"

"Uh-huh."

"That's a *lot* of food."

"Uh-huh. There's more. Let's go." He spun one hundred and eighty degrees and took off toward the rear of the house.

A swarm of laborers were laying the framework for dance floor and stage. More workers were setting up small circular tables, spreading them with dark blue tablecloths that shimmered, cerulean to black, from varying angles. The florist's people started setting out centerpieces — bright oranges, indigos, magentas, lime greens, tucked into hollowed pumpkin "vases." Lighting guys were hanging clusters of glazed-glass orbs from the gnarled limbs of the oaks.

Sammy was practically bouncing up and down from all the stimulation. "It's just so GREAT," he shouted, shaking his little arms in the air. "What a great party! You have to tell me after, okay?"

"You're coming, aren't you?" I said.

"Nope. Mommy told me I have a sitter."

"What?" I mean, I understood that he was five years old and a little unpredictable. But when was he ever going to get a chance to see another party like this? If he wanted to come —

I crouched down. "Listen to me. You want to come, you can. It's my party. Do you want to?"

"I just want to see you blow out all those candles."

" 'All those candles'?" I stood up and put my hands on my hips, doing indignation. "You yanking my chain? I'm not *that* old."

He laughed, threw his arms about my waist, and hugged hard. "You're still good."

"Well, okay, then. I guess you're in for the cake and candles."

"All *riiight*," he said, jumping a little and pumping his fist in the air.

We went back inside to see if we could find a place that was out of the way. We were being overly optimistic.

In the west wing, workers were moving an enormous amount of furniture. Using some of the comfortable chairs and tables from the sunroom and billiards room, they were refurnishing the north side of the wing — office, bath, and studio — to turn it into a dressing room and lounge for Ataxia.

More workers were setting up a casino in the two rooms on the river side of the wing. The pool table had been transformed into a craps table. It was flanked by a roulette wheel. The sunroom's remaining furnishings had been pushed to the walls to make room for blackjack, poker, and baccarat stations. One wall held a row of slot machines. My party was doing double-duty as a fundraiser for cancer research — the theory being, I guessed, that if you gathered that many rich people in one place, you should soak them for *some* cash in the name of a worthy cause.

They were setting up a bar in the library, in addition to the one on the back patio. The dining room was prepped for the food that would be spread out just before the guests arrived, with a dozen extra-long tables for food outside. Mom thought a buffet would make the guests move around more — mingle, explore the house, drop money in the casino — so she'd opted not to have a sit-down dinner.

On that thought, my stomach growled.

"Me too, Sarah. My tummy is hungry too."

There was nothing for it but to brave the kitchen again. I ducked in, wove my way through the moving workers, and snagged the paper plate Rose had left me the night before. Then Sammy and I retreated to the nautical room to eat potato salad and coleslaw with our fingers. Sammy thought it was great.

"Where's your bear, Sam?" I said, noticing its absence.

He shook his head and shrugged his shoulders.

"Mom's not gonna like it much if you lost him. He's a pretty valuable old bear."

He concentrated on the potato salad in his fingers. "No one took him?" he said.

"No, bud, nobody took him."

He shrugged again.

We were in my room reading a story from Sam's book of fairy tales when Dad poked his head through the door. "Hiding out?" he asked.

"Absolutely," I said.

"Can I join you?"

"Sure, Daddy," Sammy said graciously. "Sit next to Sarah so you can see the pictures. Do you want Sarah to start over?"

"No, thank you, Sam," Dad said, as he sat down next to me obediently. "I think I know how this one began."

We sat there, we three, cozy and calm. We finished the first tale and were heading toward the exciting conclusion of another until Mom interrupted. She stood in the door, looking around her old room like it was a habitat at the zoo and an animal might be lurking. She focused on me. "Sarah, you need to go down to my room for hair and makeup."

All business. No sign of the upset she'd experienced the night before. She'd just discovered her mother had lied to her about her father's death and prevented her from ever seeing him again, and she was still operating full steam, looking not only cool and collected, but annoyingly beautiful. Her hair was swept up into a polished French twist. Her long, slim neck was beautifully exposed, an elegant setting for the emerald necklace she'd be wearing later. Her perfect face was even more perfect. Clearly she'd already had her turn in hair-and-makeup. "Hurry up," she said, a little exasperated.

"So soon?" I said.

"It's nearly two, honey. It's not a ten-minute job."

Right. Making me presentable was going to require hours of intensive labor.

"Sam wants to watch me blow out the candles, Mom," I said, as I stood.

"That's really not going to be poss —"

I started to sit again. She said hastily, "We'll work it out, okay?"

It was mean of me, I know, but I was kind of enjoying my newfound power. What did they call it? Passive resistance? "You finish the story with Dad, okay, Sam? I'll see you later."

"Will Jackson be there, Sarah? I haven't seen Jackson for *days*."

I cringed a little, hearing Jackson's name, thinking of his possible presence at the party. Since Rose had said she wasn't coming, I'd assumed Jackson wasn't either, but I guessed he could walk on over if he wanted to. I was hoping he wouldn't want to. "I don't know, bud. I don't think so. We'll see."

"I'll find him and tell him to come, okay?"

"Don't," I said a little sharply. Dad gave me a funny look. "Sorry, Sam. But — Jackson already knows all about the party. He'll come if he wants. So you don't have to tell him. All right?"

I hoped that would stop him. I didn't want him pulling any of his special persuasion tricks on Jackson, who seemed to have a soft spot for the little guy. And who might get the wrong idea and think I had sent Sam on this mission of arm-twisting.

When I reached the door to Gramma's room, I saw four women sprawled in various poses of boredom, while one very handsome man of about thirty-five paced in the middle of the room. "Where is she? Does she have any *idea* how long this is going to —"

Angelique caught his attention and redirected it to me. He turned and smiled, teeth gleaming with an unnatural whiteness. "Ah, here's our little princess," he said. "Are you ready for your makeover, sweetheart?"

Yes. Really. Princess *and* sweetheart.

"I'm sorry if I kept you waiting," I said cheerfully, trying, really trying, to be gracious. I stuck out my hand toward Mr. Ultra-White-Teeth. "You are?"

He took my hand. "I am Mr. Poole."

"Pleased to meet you. I'm Sarah. Or you can call me Parsons." I grinned to show I was harmless. "Just not *sweetheart*. And definitely not *princess*. Deal?"

He froze a tiny bit, then smiled and thawed. "Parsons, huh? I can work with that. Okay, Parsons." He pointed. "Angelique you know. This is Kathy, the manicurist; Louise, hair removal; and Jennie, tanning *artiste*. We've got a lot to do, people, so let's get started." He tossed me a little cotton kimono. "Down to your skivvies, Parsons."

I caught it and trudged into the bathroom, the walk of the condemned.

When I returned, they sat me in a salon chair, leaned me back, and put up the leg rest. Then the three women I hadn't met before took up positions on all sides and started working. Louise waxed, Kathy polished, and Jennie buffed dead skin from neglected areas all up and down my left side. "Takes the tan wrong," she said. "You'll get spots." When all three were done, they shifted position. While they worked, they talked about the party.

"Did you see the casino?"

"Gondolas on the water."

"All those cases of champagne."

I did my best to pretend I wasn't there. I pretty much felt like a slab of meat being dressed for roasting. Then Jennie hustled me off to the bathroom shower for my airbrushed tan, inexpensive bikini thoughtfully provided.

I was soft skinned, hair free, and lightly browned all over. The trio of ladies packed up, wished me a happy birthday, collected envelopes from Mr. Poole, and departed.

I returned to the chair so Angelique could get started on my hair. She flattened, curled, combed, pinned, gave me a once-over with an acrid-smelling spray, then stepped back with a triumphant smile. I leaned toward the vanity mirror to inspect the final product.

At the back of my head sat a sleek, draping knot, held by one large gold comb shaped like a cluster of leaves. The formality of it was counterbalanced by my bangs, spiked slightly and swept to one side. "Wow," I managed, a little breathlessly.

She gave me a quick hug and whispered in my ear, "Good luck, hon." Then she collected her envelope and made her escape. That left just Mr. Poole and me.

He opened up an enormous leather-bound cosmetics case with a collection of bottles and tubes and tins of powders that even my mother would find extreme. Every product you could ever need in every shade you could possibly imagine.

"You really going to use all of that?" I joked.

"If I have to," he said grimly.

"Um, I have this bruise on my forehead —"

"Yeah-huh. Hard to miss. I'll handle it."

For the better part of an hour he worked in silence. He cleaned and prepped thoroughly, then started in with an airbrush, applying layer after layer of shading. He added false eyelashes one at a time, with tweezers. He combed on mascara with a tiny brush. He filled in my eyebrows, hand painted my lips. Finally, with a brush and some clear but shiny liquid, Mr. Poole painted curlicues around the corners of my eyes. He fixed a handful of crystals in the drying design.

"In case you don't want your face covered all night," he said. "Mask to go, as it were." He stood back to admire his work. "You clean up nice, Parsons."

I checked myself in the mirror. I didn't know how he'd done it. My too-long nose looked aristocratic and elegant. My cheeks had a lovely concave curve rising to highlighted cheekbones. My large eyes looked even larger. And my lips — I had always considered them too thin, but not now. Not under a layer of Mr. Poole's artful shaping.

"Um," I said, "can you, like, varnish this" — I indicated my facial area with my hand — "so that it stays this way permanently?"

He laughed. "I *am* a genius, Parsons, but you can learn how to do it too. You've got good bones. Just remember, there are damn few natural beauties in this world."

"Thank you *very* much."

He leaned down and gave me a little squeeze. "You are very, very welcome, princess." He grinned, all perfect teeth. I laughed. "Now let's go get you dressed."

I lifted my eyebrows.

"No," he assured me, "I am not coming in the room. Just have to check the finished product."

I led him up to the flowered bedroom, which he pronounced "gorgeous." He waited outside while I put on my party armor. Then I opened the door.

"Oh, my word," he said, "she looks absolutely fabulous. I am so proud." He made a little twirling motion with his hand, so I revolved three hundred and sixty degrees. "Is that a Marsden?"

"Yes," I said, surprised.

"Thought so. She does good work."

"Um, they gave me this with the dress." I handed him the little vial of gold dust.

He put some moisturizer in his palm, worked in the dust, then smoothed the mixture over my shoulders, forearms, and collarbone.

"There. You're Cinderella now, Parsons. Enjoy it."

"I'll try," I said.

"Do more than try. A night like this doesn't happen that many times in any girl's life." He squeezed my hand. "Got to run. Almost curtain time." He smiled and was gone.

I didn't know quite what to do with myself. I checked in Sammy's room, but Sam and Dad were gone. I walked out to the landing, to the row of windows overlooking the stone patios and river. The workers all seemed to be gone too, except for waiters in white, who milled around talking to one another, waiting. It was five twenty — the party started at six. The sun had just set and the moon was a merest sliver on the eastern horizon. When it rose, it would be full.

Just to please my mother, I thought.

The air was feeling a little thick. I reached to unlatch the window, to catch the breeze off the river. I saw my grandmother's hand meet mine in the same action. She stood a little to the right, enjoying the fresh air, her face shadowed in the dusky twilight.

A little boy came up behind her, his green eyes wide. "Who is that lady?" he asked her, pointing. "She looks like a princess."

My grandmother turned my way, but clearly couldn't see me. "You see someone, sweetheart?"

"Yes." He considered a moment. "Do you think I am awake?"

“Yes, I think you are awake,” she said, “but I don’t know if you can take my word for it.” She smiled and moved on, down the hall.

He looked at me again. “Who are you, lady?” he whispered.

I didn’t know if I should speak. How could he see me? How could he be talking to me?

“My name is Sarah.”

“Sarah,” he repeated. “Hi, Sarah.”

I saw the scars then, fresher and more vivid than the ones I knew, tracing down his hand and up his face.

The little boy, of course, was Jackson.

Chapter Twenty-Four

My mother's voice reached me before she crested the stairs. "Sarah? You ready? It's almost time."

The light changed slightly, and the little boy Jackson disappeared. My throat hurt — filled with words I wished I had been able to say to him. Something to let him know that things would be all right. That he wasn't crazy.

He wasn't crazy.

"Sarah?"

I turned quickly. She looked tired and worried and harassed. But when she saw me, her face broke into the most wonderful smile.

"Sarah," she said softly, "you look so beautiful."

I had to stop myself from bursting into tears, it felt that good. "I don't look half as pretty as you, Mom."

And she did look even better than usual. The gown clung to her figure in a way that shouldn't be allowed on mothers of teenaged girls. The green gem glittered just above her cleavage.

Mom made a brushing gesture with her hand. "I know you think I'm pretty — and I'm glad, and I thank you. But you are so much lovelier than I ever was."

I shook my head.

"You don't know," she said. "You only see the things you think are imperfections. You don't realize that my kind of prettiness is the ordinary kind, the kind you see on boxes of hair dye and can't remember ten seconds later. Your kind of loveliness is unforgettable."

I felt my nose tingling again.

"For God's sake, don't cry." She laughed. "Mr. Poole has left the building."

I gasped out a chuckle and carefully dried the corner of my eye with my fingertip.

She reached out and fingered my leaf pendant. "Is this what Robert's son gave you?"

"Yeah. Pretty nice, huh?"

"Yes," she said. "He did good." She seemed impressed. "Come on down and show your dad before everybody gets here."

"Oh, wait," I said, and I ran back to my room. I came back out with Fiona's golden mask. I held it up before my eyes.

"Good heavens," Mom said, "that's wonderful."

"It was your mom's, I think. I — found it in a drawer." I wondered why I bothered to lie.

"Must have been hers. Everything was."

She turned down the stairs and I followed, thinking about the little boy. Thinking maybe I had been too hard on Jackson, who had, apparently, known me a *lot* longer than I had known him. I felt for that kid — never knowing what was real, or what was possible. His thoughts — his *emotions* — getting tangled up in a girl he couldn't be sure even existed. It would make a person doubt his sanity.

As Mom and I hit the lower landing, the photographer from *Southern Home* yelled, "Hold it!" Mom reached for my hand and put on a brilliant smile. I tried to do the same. I hated smiling for cameras.

The photographer asked for a few shots of "the birthday girl by herself," so Mom went down and stood next to him. I focused on her eyes and smiled for her. It was easier.

Dad and Sam were watching some dinosaur program in Gramma's room. Sam saw me first and his eyes opened really big. "You look like a fairy tale, Sarah."

"Thanks, bud."

Dad stood up. He looked very, you know, secret-agent-in-an-Italian-tuxedo. Since he was one of the permanently rumpled kind of guys, I was a little amazed. He told me I looked "beautiful, so much like your mother," at which point Mom abruptly said it was time to meet-and-greet. She, as hostess; I, as the honoree. Dad was going to hang with Sam awhile and come out later.

The senator was the first to arrive, of course. He was going to stand next to Mom to help her with names and give everyone a solid dose of his charm. He clamped my hand and wished me a "magical birthday," then positioned himself strategically.

Richard shook hands with Mom before he came to greet me. His smile was so shy, it hardly got past the corners of his eyes. He reached out and touched a gold leaf.

I said, "It looks perfect, doesn't it?"

He nodded. "*You* look perfect, Sarah."

I gave him a huge foolish grin. "Oh, no," I said. "It's Parsons to you, Hathaway. You don't want to make me feel like some girlie girl, do you?"

He grinned back. "Maybe."

"Can you stand here with me?" I whispered. "I don't think I have the guts to do this by myself."

"I can't," he said. "And you do. I'll see you in a little while."

He disappeared just as the front door opened. It pretty much stayed open for the next half hour. I could glimpse through the opening a steady stream of headlights coming down the drive. The photographer crouched to the side and snapped this or that guest, I assumed based upon name-recognition value, because it wasn't for the best costumes. Only about half the people had gone all-out, with the rest in formal wear and a token mask. As I was, come to think of it.

My mother greeted each arrival with high-pitched goodwill, as if she were excited to see every single one of them. I shook hands, one after another, with a fixed smile, trying to be friendly, thanking them for their birthday wishes.

Many of them held out a present for me to take, and just as soon as I had exclaimed over it, a woman in a Pirouette costume took it from me and carried it to a table. When the table began to mound up, more party staffers moved loads of wrapped packages to some other spot in the house. It *was* going to be a mountain of gifts. I hoped my mother did not expect me to write all the thank-you notes by myself.

When the flow of people petered out, Mom told me I should go mingle. She stayed in the front hall to greet the late arrivers. I went to look for Richard.

I made my way among the throng of guests who were already placing their contributions to cancer research upon the green felt of the blackjack tables. I went out onto the patio through the open French doors. Then I stopped and marveled.

I had seen bits and pieces of my mother's party, but I had never put it all together into this, had never built in my mind's eye this — *spectacle* — that she had been able to imagine down to the very last detail.

It took my breath away.

Walking out through the French doors was like walking back across time into a seventeenth-century Venetian festival. The full moon was rising up just over the treetops, fat and deeply orange from the sunset, like the god of pumpkins come to bless the autumn revelry. A white and black harlequin dance floor spilled out in a three-level cascade, punctuated in the corners with ornate, branching gold-washed candelabras. Long tables brimming with cheeses and crudités and fruit and tiny cakes flanked the floors on every level. Beyond this, on the lawn, all the little circular tables were arranged under the oldest trees, tucked beneath a ceiling of white and gold netting that swept from branch to branch.

A purple and blue satin-swathed stage stood outside the conservatory, false-lit from the front by candles set in copper holders, but caught more securely in light from spots hidden in the trees. At the moment, it bore a trio of jugglers.

The partygoers milled and mingled, flitting about like ghosts, their costumes and masks coming in and out of focus in the glow cast by the lanterns and the tiny lights that filled the garden. Jesters in motley wandered among the guests, clowning, performing tricks, and handing out tokens. These could be traded for a ride with the gondoliers hired to pole couples amongst water-lily lanterns floating on the surface of the Severn.

It was a total fantasy. I didn't know how Mom had pulled it off. Overwhelmed, I leaned against a post and stared.

As I watched, the scene shifted. Another party played out before me — a scene of sequined flapper-era dresses and tailed tuxes. Ragtime music blared from a small band. I looked for the red-haired woman I knew must be there. And found, at the far end of the patio, someone who looked like my grandmother. Staring at me, a question in her eyes. *Wh* —

Then a high-pitched squeal stabbed my eardrums and I was grabbed from behind.

"Lordy!" Kathryn's voice cried as she spun me around and the real world came back into focus. "You look ah-mazing."

She wore a short skirt of frothy silk chiffon that had been draped around what was basically a full-body corset of pink satin ruching. I couldn't wrap my mind around how she'd been able to get into it. Almost as much of a mystery were the two pink feather wings poking out between the golden curls on her back.

"Are you — an angel?" I said.

"No," she said, laughing. "I'm a flamingo, silly!"

I laughed too. I could see it now: the pink, the feathers, the black fishnets. Kathryn beamed. You'd positively hate her for being so perfect, except, with Kathryn, it was impossible not to love her. She was like Sammy, in a way. There was some kind of innocence there, a lack of guile that charmed.

"Where's your table?" she asked.

"I haven't got one yet."

"Sit with me." She slipped her arm through mine and started guiding me along. "Just so you know," she whispered, "Morgan and I broke up — entirely mutual, really for the best — but I am actively trying to make him regret it. So I decided I am *so* making out with one of the guys from Ataxia tonight."

I almost choked.

"Well, of course, since you're the birthday girl, I'll let you have first dibs," she said quickly. "I mean, the lead singer is nice, but I've got a thing for drummers too. So either one is fine."

All I could manage was, "It's okay, don't worry about me."

She burst into laughter. "I keep forgetting: Sarah Parsons needs loosening."

Flamingo-angel that she was, Kathryn led me to the exact table I had been looking for; Richard stood to get my chair when we walked up. I tried not to blush. Kathryn sat down next to Chad, who stood belatedly to get her chair. Olivia was sitting in one of the two remaining seats.

"What are you?" Olivia asked once I'd sat down.

"I'm sorry?" I responded, confused by the accusatory tone in her voice.

She gestured to my gown. "I don't get it."

"Duh. Sarah is Autumn," Kathryn chimed in. "Can't you tell?"

I shot a glance toward Kathryn that I hoped conveyed my gratitude.

"One hell of a party," Chad offered.

"Omigod, it's *unbelievable*," Kathryn enthused. "Look at these tables. Your mother is *in-sane*."

In addition to the flowers, the shimmering cloth of each table was littered with fall leaves and tiny candles held in makeshift votives carved from mini-pumpkins. Each place was set with mismatched silver flatware from the collections of ten generations of Amber House brides — all of it polished into seeming liquidity, the gleaming surfaces dancing in the light cast by the candles.

"*Oooh*, lookit," Kathryn went on excitedly. She pointed at a woman dressed in flamboyant purple, hovering over the hand of a man at the next table. "A fortune-teller! We've *got* to get our fortunes told."

"There was another one at the tables down below," someone said.

The fortune-teller chose that moment to look over. At me. She frowned the smallest bit, then returned to the palm in front of her.

"I'm going for something to eat," Richard said, standing. "Looks like they're bringing out the main courses."

"I'm coming with you," I said. "Only thing I've eaten all day is some leftover coleslaw."

At the buffet table, servers were slicing prime rib and roast turkey. There were sides of potatoes, rice, rolls, and the ubiquitous corn cake. Six or seven different vegetable dishes, salads, sauces, and dressing. We both loaded our plates.

"Think we got enough here, Parsons?" Richard put his hand on the small of my back, and it sent a little jolt through me. My pleasure must have been apparent, because I noticed a tall, blonde-haired woman at the far end of the buffet, watching us with amusement. Or perhaps not. Hard to tell under her mask. I felt embarrassed. I linked my free arm in Richard's and started us back to our table.

When we returned to our seats, the fortune-teller was bent over Kathryn's palm. "What a love line," the woman said. "So many admirers."

Kathryn nodded and smiled. "I know, right?"

"Excellent health your whole life. You will never want. You will find your true love. Maybe someone you will meet tonight?"

Kathryn grinned at me. "That's the plan."

"That is all I can tell you," the woman concluded, and moved on to Olivia. Everyone at the table held a hand out. Everyone was rewarded with the same kind of cheery generalities.

But when she came to me, the woman frowned and shook her head, as if she were having trouble focusing. She stroked her fingers over my palm, tracing the lines with a fingertip. She kept returning to the center of my palm. "What is this mark? Is it a scar?"

I was confused. There was no mark.

She cleared her throat and started to speak, but then stopped.

"What" — I chuckled a little uneasily — "am I gonna die young?"

She motioned with her head — "No." She opened her mouth and closed it. Finally she said, "I need a small break. I am sorry." She stood and left, fast.

"Sheesh, Parsons, you short-circuited the fortune-teller." We all laughed.

"Lordy, I thought she was going to have a stroke," Kathryn said. "I'm sorry you missed your fortune, sweetie. She got mine so perfectly."

We heard the P.A. system being turned on and looked toward the stage. An emcee was at the mic, switching it on and then holding out his arms to catch people's attention. "Can everybody hear me?"

A girl closer to the river squealed "Omigod!" Then suddenly everyone my age was on their feet and rushing to the dance floor before the stage, my group included. We found a spot toward the front.

The emcee was laughing into the mic. "I can see my announcement is highly anticipated."

Another little moaning squeal started in the back and spread through the crowd like some kind of instant infection. I laughed and grinned at Kathryn, who grinned back and rolled her eyes toward heaven, fanning her face with her hand.

"All righty then," the emcee said. Then raising his voice to a shout, he got to the point: "Let's give it up for Ataxia!"

The crowd roared as four young men leapt out on the stage, the guy on bass already striking the opening chords of one of their famous songs. The drummer picked up the beat, the guitarist joined in, the amps were vibrating, and the crowd was in motion.

The costumes and gowns seemed to discourage the high-contact writhing that usually went on at every dance I had ever had the misfortune of attending, so I had the rare pleasure of actually dancing. I tried hard to move as little as possible so I didn't perspire off all of Mr. Poole's work, but in the end I just held up the train of my dress and enjoyed it. Richard was, of course, a terrific dancer. Nothing too exuberant, but every movement perfect.

The song ended, we screamed our approval, then another song began. It went on like that for an hour, the band working hard. Their tux jackets got tossed to the side, their shirts unbuttoned. My voice was a husky croak, I had been laughing and screaming so much, and the smile muscles in my cheeks ached. During the twelfth song, the adults, who had wandered away when Ataxia started its set, drifted back out onto the lawn, encircling the dance floor. At the song's end, the front man gestured for silence.

"Thank you, thank you," he was saying, trying to quiet the young crowd. "As y'all *probably* know, I'm Rafe" — more screaming — "and I want to thank you for coming out tonight to celebrate the birthday of —" He hesitated a minute, while the guy on bass whispered in his ear. "Well, it's Sarah's birthday, isn't it?"

The crowd laughed and roared.

"That's this little golden goddess over here, isn't it? Standing next to the delicious dolly in pink." He pointed, and a spot picked me and Kathryn out of the crowd.

"For our last number," Rafe went on, "I have a guest artist joining me." He gestured for the mystery performer to join him, and suddenly, there was my little brother, trotting to center stage to stand next to Rafe. The singer held out a palm for a low five, and Sammy gave him a good slap.

"If you could make a little room over here," Rafe said, pointing to the left side of the floor. The crowd parted, and a table on wheels appeared, waiters pushing it to the center of the floor. On it stood a gold and silver cake four tiers high. It was glowing with little clumps of sparklers spitting out light.

I felt an enormous grin on my face and realized from the soreness in my facial muscles that I had been smiling nonstop for over an hour. I grabbed Richard's hand for courage and went to meet the cake at the center.

What looked like a real grape vine, gilded, with small clumps of fresh gilt grapes, snaked its way up around the layers. A menagerie of gold marzipan bugs — butterflies and beetles and crickets and a spider on a golden thread — feasted on the frosting.

A jester lit the circle of candles on the top tier and put down a step for me to climb on, so I'd be able to blow out the flames.

The bassist hit a chord, and attention shifted back to the stage. Rafe crouched down with the mic, and he and Sammy crooned the opening line: *"Happy Birthday to you —"*

Rock chords on bass and guitar skittered around the familiar melody.

Rafe and Sam sang again: *"Happy Birthday to you —"*

More jarring chords, and then Sammy got a solo: *"Happy Birthday, dear Sarah —"*

The guitarist struck off a rising wail that ended in the inevitable, hanging, high-pitched note and Rafe shouted, "Everybody!"

The whole crowd sang: *"— Happy Birthday to you."*

The guests cheered. I smiled at my brother grinning at me. And as I blew out every single candle, I made the same vague wish I always made: that everything would turn out all right.

Chapter Twenty-Five

Ataxia disappeared after that, and so did Kathryn. I didn't spend much time wondering about the coincidence.

Sam, Mom, and Dad came to join me for a bite of my birthday cake. They invited Richard to stay, but he bowed out, saying he had to hunt up "the senator."

I told Sammy how amazing his performance had been. I pumped the air with my fist and served up my best Sammy imitation: "All *riiight*."

He laughed. "Not all the notes were just right, Sarah, but the other guy wasn't the goodest singer in the world."

"You're right, bud, it's tough to sing with a guy like that. You did an awesome, awesome job."

"Thank you, Sarah."

I smiled. "You're welcome, Sam. And you too, Mom," I added. "Just awesome."

She shrugged, as if she doubted my sincerity. "I know you didn't want this party, honey —"

"No, I mean it, Mom. There will never be a party as great as this one again. I am having the best time. I will *never* forget it."

"Well, thanks, honey." She pinked up a little. "You are so — thanks," she said again.

"Nobody can touch you, Anne," my father said, then looked to Sam and me. "She's amazing, right?"

"Right," we agreed.

Another band took the stage, playing music more suited to the tastes of the rest of the crowd. Older couples began to swirl around the dance floors. Richard came back and asked me to dance.

I turned a little red under the eyes of my parental units. "Thanks," I said, "but I don't know how to dance that way."

"It's easy. I'll show you."

"Sorry. I've been embarrassed enough for one evening."

"Then let's hit the casino," he said.

"Really? Are we allowed?" I asked my mom.

"Twenty-dollar limit on chips for anyone under twenty-one," my mom said, nodding. My dad palmed me a twenty.

We went down the stairs first, to use our tokens for the gondola ride. I didn't see the bribe get slipped, but something must have passed between Richard and the gondolier, because the next thing I knew, the man had jumped out on the pier. Richard began to pole the boat along the path marked by the lily lanterns.

The moisture in the air was coalescing into tendrils of fog creeping along the riverbanks. Clouds were blowing west from the Atlantic. But the moon still rode in a patch of clear sky, its twin floating on the black surface of the Severn. I trailed my perfect gold-pink nails in the water and felt like a creature from a more romantic era. Richard was busy getting the knack of poling the little boat, which I found to be an oddly endearing endeavor for someone dressed in a tux. I smiled, just as he looked over at me.

"What?" he said.

"I don't know all that much about proper gondola-ing, Hathaway," I said, "but I'm pretty sure you're supposed to sing."

"I'm not singing, Parsons."

"Oh, come on. Something, you know, Italian, about the moon and *amore*."

"I'm not singing, Parsons."

The pole stuck, arresting Richard's forward motion. He struggled to stop the boat and keep himself upright, then wrestled with the pole.

I composed my face, trying not to laugh. "And I was just about to say —" A chuckle escaped me. "— just about to say —" I started to wheeze laughter. " — that you're a real stick-in-the-mud, Hathaway." I was laughing harder. "But now I — now I —" I was getting breathless; my guts were starting to hurt. " — I just can't."

He was laughing too. "That was truly pathetic, Parsons. I'll make allowances" — the pole came unstuck and Richard staggered, still laughing — "because it's your birthday and all. But don't let me catch you making that kind of lame joke again."

"A girl's gotta have some vice. Mine is utterly lame humor."

"And mine, apparently, is laughing at utterly lame humor."

"You guys're always complaining I'm not loose enough, but see," I said, "I'm funny, I'm chill, I'm loose."

"I disagree."

"What? I'm not funny, Hathaway?"

"No. I'm not complaining, Parsons."

He pushed us on, grinning. I leaned against the cushions and went back to watching.

On the climb back up the stone steps, I pointed to the glittering trail of gold dust I'd left coming down. "I'm like some overgrown snail," I said.

Rather than cut across the dance floor, we detoured over the grass, watching our moon shadows climb the lawn before us.

We neared the sunroom doors and heard the siren call of a jackpot tinkling into a slot-machine tray. We traded cash for chips.

Richard went straight for the blackjack table. "Best odds," he told me. I stood next to him and watched for a while, then played a few hands when I was sure of the rules. But my stack of chips declined fast.

I went to play the slots and hit a jackpot after three pulls. Mindful of the charitable function of the machine, I funneled the entire pot back into its insatiable slit-mouth. When I was down a few bucks more, I went back to stand next to Richard. He was still winning. I noticed a nearly empty champagne flute at his elbow and wondered if it was his. The dealer didn't seem to question it. I put the rest of my chips with his stack, wished him luck, and told him I'd return in a few.

The rooms across the hall — the ones set aside for the band — were empty of all but a scattering of drained liquor bottles and litter, and a couple of girls rifling through the trash. Another line of girls, waiting to use the restroom, trailed down the hallway. So I headed for the bath in the east wing.

On the way back, I looked in the Chinese room. A lady was folding up the colored cloth that had been spread on a card table. It was the fortune-teller I had chased away. I started to hurry past.

"No, wait," she called to me. "You're the birthday girl, aren't you? Come in. I'll read your fortune."

"No, I — don't want to keep you."

"It's no problem. You *should* have your fortune told on your birthday. The path to the future is the most open around the time of your nativity."

"That's so nice of you," I said, relenting. "Thank you."

"I'm sorry about earlier. I don't know what came over me. Just had the weirdest sense of, like, seeing double. Had to get out of the heat. Sit," she said, shaking out her cloth and taking a deck of cards back out of a bag. "I switched to these — they're tarot cards. They're easier on me." She spread them face up. They were more colorful than a regular deck, peopled with vivid figures. She pulled out four. "These are the Pages," she said, "One card lower than Jacks. Pick one."

I chose a girlish figure in yellow holding a sword above her head.

"Interesting," she said. "The Page of Swords, who is associated with detachment, watching, maybe even spying. That card is going to represent you."

She reinserted the other Pages into the deck, and shuffled. Then she began to lay out the cards. The first one went face up on top of the yellow Page.

"Wow," she said. She took a breath. "This is the issue card — it shows the problem you're facing right now in your life, and it's represented by the Three of Swords, sometimes called the Lord of Sorrows. It signifies extreme pain, upheaval, separation, disruption, but," she said, lifting her voice, "with a positive outcome in sight. Okay?" she said. "That's your issue."

She dealt out nine more cards, all face down, the first sideways on top of the Three of Swords, the next four in a box around the center cards, and the last four in a column off to the right.

She began by turning over the card in the center. "The Magician, reversed. This represents the energy that will make solving your problem more difficult. It signifies confusion, an inability to make decisive choices. It can also mean a learning disability."

She flipped the south card. "Yeesh," she commented, looking at it. A hairy man-beast sat on a throne. "The Devil, reversed. This is the distant past, the old root of the problem. This represents . . ." She hesitated. "True evil. Bondage. Abuse of authority. Emotional blackmail. So, a long time back, something evil caused the problem you're facing now." She looked concerned. "You want to hear the rest?"

I nodded.

"Okay," she said. "This card" — she turned the card to the west — "is the newer root of the problem. The Queen of Swords. She represents a complex, courageous, and intelligent woman who has suffered some deep sorrow, especially at the hands of men. Know anyone like that?"

"No. My mother, maybe."

She revealed the north card. "This is the near future. The Seven of Cups — the Lord of Illusionary Success. It speaks of a need to reflect upon choices with great perception. It may also indicate an inspiring mystical experience.

"The far future." She flipped the eastern card. "The Tower, which is another difficult card. It speaks of the overthrow of an existing way of life, leading to enlightenment and freedom." She shook her head slightly. "This is also the third card from the Major Arcana. So this is an important lay of cards."

She went to the lowest card in the column of four. "All right, this shows something blocking you from your goal — the Nine of Swords, which has to do with premonitions, a need to wake from bad dreams, suffering overcome through faith. And that's your fourth Sword, which means this board keeps yelling 'impending change.'

"This card" — she flipped another — "is the goal — Six of Cups. New elements entering your life, linked to the past, working through the present, to create the future."

She turned the next. "How other people perceive your situation — the Seven of Wands — fortitude and courage in the face of hardship. People must think you're pretty brave."

"People would be pretty wrong," I said.

She smiled. "Last card," she said, tapping it. "The most likely future outcome of your problem." She revealed it. It was a skeleton on horseback.

Death.

She hurried to reassure me. "This is actually a good card. It means the end of an old, unfruitful way of life, and the beginning of a new way of life, due to past actions." She sat back. "I have to tell you, I have never seen a board that spoke so powerfully of change as this one. You expecting some major upheaval?"

I shrugged. "Maybe just the sale of this house."

"Well, that's major, all right. But I don't know if that's it. These cards speak of you being more central to the change. And" — she ducked her head down a little so she could meet my eyes — "they suggest you are up to the challenge. You remember, if things start to get a little wild, the cards said you have the skills to succeed. Got it?"

I smiled at her. "Thanks for sticking around and going through all this. I never had my fortune told before."

She smiled. "Well, I'll look forward to seeing you again sometime, so you can tell me how things worked out."

"Me too," I said, heading for the door.

That had taken longer than I expected. I hoped Richard wasn't looking for me.

As I walked by the gallery windows, I looked out at the party. There were fewer people now; some of the guests had already made their getaways. But a lot more had stayed to enjoy the desserts and to dance under the moon.

A bright patch in the darkness caught my eye. At the entrance to the maze.

The little girl in white stood in the gap in the hedge wall. Looking at me.

I thought briefly that I ought to be alarmed, afraid. What was she? How could she see me? Then the desire to meet, to speak to her, swelled inside my chest like pain. Without being able to stop myself, I turned and started to run.

I ducked back into the east wing and ran to the door at its end. Then I ran right along the stone paths that led to the maze. I saw the girl spin around and start running, down the tunnel of green, making the first right. I plunged in after her.

The path of flagstones shone silver in the light of the moon, still radiant through fingers of purple cloud brushing its face.

Left, skip, left, I ran, chasing glimpses of white. The sounds of the party followed me dimly, as if from another world. We were heading for the heart of the maze. I gathered handfuls of skirt to free my legs for running. The twig bones of the hedge walls plucked at the billowing tulle. The air tingled against my skin — the static of energy building before a storm.

Right, left, I ran, then dodged right and turned left again.

Ahead I saw the sketching of the gazebo, black lines rising into the purple of the night, its roof seemingly held aloft by the arms of the ancient wisterias. It glimmered softly, candlelit. The child stood on the marble steps, walking back and up, back and in.

"Wait," I cried to her.

But when I reached the little fretwork house, she wasn't there.

Jackson was.

Chapter Twenty-Six

"Did you see her?" I asked him, breathless.

He looked at me strangely. "Yes, I saw her. But I don't know how you did."

"What? Why not?"

"She isn't a ghost from the past."

"Who is she, then?"

"She —" He walked toward me a couple steps but stopped. "I've seen you in this dress before, when I was —"

And I finished his sentence with him: "— a little boy."

"You *saw* me."

"I told you my name."

"That's right," he said. He almost smiled — his eyes smiled, but his lips did not.

"I'm sorry," he began, slowly, "if what I said the other day — if it upset you. I didn't know if I should tell you. But I felt it'd be like lying if I didn't."

"Like you lied about the diamonds?" That was blunt, but pretty justified, I thought.

"Yeah, well, that was more exaggeration than lie. The diamonds *are* a local legend. And I knew you'd never believe the truth. How could you? Even I think I'm crazy most of the time."

I thought of that sweet-faced little boy I'd met in the upper gallery.

"First time, I hadn't even started school yet. Your grandmother was showing me photos she took when she visited your family." He wasn't looking at me anymore. He was looking off to one side, focused on his memory. "You were in one of them, sitting next to her beside a Christmas tree. It was that photo that did it. Set it off somehow.

"It was just sounds, feelings. I thought it was my imagination. But, over time, it got more — real. Whole memories, almost, that I'd never lived yet. Or scenes, like they were being acted out in front of me. They were always random. But they all involved you.

"And it didn't — I mean, I'd never met you. It didn't make any sort of sense. I *knew* it was crazy. I thought there was something wrong with me, that God was punishing me. And I was afraid to tell anyone. Gran isn't from here, and she wouldn't have understood. But — sometimes I thought Ida suspected. She'd try to tell me things when Gran wasn't around. About my family, and yours."

How many years had Jackson kept his gift a shameful secret? My heart ached for that boy, cut off from every other soul by the things that he saw without wanting to. I, at least, had known I wasn't the only one.

"But then I saw a vision of her funeral, and I knew how and when she died. Wasn't anything I could do about it — what was I supposed to say? 'If you don't stop drinking, you're going to die of liver failure before the age of seventy?' Was she going to believe me? Maybe part of her would have, but mostly she would have thought I was a smart-mouthed kid butting his nose in, making up stories. And even I didn't know whether what I saw would actually happen. So I — kept it to myself.

"Much later, when she did pass away, exactly when I knew she would, I saw you there at her graveside with Sam and your parents. Just the way I'd seen it all those years before. You can't imagine what that day was like for me. Because then I *knew*. I knew that it had been real all along. I started to *believe*."

It was horrifying, really. He'd been haunted his whole life by ghosts from an unknown future. Haunted by me. And then I had come, a ghost made flesh. An impossibility made almost real.

And he had treated me with such — gentleness. Such restraint. And I had treated him like a lunatic.

"I know it's not possible," he said. "You can't change the past. My parents are dead. You being here can't bring them back. I know that. Of course I know that. Except part of me just keeps thinking, maybe it *is* possible."

The night crowding the edges of the gazebo grew darker; the gathering clouds at last had covered the face of the moon. It felt like we were cut off, caught in a little bubble of lamplight trapped inside the wisteria's arms.

"I can't see much of anything anymore," he said, "besides little bits and pieces. I don't know what's going to happen."

"Why?"

"Don't know. Maybe because your mom's selling the house and you're going home, and the — *opening* — is gone." He shrugged slightly. "So many paths branch off from every choice made. I try to hold on to the thread that will lead me to the future I saw. I try to be in the right place, do the right thing. I try not to do anything that will make it all" — his clenched fingers opened, releasing nothingness — "make it all disappear." He shook his head. "Maybe what I saw all my life was just a might-have-been, if things had happened differently."

"An otherwhen," I said.

He looked at me and nodded, wistful. "It was — a good life that I saw. Worth fighting for." He shrugged again. Then a smile coaxed one corner of his mouth up. "Do you dance?"

And, as if on cue, I heard the wisps of music from the party he hadn't attended.

"Not really," I said. "I never learned. I'm like the least graceful person on the planet."

"A friend of my mother's taught me. They both went to New York to be dancers."

"Where your dad first met your mom," I remembered.

"That's right," he said, smiling. "I learned to dance so I could be a little more connected to her."

"What was your mother's name?"

"Cecelia." He stepped forward, his hands raised, his arms open. "Would you dance with me?"

He stood there, vulnerable, waiting for my answer. This boy, who'd known I loved cherry Coke. Who'd taken me crabbing, and pulled me back from the cliff, and dried my tears when I was brokenhearted. This boy, who was as damned as I was with voices from another time.

Of course, I thought to myself. Of course I'd dance with Jackson.

I reached out and took his hand.

"It's easy, really," he said. "You just step, one-two-three, and go where my hands lead." He put his hand on the small of my back. "Catch up your train," he advised. He listened for the beat. "Now, one-two-three, one-two-three, one-two-three, one-two-three."

My feet fell into the pattern of the music. We spun slowly in a circle. I could feel the pressure of his right hand, more in his fingertips, less in his palm, urging me in a counterclockwise twirl, talking to me without words; his left hand agreeing with the smallest pull.

I closed my eyes, to concentrate on the whispers of his hands. The pressure changed, and we turned in a new direction. Our steps grew longer. I relaxed back into his palm so that I could listen more closely. It was lovely to be part of a conversation so quiet, so subtle.

"See?" Jackson said. "You *are* graceful."

I *felt* graceful, floating on my toes. I wasn't thinking about the steps anymore. I was sailing on a river of sound, with Jackson's hands guiding me from this current to that. Music and motion filled the endless spaces behind my closed eyes with color and radiance. I felt like I was dancing on a carpet of stars.

Then strong fingers wrapped around my arm, and we were ripped apart.

"What are you doing?"

Richard stood there, breathing heavily, his face twisted with anger, and hurt, and disbelief. "What the *hell* are you doing?"

I could smell the sour notes of champagne, and I could hear it in his voice. I didn't know what to say to him.

Jackson spoke. "I was just teaching her to d —"

Richard turned and struck him in the face. "Shut up!"

Blood beaded on Jackson's lip, purple-red in the half light. His hands clenched and his eyes darkened, but he otherwise might have been made of stone.

I lunged forward, furious, my hands shaped into fists. "Are you out of your —" The look on Richard's face stopped me cold.

"You told me you couldn't dance," Richard accused me. His face was ugly, but he looked like he might start to cry. "I thought — you and I —"

I was mute with horror. I wanted to say — *something*, but the words were sticking in my throat, jammed behind the painful lump that had formed there. What he had done to Jackson was beyond unacceptable. But the truth was, the wild infatuation I had felt for Richard was gone, had evaporated some time in the middle of that dance. The truth was, however unintentionally, I had betrayed this boy.

The sky took that moment to give way, to release its burden. Fat drops of rain started to detonate on the metal roof above us.

Quietly he said, "How could you do this to me?" Then his hand shot out, his fingers closing around the gold leaves at my throat. I cried out as I was jerked forward, the chain white-hot on the back of my neck before the clasp gave way.

He stood there, swaying the slightest bit, staring at the dead thing in his hand. "Oh, God," he said dully. "I'm so — Please. Forgive me." He turned and walked out into the rain and darkness.

I felt sick with disbelief and anger and sorrow and mortification.

"I'm so sorry," I whispered to Jackson. I moved to inspect his lip. "There's so much blood —"

He turned his head to one side. "It's all right," he said.

"We should get inside. We'll get my dad to —"

"It's all *right*," he repeated. "There's something else you need to understand." He walked to pick up something leaning against a post. He turned back, opening an umbrella he held out.

I stared at it. "You *knew* it would rain."

"Yes," he said.

"Did you know Richard would come too?"

He shook his head. He seemed to be searching for words to explain. He finally shrugged. "I knew he *might*. But I knew I had to be here. I knew we had to talk. I'm sorry. I can't see it all — I can't even see most of it. I'm just trying to hold on to the right thread."

The black umbrella fascinated and repelled me. I felt sad. The past and the future had gotten confused somehow, here in this place. I didn't like it. I just wanted to be my old self again. Someone simpler. Someone *innocent*.

"Thanks for the umbrella," I said, holding out my hand without looking at him. He put it in my fingers. I took it and left.

❧

The party was over. I saw Mom in the front hall saying good night to the last of the guests. She raised her eyebrows. I must have looked like hell. I would tell her tomorrow about what had happened. When I could talk about it.

As I passed the mirror, I saw I had a red welt around my neck. Most of Angelique's bobby pins had fallen out and my curls were hanging limply about my shoulders. All the gleam had sweated off my skin, and my makeup was streaked where tears had started to mix with mascara.

But my insides felt worse than my outsides.

I retreated up the stairs, afraid I would start crying at any second. I shed my golden gown and draped it over a chair, then slid into my pajama bottoms and a T-shirt. I washed off the rest of Mr. Poole's handiwork and curled up like a small animal under the tree on my quilt.

I felt as tired and old as a brand-new sixteen-year-old possibly could.

The moon sailed high overhead. I was dancing with Jackson, dancing on a black and white floor that floated in the middle of the ocean. A huge fish rose from the depths and swallowed the moon that sailed upon the water's surface.

Then Jackson was gone and there were walls all around me, with three tall windows to either side. The windows were open, and I had to close them so the little girl would not climb out and jump into the sea. All the corners of the room were soft with spider silk.

The room was full of school desks, and I — Deirdre — sat at the head of the room in a throne, holding a sword. The blond man wearing a captain's coat smiled cruelly. "Please give me back my child," I begged. And the Captain said, "You'll have him nevermore."

The spider spun a shining thread, and the pale woman followed it, down and down the secret stairs, and at the bottom, through a trapdoor and down again, into a darkened house where seven golden cups sat on a dust-laden table, and nine swords pierced the wall. The thread led on into a maze full of moon shadows, where a little boy ran, crying, "Sarah, Sarah, where is my box?"

But my mouth was sealed with spiderwebs that I had to tear away. My lips were joined with spider silk, but I forced them apart, forced them open. And I willed a word to fly out of my mouth, emerging hard like a dark bat —

"Sammy!"

I opened my eyes to morning, still hearing the sound of my little brother's name.

Chapter Twenty-Seven

I felt stiff when I woke the next morning — like I'd been in a fight with a pro. I went to dig some clothes out of the dresser and was surprised by what I found in the top drawer: Fiona's journals, Ida's notes, the old photos. With the amber pendant sitting on top.

Who had fished them out of the trash? Not my mom, never her. Rose, maybe? Or Sam. Maybe Sam.

I put the amber back around my neck. It hurt a little, because it rubbed the raw spot from the gold chain. But I left it there anyway.

When I went down to breakfast, Mom was at the kitchen table, hunched over her cup of coffee. The night's festivities had taken their toll on her too — she looked almost sick from exhaustion.

"You okay?" I asked.

"Oh, sure," she said, smiling wearily. "Just let me get my morning cup in me. How about you? You looked kind of upset when you came in last night. And a little worse for wear."

"I'm —" It flashed briefly through my mind to tell her about Richard, but then I thought that I could wait, I shouldn't dump that on her now. "I'm a little tired, I guess. Just like you. That was some party."

"That it was." She drained her cup. "But it went pretty well, I thought."

"Nobody'll see another party like that for the rest of their lives."

She shook her head, smiling again. "I dunno, hon. Party throwing is a competitive sport."

"Where's Sam?"

"Haven't seen him."

"Huh," I said. "That's weird. He never sleeps in."

"It was a pretty big night for him too."

I smiled, remembering. "He was great."

"That he was. He's a pretty great kid."

That's right, I thought, surprised she knew it too. "Think I'll go wake him up."

"There's something I should —" She stopped herself. "Never mind. Find Sam. Then I can talk to the both of you at once."

I pushed myself back up the stairs, remembering Sammy on that stage, crowding the mic, edging Rafe to one side. My man, Sam, a firm believer in the old adage that if you wanted something done right —

He wasn't in the nautical room. I went back downstairs to check the TV in Gramma's room. He wasn't there either.

I stood for a moment, trying to sense him. I conjured him up in my imagination. His sweet face. His grin.

Only the Sammy I imagined wasn't smiling. His face was — smooth, like it had been wiped blank. I couldn't get a sense of where he was.

"Sam?" I called, as I started checking all the rooms in the east wing. "Sammy?"

I hurried back to the entry and climbed the main stairs, two at a time. I checked the flowered room. I checked the Captain's rooms. I opened Deirdre's door.

"Sammy, where are you, bud?"

I trotted through the west wing, into Fiona's room, to look out the window at the tree house. Out the doors to the conservatory, down the stairs, and along all the paths. A quick check of the ground floor, then outside by way of the sunroom. I wasn't worried about the river this time — he was *some*where. I could feel him. I just had to find him.

Workers were dismantling the remains of the party — the stage, the dance floors, the lighting. I called to them, "Any of you guys seen a little boy?" I shouted down the stairs to the dock. "A little boy down there?" They all shook their heads.

He had to be in the maze.

I didn't want to go in there. It brought to mind things I wasn't ready to think about. But I concentrated on Sammy and ran in, sliding a little on the flagstones, still slick from the night's rain.

Traces of gold glinted in the wet grass. That must have been how Richard had found me. Followed my snail trail right to the center —

I made the last turn. A limp mass lay across the steps of the gazebo, the small brown lump of Heavy Bear a few feet beyond.

"Oh, my God!" I yelled. "Sam!"

I knelt next to him, took his little pajama-clad body in my arms. "Sam," I said, stroking his face, patting his arm. His cheek was cool to the touch, his lips slightly open. He was breathing shallowly.

I tried to raise him up, to sit him on my hip so I could carry him like I used to, when he was a toddler. But it was impossible without his legs holding on to my waist. "Come on, buddy, we've got to get you out of here." I stood there crying, hugging him to me, his head lolling back, his arms hanging. I yelled to the sky, "Help me! Somebody please help me!"

Then Sam was lifted from my arms. Jackson had come. He turned and started to jog out of the maze. I grabbed Heavy Bear and followed.

Mom screamed when we came through the kitchen door. "Sammy! Did he fall? Was he in the tree?"

"He didn't fall, Mom. I don't know what happened. I found him lying in the maze." What *had* happened? Why had he gone in there?

She grabbed the kitchen phone. "I need an emergency airlift," she directed. "My son is unconscious. I want him taken to his father at Johns Hopkins."

When we heard the helicopter coming down, Jackson carried Sammy to the door. The medics met us there with a gurney. They said they only had enough room for Mom to go with Sam. She looked at me. "You go," I told her. "Rose'll drive me."

She nodded, climbed into the chopper, and they took off.

We went back in so I could grab a couple of things — my jacket, some cash. As I headed out the door, I saw something in the corner of my eye. Something in the hall mirror. I stared.

My legs gave way. I sat down heavily on the floor. Jackson knelt next to me.

"What is it?"

I was shaking and gasping. The little face, smooth and blank, surrounded by a darkness that seemed to have no depth, like the inside of a closet with no closet around it.

"Tell me," Jackson said.

I could hardly get the words out. "Sammy's in there," I said. "Sammy's in the mirror."

It was a measure of what Jackson had lived with all his life — he never even doubted me. He helped me up and said, "We'll figure this out."

"'We'll figure this out'?" I repeated with rising hysteria.

"We have to," he told me. "We're the only ones who can." He sat me in a chair and crouched down in front of me.

"Sammy told me he saw people in the mirror," I babbled, weeping steadily. "I didn't believe him."

"There's an old superstition that spirits can be trapped in mirrors. You're supposed to cover them when someone dies."

"Rose said — it's not that they're *in* the mirror, but that the mirror shows you the other side. A place where the dead can get stuck. But — Sam's not dead."

"No. He's still alive."

That word, *still*, slammed into me. "You think he's dying?"

"I think we have to get him out of that mirror-world. The sooner the better."

A thought struck me then, a horrible thought. I grabbed Jackson's shirtfront with violence boiling inside me. "Did you know this would happen? Did you know and do nothing to stop it?" I was nearly shrieking.

He covered my clenched hand with his own. He shook his head and spoke softly, forcefully. "No. I swear I didn't know, Sarah. I wouldn't have let this happen to Sam without trying *some*thing to stop it."

"No," I said, still furious. "You knew Richard might come. How could you *not* know about Sam?"

"That point of darkness I've always had to travel through — it's like Sammy was in the middle of it and I couldn't see him." He ducked his head to look me in the eyes. "I didn't know, Sarah. I didn't see it. *Please* believe me and let me help you now."

I didn't want to believe. I wanted someone to blame. Shaking off his hand, I snarled a reply, "How can you help me if you can't see Sammy?"

Who could help me? Maybe — someone who had helped me before. Someone who, oddly, had asked me twice if Sammy was all right.

I jumped up and started out the door. Jackson followed. "Where are you going?"

I didn't answer him. I couldn't. I could hardly breathe around the knot in my chest, and I had to save my breath for running. I sprinted across the meadow and plunged heedlessly into the woods, leaping fallen logs, crashing through the brush.

Nanga had asked about Sammy. Nanga might know what to do.

I staggered up the hill face, and Jackson was beside me. I felt his hand under my arm, helping me on. I broke into the clearing.

And found a ruin. Four sagging walls. Broken glass, broken chimney. Young trees growing up in the middle. It was the same cabin. Only, nobody had lived there for a century.

I sobbed for air, utterly defeated. "I saw her. Sitting on that porch. With smoke coming up from that chimney."

Jackson held me up.

"She was dead," I said. "I've been talking to a ghost."

"You said there are no ghosts in Amber House."

"*She* told me that. How else could she talk to me?"

"You talked with me in the past."

"Because you could see the future," I said, and then pieced it together. "*She* can see the future. And because I can see the past, we could talk to each other. Then she's got to know how to help. Do you know who she was?"

"She was a slave," he said. "She belonged to the Captain. She was my grandmother, seven times removed. The children called her Nanga, but she called herself Nyangu."

The woman, I realized, who'd been raped by the Captain. It was too horrible to think about right now, when Sammy needed me. I went to the rotted steps and started up them.

"Don't —"

"Don't tell me 'don't,' " I snapped. "You already said we might not have much time."

I crawled across the remnants of the porch boards, spreading my weight, praying that I didn't break through. I touched the seatless, broken frame of an old rocker, hoping it was the same.

"There, there, Sarah, girl," I heard her say in her strangely accented voice, but it wasn't to me she was speaking. The chestnut curls of Sarah-Louise spilled across Nanga's lap as the slave stroked the girl's head.

The woman who sat there offering patient comfort wasn't aware of me, and she wasn't my old woman. She was younger by decades, but older than when I'd seen her last — saving her drowning baby. She was a beautiful woman, with high, strong cheekbones and large, dark eyes. Nanga and Nyangu both, I realized now.

"She won't wake," Sarah-Louise sobbed. "It's been ten days now. Each time she sleeps, Mama takes longer to wake, and each time, she grows weaker."

"She has happiness in her dreaming, child — happiness she never found here."

"She didn't recognize me when I roused her. She pushed me away and told me her 'little ones' were calling her."

"You need to be ready, Sarah-girl. You know what I've seen. I don't think she will wake ever again."

"How can I deal with the Captain without her? He and Camilla will take everything. Amber House will be lost. You and I will be lost."

I felt sick trying to intrude on this scene of grief, but Sammy needed me and I needed Nanga. Putting all my focus on trying to get through to her, I reached out my hand to touch hers. *"Nanga,"* I whispered, and felt a spark of static at the tip of my finger.

Her head lifted, as if she heard, and she said, "Hush now, Sarah-Louise, there be someone here who needs me." The girl sat back, trying to quiet.

Nanga turned toward me, blindly, and said, "Speak my name again, friend."

"Nang —" I started, but it seemed disrespectful to call her that. I tried again. "Nyangu."

Her head jerked and she stiffened, gasping. *Like Jackson*, I thought. And then a bubble opened and I realized I had, until that moment, been in the *wrong space*, but we were now together. As we had been before. Nyangu's eyes widened, and she seemed to see me for the first time.

"Who are you?" she said.

"I'm Sarah. You said if I needed help, I could ask you."

"We spoke?"

"Twice. You were a lot older."

She thought about that for a moment. "Then I'm thinking, Sarah, maybe you need to find the Nanga you met, because I don't know how to help you yet."

Sarah-Louise interrupted. "She has my name?"

The bubble burst. I could still see them both, but I knew Nyangu could no longer see me.

"Maybe named after you, child," she told Sarah-Louise, "but you ought not to have spoken." Nyangu talked to the air. "Hope you can still hear me. You go back to Amber House and find me, Sarah. The power's the strongest in that house. I'll be looking for you in Sarah-Louise's room, touching the canopy bed. You come find me, and I'll try to help."

I started walking, started trotting. "I have to find her again. She said she'd meet me in the flowered room. I wonder," I said, as I started to run, "if she'll remember."

Back at the house, Jackson followed me upstairs. "What do you mean, 'if she'll remember'?"

"Been five minutes for us," I said grimly, "but maybe twenty years for her." I asked him to wait outside. "Please don't make any noise — don't break my concentration."

I dropped to the floor and touched a corner of the bed. The atmosphere shifted, and I could see Nyangu sitting, her hand gripping the bedpost. It seemed she had gotten here before me. Two centuries before me. "Can you hear me, Nyangu?"

"You call me Nanga, child, like they all did."

"It's not your name."

"Neither is Nyangu. Was the name of him I loved. What help you need, Sarah-to-come?"

"My brother — I found him unconscious in the maze, and then I saw him in the mirror."

"In the mirror? Is that how it happened?" She was genuinely shocked. "Never heard of the gift in a boy child."

"Sammy has visions like I do?" How had I missed that? How had I not known?

"It may be so. If he is in the mirror. If he's stuck in the in-between world."

"Stuck? How did he get stuck? How do I get him out?"

"He is lost somehow. Like a spirit that can't find its way to the next world," Nyangu explained. "You've got to find him. Help him remember the way back. Or he will die. Can't be separated from your spirit for too long."

"But how do I do that?"

"Can't tell you how, child. Never done it myself. Find him. Help him remember he is alive."

Sarah-Louise came in. "Nanga, I've been looking for you. Come down to supper with me." Nyangu startled and could no longer see me.

"No, wait," I cried, "I don't know how to do this."

And in my upset, I could no longer see her either. I went to the door. "What did she say?" Jackson asked.

"Sammy has the gift," I recited flatly and hopelessly. "He went into an in-between world and lost his way. I'm supposed to help him find his way out. Fast."

"An in-between world? What is that?"

"I don't know. She said it was like the place where spirits get stuck if they don't go where they're supposed to." I was angry and crying. I needed better help.

"So how do we get him?"

"I don't know," I repeated miserably. "Try to find out how he got lost?"

We knew Sam had wandered into the maze late the night before. I just had to connect with something that would allow me to see the moment when he went — *away*. Something, I thought, from his bed. I grabbed the door handle for the nautical room and saw another hand grabbing it before me. Nyangu was there.

She was as old and eroded as the Sphinx. White-haired. Her skin emptied into folds. Her eyes, cloud-cast with cataracts. But she would not have been able to see me even if she weren't blind — I was looking into the past, but I could feel she was not looking forward.

She spoke to the empty air.

"Sarah, child. Been waiting to see you once more. Been looking for the right moment for a long time, but it never came. So I'm trusting you'll see me here, before you go to find your little brother. Like I told you, long time ago for me now, Amber House got a way of answering a need."

I didn't answer her, since I knew she would not hear.

"Something else you got to know." Her hand stayed on the knob, her fingers touching and not touching mine. "You have to find the box. You hear me? It's the needful thing." And she was gone.

Chapter Twenty-Eight

I returned to myself with my hand on the door to Sammy's room. I couldn't go in yet. "Nanga said I would need the box."

"She came back?"

"She was a lot older. Maybe thirty years older. It was like — she had something she had to add, something she figured out after we talked in my room, and she had to tell me before I went after Sam."

"What box?"

I remembered the night Sammy came into my room sleep-walking, and Sammy's presence in my last dream. Both times, he had been looking for a box. I realized, finally and much too late, that the whole time we'd been here, Sam had been caught up in something I hadn't seen. Because I wasn't paying enough attention. I'd been so involved in my own drama, I hadn't once thought that Sam might have this "special" gift too. That maybe he had it even stronger than I did. That maybe I wasn't as special as I thought.

I was an idiot. I'd let Sammy down.

"I think — I think it's Matthew's box. The Captain's son." I described the box to Jackson, using my hands to show him the size. "The very last place I saw it was in the tree house. My mom and Maggie were hiding it up there. But it was gone when we looked the other day."

"Someone moved it."

"It must have been my mom. After Maggie died. But I have no idea where she put it."

"Call her. Ask."

I was afraid to ask my mother. Afraid I'd reveal to her that I knew more than I should. That I'd — *heard* the house. Gotten involved with it. Woken it up. She hadn't wanted to stay, wouldn't have stayed if we hadn't tricked her.

I didn't want her to guess it was my fault that Sammy was lost in Amber House.

When I went to lift the phone to my ear, I slipped again into resisting space and saw a different hand on the receiver — my young mother's. Her other hand held down the disconnect button, which she let up slowly, quietly. She was going to eavesdrop on the line.

I leaned in close, my head next to hers. I could hear the words coming from the receiver, small and tinny, like an insect's voice.

"Margaret's condition has not stabilized. We had to insert an endotracheal tube."

A doctor, talking about Maggie.

"When will she wake up?" That was Gramma.

"The average coma lasts anywhere from a few days to a few weeks. A patient either recovers, progresses to a vegetative state, or — dies."

"She's not going to die." Silence. "Tell me she's not going to die."

"At this point," the doctor hedged, "we can't be sure of the extent of the neurological damage caused by Margaret's fall. Judging from her X-ray, I wouldn't say that this was caused by head trauma at all. There's little indication of hemorrhage. She shouldn't have experienced anything beyond a transitory lack of consciousness. We need to run more tests. But — at this point," he repeated, hesitating, "I can't tell you that I expect her to make a recovery."

"Oh, God," I heard Ida say, before my mother quietly returned the phone to its cradle.

"Oh, God," my mother echoed as she disappeared.

Maggie had fallen into a coma before she died. A coma they couldn't figure out.

The house had taken her too.

The helpful nurse on the other end of the line found my mother in the Pediatric Intensive Care Unit waiting room. They'd done an MRI on Sam.

"They find anything?" I asked.

"Nothing," my mother said, her voice lifeless. She was back again with Maggie, I thought. Back again with the loss that had taken everything with it. "Your father's in with Sam, consulting with the other doctors. They don't know what's wrong yet."

I knew what was wrong. I exhaled heavily.

"There was a drawing," I said, "in the nautical room. Of a puzzle box. I need to know where that box is."

"Why?" Mom's tone was suspicious.

"Sam . . . wanted it. I need to find it for Sam." The words sounded unnatural coming out of my mouth. I wished I was a better liar.

I could hear her thinking, piecing things together. "What are you hiding, Sarah? What have you and Sam been doing?"

Do I tell her? I wondered rapidly. Maybe she could help. Maybe —

Her voice was completely hard. "I want you out of there. Right this instant. You understand me?"

"Mom, I've got —"

"Right this instant. Tell Rose you have to leave now. If you're not here in the waiting room in thirty-five minutes, I'll call the police to come get you. You understand me? I want you out of that house."

And I knew there wasn't a single thing I could say that would persuade Mom she was making the wrong decision. If I mentioned the box again, it would just make her want me out of there faster. The only thing I could do was squeeze out a little more time.

"Okay. I'm on my way. But — I'll need a few minutes to change my clothes, grab a couple things."

"You've got forty-five minutes, then. But that's it. And when you get here, you and I are going to talk. You're going to tell me, in detail, what you and Sammy have been doing."

I was about to hang up, but my mother spoke again. "And I was going to tell you and Sam together, but you should know." She cleared her throat. "Amber House is sold."

Sold?

"A woman I've known since high school. She was at the party. I didn't even realize. She made me an offer I just couldn't turn down. Much more than the place is worth. Sarah, Claire Hathaway — Richard's mother — is the one who is buying Amber House."

The blonde in the mask, I thought, unreasonably, but with absolute certainty. Why did the idea of Richard's mother taking ownership of Amber House give me a feeling of dread? *Poor house.* I wondered if Richard had any idea. Grief hit me with such a force I doubled over, breathless. I could have wept.

"Are you still there?" I must've made some affirmative noise, because she went on. "She wants it furnished, with everything in it, as soon as we can close an escrow. So we'll take a few personal things and that's that. Meanwhile, you get yourself up to this hospital on the double. I've got to go. Your father's come out to speak to me." I heard the click on her end of the line.

No time for this. I straightened up, wiping tears from the corners of my eyes, and turned to Jackson, all business. "We've got an hour, tops, to get this done. Then a policeman will be here to take me to Baltimore. And I don't think I'll ever be back. Amber House is sold."

The pain in his face matched my own. He looked like he wanted to ask questions or protest. But he just nodded.

"First, we need to go back to the tree house."

I was pretty certain the box wasn't up there any longer, but I was going to double-check. And then I'd see if I could summon up a vision of the person who'd moved it.

When I touched the tree to climb it, the past opened. A flash exploded — a woman and a child were posing for a photograph. *The photograph from Heart House*, I thought. I was just close enough to recognize that the child wasn't the little girl in white after all. They were much alike — both beautiful and both of mixed-race parentage. But that little girl — Maeve's daughter — was not my little girl.

No time for this. I snapped back and started climbing. I had the tree-house floorboard pried open before Jackson poked his head above the ladder. "Definitely not here," I said. I concentrated, touching things, trying to find a key to the right moment in the past. But I couldn't see a thing.

Except. Something I hadn't noticed before. Wedged between the end of a board and the branch it rested on, the remnants of a string of beads. Carefully, I lifted the rotting string and saw the beads as they once were — whole, glittering on the floor of the tree house among a mess of other childish treasures spilled from Matthew's upended box.

A woman's hand lifted the box. Then her other hand swept viciously through the treasures, knocking them off into space. I heard sobbing. "So stupid," she said. "Like a lure to bring her here."

My grandmother's voice.

"Oh, God," I said, holding my head in my hands. "What did she do with it? Where would she have put it?"

And then it hit me. There was only one place in Amber House to put something that had caused my grandmother so much pain.

"It's in the trunk in the attic."

He must have seen something tighten in my face, something that betrayed the horror I felt at going back to that lonely chest. "You don't have to go," Jackson said. "I'll get it."

"No. I might see something else, something that will help. I'll go."

I climbed down from the tree and took off running again. Time was slipping away. At the second-floor landing, Jackson grabbed my arm and pulled me toward the east hall. "Faster this way," he said.

At the wall with the secret panel, he stopped and leaned with his palms against it. I saw his body stiffen, his head jerk back slightly, as a groan escaped him. Then he unclenched. With surety, he reached for a piece of molding that clicked under his fingers, and the wall panel popped in and open. I realized he had just seen the future, had seen himself finding the way in. I did not have time to wonder how that worked.

"It hurts you?" I asked him, as I climbed up and inside.

"Not enough to matter," he said. "Can't push it too much. Can't push it too far. Wait one second." He dashed into the nautical room, dumped something on the floor, and came back a half minute later with Sam's flashlight. "Here."

When I knew to listen for it, I could hear the weeping that filled that long room at the top of Amber House. Even though I was in a deadly rush, I walked quietly to the chest, so as not to disturb the gathered sorrows. I knelt to undo the lock, and Fiona was there with her tears, and my grandmother with her tears, and many grandmothers, with a river of tears.

The wooden box I remembered from our last visit was buried under a layer of things I had to shift aside. At my touch, the griefs of centuries crowded my sight: a dusty-blue baby in a coffin; a man screaming as a surgeon sawed off his leg; a woman in the tub of the rose-tile bathroom, a puddle of blood below her slashed arm. I squeezed my mind closed against them, forcing myself to see the present moment. And there it was.

Matthew's box.

I opened the lid, desperate to find the thing that would help me save Sammy. But the box was empty inside, except for the mirror in the lid.

I shook my head, incredulous. This had to be it. This had to be what Nyangu had sent me for. "Wait," I said, remembering. "It's a puzzle box." I started pushing at the sides, trying to identify the piece that would move.

"Let me try," Jackson said. He inspected the edges carefully, then pressed firmly on the rear edge of the right side. The whole side panel slid forward.

"Yes!" I said. "That's how he did it." Jackson slid all the pieces in turn until the front came entirely free, revealing the little hidden drawer. Inside lay a brooch made of two intertwining locks of hair, mounted under glass on a silver backing.

"That's a love knot," Jackson said. "A snip of hair from two people woven together. It's a kind of charm."

I picked it up to look at it. Words were scratched into its silver back: ANNIE AND MAGGIE FOREVER.

Was this what Nyangu had wanted me to find?

It was or it wasn't, but I didn't have time to look for anything else. A little over half an hour left. I dropped the love knot into the main compartment of the box and stood. I had to keep moving. "We still need to find out how Sammy got lost," I said. "Let's go to the nautical room. And — if I find a trail, I can't lose it. Because I might not be able to get back to it again. I can't have anything break my concentration. No noise. No furniture in my path. No closed doors. Can you help?"

"I'll handle it," he promised.

I tucked Matthew's box into Sammy's backpack and hooked an arm through one of its straps. Then I lay down in the berth in the nautical room with Heavy Bear in my arms. I closed my eyes and imagined Sammy, trying to get back to where he had been last night.

I imagined him lying small under the covers with Heavy Bear clutched against his chest. I imagined his breath moving softly in and out, his eyes darting behind his lids, his brow furrowed with the burden of a dream. And I heard him speak.

"No one?"

I opened my eyes to the darkness of an echo. Beside me, Sammy stood without waking and went to the door. I did the same in my vision of Sammy's past. Dimly I heard Jackson following along behind us.

He padded down the hall in his footed pajamas. His eyes were open, but I knew he wasn't awake. He stood at the top step, teetering. Uselessly and helplessly, I worried for him, standing there surrounded by night, at the top of those long stairs. Then he continued down.

I shadowed him into the east wing and down to the door at the end of the hall. Sammy opened it and seemed to see someone. "No one," he said again, and jumped down onto the stone walk. He trotted, as if chasing somebody, toward the entrance to the maze.

We jogged down the leaf corridors, filled with light and shadows cast by the full moon of the night before. The fabric feet of Sam's pajamas got soaked by the remnants of the rainfall, but he didn't wake or slow down. Even in his sleep, he knew his way to the center.

He stopped at the end of the last corridor, where the hedges opened around the iron gazebo. As I slipped up behind him, he started forward again, to the marble steps, where he bent and reached for something.

Sam stood, holding the thing in front of him, then looked deeper inside the gazebo. He walked forward a couple of steps, his hand outstretched, as if he were about to take the hand of someone taller. Then he crumpled, like a marionette whose strings had been cut.

"Sammy," I cried, as I ran forward to kneel by him, unable to touch his little body, fallen there the night before.

He'd seen someone. He'd picked up some object, and it had triggered a vision of a person who had offered him a hand. How could that be? Was the gift different for Sam? And the person he'd seen — was she one of the ones who could see the future?

I needed to see what Sammy had seen.

I glimpsed, in this vision of the night before, a patch of gold on the gazebo floor near where Sam lay. It was my mask, from the party. I reached for it, but all I felt was the cold marble tiles. I could see it before me, but in the time where my body was, the mask was someplace else.

Full daylight flooded my eyes. I squinted. I was in the gazebo, and Jackson was crouched over me.

"Sam touched my mask and then he seemed to see someone,"

I told him. "He reached out his hand like he was going to take someone else's. I need to find —"

" — the mask." He'd already found it where it was lying. He held it out to me.

"I don't understand how this is possible," I told him. "I can't touch anything in a vision. How could he take somebody's hand?"

He thought a moment. "Sammy was sleepwalking. Dreaming."

He touched someone in a dream? He touched . . . and crumpled. I got it. I finally understood. The touch was the moment he got lost. No. The touch was the moment he got *taken*. Someone had coaxed his dreaming spirit right out of his body.

"Oh, God," I said, shaking my head. "How am I supposed to follow him there?"

"That game you played — Hotter, Colder — you weren't sensing his body, Sarah. You were sensing his spirit. That spirit is still here, trapped in Amber House. You'll find him," Jackson said. "You always do."

I nodded, swallowing my doubt like a lump in my throat. Then I took the mask from him, held it in both hands, and closed my eyes to daylight.

And opened them to dusk. The green walls around me were noisy with crickets and frogs, the wisteria in full bloom, and the hedge tops weren't yet grown any higher than my shoulders. I was in a time when the maze was still young. I looked all around, but I couldn't see Sammy.

Except — I could sense him again. He had been there. He was still close. I could feel that heat. I just had to focus.

A young woman emerged from the maze, black-haired and lovely in a gold and silver hoop-skirted gown. Deirdre. On her face, my gold mask. The man who walked beside her wore a tailcoat trimmed in gold braid — a military uniform. Tall, blond, blue-eyed, with full lips and a slightly curving nose. The

Captain, as youthful as I had ever seen him. He seemed attentive and flirtatious, but also detached, as if he were dancing and admiring his own steps. I loathed him. He leaned in to murmur something in the girl's ear, then reached up and pulled off her mask.

She was maybe sixteen, an ivory-skinned beauty. She looked at him with shy longing. He laced his fingers in her hair and tipped her lips to his.

Movement caught my eye. A little girl in a white gown was climbing down through the trapdoor of the newly-built gazebo. It wasn't who I expected — it wasn't my little girl in white. This child had pale skin and blue eyes. And my mother's features.

"Maggie," I said.

She looked at me. She looked right at me. This wasn't like Nyangu, looking into the future at me looking into the past, or even Fiona, guessing at my presence. Maggie was *from* the future here, just the same as I was. So how could she *see* me? Or I her?

There seemed only one possible answer. Though her body was long dead, somehow her spirit still wandered Amber House. And because she had traveled into the same moment in the past as I had, her spirit was somehow aware of mine. As I was of hers.

If that was true, then that had to mean that when Sam had come to this same moment the night before, some *other* Amber House woman must have traveled back here as well. Must have seen him. And led him away.

I thought furiously. Why was Maggie here? What kind of insane coincidence would bring her to this same moment as Sam and his — soul-snatcher? And I realized, it wasn't coincidence. *Maggie* must have brought Sam here. What had I heard him say in his sleep, when he rose from his bed? He'd said, "No one?" That was his name for her. The imaginary friend who played hide-and-seek with him, and showed up in mirrors all over the house. No one. It made my skin crawl.

Maggie had led Sam here deliberately. But why? Whatever she was, Maggie could not be the person who had taken him. Sam had reached *up* to take that invisible hand.

I had no idea what was going on, but it seemed like I needed to talk to Maggie. If that was even possible.

Just then, she beckoned to me to follow. And jumped down into the hole in the heart of the maze.

Chapter Twenty-Nine

"Maggie! Stop," I said, running after her. I swung my feet around to the ladder and descended behind her.

Part of me wondered how I was able to do this, to pass through a door in my vision that wasn't open in the present. And I realized that Jackson was doing as he'd promised — making it possible for me to stay within the vision. He must have foreseen the need for me to go down through the trapdoor and opened it up. I blessed him and wondered what it cost him, but I stayed focused on following Maggie. Maggie, who clearly wanted me to follow. Maggie, who was heading toward that faint feeling of warm energy that drew me on.

She was gone into the darkness when I touched bottom. I wished for light, but knew I would have to do without. The tunnel was straight and its floor fairly even. I forced myself to start walking, trailing the back of my shirt-sleeve-covered wrist along the wall to help keep me on track. I heard Jackson again following behind me.

My hand bumped against wood. I had reached the door to Heart House. It was open. I went in blindly, my hands outstretched, afraid I'd collide with something. The door to the farther room was ajar, filled with a faint light. Hugging my hands to my chest, I walked through it.

Maggie was there, holding a candle, looking back at me. Perhaps even waiting for me. She turned and pressed a hidden lever, revealing an opening I had never seen before. She went in, and the light went with her.

"No," I moaned. "Another secret door" — one that wouldn't be open in my time. But then I remembered Jackson. "The lever is about five feet up near the center of the wall." And I heard, from far away, a click, a creak. I felt, smelled, a weight of stale air wash over me. The passage was open.

The dark that shouldered around me from behind was cold and featureless; the pitch-black that snaked down out of that passage was thick, repellant. I did not want to go into it. But Sammy was up there, on the other side. I slid my right toe up the rise of the first step until it cleared the edge. Then I stepped forward. Both feet on the first step, I repeated the process, and climbed the second.

I could feel — on my face, on my arms — soft, hair-thin touches that clung and grew thicker with each step I took. It seemed the spiders of Amber House had done their best to close and seal this passage. *Good mothers*, I thought. A staccato of tiny feet ran from my temple down my cheek. But I did not scream. I followed the faint thread of my connection to Sammy, up and up again.

More than a dozen steps up, my head bumped wood. I waited, afraid to push with my hands, hanging on to my sense of Sammy, thinking and not thinking of Jackson. I refused to hear the muffled sounds of movement above me. But when fresh air fell upon me, I started forward again, up into the closet in Amber House's kitchen, its door open to the light of a fire in the hearth in whatever time I now traveled.

Some part of me, some physical part, felt the shroud of webs I was wearing. I looked at my hands, and saw them clean, but *felt* them sticky with spider silk. I passed them over my face and hair, feeling and not feeling the gray trailings that hung there, swept up by my fingers. I would not see the spider that ran down my wrist to my palm and sank fangs in its center, pain a blossom in my hand. I only brushed her off and went on.

Through the dining room and into the entry. I felt with my heart for my path, and knew it was up the stairs. I looked to the top and Maggie was there, looking back. She turned and ran on.

Halfway up the staircase, my attention was pulled by a disturbing blankness on my right — the mirror that hung there. I saw my reflection draped in webs, standing in a day-lit hall, with Jackson behind, his face creased with worry, his hands partially raised, as if he wished he could help. My sight was filling with sunlight — I was losing the connection.

I squeezed my eyes shut and again concentrated on Sam. I waited for the warmth to grow, turning my face from the mirror. When I opened my eyes, I was back in the shadows of a long-ago evening.

And I could feel Sam, getting hotter. He was — above.

On the second-floor landing, I saw movement in the portal of the eastern wing. Someone standing there, someone watching me. I could feel her presence like an ice statue, like cold fury. I backed up two paces, then turned and fled up the farther staircase.

Darkness pooled in the narrow steps at the top. When I reached the last landing, light fanned sideways into the hall from the partially open door at its end. I slipped in.

The large garret room that in my time had been dust-laden and packed in all its eaves with taped boxes was in this time set up as a nursery, empty and abandoned. Two iron-framed beds sat naked under the far window; two children's chairs stood in the middle of the floor before a simple trunk of unpolished wood. The rest of the space was bare.

Sammy and Maggie, sitting in those chairs, looked up at me when I walked in.

"Hello," said Sam, and Maggie said, "Hello."

"Sam?" I said.

"Sam is my bear," my brother told me. "He's five years old. Who are you?"

Who am I? I repeated to myself, feeling chilled. "I'm Sarah, Sammy. Don't you remember?"

"Sarah?" Sammy laughed. "My sister's name is Sarah too." He gestured toward Maggie.

"Sarah too." Maggie nodded.

"You're Sarah?" I said, confused.

"Did you see my toys?" Sam asked, jumping up to flit about the room, pointing. "This is my horse. And this is my ship. And this is my tiger."

He did not seem to know that every place he pointed was empty.

I reminded myself that he was sleeping, dreaming. True, he was in the same past as I, or else I couldn't have spoken to him. But he had come here in his dream, and in his dream he stayed. In that dream world, reality had no bounds. Where I saw an abandoned nursery, he saw a room filled with toys that didn't exist. I wondered if Maggie dreamed them too.

"Your toys are wonderful," I told him. "What's your name?"

"My name is Matthew."

Matthew. Whose sister's name was Sarah. Sammy was dreaming he was someone else, just as I'd once dreamed I was Sorcha and Fiona and Sarah-Louise.

I needed to wake Sam up. I needed to make him remember who he was, make him remember the real world. But I couldn't even touch him. How could I wake him?

I dimly sensed Jackson watching me, and felt grateful for his presence. But then I turned my attention back to the children.

"How did you get here?" I asked Maggie.

She struggled to find a few words on her own. "Mama took me," she said.

Mama. Deirdre. She took Maggie down into death, I thought, and in the next thought realized: *Persephone.* Maggie had gone into the underworld, never to come out.

How could it have happened? Somehow, when Maggie had fallen from the tree — had fallen into unconsciousness — her dreaming spirit had traveled into the past, as Sam's had, as I had myself those few times. Her spirit had gotten trapped here, unable to find her way back to her body, back to her life. Her body had died because of it.

And now the same thing was happening to Sam.

And "Mama," Deirdre, had done this. Deirdre, the woman who'd been driven insane by the loss of her own children. I remembered that she'd spent the last weeks of her life barely waking, even though Sarah-Louise had tried so hard to wake her up. Perhaps Deirdre's dreaming spirit had stumbled upon Maggie's and wrapped it up in her own mad vision. Then she'd looked for a Matthew too, to have both her lost children restored to her. And she had found Sam at that moment of her first kiss.

I needed to get Sam out of here. I needed him to wake up, before what had happened to Maggie happened to him.

"Does your mama let you go out?" I asked Maggie.

"Nope," Sam said. "We never go out. It's not good outside. There are dark things. And spiders."

"Spiders," Maggie said.

"Mama locks all the doors," Sam said.

"Not *all* the doors," Maggie said.

No, not all, I thought. Not the secret door that led to Heart House. Which Maggie had found. *Clever girl.* That was how she wandered through the past, I thought, and met Sam, and became Fiona's Persephone.

"You looked for someone who could help," I said to her.

She nodded, her eyes pained. "Someone who could help."

"Who?"

She shrugged a little and shook her head. "Who," she said.

No one she could remember, I thought to myself with anguish. But maybe she'd been searching for her beloved older sister. Who wouldn't walk those paths in the past anymore.

Sam spoke up, his voice a little angry. "We don't need help. Mama gives us *everything*." He brightened at a thought. "You want to see the bestest thing of all?" He skipped forward to stand near me and indicated an invisible something, standing upon the chest. He made the motions of winding a key. "See?" he said. "A carousel! With a song in it!" He hummed along.

I closed my eyes and tried to hear through Sammy's ears, see through Sammy's eyes. Tried to imagine a carousel set with tiny animals that spun in a circle around the center, while a melody poured from its heart.

When I opened my eyes, I could almost see Deirdre's dream nursery, like glimpses in my peripheral vision. A zoo of animals tucked in their cages. A rocking horse, hand painted. A model of a three-masted ship. Toys and balls and books and puzzles of every shape and size.

The bare walls became, at the edges of my sight, cozy with draped fabric patterned in red and yellow and white. A braided rug warmed the floor and a table stood in the middle of the room, covered with a cloth. A fantasy nursery, decorated with mad splendor, for two children who had come here in their dreams and now could not wake.

And in the center of it all, the china carousel, playing a melody I knew very well. A melody of six notes that Sammy had been singing since before he could talk. How could that be?

I was cold to the pit of my stomach.

"That's beautiful," I said, struggling to keep my voice even.

"Thank you," he said cheerfully.

"You're welcome," I answered in the rhythm of our old joke, dipping my head to catch his eye. And he looked at me swiftly, a tiny furrow between his eyebrows.

From far away, through an echoing tunnel, I heard the knocker rap against the front door of Amber House. It had to be the police. I was out of time. The nursery slipped sideways and blackness ate the edges.

I focused on Sammy. I held on to Sammy. The music had stopped, the shadows were empty, but I was still there. And Sammy was still there.

"I'm going to have to go soon," I told him.

"That's too bad," he said.

"I want you to come with me."

"Want to come," Maggie said softly.

"Nope," Sam said. "Can't go out."

"Look at me, bud." I sank down to the floor, where the world was more solid, and I could look Sammy in the eye. "I'm your sister. Sarah."

"I don't think so," he said. "I'm pretty sure I would remember."

"You've got to remember, Sammy." I reached out a hand. And stopped myself. My fingers hovered over his, but could not touch them. "Samwise," I said, pleading. "Sam-my-man."

He hesitated, then — "Nope!" he shouted.

My hand hurt in the center, and the pain seeped up into my arm. Jackson had said the good mother was poisonous. I was tired, so tired. I set down Sam's pack. And remembered what it held — *the needful thing.*

I opened the pack and got out Matthew's box. Lifted the lid. And I saw myself looking back at me, sitting in an empty attic. *The mirror'll show you true,* Nanga had said to me, long ago.

I could hardly see Sam anymore. A boy of smoke. I closed my eyes and sensed for him. *Warmer, warmer.* I turned the mirror toward him, imagining him there, seeing Matthew's looking glass. Conjuring that belief in my mind, I struggled to keep hold of both thoughts — Sam and the mirror. "I brought your box. Weren't you looking for it? Can you see it? Can you see yourself in the mirror?" I forced my eyes back open and he was there, solid.

He was looking at the thing in my hands. Worry had settled in his eyes. He looked closer. "I'm not in the mirror."

I nodded tiredly. "Because you're not really here, bud. You're asleep. You have to wake up."

"It's dark in the mirror."

"I came to find you, Sam."

He looked at me. He whispered, "You're my Jack."

The door opened. There was cold behind me. I turned my head to see. It was the woman from the attic — mad Deirdre, dressed in a sack shift, her wild and matted hair gone to gray.

"You shouldn't *be here*," she said, frightened. "Who are you?"

"I'm Sarah." I gestured toward Sam. "He's not . . . your son."

"You dare suggest I mistake my own son?" she said, outraged. "My husband sent you, didn't he? He is always trying to confuse me."

I'm tired, I thought. *I need to sleep.*

She bent close and peered into my face. I didn't know why I'd found her frightening. She looked nicer now. Beautiful. And kind. "Lay your head down for just a little while," she said soothingly.

I was forgetting. I turned back to my brother. He was fading into darkness. "Sam?" I said.

Maybe he answered. "I have to go."

"Matty?" Deirdre cried, fear returned to her voice. She stretched out her arms to him.

"Nope," my little brother said. And part of me smiled. *All right, Sammy.*

Dimly, I saw him pad toward the door in his footed pajamas. “Come, Sarah,” he said. Then he disappeared.

Maggie was there still. Tears leaking from her eyes. *Persephone*, I thought again. I felt vexed. I wanted to sleep.

“It’s dark in the mirror,” she repeated. The shadows were crowding around her, blotting her out. Maggie, whom I had never known, her spirit trapped here in this past before I was even born.

I remembered the thing inside the box Nanga had sent me to find. The love-knot brooch. I could do this last thing. I pulled it from my pocket and set it on the trunk in front of me. Maybe I saw Maggie look at it. Maybe I saw her mouth shape a word. “Annie.”

The darkness was growing. The room was tilting backward, a house in a tornado. The smoke girl went up the floor to the door, where she stopped to look back down at me. Then she too was gone.

“He was not Matty; she was not Sarah,” the lady said, sorrowful.

“I’m Sarah,” I said, laying my head on the woven rag rug in the room of red and white and yellow.

The beautiful lady knelt beside me, to stroke my cheek. “Sarah,” she said, as if seeing me for the first time. “Sarah-Louise.”

Once, I thought dully, *I’d been Sarah-Louise. But that had been a dream, hadn’t it?* One more person who needs to wake, I realized with dreadful reluctance. I felt like crying. My tongue moved thickly. “I’m not,” I said. “Your daughter.”

“My daughter,” the lady said softly, her touch light on my head. I couldn’t remember being touched like that before. So sweet. So gentle. A good mother’s touch —

“No!” I tried to shout, but it came out a whisper. It hurt to speak, and tears leaked from my eyes. But I had to try. “Not — daughter.” *What was the other thing? Oh, yes.* “You. Are sleeping.”

"Sleeping?" She looked at me, uncomprehending. *Stupid woman.*

"Just a dream." I wanted just to dream. The salt of my tears reached the corner of my lips. A real thing. I jerked my head up again. "Sarah-Louise. Holding your hand. Can't you feel her?"

"I feel you, my sweet girl," she said.

"Wake up," I snarled. I had hardly any air left to make words. "She needs you. She's afraid. Of the Captain."

"I'm afraid of the Captain."

"Have to. Help her." *Wake up!* "She needs. Her mother."

"She needs her good mother," she repeated. "Yes." And then understanding finally reached her eyes. "My God. What have I done? I made myself forget, but — she should not have to face him alone." She seemed to see me anew. She stroked my head again, tenderly. "You are like my Sarah. I am sorry for you. But I have to go now." She looked toward the door. "Sarah-Louise needs me." Her words faded away, like an echo. And I couldn't see her anymore.

I knew I lay on a dusty floor in an empty attic. I couldn't feel my body, and a coldness had seeped into my head. I thought, uncaring, *This isn't a dream you wake up from — if your spirit lets go, you will go out forever.*

Then that thought slipped sideways from my mind, and I could not get it back. The contents of my head — images flat and shrunken — were sucked away in a funnel wind, and I could not get any of them back.

The walls pressed in; the light grew dim and dimmer still, and was shut behind a door too small to pass through. I huddled tight and listened to the storm howling beyond the edges of this tiny room. Darkness inside me was filling all the spaces. The walls pressed up against my sides. The ceiling crowded my head. Amber House was folding down upon me. It was time.

Time to let go.

A hand — large, warm, strong, sturdy — took mine and pulled me to my feet into the circle of his arm.

I looked up into green eyes I knew. We were connected, he and I, weren't we? I could feel it. A current like breath flowing between us as we met in this place, this last place that would ever be. We stood in the center, and a storm circled all around. I said, "Jackson —"

"— Jackson." A little boy with green eyes. The car was slipping sideways, the tires screeching, the woman screeching, reaching behind, her fingers working frantically to pop the buckle of the car seat. Fire filled the world —

And there was pain, searing pain, blistering pain. I sagged, held up by him — the boy with the green eyes. "Shh, shh," he told me, his scarred arm wrapped strongly around me. I felt the thousand touches of other times, other possibilities, pulling at me irresistibly, and he was the only solid thing left in the world. He stroked my hair with his long surgeon's fingers. "Don't slip away," he said. "Stay with me. Stay awake —"

"— awake. Mama just opened her eyes, Nanga, just like that." Sarah-Louise was hugging Nyangu, who looked blindly for me. I could feel her searching. "You hear me, Sarah, girl? It is possible. You got to remember —"

"— You've got to remember," Gramma said as she tucked the piece of amber inside the hole under the bear's arm. Then she began to stitch him shut again. She ducked down to look into Sammy's face and told him, "Nanga said you'll be the only one who doesn't forget. Tell her: You changed things once, you can change it again, it is poss —"

" — possible," the boy finished, still holding me. His strange green eyes were filled with such hope, it was painful. "I see it too. I see what you're seeing, Sarah. We just have to remember —"

"— have to remember," my crazy great-grandmother said, laying The World upside-down on a cloth-covered table, "that when the card is reversed like this, it means that events have not yet come to a conclusion." A little girl with green eyes and honey-colored skin stood just behind her, watching me. "But they are nearing completion," Fiona finished. She looked in my direction, her face shadowed, but her eyes oddly bright. I saw pity in them. "Are you —"

"— Are you asleep, Sarah? Sarah? Honey? Wake up."

Epilogue

My ears felt empty, as if there should be noise, but there was not. Just birdsong. A peaceful sound. I was lying on the grass beneath the old oak, and someone was gently patting my hand. I felt air fill my lungs in a gasp, like I hadn't been breathing, but now I was. It hurt a little.

I looked up into the face hidden by the sun behind it — a shadow face haloed in light. A face so like my mother's, but softer, simpler.

"Maggie," I said, remembering where I was, and why. "Did Mom send you to look for me?"

"Yes," my aunt said. "Your mom sent me."

"It's time?"

"Yes," she agreed again. "It's time."

"Then I guess we should go in." I took Maggie's arm. I reached up to touch the brooch on her collar, the one she always wore: a love knot she and Mom had made when they were girls. She'd nearly died once; a fall had left her in a coma, and when she woke up, she'd asked for this pin, and had worn it ever since.

"Your lucky pin," I said.

"Yes," she said. "Very lucky."

We stood on the hill, inside the iron fence of the family graveyard. It was late October, and winter had come early. In one weekend, the air had turned frosty and the trees had begun to drop their leaves, damp blankets around their feet.

We clustered around the open grave like a flock of starlings. The priest intoned in a somber voice. My little brother, Sammy, played a solitary game of hide-and-seek among the tombstones, just he and Heavy Bear. The rest of us seemed frozen, including my mother.

Dad reached out and took her hand, and I saw her squeeze back. *It must be nice*, I thought for the thousandth time, *to love someone like that.*

Outside the fence, Rose and Jackson stood apart. When I glanced at them, Jackson looked away, like he'd been caught staring. Up the hill a bit, apart from the group, there was a family trio, all tall and blond, father, mother, and son. I noticed a few of the other mourners covertly pointing them out to one another. They were my mother's old friends, Senator and Mrs. Hathaway, and their son, Richard.

" 'For there shall be a time for everything under the sun' " — the priest's voice raised on a conclusive note — " 'a time to laugh and a time to dance.' I believe, even now, Ida is dancing in the moonlight, in the arms of her beloved Mark."

I looked beyond the graveyard, at the fields and woods of my family's home, at the house crouched behind the thick border of gardens. A gust blew my hair into my face, whispering in my ears. The naked branches of the graveyard willow rattled one against another. I heard an eho of voices, perhaps rising from some boaters on the river.

Sammy and I were the only ones who seemed to notice.

We filed down the hill to the house for a luncheon Rose had prepared. I was one of the last through the door. I'd had a headache ever since Maggie woke me, thick and dull and numbing.

The house was packed with people, many with full plates already in hand. They talked quietly in small groups, I assumed about my grandmother. She had been a fixture in these parts. Active in her church, active in the community. A big fund-raiser for research into brain function and neurological abnormalities.

Even with all these people in it, the house seemed desolate without her. For the first time, I felt all its empty places. For the first time, I noticed how the high ceilings and long halls and shuttered, vacant rooms seemed to catch sound and hold it there, a dim echo.

Maybe it was just my headache.

I located Mom in the parlor to the right of the stairs. She sat alone on the sofa, an untouched plate of food in her lap. She motioned for me to sit beside her.

"Where's Dad?" I asked.

"Helping Mrs. Whipple to her car."

"How come the mirrors are draped? All over the house."

"Rose must have done it," Mom said. "Southern custom. To help Gramma's spirit cross over." She took a deep breath. I put a hand on her arm. "She had a good life, don't you think?" she said. "It happened so suddenly, you know? A stroke. Just like that. I never expected it."

"Yeah," I said.

"But I woke up today, and it was like I wasn't surprised anymore. It was like I'd . . . known about it for weeks." Her voice broke a little, but she steadied herself. "I'm glad, you know, that we were able to celebrate your birthday before we got the news."

"Yeah," I said. "Me too."

She rubbed her temple with her palm. "I have such a headache. Would you get me some aspirin, honey? Please?"

I squeezed through the crowd, making my way toward the swinging door at the end of the hall. I pushed through to the kitchen.

Rose turned to stare at me.

"Oh," I said. "Sorry." There was a ringing in my ears, and I felt a little dizzy.

"Something wrong?" Rose asked.

"No. I, um — I . . . Shouldn't Jackson be here?"

I had no idea why I'd said that. Neither, apparently, did Rose.

"You need something? Maybe some pop?"

"I'd kill for a cherry Coke."

She went to the fridge and rummaged through its contents. I went to the narrow cabinet where Gramma had kept the aspirin.

"You not feeling good?" Rose asked, noticing the pills as she handed me the drink.

"Mom has a headache."

"Seems like it's going around."

"Yeah," I said. "Thanks for the soda."

"Gotta get back out there, collect up some of those dishes. Getting crumbs everywhere. Gonna have —"

"— cockroaches living in the sofa," I concluded. She stared. "Sorry," I said again, "didn't mean to finish your sentence."

"Don't forget a glass of water," Rose said, eyeing me strangely.

"Huh?"

"For your mama."

"Right," I said.

I went looking for Sam after I gave Mom the aspirin. I found him where I knew I would — in the nautical room upstairs. It was his room whenever we came to visit.

Sammy was at the desk, sitting in the swivel chair, pushing himself in slow circles. He looked at me questioningly.

"You doing okay, bud?" I said.

"My head hurts," he said finally, "but I'm okay."

"Okay," I said. "I guess I'll go back down." I turned to leave.

"It's better now than it was before," he said.

"Better?" I repeated. "What's better, bud?"

"Things," he said. That was Sam. The master of specificity. "I have to give you something, Sarah. Something I found."

"What you got, Samwise?"

He pulled Heavy Bear to him and poked a couple stubby fingers into a hole under the stuffed animal's arm. He fished out the end of a chain, which he drew from the bear. The pendant on the end popped loose from the hole.

Treasure, I thought, foolishly. "What is it?" I asked.

He put it in my hand. It was a smooth stone, yellow-orange and translucent. Amber. And at its heart was a spider, with long spindly legs. My skin crawled. I'd always hated spiders. "These are poisonous. The bite never goes away."

"I know, Sarah."

"It's amazing," I said.

"You're welcome," he said, nodding.

"Yeah, thanks, bud." I slipped it over my neck. It struck me, then, that there was someone I needed to see, something I needed to say. "I gotta go, Sam, okay? I gotta find — Jackson."

He looked at me, measuring. "Yep," he said. "You gotta find Jackson."

I went outside. I walked to the stable and peeked in. The horses nickered softly. I wandered across the front lawns and through the gardens. Trotted down the stone steps to the dock where the *Amber* floated.

Climbing back up the hill toward the house, I veered to one side and entered the maze. I found my way to the heart and climbed the marble steps of the metal house.

And there he was.

He smiled. I liked his smile. It fit him. Warm, friendly, honest.

I had known Jackson forever. We had played together sometimes when we were littler, the times my family came to visit. I didn't even see his scars anymore — Jackson was just Jackson. So it was odd, me noticing his smile. And the muscles under the fabric of his shirt. And the way his hands were like my father's — a surgeon's hands, huge and square, with long fingers. It was odd, me wondering what it would feel like to have those hands cradle my face, to —

I stopped that thought. I saw that he was watching me, almost like he knew what I was thinking. I stepped away from him.

"I'm hoping we'll move here now," I said.

He gave a little nod. "You will."

I smiled at his confident tone. "You know something I don't know?"

"Oh, man, *so* many things," he said with a grin.

"Shaddup," I told him, chuckling. I rubbed my forehead. Where once I'd had an enormous lump. Hadn't I? And now it was cool and smooth. "I had this dream. I wish I could remember it. But it's like it's floating just beyond my grasp, you know? And there was something . . ." My voice trailed off. "Something important."

"Tell me," he said.

The words slipped loose. "It *is* possible."

His eyes widened. *Green eyes filled with hope.*

Why had I thought that?

"What's supposed to happen?" I asked, feeling an urgency I couldn't understand.

It seemed for a moment like he had something he wanted to say, but then he only smiled. "We're just gonna have to wait and see. Right?"

He reached up, touched beside my eye, showed me his fingertip. "A tear," he said.

It glistened, catching the light. I closed my eyes.

What if he slid his hand along my chin? And parted my lips with his thumb? And leaned in so close that my breath became his breath, his breath became my breath?

What if he finally, finally — gave me that kiss?

TO BE CONTINUED IN BOOK II

NEVERWAS

Acknowledgements

We have learned that it apparently takes a village to do quite a few things in life, including getting a story idea onto a book shelf. We owe many people thanks for turning *Amber House* into a book.

First among those, our Gramma and Commander, Lore and Lundi Moore, who shared a love of old things, and our Boy, Sinjin Reed, who shares a love of storytelling and who contributed many helpful ideas to this book. These three have always backed us in all our endeavors, no matter how insane. Next, to our earliest reader and "Negative One," Jessica Wanderscheid. Jecie — your enthusiasm gave us the will to keep on, even during the daunting submission process.

Endless thanks to our first heaven-sent blessing, the amazing, gentle, insightful, patient, fearless agent Jennifer Weltz, of the Jean V. Naggar Literary Agency. *Amber House* is a much better book for her criticisms and suggestions. Thanks also to the wonderful Jessica Regel and Laura Biagi at JVNLA.

We further thank Heaven for our second blessing, Cheryl Klein, whose keen, meticulous eye is simply staggering. Unceasingly cheerful and encouraging even while delivering dagger-sharp criticism, Cheryl is the kind of editor every writer should be so lucky to have. Also at Scholastic, we must thank our tenacious production coordinator, Elizabeth Starr Mayo; our designer, Whitney Lyle; and our publicist, Lauren Felsenstein.

Finally, our thanks to other friends who took the time to read and comment: John Hicks, David Leiwant, David Naggar, and Tammie Stickney. Thanks to Maureen Grady and Nancy Harewood, who helped to imagine an early version of this story. Thanks to Deborah, who made sure all things nautical were shipshape. And thanks to the folks at Annapolis Small Boat Rentals, who gave us a map and a boat with which to explore the beautiful waters of the Severn River and the Chesapeake Bay.

And thank you all, gentle readers — we are grateful.

About the Authors

Kelly Moore first conceived of *Amber House* while in law school, and an early draft of the story was written in the mid-1980s. When her daughters Tucker and Larkin Reed discovered the manuscript a few years ago, the three decided to rewrite it together. Tucker currently attends the University of Southern California, while Kelly and Larkin live in Jacksonville, Oregon, in a house full of antiques. Please visit their website at www.theamberhousetrilogy.com.

This book was edited by Cheryl Klein
and designed by Whitney Lyle.
The text was set in Perpetua,
and the display type was set in Phiastos.
The book was printed and bound at R. R. Donnelley
in Crawfordsville, Indiana.
The production was overseen by Cheryl Weisman and Starr Baer.
The manufacturing was supervised by Adam Cruz.